TIGER IN THE MOUNTAINS

TIGER IN THE MOUNTAINS

by

Franklin M. Proud

and

Alfred F. Eberhardt

ST. MARTIN'S PRESS   NEW YORK

Manufactured in the United States of America
Library of Congress Catalog Card Number: 76-25849
ISBN 0-312-80430-X
Library of Congress Cataloging in Publication Data

Proud, Franklin M ˙1920-
    Tiger in the mountains.

    I. Eberhardt, Alfred F., 1939- joint author.
II. Title.
PZ4.P969Ti5 [PR6066.R625] 813'.5'4 76-25849

Having climbed over steep mountains and high peaks,
How should I expect on the plains to meet greater danger?
In the mountains, I met the tiger and came out unscathed.
On the plains, I encountered men, and was thrown into prison.

From: *"Hard is the Road of Life"* *
Written from a prison cell
in China, 1942-1943.

Ho Chi Minh

* *Poems from a Prison Diary*
Hanoi: Foreign Language Publishing House, 1959

Mandalay

BURMA

Rangoon

Yen Bai   Phuc
NORTH
Hanoi
Hai Phong

Than Hoa
VIETNAM

LAOS

Ventiane

Chiang Mai

Udorn   N K P   LAO

THAILAND

Ubon

Takhli   Korat

Bangkok   CAMBODIA

Bang Saen

Phnom Penh

Songkhla

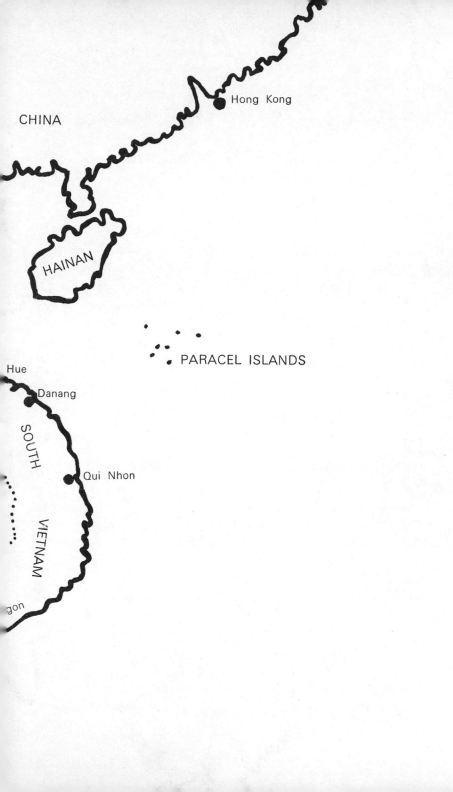

CHAPTER ONE

Phnom Penh's Pochentong International Airport was bathed in the harsh midday glare of a white-hot December sun. The Air France jetliner of the Paris to Tokyo flight sat on the concrete parking apron in front of the low terminal building.

Court Palmer hadn't disembarked for the 45 minute stopover. He gazed out the port side window, beyond the silver wing, towards the mesh-wire fence which separated the arrivals section from the transit and departure area. On the far side of a wide stretch of sun-scorched lawn, was the terrace restaurant. It was too far away and distorted by shimmering waves of heat rising from the concrete for Court to distinguish individuals at the canopy-shaded tables. He waited impatiently.

There was a stirring of movement in the terminal. Transit passengers straggled lethargically back along the walkway towards the waiting airliner. Palmer disregarded them. His eyes were fixed on a small group of boarding passengers emerging from the terminal building.

He readily identified the towering figure of Anderson, but searched in vain for Gracier.

Palmer experienced a sinking sensation. Something must have gone wrong. Without Gracier, the project would have to be abandoned. The weeks of careful planning would have been to no purpose.

A man emerged through the glass doors, paused to drop a cigarette butt onto the cement, and grind it under his foot, then strode purposefully to overtake the boarding passengers. Court recognized Gracier and felt a momentary flood of relief, oddly mixed with a surge of apprehension.

Palmer followed the approach of the two men reflectively. He noted the camera slung carelessly around Anderson's neck. Both men carried airline flight bags. Gracier's was suspended from his shoulder by a strap, leaving his right hand free for the bulky brief case. Palmer's gaze was attracted magnetically to the brief case, which he followed with his eyes until the men were obscured from his vision by the aircraft wing.

As he turned from the window and settled back in his seat, Palmer noted with surprise that despite the comfortable temperature of the aircraft's interior, his palms were sweating. He grinned wryly and wiped his hands against the seat fabric.

Well, he mused, this is it. In spite of the weeks of preparation, there had been a quality of unreality about the adventure. That was no longer true. Barring the unlikely advent of some mishap on take-off, what had all started with a wild idea voiced in casual conversation in a booth of the Derby King on Bangkok's Patpong Road was now about to be translated into action.

As the first class passengers filed into the cabin, Palmer regarded them idly.

The middle-aged man in the creased lounge-suit had boarded the flight before Bangkok. From the cut and material of the man's suit and the heavy topcoat in the overhead rack above his seat, Palmer judged the man to be a European who had probably embarked at Paris.

A young mini-skirted, auburn-haired girl had also joined the flight at some point prior to Bangkok. Palmer didn't consider her to be beautiful, but she was certainly attractive. She was probably on her way to join family, friends, or possibly her fiance, for Christmas in Hong Kong. Had she been traveling economy class, Palmer might have labeled her as a model or an entertainer, but it was unlikely that an agency would provide a first class ticket. She could have embarked at Paris, Tel Aviv, Teheran, or New Delhi.

Considering her becoming suntan, Palmer favored Tel Aviv.

The remaining three passengers in the first class compartment aroused no speculative consideration in Palmer. Although he was not personally acquainted with any of the trio, they had, like Palmer, boarded at Bangkok. They were, in fact, the reason for Palmer's selection of this particular flight. The group consisted of the Indian Ambassador to Thailand, his dumpy sari-clad wife, and a young man acting in the capacity of aide or secretary to the diplomat.

As they entered the cabin, it was apparent that the ambassador was agitated. Palmer couldn't help but overhear snatches of the one-sided discourse. He gathered that some informal meeting had been scheduled during the brief Phnom Penh stop. Evidently, owing to some foul-up in advance communication, some of the people the ambassador had expected had not been in attendance. For this, the ambassador was berating his nervous and embarrassed aide.

Palmer smiled faintly. If the ambassador displayed such distress over such a relatively minor contretemps, what would His Excellency's reaction be to the harrowing experiences about to befall him?

Across the aisle, the girl was adjusting her make-up case and a hat box. She must have noticed Palmer's amusement concerning the ambassadorial display of pique. Glancing in her direction, Palmer caught her eye. She inclined her head slightly in the direction of the Indian Ambassador and raised her eyebrows. Palmer's smile widened to a broad grin.

The stewardess moved down the aisle drawing attention to the lighted smoking and seat belt instructions.

As Court Palmer snapped his belt across his waist, he reflected that under normal circumstances he would have contrived to get acquainted with the girl opposite him during the hour-long passage from Bangkok to Phnom Penh. He would have accompanied her to the transit lounge, and by this time the relationship would hold promise for interesting developments in Hong Kong — if that was indeed her destination. Granted, these were hardly normal circumstances. Still, he would have time after take-off to rectify the oversight and resolved to do so.

As the Boeing 707 moved out onto the taxi strip, the honeyed voice of a stewardess intoned in French and English over the broadcast system. Boarding passengers were welcomed to Air France's flight 194 with destinations of Hong Kong and Tokyo. They were advised that the aircraft would be flying at an altitude of 37,000 feet; that the flying time to Hong Kong would be two hours and fifteen minutes; and that luncheon would be served shortly after take-off.

The thin whine of the jet engines deepened to a throaty roar. As the airliner gathered speed down the runway and lifted off, Palmer's eyes were fixed on his wrist watch. When he heard the faint thump as the undercarriage homed in its housing, he noted the exact time.

As the jetliner banked in a steep climbing turn, Palmer gazed reflectively at the patchwork quilt of paddy fields dotted here and there with palm trees, the red-tiled roofs of the city, and the muddy expanse of the Mekong. He caught himself wondering when next, if ever, he would see again the river.

Palmer shrugged, unclasped his seat belt, and reached into the pocket of his shirt for a cigarette.

Of one thing at least, Palmer had sure knowledge. The confident pronouncement of the stewardess concerning the flight time to Hong Kong was gravely in error.

CHAPTER TWO

Courtney Jerome Palmer III made a squalling entrance into the world at 8:17 in the morning of October 12th, 1942. This momentous event took place in the big house at Darien, Connecticut. Attending Kathleen Bisley Palmer were a doctor and two private nurses.

It was a gray day, with fog from the sound obscuring the rocky point and the small crescent of beach. In spite of the dreary weather, there was general jubilation in the household on the announcement of the birth.

Commander Courtney J. Palmer Jr., was up from Washington on leave for the occasion from his duties with Naval Intelligence. He received the news that his wife had presented him with a son and heir with quiet satisfaction. His first question was whether the child was sound, then, as an afterthought, he inquired of his wife's condition. Reassured on both scores, he went over to the small bar in his study and poured himself a healthy slug of bourbon. As he savored the drink, he smiled at his dim reflection in the glass facing of the bookcase. After four daughters in quick succession, Palmer had secretly harbored the suspicion that a male child was to be denied him. He had considered this to be some hereditary defect on the part of his wife since the Palmer line was amply endowed with male offsprings. Now, however, the line of succession was assured. Commander Courtney J. Palmer Jr., USN, was well pleased.

The baby's sisters were delighted. To Kathleen, Patricia, Helen, and Sharron, aged respectively 7, 5, 4, and 20 months, the infant represented a new and vastly interesting plaything. To the three older girls, the advent of a birth in the family was no novelty, but this was the first time the event had taken place within the confines of the home. Somehow, this added immeasurably to the mysterious proceedings. The nurse had informed them that their mother was resting, but that they could expect to view the new arrival a little later. They were impatient for their first glimpse of their new brother. Little Sharron was too young to grasp the significance of the happening, but was caught up in the general air of excitement and chuckled happily in expectation of some as yet unexperienced wonder.

Upstairs, Kathleen had been transferred from the guest room, where the delivery had been effected, to her own room. She lay propped against the pillows, contentedly cradling her swaddled red-faced son. She was still a bit fuzzy from the after-effects of the anaesthetic. Her mood was one of glowing euphoria. She was infinitely happy that the baby was a boy.

Although nothing had ever been directly discussed between them, Kathleen was well aware that her husband considered their lack of a male child as due to some congenital flaw in her construction. She had read books on the subject and could have advised Court that it was generally conceded that the sex of a child was determined by the father's sperm. She had refrained from mentioning the fact. Now, the subject need never be broached.

There was yet another compelling reason for Kathleen's happiness. She had been a vivacious and popular post-debutante of 25 when she had married Court Palmer in 1935. She had at that time every reason to believe she would be embarking on a gay social career. It hadn't worked out quite that way. Life had seemed an endless procession of pregnancies. Perhaps now that she had produced the desired son and heir, she could look forward to a respite from child-bearing. At 33, she was an extremely attractive woman. Her errant thoughts dwelt pleasurably on visions of travel and a fuller social life.

As she lay in state, awaiting the arrival of husband and family to pay due homage, Kathleen Palmer's euphoria might have been considerably lessened had she been able to divine her husband's thoughts.

To Courtney Palmer's way of thinking, his wife had now vindicated his selection. She had fulfilled her function as brood-mare. She could now be relegated to duties of rearing the offsprings. His paternal obligations having been discharged, he would be free to roam further afield. Discreetly, of course, as befitted his position, Palmer intended to explore greener pastures.

*   *   *   *

Early in life, the third male of the line to bear the name of Courtney Jerome Palmer, was exposed to selective indoctrination. He was taught that he had certain obligations and responsibilities to his illustrious forebearers, the Republican Party, and to flag and country. Unswerving allegiance was expected in that descending order.

He understood that he would one day inherit the mantle of family interests which had been the fruits of the diligence and devotion to duty of the three generations preceding him.

His great-grandfather, Jerome Palmer, had founded the prestigious dynasty.

Coming from England at the tender age of 16, Jerome Palmer was apprenticed to the ship chandlery firm of Wainright and Pugh of Philadelphia. That was in the year 1839. By application and thrift, young Jerome advanced rapidly within the firm. The crusty old bachelor who was the firm's senior partner, Ephriam Pugh, developed a paternal interest in the young English apprentice. When the old man passed

away in the winter of 1846, it was revealed that he had willed
his share of the business to Jerome. At the age of 23, Jerome Palmer became a full partner in the chandlery
company. The name was changed to Wainright, Pugh & Palmer.

Largely on Jerome's urging, the company expanded its
interests into ship brokerage and the factoring of cargoes.
These ventures were to prove profitable.

During the course of a business trip to Baltimore in
1850, Jerome met Anne Courtney. With the singleness of
purpose which marked all his endeavors, Jerome paid court
to this youngest daughter of a proud family of Maryland
landowners. By 1851, he had overcome the objections of her
family. In the early summer of that year, Jerome and Anne
were married with all due pomp and ceremony at the Courtney plantation, Nine Oaks. Anne brought to the union not
only a family name boasting an American heritage of pre-
revolutionary vintage, but a substantial dowry.

The first of their four sons was born in February,
1853. He was christened Courtney Jerome Palmer. Over the
next seven years, his birth was followed by those of William, Edward, and Justin. And as his family grew in size,
so did the fortunes of Jerome Palmer prosper. Using his
wife's contribution to his coffers, Jerome bought out the
original surviving partner, Johnathan Wainright. The company became Palmer Shipping Company. By the time Justin
was born, the company owned and operated a fleet of five
sturdy clipper ships, had shares in the cargoes of many
more vessels, and had under construction on the ways at
Trenton a steam side-wheeler designated as flagship of
the line. That was also the year in which Jerome started
construction on the big house in Philadelphia.

It was the advent of the Civil War which presented Jerome with the opportunity to parlay a position of solid wealth into a truly sizeable fortune. Shipping was at a premium and cargo rates soared. Jerome had ships. He also had valuable commodity connections.

In the chaotic period which followed the conflict, Jerome found himself in an enviable position of power of both a financial and political nature. When the Courtney's Maryland landholdings were in jeopardy, Jerome stepped in with alacrity and ready cash. Nine Oaks became the Palmer plantation — staying more or less within the family.

The Nine Oaks acquisition alerted Jerome to the potential in the South where vast acreages were going at sacrifice prices and levied tax arrears. Working through agents, Jerome quietly began to accumulate plantation after plantation.

Jerome shrewdly foresaw that once deprived of slave labor the staple crop of cotton would go into decline. He commenced conversion of his holdings in Virginia and the Carolinas to the more profitable tobacco. He established processing plants for the leaf in a number of strategic locations.

Shortly after his eldest son Courtney had celebrated his sixteenth birthday in 1870, Jerome founded the Philadelphia-based Knickerbocker Trust Bank. He was to devote the major portion of his time and remaining years to the consolidation of a banking empire which was to elevate him to the ranks of one of the ten richest men in America.

Courtney Palmer graduated from Princeton in 1876. Following a year of traveling in the hemisphere and Europe, an itinerary designed to broaden his education, he joined his father in the bank.

When William, and in turn Edward, graduated from Princeton and completed the ritual continental sabbatical, they were introduced into the shipping company. Justin followed the same scholastic schedule, but varied the pattern by spending three years and a good deal of money in Paris and the south of France. A sharply reduced allowance finally persuaded him to return home, where he was safely installed in the Palmer Tobacco Company in Richmond.

Although his younger brothers all married before the age of 30, Courtney remained a bachelor and lived with his parents in the big house. When he finally bowed to the inevitable, the year was 1892 and Courtney was 38. His bride, Lucinda Stainbridge, the second daughter of a socially prominent Philadelphia family, had just turned 18. After a brief honeymoon in Bermuda, Courtney returned home and established his young wife in the big house.

In honor of his eldest son's nuptial status, Jerome relinquished the presidency of Knickerbocker Trust Bank to Courtney, but retained his position as Chairman of the Board.

For a number of years, Anne Palmer had been bedridden with consumptive fever. She died quietly in her sleep less than a month after the arrival of the new bride. At 18, Lucinda found herself mistress of the big house. It was not too heavy a responsibility since the servants ran the establishment with quiet efficiency. Her father-in-law occupied one wing of the rambling mansion and required no special attention. The household virtually ran itself.

Lucinda fully appreciated that she was expected to produce a son and heir. She was a healthy young female, but in this simple endeavor she experienced some difficulty. In 1893, and again in 1895, Lucinda suffered miscarriages in the fourth month of pregnancy. When she became pregnant again in 1897, every precautionary measure was adopted. Courtney Jerome Palmer Junior was born in the spring of 1898. In the late fall of that same year, Jerome, with no prior warning of illness, died of a massive coronary occlusion. Courtney was left undisputed head of the family. The infant Courtney Jerome Junior was heir-apparent.

Lucinda didn't immediately abandon her plans for a larger family, but when a male child — who would have been christened Justin William — was stillborn, she bowed to the inevitable and devoted herself to the rearing of her only son.

Courtney Jr. was attending Princeton when Europe erupted into war. He was in his Junior Year when the American Expeditionary Forces embarked for France. Although a good many of his college friends volunteered and were granted military commissions, Courtney Jr. did not number in their ranks. By the time he graduated, the war was over, providentially allowing him a year in postwar Europe before returning to continue his studies at the Harvard School of Law.

Courtney Jr.'s best friend at Harvard was Arthur Bisley, a Bostonian. During vacations, Arthur visited at the Philadelphia home, or at Nine Oaks, while Courtney was as often a guest at the Bisley residence. Although Arthur's youngest sister was barely emerging into her teens, Courtney decided she would one day make him an admirably suitable wife. In January, 1935, he was to realize this long-contemplated ambition.

Upon passing his bar examinations, Courtney Jr. joined the legal staff of the Manhattan branch of the Knickerbocker Trust Bank. He established his bachelor residence in a brownstone on West 78th. The year was 1927, and the gaunt girders of the new Knickerbocker Trust Building were rearing against the Park Avenue skyline.

Established on a rock-solid base, the Knickerbocker Trust Bank weathered the 1929 crash relatively unscathed.

Courtney Jr. was by now a director, with Courtney Senior occupying the positions of both President and Chairman of the Board.

In 1931, Courtney Jr. embarked on a new venture. The Wall Street brokerage firm of Crandell, Topeler & Fitzpatrick was in serious financial difficulties. Courtney studied the reports and financial statements of the brokerage concern. He had the bank's auditors run a thorough check. His conclusions were that the moment was opportune to step into the picture. It was also his considered opinion that the depression-ravaged economy would bottom out and commence a dramatic upsurge within a maximum period of five years. At relatively little cost, Courtney Jr salvaged the foundering brokerage house. In return, he acquired the controlling interest, a directorship, and the satisfaction of seeing his name appe.xied to the firm as Crandell, Topeler, Fitzpatrick & Palmer.

In 1934, with real-estate values still depressed, Courtney Jr. purchased the large house on the promontory at Darien, as well as a sizeable estate in Palm Beach, Florida. It was at this time that he began to seriously contemplate marriage.

He had maintained contact with the Bisley family, and now paid ardent court to Kathleen. The family was flattered. Kathleen had always considered her brother's college friend as rather dull and stuffy. She had never looked upon Courtney as potential husband material. But any reservations she may have had were overridden by the facts that Courtney was one of New York's most eligible, and certainly one of its wealthiest, bachelors. These proved to be compelling credentials. Kathleen accepted Courtney's suit on New Year's Eve.

The wedding in late January and the honeymoon of a

Caribbean cruise with a two-week stopover in the Bahamas
were dictated in timing by Courtney's business commitments.
The couple returned in late February to set up residence
in the house in Darien.

In an admirable display of fecundity, Kathleen was pregnant on their return from the honeymoon cruise. Courtney
Jr. was delighted.

In October, when Kathleen dropped the first of what was
to be a quartet of distaff contributions, Courtney's elation
was tempered by disappointment. With characteristic zeal,
he set about rectifying the obvious error. Over the course
of the next six years, as his efforts continued to be rewarded with female progeny, his disappointment increased progressively. His uncles, William and Edward, had married
at a much earlier age than his father and been rewarded
with both sons and grandsons. Only Uncle Justin could be
counted out of the race. Justin's marriage in 1888 had
lasted less than a year, ending in separation and some
years later in divorce. The marriage had been childless.
Justin seemed quite content to live in celibacy, his interests absorbed by the tobacco company, art, philanthropy,
and, it was rumored, little boys. In any event, at the age of
79 there was little likelihood of Justin's sudden emergence
as a contender. But even discounting Uncle Justin, there
were more than enough males in the clan to assure conti-
nuity. Courtney Jr. had no wish that the succession should
pass from his own direct line. Under the circumstances,
he considered a son and heir imperative. Any attraction
Kathleen had held for him initially had long since waned. In
fact, until his son's squalling emergence on the scene,
Courtney had been secretly harboring thoughts of a divorce.

By odd coincidence, the male members of the Palmer
line did not long survive the advent of a child born to the

eldest son. It was as though this event triggered some mysterious cosmic mechanism which dictated an immediate thinning process. Jerome had passed away within eight months from the birth of Courtney Sr. Both William and Edward had lasted less than a year from the birthdates of their grandsons on the Palmer side. Now it was Courtney Sr.'s turn. It could be argued that at 88 Courtney Sr. had already lived well beyond his allotted span, still it was passing strange that the old man, who had seemed indestructible, should contract influenza, complicated by pneumonia. He had been rushed to Philadelphia's Presbyterian Hospital. He did not live through the night. His grandson was three weeks old.

The significance of such coincidence was not lost on Courtney Jr. He had been advised by telephone at his New York apartment of his father's death. Now, as he sat in the club car of the train, bound for Philadelphia, his thoughts turned to a vision of his infant son in the crib at Darien. Could it be that his own days were to be numbered by his son's eventual marriage and fatherhood? It was a distinctly disturbing thought. The events, however, were too far in the future to cause undue alarm. Of more immediate concern to Courtney, were the terms and conditions of his late father's last will and testament.

On the reading of the will, Courtney Jr. was little surprised that the Philadelphia mansion went to his mother, as did Nine Oaks. With the family bank acting as trustee, a trust fund had been established from which his mother, himself, and his children would derive income on an equally shared basis. Listed in the trust was a bewildering array of stocks, bonds, and income properties, many of which were being revealed to Courtney Jr. for the first time. A second, and even larger trust, had been established from which the income was to accrue to a Courtney J. Palmer Foundation; the terms of reference and those named to the initial board of directors for the foundation being outlined in a separate codicil. In addition, there were a number of endowments to institutions and lump sums bequeathed to individuals such as loyal servants and trusted employees of long standing. Amongst these was a bequest of one hundred thousand dollars to a Mrs. L.M. Spencer. The name was unfamiliar to Courtney, which, considering the size of the legacy, he found surprising. Glancing in the direction of his mother, he detected a twitching of her lips in a semblance of a smile.

Courtney found the provisions for the administration of the Palmer family trust revealing. While the trustee had discretionary powers over the conversion of stocks and bonds, the disposal of properties, and the acquisition of new holdings, the legatees did not. It was further stipulated that under no circumstances were the shareholdings of either The Palmer Line — as the shipping company was now called — or Palmer Tobacco Company to be disposed of. Income was to be shared equally. Upon new births within the family, the earnings would be divided accordingly. When deaths occurred, the income was redistributed between the surviving members. Payments were on an annual basis, with a further provision that until a recipient reached majority the annual amounts would be deposited to savings accounts established in the Knickerbocker Trust Bank. The trust itself could not be liquidated for a period of fifty years, and then only at the discretion of the trustee. Courtney smiled thinly. The old man had taken no chances that the fortune would be dissipated outside the family. Fortune hunters might be discouraged by the fact that they could only anticipate increments of the income but could never get their hands on the capital. Still, at least initially, that income would be substantial. In time, as his descendants, multiplied, the individual returns would grow progressively smaller despite the growth rate of the capital holdings. If his daughters followed their mother's example, Courtney thought glumly, the proceeds of the trust could be spread over half the eastern seaboard by the turn of the century.

Courtney Sr.'s shareholdings in the Knickerbocker Trust Bank had not been included with the trust funds. Courtney Jr. had known this would be the case from previous discussions with his father. On his father's retirement from active participation in the affairs of the bank in 1934, Courtney Jr. had become Chairman of the Board, a position he still occupied. He had fully anticipated that his father's shareholdings would pass into his hands to give him undisputed control. He received a shock. The shares were bequeathed instead to his mother. He would still exercise control, of course, through his mother's proxy, but it wasn't quite the same thing as having the power firmly within his own grasp. He glanced sharply at his mother, and surprised an expression suspiciously like amusement.

*　　*　　*　　*

The family history was imparted gradually to Courtney Jerome Palmer III over the course of his formative years.

By the time he had entered his teens, young Court had formed a mental picture of the Palmer men as epitomizing conspicuous virtues. They were all, especially his father, men of probity and vision. As such pillars of the community and nation, the wealth they had accumulated was a fitting and just reward.

Other tenets were indelibly impressed upon the boy. He was led to understand that whatever temporary setbacks might afflict it, the Republican Party was destined to guide the nation to ultimate glory; that he would one day attend Princeton University; and that, in the fullness of time, he would inherit the reins of family authority and that under his stewardship the house of Palmer would flourish and achieve even greater fortune and renown.

These facts, Court held to be as immutable as death and taxes.

*　*　*　*

CHAPTER THREE

The seat belt warning light blinked out. Court unsnapped the locking clasp and stretched his arms.

The stewardess passed through the cabin taking orders for pre-lunch drinks. Court requested a bourbon and water. Across the aisle, the girl asked for a dry martini.

When his drink was served, Court carried it in his left hand as he stood up and moved into the aisle. Looking down on the seated girl, he said, "Hello. Mind if I join you?"

"Not at all," she answered. The accent was English.

"My name's Court·Palmer." He extended his right hand.

She smiled as she clasped his outstretched hand lightly. "Lucille," she responded. "Lucille Mongomery."

As he settled into the seat beside her, Court grinned. "Do they call you Lucy?"

"Yes. Most of my friends and the family do." Noting his broad smile, she added, "You find that amusing?"

"No, no. Not at all. It's just a coincidence. My grand-mother's name was Lucinda. She was called Lucy. But I assure you that's the only point of resemblance."

Over their drinks, and during the luncheon service, they became acquainted. Court's earlier guesswork had been wide of the mark. She was an actress. She had just complet-ed a small part in a French-Italian produced western with location shooting near Almeria on the Spanish Costa del Sol. She now had a slightly better role in a film which was to commence its shooting schedule in Hong Kong within a few days. She had boarded the flight at Paris.

As they flew northeastward, the weather beneath them changed. At this time of year, the Northeast Monsoon was well established along the eastern coastline of Viet-Nam. The highlands and mountainous spine over which they passed were obscured by massively banked clouds.

As they neared the coast, the cloud mass thinned a

little. Through the overcast, Court was able to distinguish the line of beach and Qui Nhon. He checked the time. The aircraft captain would be reporting his position to Saigon Control. They were now altering course slightly to the air corridor designated as Amber 70. When they had proceeded another 130 nautical miles seaward, in 15 minutes time, the captain would report the position at a point known as Papa Echo Eight. The next report would come 102 nautical miles later at North Reef as they overflew the Paracel Islands, changed course again slightly into air corridor Amber 1, and switched Flight Information Regions, reporting to Hong Kong Control.

Court sipped his glass of wine, and ordered another cup of coffee. He still had sixteen minutes to go.

The image of his stern-faced grandmother appeared on his mental screen. Well, Lucy, he thought, you wanted me to display a little individuality. You felt I should break the mold. Wherever you are now, I hope you're watching. See how this caper grabs you.

*　　*　　*　　*

For young Court Palmer, the road to manhood lay along well-defined geographical routing. There were deviations dictated by schooling and holiday travel, but in the main he adhered to the established path. It was a pleasant thorough-fare smoothly paved and tastefully landscaped along its course by the judicious expenditure of family funds. And along the way were milestones. Some of these, such as the preordained markers of educational advancement, were readily distinguishable. Others, chance mileposts of ex-perience, were less easily identified, glimpsed only fleet-ingly in passing, or undetected altogether in obscuring foliage.

From the first week in January until a few days after Easter, the family was officially in residence at Palm Beach. For the duration of the spring and early summer, the venue shifted to Darien. July and August were divided between Darien and the Maryland plantation, Nine Oaks. This summer pattern was the most flexible of the seasonal routines. As Court grew older, visiting with relatives, staying with friends in New Haven or the Hampsteads, and, during the summer before his entrance into university, bumming around Europe with three of his buddies, added variety to his holidays.

During the autumn months, family activity was based on Darien, although his mother invariably traveled to Europe for October and the early part of November. Court's father rarely accompanied his wife on these junkets. Instead, one or more of the children were included on the continental visits as companions for Kathleen. Court's first exposure to England and France occurred during his second year of Junior High School. He was delighted to miss seven weeks of school. Justification for this scholastic hiatus was on the grounds that the cultural exchange benefits would outweigh any lost classroom instruction. But as far as Court could determine, his mother's chief interest was in a shopping expedition. There could have been some broadening of viewpoint derived from exposure to the many social functions attended by his mother, but at 13, Court was excluded from these activities.

Whatever departures might be introduced into established routine throughout the rest of the year, Christmas was rigidly ritualistic. The entire family journeyed to Philadelphia to the old mansion on West Philadelphia's Spruce Street where Grandmother Palmer held matriarchal sway.

Court's memories of Christmas, at least until his freshman year at Princeton, were not particularly happy ones. He had found the old house and the neighborhood gloomily depressing. The big tree in the sitting room was a splendor to behold, and the gifts were indeed marvelous, yet somehow the autocratic and forbidding presence of his grandmother cast a pall on the festivities. And the traditional Christmas dinner was too stiffly formal to be truly enjoyable. Court had always found himself looking forward to the return to Darien, and a much gayer event, the Palmer New Year's Eve party.

From his mother, Court inherited his dark blond hair, blue eyes, and amiable disposition. His father's contribution was a sound body and excellent physique. From neither parent, or perhaps by some happy combination from both, he was endowed with above average intelligence and a keen, inquiring mind.

With four sisters who lavished affection on their only brother, an indulgent, if somewhat vague, mother, and the attention and homage of the servants, it would have been miraculous had Court not been spoiled. To a degree, he was, accepting such adulation as his right. That he did not become insufferable was largely due to the fortunate trait of adaptability and a healthy sense of humor.

What little discipline that was administered to young Court was meted out by his father. These occasions might have been more frequent, but the elder male of the household spent little time with his family. It was understood that the rearing of the brood was the province of the mother. Courtney Jr. spent a good deal of his time in New York. Following the war, he had moved from the 78th Street brownstone to a large apartment on Central Park

West. This he utilized as his base of operations in preference to the house in Darien. Weekends, when he wasn't in Philadelphia or Washington on business, he spent at Darien. For Easter, he joined the family in Palm Beach. And, for the Yuletide festivities he was invariably present at his mother's Philadelphia house.

To young Court, his father wasn't a forbidding figure so much as he was curiously remote. As Court advanced into his teens, his father took a more direct interest in his son's activities. This attention to paternal responsibilities took the form of instruction and counsel to the growing boy. From these sessions, Court was acquainted with some of his father's business activities, and led to understand the responsibilities which would one day be his. Not all of this indoctrination was confined to Darien or the Palm Beach estate. Young Court was afforded the privilege of spending some of his weekends at the Central Park apartment, and, upon occasion was allowed to accompany his father to Philadelphia, Washington, and Richmond. Young Court was suitably impressed. He felt affection for his father, and pride, but there was little empathy or understanding between them. In all honesty, Court found the world in which his father moved a sterile and cheerless domain.

In the matter of education, it was clearly understood that Court would attend Princeton. The pre-university years, however, had been the subject of some discussion. His mother wanted Court to attend a military academy in Virginia, the same school which had been attended by his uncles, Arthur and Clifford Bisley. Kathleen was overruled in this academic selection by her husband. Courtney Jr., contended that while private schools, such as Miss Fine's in Princeton, were admirably suited to the needs of his daughters, the boy would be better served by an introduction to life through the co-educational and democratic mixing process of the public school system. That the validity of his argument was open to question within the immediate confines of Darien, escaped the senior Palmer.

Through elementary, junior high, and high school, Court's scholastic record was mediocre. He achieved no better than passing grades. The only subjects in which he displayed even the mildest interest were mathematics and science.

In the realm of sports, the picture looked more promising. Court was big for his age and possessed a high degree of muscular coordination. He played on the school basketball, baseball, football, and ice hockey teams. He could easily have become the star player of both basketball and football had he exerted himself and devoted more time to practice.

His father attributed Court's failure to attain academic or athletic honors to indolence and lack of team spirit. He was wrong in both assessments. Early in his school career, Court had remarked two phenomena of group behaviour. The student with the top grades evoked not only envy, but opprobrium in the student body. The star athlete, while he certainly gained a measure of adulation, was also set apart from the rank and file of his fellow students. Court decided that he had no desire to be labeled as either a "brain" or a "jock-strap". Had his aspirations run in that direction, he was perfectly capable of being either, or both. He displayed discernment and the exercise of restraint beyond his years, and was neither. In consequence, Court was one of the most popular members of the student body throughout his school career.

That Court was not lacking in competitive spirit was amply attested by his achievements in other extra-curricular activities. While his father was justifiably proud of his son's record in at least two of these areas, he failed to grasp the significance.

From the summers in Maryland, Court had learned to ride almost before he could walk. The family kept riding stock and hunters at a nearby stable in Connecticut. Court exulted in his ability to master and coax superlative performance from the majestic beasts. Both he and Sharron walked off with an impressive array of blue ribbons from the Connecticut summer fairs, and later from competitive show-riding throughout the eastern States.

Court learned to sail almost as soon as he did to ride. The challenge presented by the tricky winds and choppy waters of Long Island Sound fascinated him. As he graduated upwards from Snipes, through "L"s, and Dragons to 12 Meter craft, and from relatively sheltered waters to the bluewater classics of Bar Harbor, Halifax, and Bermuda, Court accumulated a mantle-piece crowded with silverware.

The obvious lesson which should have been self-evident to his father was that Court excelled where he considered the personal challenge demanding enough to warrant the effort. That the import of his performance in these sports had not escaped his grandmother, Lucinda Palmer, Court was to learn later.

In yet another area of highly individual achievement, Court brought a formidable talent. In the competitive field of amatory conquest, Court chalked up a record which was the envy of his less gifted companions. Of this particular realm of preeminence, most of his family remained blissfully ignorant.

Court's sex education was something akin to osmosis. His mother had given early instruction to her daughters concerning the advisability of keeping their legs crossed — an admonishment which accomplished little other than whet their curiosity. But when it came to advising her son, the delicacy of the subject defeated her. Court's father was called upon to impart this vital knowledge.

The senior Palmer started out bravely with a dissertation on birds, insects, the fertilization of flowers, and the mating habits of lesser vertebrates. Here, he ran into difficulties. When he moved onwards and upwards to deal with the primates, the frank father-to-son talks degenerated into a discussion of the horrible consequences visited on the unwary by virulent strains of venereal bacteria. As a curtain-dropping finale, the father produced a condom. Utilizing his thumb as a phallic surrogate, the senior Palmer demonstrated the purpose and usage of this boon to mankind. Court listened politely, privately concluding that his father looked pretty silly with a latex-draped digit. Since this illustrated lecture was conducted in Court's tenth year, the boy had already acquired a grasp of the subject well beyond the scope of his father's presentation.

With four sisters relatively close to his own age, the female anatomy held little mystery for Court. He was thus enabled to add certain clinical details to the discussions between himself, his closest pals, Kevin and Frankie Crane, and others of the select neighborhood coterie. The discussion group felt the need of wider experience. Sally Lang and Enid McBain, who were active participants in such preliminary enterprises as spin-the-bottle, proved willing accomplices in a progression to more sophisticated games. There was a good deal of giggling, and furtive probing over an extended period before they arrived at the group therapy of masturbation. Without doubt, the experimentation would have proceeded into more fruitful channels had not one of the sessions been disconcertingly interrupted. This incident, which was discovered in progress in the McBain boathouse, precipitated something of a suburban crisis. It also brought about the rather belated lecture delivered by Court's father.

While neither the Crane boys nor Court abandoned their field research, they were considerably more circumspect in their pursuit of knowledge and experience.

Court was 14 before he actually made out with a girl. He plotted the deflowering of Mary-Lou Kenear with infinite patience and guile. As a result, he very nearly didn't score at all.

The Kenears owned the adjoining estate to Nine Oaks. Court had known Mary-Lou as a summer playmate for as long as he could remember. Since she was only six months his junior, it was only natural that he and Mary-Lou would share many of the pleasures of childhood. They fished, rode, tracked imaginary Indians, sneaked smokes, swam in the Kenear or Palmer pools, and played tennis on the Palmer or Kenear courts. Until the summer he was 13, Court thought of Mary-Lou as a companion and pretty good kid rather than as a girl. But that summer he discovered she had taken on an added dimension. She had developed boobs. Court's attitude underwent an abrupt change.

While Court was determined to explore the possibilities of a new relationship with Mary-Lou, there seemed to be little opportunity that summer. Mary-Lou had suddenly acquired some new friends who occupied most of her time. What little time she allocated Court was devoted to swimming and tennis in the company of others. The best Court could manage was a hurried session of kissing with appropriate but amateurish frontal massage. Mary-Lou had offered no resistance to his fondling of her budding breasts. Time, however, worked against Court. No second chance presented itself before his return to Darien.

The thought of Mary-Lou was much with him. The fact that she had not objected to his caressess lent him hope which sustained him through a dull trip to Europe, a bleak winter, and the spring term of school.

His operational plan was simple. On arrival at Nine Oaks, he would telephone Mary-Lou and invited her to go riding. He would steer a circuitous course which would bring them eventually to the deep pool of the creek. In the hot afternoon sun, a skinny-dip would be appealing. From that point, he was sure events would shape up to his advantage. There was but one flaw to his scheme. He had devised no alternate. It was a mistake he was never to repeat in future conquests.

Mary-Lou was physically attracted to Court as far back as the summer before he evinced any interest in her awakening desires. He had been oblivious of her timid advances. She began to feel that perhaps Court was a little too young to appreciate her needs. In consequence, the following summer she gravitated towards the company of a slightly older group. 16 year-old Nate Bradly satisfied her curiosity.

As the summer neared an end, she became aware of Court's quickening interest. She both welcomed and enjoyed the all-too-brief necking session in the Palmer bathhouse. Mary-Lou looked forward to the summer of their mutual 14th years with almost as much ardor as did Court.

She was aware of Court's arrival at Nine Oaks at the beginning of August, and was surprised and disappointed when he did not contact her immediately. She had no way of knowing that an unseasonal week of rainy weather was proving an insurmountable obstacle to the execution of Court's mentally-rehearsed master plan. Mary-Lou was on the verge of admitting defeat and seeking solace with Nate Bradly, when the weather resumed its normal August character and she received an invitation for a morning ride with Court.

Up to a point, everything proceeded exactly according to Court's plan. The departure came in the final moments. Overly-excited, Court ejaculated after he had achieved only partial penetration. He felt cheated. The anticipation was superior to the realization.

Had it not been for Mary-Lou's experience and instinctive reaction, the summer romance could have died aborning. Court had mumbled something about it being his first time. She kissed him, and fondled him as she claimed it to be her first experience as well and that it had been wonderful. Court had been led to understand that the rupture of the hymen should be painful and produce bleeding. Of course, he hadn't gone in very deeply, but he had encountered no obstacle to his progress and there was no sign of blood. He questioned Mary-Lou, who lied convincingly that the impediment had been eliminated long ago through horseback riding. Court readily accepted her explanation.

In the weeks that followed, Mary-Lou subtly forced the pace until Court took over the initiative. They were young and healthy animals. Adjustment came naturally and quickly. It was an enjoyable and satisfying August for them both.

As a result of that memorable August, Court went into his first year of high school confident of his sexual prowess. That distinct psychological advantage was coupled with the tactical edge provided by his own sports car and more than ample allowance. His success in at least one popular high school activity was assured.

*　　*　　*　　*

Court's introduction to sex by Mary-Lou was a milestone on his road to maturity. An encounter with a much older woman three-and-a-half years later was to have an even greater impact. The woman was his grandmother.

The day after Christmas was cold and bright. Court had been visiting some friends in the suburbs. He returned to the old house on Spruce Street about three-thirty in the afternoon.

He was preoccupied with his thoughts as he let himself into the front hall and walked towards the wide central staircase. At the foot of the carpeted steps he stopped, his attention drawn to the full-length oil painting of his great-grandfather which dominated the landing above.

Normally, Court paid scant heed to the painted likeness of the dynastic founder. It was remarkably similar to the painting which graced the board-room of the Knickerbocker Trust Bank. Court found both portraits singularly lacking in asthetic value. What had given him pause this time was an odd trick of lighting which imparted a curious lifelike quality to Jerome Palmer's countenance.

The artist had employed somber hues. Jerome's frock coat was of a dark gray which closely matched the hair and mutton-chop sideburns. The contrasting background was a dreary green-black. Even the flesh tones of the features had a grayish cast. To Court, the impression imparted by the portrait had always been one of austere disapproval of the house and its occupants. Now, however, the late afternoon sunlight slanted through the stained-glass window at the turn of the landing and touched the stern visage with a ruddy glow of health.

For a fleeting second, Court imagined that the dark eyes beneath bushy black brows were staring directly into his own. He grinned, and shrugged the fantasy aside.

The unmistakable voice of Court's grandmother grated behind him. "Don't stand there gawking at your great-grandfather, Boy. Come here."

He hadn't noticed his grandmother when he crossed the hall. She must have been just inside the archway leading to the sitting room. He turned. She was in her wheel chair, which she had propelled part way into the hall. For the past few years, his grandmother had been partially crippled with arthritis. She could walk with the aid of a cane, but preferred the wheel chair. Instead of evoking any effect of helplessness, her infirmity seemed only to increase her forbidding aspect. "Yes, Grandmother," he replied dutifully, crossing to her side.

"Wheel me into the conservatory," she commanded imperiously.

Court complied. When she was settled amongst the plants, with the sunlight filtering through the steamed glass panes onto her snow-white hair, there was an air of regal splendor about the old lady. Court pulled the small marble-topped table to her side. She had an unopened book in her lap, and was searching in her beaded handbag for her reading glasses. Court started to leave her to her pursuit, when her voice halted him in mid-stride.

"Fetch me a glass of sherry." Then after a brief pause. "You may have one yourself, unless your would prefer something stronger."

"Sherry will be fine," he said, leaving to do her bidding.

When he returned, the reading glasses were perched on the thin high bridge of her nose, but the book was still unopened in her lap. He started to hand her the crystal glass with its amber contents.

"Just put it on the table," she ordered.

Court obeyed. "Now," she said, "pull up that footstool

and sit here beside me, Boy."

He placed his sherry glass carefully on the table. As he moved to pick up the stool, his thoughts were mixed with sudden resentment. For as long as he could remember, his grandmother had never called him anything but "Boy". He should be used to it. He was, but had never liked it. Now that he was a freshman at Princeton, the appellation seemed not only unsuited but somehow demeaning. He had never spoken up to his grandmother, but was resolved to do so now.

He sat stiffly erect on the edge of the ottoman. "Grandmother," he said evenly, "I was christened Courtney."

Over the top of her reading glasses, her eyes swung to rest on Court's face. He thought he detected her lips twitch in a smile.

"Do you think I'm so steeped in senility that I don't know the name of my only grandson?"

"Well . . . . no, but . . . "

She interrupted him. Her voice was not unkind. "All my adult life I've been surrounded by Courtney Jerome Palmers. When you father was born, I wanted to name him Jonathan Duncan. Would have found Jonathan Courtney acceptable. I've always thought that carrying Christian names into the second and succeeding generations errant nonsense. It has a tendency to stifle individuality. The son is expected to be a carbon copy of the father. I was opposed to your being christened Courtney Jerome. Your father's wishes prevailed. You have probably always detested my calling you, Boy, but it wasn't meant to cause you hurt. Do you understand what I'm driving at?"

Court was disconcerted. His grandmother had never talked in this manner to him, and he wasn't at all sure what she was driving at. He nodded, but remained silent.

"You don't look like a Palmer," his grandmother continued. "With your excellent display of horsemanship, and a shelf groaning with yachting trophies, I was of the opinion you were more like your great-grandfather than your Courtney J. predecessors. Perhaps I was mistaken. Here you are, seventeen, enrolled in Old Nassau, resident in Brown Hall, and next year without doubt a proud member of the Pudding Club. Why did you choose Princeton? Didn't you ever consider another college?"

Her throwing such direct questions at him disturbed Court. "Yes," he answered, "I think I would have preferred a smaller school such as Amherst. But Princeton was expected of me. . . .and that's where I am." He ended on a faint note of defiance.

"Yes, there you are. I suppose it would have been too much to expect you to rebel on that issue. What courses are you taking?"

"Oh, Physics. . . .History."

"And when you graduate, which family enterprise is it to be, banking or brokerage?"

He was finding the interrogation irritating. He answered with more asperity than intended. "Look, Grandmother, I don't know yet *what* I'm going to do. I'm only a freshman. May never graduate. But even if I do, I'm in ROTC and will be another few years in the Air Force. So, in another eight or nine years I'll make up my mind and let you know."

She regarded him for a moment before speaking. "In other words," she rasped, with a curious edge to her voice, "it's none of my business. Is that what you're trying to say, Boy?"

What the hell. He'd gone too far already anyway. "You've got the message, Grandmother."

He regretted the words even as they left his mouth.

He fully expected to be soundly berated for his disrespect, and dismissed from her presence. He would welcome the latter. He felt foolish and uncomfortable under her unswerving scrutiny. Her response, when it came, startled him.

She chuckled. "So, it *is* possible to strike sparks from the dauphin. But you're quite wrong. It *is* my business; very much my business." At his look of bewilderment, her short laugh subsided into a thin smile. "I doubt if your father has outlined to you the provisions of your grandfather's will. Apart from properties and securities establishing trusts, the Maryland properties, this house and property, and shareholdings in the bank amounting to a controlling interest were left to me. In addition — and your father isn't even aware of the extent — a number of properties and securities were deeded to me prior to your grandfather's death. I have considerably more personal wealth than your father. Much more than he suspects. The disposal of this is entirely at my discretion. I have, therefore, a not unnatural interest in those nieces, nephews, and grandchildren who will survive me. You, Boy, as my only grandson, fall into a rather special category."

All this was a revelation to Court. He had known that his grandmother was wealthy. He had heard this discussed beween his parents. But while the old mansion was impressive, it had never led him to believe it symbolized any great fortune. Involuntarily, his eyes swept the conservatory.

Sipping her dry sherry, his grandmother noted the inventory and read a measure of disbelief in her grandson's eyes. She placed her glass primly back on the table, and broke into Court's speculation.

"This old mausoleum doesn't impress you, does it?

You have been a somewhat unwilling guest in this house for the past seventeen Christmases. You must have overheard your father importuning me to move to an estate in one of the more fashionable "main line" suburbs. You probably wondered why the stubborn old lady refused to move. It will very likely be difficult for you to understand my attachment. For me, it holds a host of memories, some good, a few bad, but they are my only real companions. I could not leave them to wither alone in this outdated old house.

"I came here as a young bride sixty-seven years ago. I was only a girl, a year older than you are now. The house was 38 years old even then. It was considered a magnificent mansion, and a landmark. It was to your great-grandfather, who had had the house built in the best traditions of Victorian architecture, a fitting symbol of his wealth and position. The house frightened me, and all the more so because of the circumstances of my marriage. My husband, your grandfather, was twenty years my senior. Our marriage wasn't based on romance, it was a simple matter of barter. My family, the Stainbridges, were socially prominent, but virtually penniless. I was a suitably acceptable bride for Courtney Palmer, who was then thirty-eight and desirous of producing a son and heir. He was not unkind, then or ever, but he was not a very romantic figure. His chief interest and dedication was in the bank. It was always his driving ambition to amass more wealth than your great-grandfather had managed to accumulate, and to ensure that the family name would have a secure place in American history. I believe he succeeded. For him as well, this house represented a symbol of status. To me, it was an oppressive trap. It took me a good many years to come to terms with this house.

"I hadn't been in this house a month when your great-grandmother died, leaving me the reluctant and very scared mistress of the household.

"Your great-grandmother had been ill for a number of years, so her death was no great shock. Nevertheless, Jerome was very close to his wife, and grieved at her passing. Gradually, the old man transferred a good deal of his affection and confidence to me. I sometimes think that I meant more to him than his own sons. I grew very fond of him, and through him the house lost its strangeness and started to become my friend. It is probably a strange admission, but I grew to have a stronger affection for my father-in-law than I ever had for my husband. Certainly, when he died suddenly a few months after your father was born, I was grief stricken."

Court was fascinated. He sat on the edge of the footstool, leaning forward to catch his grandmother's every word. Her voice had become softer, and her eyes misty as she became lost in the reminiscence. She stopped talking abruptly as she was wracked by a fit of coughing.

Court was concerned. "Can I get you anything, Grandmother?"

She recovered quickly. "No, no. It's this draughty old house. A touch of bronchitis . . . Always afflicts me this time of year." She took a lace handkerchief and patted her lips delicately. She smiled at Court. "I may have grown very fond of the old place, but I'll have to admit it has a few drawbacks. It's only twenty years older than I am, and almost as creaky."

Court was lost in thought. Suddenly, the old house had taken on a personality. He imagined the rooms as they must have been, filled with three generations of Palmers and their guests. Over a century, the house had stood, offering shelter, warmth, and hospitality to a pantheon of notables long since ghosts. He tried to imagine his grandmother at his own age. He looked down at her hands clasped in her lap; at the pale, liver-spotted skin stretched over prominent blueish veins and the swollen, distorted arthritic knuckles. And he glanced at his own strong hands, trying to imagine them as they might look in another seventy years.

She broke once more into his thoughts. Her voice had regained all its former strength. "I shall live here until I die. Then, the house will be yours. You can do with it as you please, but I wanted you to know something of its history."

Court murmered an expression of thanks, as he cleared his throat.

"But there is something else I wanted to tell you," his grandmother continued. "It concerns your great-grandfather. What do you know of him?"

Beyond the fact that his great-grandfather had always been held up as a model of what hard work and honest virtue could achieve, Court suddenly realized he knew very little. He didn't know how to answer the question. He was saved the embarrassment of an admission of ignorance by her next question.

"You knew he came from England as a boy. Was it ever suggested he might have been of noble birth?"

"Well, not nobility, exactly. Father has suggested that he came from an excellent background — that the Palmers have been noted parliamentarians, and that the family traces back to the Crusades."

His grandmother snorted. "Hogwash. It would have amused the old man to hear such a description of his family tree. As a matter of fact, any such myth that exists is largely his own fault. When he was courting your great-grandmother, he was considered an upstart by the Courtneys. To assist his cause, he hinted strongly at an illustrious lineage. There could have been Palmers with the crusading knights, and prominent in politics, but they weren't in your great-grandfather's immediate family branch.

"He was raised in a foundling home in Bristol. At about your age he was shipped to America as indentured labor.

"Some years later, he spent a good deal of money in an attempt to trace his parentage. He was only partially successful. His mother had been a waterfront whore named Jenny Palmer. He could never determine who had fathered him. In all likelihood, Jenny didn't know herself. However, from the district where she employed her professional talents the odds would favor a dockhand or a seafarer rather than an aristocrat. In short, Boy, your great-grandfather was a bastard.

"That could well have been a contributing factor to his determination to succeed. He was intelligent, cunning, and unscrupulous. He got his start by ingratiating himself with silly old Pugh. And, although he never admitted such an act to me, he was perfectly capable of hurrying along the old man's death.

"Those were the days of wooden ships and iron men. To carve out a stake in the shipping business, one had to be tough and ruthless. Since your great-grandfather rose rapidly in his chosen field, you will have some idea of his character.

"His big chance came with the Civil War. I have heard my husband, and your father prate about patriotism, flag, and country. Your great-grandfather was hampered by no such clap-trap. He charged the Union all the traffic would bear to ship armaments and supplies. And, at the same

time, he financed a fleet of blockade runners for the Confederate States. Through shipping connections in London,
he obtained arms and supplies for both sides. For the
Confederate States, he arranged barter cargo exchanges
in Bermuda. Whichever side triumphed, Jerome Palmer
stood to profit and emerge a winner.

"After the Civil War, your great-grandfather was nothing
more nor less than a carpetbagger. He acted through agents,
of course, but the end result was the same. He acquired
more damned property in the south than the Courtneys
ever dreamed existed — and in the same process dis-
possessed his own brother-in-law to pick up title to
Nine Oaks.

"He founded the Knickerbocker Trust Bank to finance
his own reconstruction in the south, and lend money to
other financial projects at usurous rates of interest.

"That is the manner by which our fortune came into
being. Jerome Palmer was a grasping, crafty bastard,
but he had guts and was above all a man. A man the measure of whom this family has not seen since."

Court digested what she had just told him. The painstakingly woven tapestry depicting family background
unraveled before his eyes. At least one icon proved to have
been erected on a pedestal of basest clay. He suspected
that others were similarly flawed. Yet it was a relief to
find that these figures were after all men imbued with
human frailties.

He did not for a moment doubt the truth of her account,
but a number of things still puzzled him. "Does my father know of this?" he questioned.

"He does not. When old Jerome confided his story to
me, he did so on the condition that I never divulge it to his
sons. Their own mother was not aware of his illegitimacy,

or many of his more reprehensible business dealings. My husband was by no means a stupid man and I believe he knew at least part of the story. It led him to strive doubly hard to cloak the family name in a mantle of respectability. I kept my trust with the old man. During your grandfather's life, I told no one the story. When your grandfather died, your father was well into his forties. Had he been younger, with less overweaning pride in his heritage, I might have told him. I did not."

"Why have you told me?"

She rested one claw-like hand on the sleeve of his jacket. "For several good reasons," she answered. "Through no fault of your own, you are being cast in a mold I believe ill-suited. Princeton has nurtured some of the finest brains of this country, but it has also produced some of the stuffiest snobs who ever graced a corporate board room. I have no wish to see you enter those ranks. And I also feel that you possess some of your great-grandfather's character and strength."

Court was not convinced that old Jerome Palmer's qualities were admirable, but he realized his grandmother had paid a sincere compliment. He brought his hand to rest lightly on the frail hand of the old lady. He squeezed gently and felt a tremor in response.

Twilight had descended, casting deepening purple shadows in the conservatory. Court could barely distinguish the time-creased countenance of the old lady. Now he could almost visualize her as the young and frightened girl who had first come to this old house. The many decades which separated them melted away, and Court felt both sympathy and understanding.

She withdrew her hand from beneath his. "It has been many years since I have been called by my proper name in this house," she said. "I will make a pact with you, Boy. From this day, but only when we are alone, I shall call you Court. You shall call me Lucy. Is it agreed?"

"Yes, Gra. . . Lucy."

"Good. Then I suggest, Court, that you wheel me into the study. I think we both need something a bit stronger than sherry."

* * * *

CHAPTER FOUR

The stewardess retrieved the luncheon tray from in front of the passenger in seat 31C of the economy class section. The occupant of the seat, Tony DeSantis, smiled up at her. She smiled automatically in response and moved to the seats ahead.

Tony raised and secured the drop-table. Leaning forward, he pulled the flight bag from beneath his seat and unzipped it. As he poked within the contents of the bag in search of some desired object, he edged the bag forward until it was partially hidden under the seat ahead. His groping fingers located the cloth-wrapped cannister. His glance darted to the fellow passenger in the window seat on his side, and to the single passenger in 31F across the aisle. Neither evinced the slightest interest in Tony's activity.

Taking care to avoid contact with the metal surface, he partly unwrapped the cannister until he could peel back the attached strips of adhesive. In one motion, he raised the can against the underside of seat 30C and smoothed out the securing tape. Letting the cloth wrapping fall back into his flight bag, Tony extracted a pocket book as the object of his search. He settled back in his seat, leaving the unzipped bag at his feet. The operation had taken only a few seconds.

Tony checked his watch. When the sweep second hand came up to twelve, he had exactly six minutes before he must reach down and twist the top of the hidden cannister.

In case a customs check might have found the device questionable, it had been constructed in an innocent looking can of foam shaving cream. It was a simple apparatus. It was filled to one-third of its capacity with a mild acid solution. A half turn of the top would drop the chemical into the acid bath. The resulting reaction would produce a pungent, but harmless, black smoke. From the moment the top was twisted, there would be a lag of 30 seconds before there would be sufficient pressure within the cannister to operate the spring-loaded release valve built into the spout. Then, the smoke would start pouring into the economy class cabin, and would continue for a calculated duration of 90 seconds. The 30 second margin would allow ample time for Tony to take up his position at the rear of the aircraft before the panic and confusion started.

He leafed absently through the book, hoping he appeared unconcerned. In spite of the many times they had rehearsed the action, and the anticipated reaction of the aircraft crew and passengers, Tony was nervous.

* * * *

In the first class compartment, Court went through a five minute period of mounting concern. The Indian Ambassador's wife had gone forward to the lavatory and had remained there for what seemed to Court an agonizingly long stretch of time. As she emerged to waddle back to her seat, Court checked the time for the fourth time in as many minutes.

Lucille had noted his preoccupation with amusement. "Going someplace?" she questioned.

Court grinned. "Was beginning to think our fat friend intended to ride out the rest of the flight in the can. Have a pressing need for the facilities myself." The latter part of his statement was indeed true. He had a little less than four minutes in hand. Running his hand over his face, he added, "While I'm there, I think I'll grab a quick shave. Will you excuse me?"

"Certainly."

Returning to his original seat, Court retrieved a soft leather bag. No panic, he admonished himself mentally, play it cool. All he really required was two minutes in the lavatory, but the timing was vital. He couldn't afford to have anyone else get there ahead of him now.

Once in the washroom, Court secured the door latch, placed his bag on the sink shelf, unzipped the bag, and went to work with the swift sure movements of practice.

At the bottom of an inner pocket, a concealed catch released the false bottom of the bag. From this hidden compartment, Court removed a number of articles.

Covering shoes and trousers, he pulled on black muslin leggings, tying them at his waist. Next, he shrugged into a black, sleeved frock, somewhat like a surgeon's gown, which came to well below his knees. He took out a wire contraption which unfolded into a basket-like framework. He placed this over his head onto his shoulders, where it snapped onto fittings of the cloak. Over the wire bracket he pulled a loose black hood. The face-piece of the hood was of lighter material which allowed only slightly obscured outward vision while still effectively disguising his features. Fully clad in this bizarre sable outfit, Court surveyed his image in the mirror above the washbasin.

"If I didn't know it was you inside this rig, old buddy," he murmured, his voice muffled by the cloth, "I'd be scared shitless." The wire framework beneath the hood added two inches to his height. He had designed the weird ensemble to provide not only a complete disguise for the wearer, but also to present an awesomely-looming apparition calculated to inspire fear in the beholder. In this dual purpose, the outlandish get-up was remarkably effective.

Court had but three tasks to complete in the time remaining. He took off his thin gold Longine wrist watch, switching it for a stainless steel Seiko. Slipping his hands into black gloves, he took the snub-nosed 38 revolver from the bottom of the bag and transferred it to the pocket of his cloak. Then he folded his bag and stuffed it well down in the used-linen disposal bin.

As he slipped the Longine wrist watch into an inner pocket, he noted with satisfaction that he had one minute to spare. He had expected to be nervous, but was surprised that he felt calm. He sat down on the toilet to wait out the remaining seconds.

Court was aware of the gentle vibration of the speeding jetliner. It was a familiar sensation. His mind flashed back to the days when he had jockeyed a different and much faster jet — an Fl05 fighter-bomber — and to Deke Maloney.

*   *   *   *

Court's years at Princeton passed all too swiftly. They were memorable years.

Plunged into a world of new experiences, Court found life absorbing. Naturally gregarious, he found that the communal life of the campus suited him. He also discovered that now that the subjects were no longer spoon-fed as they had been during his elementary and high school education, he had both the inclination and aptitude for study. He still wasn't setting the academic world on fire, but his achievement level improved dramatically. Physics presented to him almost as much a challenge as had show riding and yacht racing.

He still did not aspire to athletic eminence, preferring the role of enthusiastic supporter to that of active participant. When approached to turn out for the hockey team, he declined. It was still his thesis that time devoted to team practice could be better employed in other pursuits. Lest his interpretation be construed as scholastic endeavor, he averred: "I'd sooner gain renown as a boudoir bandit than as star of track and gridiron."

Both Palmer Square, in the town, and Palmer Stadium, on campus, were a source of mild embarrassment for Court. It was assumed by many that he was a descendant of the Palmer whose contributions to college and community had been immortalized. It was purest coincidence, but Court's disclaimers to relationship met with skepticism. "Suppose," as he put it, "my name happened to be Firestone. Would the library have to be named for some forebearer?" Since the answer was as often as not, "Yes", in time he abandoned the analogy. He took the line of least resistance and confined his answer to the oft repeated query to a noncommittal shrug. He supposed that his father had been exposed to the same problem and wondered how he had handled it. He meant to question his father on this score, but somehow he never did.

His studies were not so arduous that social life was excluded. Court enjoyed this aspect of college life to the fullest. There were hockey and football weekends, forays into town to visit the Garden Theatre or Playhouse, followed by the Nassau Tavern in Palmer Square, furtive assignations at motels along the highway to Trenton, and of course the coveted weekends in New York. To the latter, Court had impressive credentials. He was already familiar with many of the delights of Manhattan, his credit well established through his father's having exposed Court to the night-life of the city. Headwaiters and bartenders treated Court with all due deference, which enhanced his reputation with those college friends who accompanied him on these weekend excursions. Then too, when he knew his father would be out of town, Court utilized the Central Park West apartment to advantage. On these occasions, he was careful to ensure that any incriminating evidence, such as empty bottles, bobby pins, or stray lingerie, was removed before his return to Princeton. Court's reliance on the discretion of the servants was misplaced. Court's father generally received an account of the festivities. Court would have been astonished that instead of being angry, his father was amused.

For all his vaunted reputation as "The Swordsman of Darien", Court's box-score was not all that impressive. To other than Court, this was not known. To explain his not-infrequent solitary trips to Philadelphia, Court made casual reference to a mistress. By this simple deception, he racked-up undeserved points. The "mistress" was his grandmother.

Court's familial attachments had never been very deep. The strongest bond had been between himself and his sister Sharron. As they grew apart due to schooling and diverse interests, this tie became attenuated. An additional and much stronger linkage with the family had been forged by Lucinda's unexpected disclosures on the Christmas of Court's Freshman year at Princeton. There was, in the new relationship, something in the nature of a conspiracy. In the presence of the rest of the family, during the annual Christmas pilgrimage, a rigidly formal facade was maintained, where Court was still "Boy", and Lucinda, a respectful "Grandmother." In private, they lapsed easily into the agreed "Court", and "Lucy."

The relationship was mutually rewarding. Court delighted in Lucy's anecdotes from her youth and her association with the Palmer family. With purpose, she stripped away the veneer of pomp and pretense to expose the human foibles and frailties beneath. She did this not with malice, but with charity and a keen eye for the humor in the situations. The skeletons she caused to emerge from the family closets pranced forth as loosly-jointed comics rather than tenebrous specters.

Through Lucy, Court appreciated the glee with which his great-grandfather would recount a sharp practice or act of particular chicanery. He became a spectator to a number of events in Lucy's life which had been closely guarded secrets. He learned, for example, that his grandfather, at the age of sixty, succumbed to the allure of his secretary, Lydia Spencer. The affair had been short-lived, but had resulted in a child whose relationship to Court would be half-uncle. Courtney had never known that Lucinda was aware of his brief infidelity. In the retelling to Court, Lucy expressed not only a sympathetic understanding of her husband's late blooming romance, but regret that he had been guilt ridden for the remainder of his life. In her late thirties, Lucy herself had been guilty of an indiscretion with a vividly remembered, though profitless romance in Atlanta.

There was one thing Court noted, though he refrained from comment. Lucy rarely mentioned episodes involving his own father. He took this as a natural discretion on her part; a desire to preserve his image of his father. In part he was correct. Lucy's sparing reference to her son was dictated by the fact that she had never held him in high esteem and could find little good to say of him.

And in turn, Lucinda profited from the association. Court gave her the confidence he had never shared with his parents and sisters. She learned of his hopes, fears, aspirations, triumphs, and tragedies. Through his experiences, she vicariously returned to her own youth. In addition, if only for the duration of Court's visits, she was reprieved from her self-imposed isolation and able to drop the pose of matriarchal curmudgeon.

Court told Lucy of his initiation to sex by Mary-Lou Kenear, and his keenly-felt disappointment in a more recent encounter. In his freshman year. Court invited Mary-Lou down from Radcliffe for a football weekend. He drove her back to New York to make the train connection for Cambridge, allowing sufficient time for an overnight romp on the town. At the hotel, they picked up where they had left off in their summer encounters. For both, it was a peculiarly disappointing experience. Mary-Lou returned to Princeton several times over the next couple of years, but as a guest of Ted Cranston, an upper-classman and distant cousin of Court's. Lucy's dry comment was that trying to relive a youthful romance was like watching a rerun of an old movie on the late-late-show. It might evoke nostalgia, but invariably failed to bring back the pleasure of the original performance.

Lucinda lived through the ecstacy and despair of Court's affair with Marcie.

Without warning, love came to Court in the fall semester of his junior year. It came wrapped in the exotic packaging of Marcie Kirk.

"The Wayward Warlock" was being presented in New Hope, Pennsylvania on its pre-Broadway tryout. Court was persuaded to run down to take in the play. From the opening curtain, he regretted his decision. He found the acting mediocre, the lines trite, and the comedy contrived. In the second act, a girl playing a junior-grade apprentice witch called Sybella made an entrance. Court was jolted upright in his seat as though he'd been plugged into a live socket. He suffered through the rest of the play, his interest quickened only when Sybella was on stage. Unfortunately, hers was a minor role.

After the performance, Court contrived to go back stage.

When he was introduced to the actress who had played Sybella, his customary confidence suddenly deserted him. Marcie Kirk, who was playing this small part, found something appealing about the inarticulate college junior.

The play opened on Broadway in October to such rave notices as: "It Stinks!" and "Avoid it at any cost." Court was indignant. Marcie adopted a more philisophical attitude. "It *was* a turkey," she said in full accord with the critical acclaim. "It even bombed in New Hope."

Marcie was an entirely new experience for Court. She had money. The theatre was only a passing interest. She lived in a four-level apartment off Washington Square. Court moved in with her, commuting from New Jersey. He very nearly failed his junior year.

Her grandfather was Senator Kirk. There was a solid background of wealth in the family. Court expected that this similarity would contribute to a community of interest. Apart from sexual compatibility, he found they had little in common. Even in this area, Court found himself slightly confused. Marcie was a wildly uninhibited sexual partner with an avid interest in experimentation, but there were times, sometimes weeks on end, when she would practice total abstinence from intercourse. These periods, generally but not exclusively, coincided with Marcie's quickened interest in some new doctrine or cause. Whatever the reason, these stints of enforced celibacy drove Court to near desperation.

By tradition, rather than conviction, Court was a Republican. He could not agree with his father that the election of John Fitzgerald Kennedy spelled doom for the nation. Essentially, Court was politically noncommitted. He was not swayed by Marcie's arguments that the Establishment must be overthrown, or that the whole country and the world were going to hell in a basket. He could not bring himself to like many of her friends who espoused revolution, free love, the emancipation of the downtrodden female, equal rights for the oppressed negro, herbalism, scientology, the unrestrained use of drugs, or any number of bewildering isms. Her friends fell into two main categories. They were either long-haired, unkempt, and given to weird garment; or equally obnoxious intense young executives. In either case, her companions were equally patronizing to a Princeton under-graduate and contemptuous of Court's wealth and background. Marcie joined with the latter opinion, being as self-flagellating concerning her own antecedents. In defense of his family, Court told Marcie something of his great-grandfather's history. He regretted the impulse. Marcie invented an episodic series of movie scenarios which she entitled "Robber Baron", "Son of Robber Baron", and "Grandson of Robber Baron." She was, as she stated, currently working on the script for "Great-Grandson of Robber Baron", using Courtney J. Palmer III for the required research. Court even went along with some of the fantasies, but at times her open derision hurt and angered him.

Court's months with the mercurial Marcie were a time of both joy and misery; of heated arguments, violent quarrels, recrimination, tender reconciliation, and deep sexual fulfillment. He was being introduced to a world well beyond the confining scope of his sheltered youth and tradition-bound Princeton. It was a disturbing, frenetic explosive world brimming with raw passions. It was both exciting and frightening.

Under the tutelage of Marcie and her friends, Court experimented with the escapism provided by narcotics and hallucinogens. He found that marijuana, and its stronger cousin hashish, stimulated him and released him from inhibition. In moderation, amphetamines seemed to enhance his sexual pleasure. Peyote and LSD were mind-blowing encounters, but frightened him. As for hard drugs, such as cocaine and heroin, Court witnessed too many examples of their devastating effects for there to be any appeal in the fleeting euphoria they imparted. He came to the conclusion that drugs were a sick scene, and confined himself to the occasional indulgence in pot.

Through this exposure to wide spectra of experience and challenging ideas, Court was arriving at a new awareness. He was making the painful transition from youth to manhood. The process of questioning appearance and dogma, initiated by his grandmother, was carried even further by his association with Marcie.

To display consideration for Court's feelings was not one of Marcie's conspicuous virtues, yet she refrained from provoking him when he was under stress as the final examinations approached. She delayed informing him of her pregnancy until after the exams.

Court received the startling news with decidedly mixed emotions. He suddenly discovered that he wanted Marcie to bear his child, but the complications arising from such an event at this time were truly dismaying. Beyond the immediate objectives of graduation and a stint of reserve military service, Court had formed no very clear ideas concerning his future. Eventual marriage and fatherhood, when he thought of them at all, had been relegated to somewhere in the region of a decade hence. Marcie's disclosure radically altered his thinking. He decided that the only honorable course was an immediate marriage. He would sort out the remaining problems later.

Marcie's reaction to his proposal stunned him. She was

indignant of the implication that she was using pregnancy to promote marriage. In no uncertain terms, she told him that she had no desire for the state of matrimony, either now, or in the foreseeable future. She had decided that she wanted a baby — his baby. It was no accident. Had she wished to avoid pregnancy, she could easily have done so. He should be damned grateful that she had selected him to sire the child, but not stupid enough to feel she required a husband to go with it. She valued her freedom too much to even consider such legalized slavery. If Court wanted to continue living with her, and share the experience of parenthood, he'd better get any ideas of marriage out of his cotton-picking head. In addition, she advised him that she was planning to go to Europe with friends sometime before the end of the summer.

In August, Marcie announced that she was leaving for Spain. Court wanted to accompany her. She vetoed his suggestion angrily. She softened, and assured him that she would keep him advised of her progress.

Court returned to his senior year, confused and bewildered by the events of the summer, missing Marcie desperately, yet relieved that she had absolved him, at least temporarily, of responsibilities.

It was November before he received a postcard from San Antonio on the island of Ibiza. Marcie scrawled that in spite of increasing girth, she was having a marvelous time. As a postscript, she added: "Yanqui No, Cuba Si!"

Court sent a long letter containing a check to the address given in Ibiza. Shortly after Christmas, the letter was returned, marked "Address Unknown".

1963 was a turbulent year, marked by momentous and tragic events.

In late February, Court received his second letter from

Marcie. She announced that a healthy young son had arrived on schedule in early January at a hospital in Malaga. He was, she said, the very image of Court. In honor of another illustrious bastard, she had christened the baby Jerome. To avoid any patriarchal confusion, she added, the surname was Kirk. She stated that she was working in a boutique in Marbella, that both she and the baby were well and happy, but that the February weather on the Costa del Sol left a good deal to be desired. She closed with love to Daddy from Marcie and Jerry.

Court wrote and enclosed a cashier's check for a substantial amount. The check was not returned, but his letter went unanswered.

*   *   *   *

"Bastard to bastard in five generations," he said glumly.

Lucinda looked at him for a moment before commenting. "I will admit that by the standards of my youth, I should find her attitude incomprehensible. Still, over the last three or four decades I have noticed a definite trend developing. The so-called sanctity of marriage has almost become meaningless in most of this country. Divorce has become an accepted fact and carries with it virtually no stigma. In all likelihood, illigitimacy will become equally acceptable."

Court hadn't expected his grandmother to defend Marcie's action. He had been prepared to enter a plea on Marcie's behalf, even though he couldn't quite understand or condone her decision.

Lucinda noted the confusion in her grandson. She chuckled. "We old people are supposed to be hidebound and inflexible. I suppose we do become slaves to habit. But I happen to have given the institution of marriage considerable thought over the past few decades. It seems to me that the economic advantages of a tightly-knit family unit in a pioneering and agrarian society have largely disappeared. The days of economic empire building, which founded dynastic structures such as ours, are a thing of the past. In a rapidly advancing technological society such as we now live in, strong loyalties to family may not even be desirable. The need, or even the desire, for the traditional family unit could well become an anachronism. If that is so, legitimizing the progeny becomes the only valid excuse for continuing an outmoded practice. Habit dies hard, but it might well be that the path chosen by Marcie could become the rule rather than the exception."

Court had heard arguments of a similar nature advanced within Marcie's circle of friends. They were not without logic, but he had considered them impractical. That Marcie subscribed to such views hadn't made them any more palatable. To hear them issue from the lips of his grandmother, was akin to heresy.

"But, Lucy," he protested, "he's my son. He should at least bear my name."

"He's also my great-grandson," she remarked drily. "He carries your blood — our blood — which I hope will prove an advantage. He is also of your Marcie's blood. I may not think her actions wise, but she's displayed courage. In the naming of the child, she's demonstrated a sense of humor. If little Jerome inherits those two qualities, he's well equipped to handle life."

He nodded agreement. She was right. If the child lucked-out on genes from both parents, he was off to a good start. All that remained was to see to it that he wasn't neglected. From what he knew of Marcie, he wasn't sure on this point.

He resolved that immediately after graduation he would visit Spain and satisfy himself that the baby was receiving her love and attention.

A morbid thought struck him. "If there's any truth to the family superstition, Father doesn't know it but he won't last out the year."

"Hogwash," she said, with a flash of annoyance. "Jerome was 75 when he died; your grandfather 89. Do you think Palmers are supposed to live forever?

Court grinned. "Hope you're right Lucy. If the little bastard takes after his old man, I'll be a grandfather by the time I'm 40. I'd hate to get cut off in my prime."

*   *   *   *

Court graduated in late May. At the same ceremony, he received his commission as Second Lieutenant in the Air Force.

His parents attended the graduation. In a Givenchy ensemble, Kathleen looked radiantly lovely; no older than 40 instead of 54. His father, tanned, erect and handsome, was impressively distinguished. Watching them, Court suddenly wished he knew his parents better.

He was to report for active duty at Vance Air Force Base in Enid, Oklahoma by the 15th of June. It didn't give him much time to visit Marcie in Spain.

He arrived at the Malaga airport on June 3rd. Renting a U-Drive, he drove the 57 kilometers down the coastal highway to Marbella.

He located the boutique at the address Marcie had given him. She was no longer there. He was informed that she was managing a small bar-restaurant on the Paseo Maritimo in Fuengirola. His informants were not sure of the exact location.

Court checked into the Mare Nostrum hotel on the out-
skirts of Fuengirola. The following morning, he set out
along the wide promenade, checking the bars and restaurants fronting the sea. He found her about noon, not properly on the Paseo Maritimo, but at a beach bar called
The Clipper.

Marcie was casually dressed in shorts and a halter;
tanned a golden brown, bubbling with health and good
spirits, and delighted to see Court. She proudly displayed
the rustic open bar, small attached kitchen facility, and the
stretch of beach with lounge chairs and small circular
palm-frond umbrellas to provide shade. She explained that
the rush of European summer visitors wasn't due for another
few weeks, and that she was rushing a changing room and
shower to completion. The whole enterprise, he was led to
understand, was partly his, since it was his February check
which had financed the undertaking.

After lunch, Marcie took Court along to a small villa
on the Avenida Nacional. There he was introduced to a
gurgling, chubby infant who was his son. He was also introduced to a hulking blond Norwegian giant named Eric. Court
never did catch the last name. Offhandedly, Marcie explained that Eric was an artist who was living with her temporarily.

The baby was well cared for by a small dark maid, who
obviously adored the infant, and by his equally proud and
attentive mother.

With no false modesty, Marcie slipped out of her halter
to breast-feed little Jerome, at the same time keeping up
a running chatter with both Court and Eric.

Court stayed only three days. He felt like an intruder.
Satisfied that the baby was receiving every possible atten-

tion, yet disturbed by the presence of the big Viking, he left for Malaga. He flew to Madrid, and directly to New York.

Second Lieutenant Courtney Palmer was well into his initial introduction to flight training, flying T37 subsonic trainers. The tragic news interrupted his instruction. He was granted leave, and flew home for the memorial service.

Kathleen had been on her annual shopping expedition to Europe. In late October, she had flown to Rome to visit with Helen and Sharron. On the return flight, the aircraft had crashed in the French Alps, killing the entire crew and passenger load.

At the funeral service, Court found himself wishing fervently that he'd been closer to his mother. He was saddened by her passing, but experienced none of the acute grief exhibited by his sisters. He was thankful for one mercy. His mother couldn't have suffered much in the few seconds preceding her abrupt demise.

The year's quota of tragedy had not been exhausted. On the first day of November, a military coup d'état toppled the Ngo Dihn Diem dynastic regime in Viet-Nam. The Brothers, Diem and Nhu, were brutally assassinated. Although hotly denied, the nation suspected its Administration of complicity. There was an uneasy feeling of guilt surrounding news of the remote event.

Some three weeks later, the nation was horrified and plunged into grief by the assassination of John F. Kennedy in Dallas.

During these months, Court discovered that he possessed a natural aptitude for flying. He thoroughly enjoyed the training and was delighted when, in mid-December, he graduated from the slower T37s to supersonic T38s.

Court's father had not objected to ROTC at Princeton

although he would have preferred that Court opt for Navy rather than Air Force. In 1964, however, the picture on the international scene was changing alarmingly. In Viet-Nam, the November coup d'etat was followed in rapid succession by a series of coups. During this period, known as 'the waltz of the generals', the situation in Viet-Nam steadily deteriorated. The American AID and military commitment grew apace. Through his connections on 'the hill', Courtney Jr. was more aware of the gravity of the situation than the average citizen. He became concerned that Court could not long escape involvement.

Without consulting his son, Courtney Jr. quietly arranged through Vice-Admiral Parker at the Navy Bureau of Personnel for a transfer of Court from the Air Force to Naval Intelligence.

When Court learned of his father's action, he was furious and rejected his father's well-meaning intervention out of hand. Court would not even consider the transfer.

Court earned his wings in June. During his leave, there was a bitter scene between his father and himself. Courtney Jr. could not understand why his son had rejected the proposed transfer, and was understandably angry. Eventually, however, he resigned himself to the fact that Court could not be persuaded from his intention to continue his reserve military career as a flyer.

From his year of basic training, Court had emerged in second place out of his class of 40 trainees. Court was assigned to more advanced training as a fighter pilot at McConnell Air Force Base, Wichita, Kansas.

Court was introduced to the F105 Thunderchief fighter-bomber. His Instructor Pilot for this training was Captain Desmond Kevin (Deke) Maloney.

There was an almost instant rapport between the two

men. Deke Maloney and Court Palmer, became not only instructor and pupil, but fast friends. If it was an unlikely affinity; a close association between the son of a third generation Irish son of a Brooklyn cop, and the scion of one of America's most prominent WASP families, neither of them noticed it.

The growing friendship was interrupted when Deke Maloney was assigned to Nellis Air Force Base, Las Vegas, Nevada in January, 1965. Court stayed on at McConnell, becoming an Instructor Pilot in his own right.

The two men kept in touch by correspondence. In April, 1965, Deke was transferred to the Danang Air Base in Viet-Nam. Thereafter, the letters became less frequent. It was to be July, 1967, before the two men would meet again, at an operational base in a different country, to continue the friendship from the point they had left off two and one-half years earlier.

* * * *

CHAPTER FIVE

Tony DeSantis closed the paperback and dropped it into the unzipped bag at his feet. Leaning down, he rummaged within the bag as though rearranging its contents. With a cloth protecting his fingers from direct contact, he grasped the knob of the gas cannister taped beneath seat 30C. When the sweep second hand of his wrist watch indicated the exact minute, he twisted the knob the required half-turn.

Whistling softly to mask his nervousness, DeSantis picked up his bag and sauntered the few yards past the after serving galley to the lavatories. The lighted signs on all three doors indicated that the washrooms were occupied. DeSantis grasped the handle of the forward door and twisted it sharply three times, then once more, slowly.

Inside the lavatory, Anderson was waiting for this signal. He unlatched the door. Fumbling at his belt, he emerged. With no sign of recognition, he eased his bulky frame past DeSantis with a muttered apology.

Sidling around Anderson, DeSantis stepped into the washroom, closed and locked the door, and placed his flight bag alongside the one Anderson had left on the sinkboard.

Working quickly to don the black costume, DeSantis could already hear sounds of mounting confusion from the other side of the locked door. He didn't have to switch wrist watches, his already being the standard synchronized Seiko. As he adjusted the hood, he said a silent prayer that everything was going according to plan with Palmer up forward in first class.

Taking Anderson's bag in his left hand, he unlatched the door. Easing the door ajar, he checked to see if the other two lavatories were now vacant. They were. Having ensured that he could not be surprised from that quarter, he swung open the door and stepped out into the passageway. Revolver grasped in his gloved right hand, DeSantis faced forward. By now, the cannister had ceased to generate smoke and the billowing clouds within the cabin were thinning. The passengers and crew members crowding at the rear of the aircraft were intent on the activities of the flight engineer who was on his knees groping beneath seat 30C.

*   *   *   *

Court assumed his duties at McConnell Air Force Base in January, 1965.

Over the months that followed, the giant base became increasingly active. Tension had been growing steadily since the preceding August 2nd when North Vietnamese PT boats launched an attack against an American destroyer in the Gulf of Tonkin. The Gulf of Tonkin Incident was followed on August 4th with retaliatory strikes against PT boats and coastal installations in North Vietnam. Then. on the 7th of February, bombing raids north of the 17th parallel commenced in response to a Viet Cong attack on a U.S. military base in the South Viet-Nam highlands at Pleiku. By March, the decision was reached to commit U.S. forces in active support of South Vietnamese forces. On June 18th, the first B52 bomber raids against Viet Cong and North Vietnamese Army concentrations were launched from Guam. In effect, a state of war existed and the Stateside Air Force Bases accelerated training and took on the function of staging areas. McConnell, being essentially a fighter-bomber base, and since the adjoining Boeing plant and runways were devoted to the reconstruction and testing of monster eight-engined, droop-winged B52 strategic bombers, probably saw more activity than most bases.

Court was caught up in the pace of events. Like most

of the younger pilots, he wanted to be where the action was. While it was infinitely better than the administrative work which Court detested, the simulated tactical nuclear weapons delivery runs at Phillips Bomb Range seemed a pretty poor substitute for payload strikes over North Viet-Nam.

When he learned of Deke Maloney's posting to Viet-Nam, Court was more dissatisfied than ever. He asked for transfer to the Southeast Asian theater of operations. His request was rejected.

*   *   *   *

Early on the morning of October 8th, Court received a long-distance call from his father advising that Grandmother Palmer had passed away quietly in her sleep the previous night.

Her death should not have come as a surprise to Court. After all, she had been in her ninety-first year. Over the past few years, the old lady had been virtually bedridden, with a trained nurse in attendance. From the time he had gone on active duty, his visits with Lucy had been much less frequent. On each occasion, he had noted her physical deterioration. Yet even as her body wasted her mind remained actively alert. With the exception of a rare expression of waspish exasperation, she never complained of either age or ailment. The unfailing humor and indominable will she projected from within her eroding exterior had lulled Court into discrediting the evidence of his eyes. Her passing came to him as a wrenching shock.

To the rest of the immediate Palmer family, Lucinda's departure came as neither surprise nor shock, but as a welcomed relief from the tyranny of the crusty old martinet.

Any sadness Court's sisters may have experienced was submerged by anticipation of material benefits. With scarcely
a twinge of conscience, Court's father considered his
mother's demise a blessing. In his eyes, apart from a
symbol of family solidarity, she had long since outlived
any useful function.

Court was granted emergency leave to attend the funeral
rites.

Throughout the ceremonial eulogies at both chapel and
graveside, Court maintained his outward composure. Only
once did his control slip. As the coffin was being slowly
lowered into the open grave, he was distracted by the open
sobbing of the old housekeeper. A sense of the magnitude
of his own loss flooded over Court. Angrily, he suppressed
his impulse to cry. Lucy would have been the first to
deride such a display of self-pity.

Fleeting as was the betrayal of Court's anguish, it did
not go undetected. His father was surprised and puzzled
by the momentary exhibition of emotion. Later, he would put
it down to remorse.

At the reading of Lucinda's will, there were a number
of surprises in store for the family. Even Court, who had
enjoyed Lucy's confidence, was not prepared for some of
the revelations.

The estate consisted of many more securities and
properties than anyone, with the possible exception of
Court and her lawyers, had imagined. But it was not her
holdings so much as the manner in which Lucinda had
chosen to dispose of them that caused dismay.

It was hardly surprising that the bulk of her estate went
to the Courtney J. Palmer Foundation. What caused consternation was the disposition of the substantial residue.

The old house on Spruce Street and Nine Oaks were bequeathed to Court. He had known about the Philadelphia mansion, but the estate in Maryland was a surprise. That was nothing, compared with the next startling disclosure of which Court had not had the slightest intimation. Instead of being willed to his father, Lucinda's shareholdings in the Knickerbocker Trust Bank were bequeathed directly to Courtney J. Palmer III.

His father was visibly shaken, but Court could not but admire his father's quick return to a pocker-faced acceptance of the fact.

Court was not amused by the old lady's whimsical caprice. He fully appreciated the undesirable aspects. And knowing Lucy as he had, he discarded the thought that her action had been any whim. It was a calculated move. Had he had the barest hint that anything like this was in her mind he would have done everything possible to disuade her. She had known full well that Court had no intention of taking up banking as a career. By skipping the logical succession, she had unsubtly indicated a lack of confidence in her own son. She had widened the gulf which already existed between father and son. And to compensate against the event that this rift should one day become an open break, she had prevented Court's exclusion from a voice in the affairs of the family's major enterprise.

Among the bequests to relatives, friends, and servants, were two which were a total mystery to all in the family but Court.

A sum of one hundred thousand dollars was settled on a California resident named Wesley Spencer. Court presumed this to be his illegitimate half-uncle. He wondered if Spencer would have any conception of the reason for such good fortune. Probably not. Even if he knew of his relationship to the Palmer family, he could not have anticipated an old lady's belated gesture in granting absolution for her long-dead husband's infidelity.

The second strange bequest was in the form of a fifty thousand dollar educational trust fund established in the name of Jerome Leslie Kirk, American, aged two and one-half years, resident at 22 Avenida Nacional, Fuengirola (Malaga), Spain.

Court felt warmth and gratitude well within him. While he had recounted to Lucy his trip to Spain and short visit with Marcie and the baby, he had not mentioned the Fuengirola address. Lucy must have employed an investigator to report on her great-grandson. Until the reading of the will, Court hadn't even known his son's middle name.

After almost a decade of secrecy, Court's relationship with his grandmother would be next to impossible to explain. He knew this, and appreciated that by the provisions of her last will and testament Lucinda had invited, nay, demanded speculation. He was resigned to the fact that eventually the servants, or the nurse, would disclose the unlikely association. That this would be construed as a scheme of Court's to ingratiate himself with a senile old lady to further his own ends, was inevitable. The material benefits accruing to Court upon her death would be taken as damning evidence. Who would believe that his grandmother had initiated the relationship? Nobody Ruefully, he accepted the fact that any chance of logical explanation had been buried along with Lucy's casket. In setting out to wean him from what she felt to be the placebo of family tradition, she had done a remarkably effective job.

*   *   *   *

Throughout his two and one-half year tour of duty at

McConnell Air Force Base, Court periodically repeated his request for transfer to an operational squadron in Southeast Asia. His importuning met with negative response.

The initial enthusiasm for combat which had pervaded the Wichita airbase in early 1965, had not been shared so wholeheartedly by veterans of the Korean War and had been embraced even less by those of World War II vintage. Now, as the struggle in Viet-Nam carried into its second year of full-scale American participation, veterans of this conflict commenced to filter back to McConnell. For the most part, they had matured rapidly during their exposure to 100 combat missions or full year under the stress of combat conditions. They spoke disdainfully of the reluctance of MIG fighters to join in aerial combat, but related with awe the devastating effects of the intense and highly accurate anti-aircraft defenses ringing the North Viet-Nam target areas. Of the comrades they had seen winked-out in a ball of fire, or streaking earthward with mortal wounds, or that they knew or suspected were prisoners of war, they spoke but little if at all. At McConnell, as at countless other airbases throughout the states, the desire to join battle commenced to wane.

Perversely, Court's own personal wish to see action did not dimnish. If anything, it increased in inverse proportion to the discouragement of combat-weary pilots. It wasn't that he was a war lover, or had any burning desire to reduce the enemy terrain to smoldering rubble. The truth was that he was haunted by a sense of shame. He was acutely aware that the Palmer posture of patriotic duty was an empty sham. His great-grandfather had profited by playing both sides against the middle during the Civil War. And while his grandfather had been admittedly too old to participate in World War I, he could have, but didn't, take any part in the Spanish American War. Court's father could have volunteered with the Expeditionary Force of World War I, but once again, didn't. His duty with Naval Intelligence during the Second World War may have been necessary, even essential, but he faced nothing more hazardous than choking on a martini olive on the Washington cocktail circuit. Court wanted to balance the record by being the first of his line to see duty in combat. While he recognized his compulsion as naively stupid, he could not shake it off. He was desperately afraid that the Viet Cong and North Vietnamese resistance would be crushed before he could see action. He need not have worried.

When his transfer did come through in January, 1967, it was indeed to Southeast Asia, but to an administrative job at Clark Field in the Philippine Islands.

Proximity to the medical evacuees streaming into Clark should have cooled Court's ardor. He was repelled, even frightened, by many of the ghastly examples of what war could do, yet somehow he remained curiously detached. The ability to gaze upon the mangled remnants of what had once been a whole and healthy man; and say: "Yeah, sure, maybe him . . . but not me.", is not unique. In Court's case, however, it was a deep conviction. He *must* see combat, and he *would* emerge unscathed.

He continued to plague his superiors with requests to be assigned to an operational unit in either Viet-Nam, or the new airbases in Thailand. Finally, his wish was granted.

On the 28th of July, 1967, Lieutenant Courtney J. Palmer arrived at the Thai Air Force Base of Takhli. And the first person he met was one who had been impatiently awaiting him — Major Deke Maloney.

"Hi, kid. Saw your name on the list and figured there could only be one with a crazy name like Courtney J. Palmer."

Court grinned. It had been a private joke between them. "There are three Courtney J. Palmers, Major, two living, but only one dumb enough to be a member of this freaked-out flying circus."

Maloney had a pickup waiting on the apron. As they loaded Court's gear into the back, their fragmented conversation skipped erratically over the highlights of their lives since they had last seen each other.

As they conversed, Court observed Maloney. After exposure to combat conditions, he had expected to find Deke changed; older looking. Deke was a little thinner; a few more lines around the eyes and more deeply tanned, but the freckles still showed through the tan, the unruly shock of reddish-brown hair was unchanged, and he still flashed the same irrepressible grin. With the exception of a major's gold oak leaves, it was essentially the same Deke Maloney he remembered from their days in McConnell. Deke wore his 36 years lightly.

"Soon as we get you checked into the BOQ, I'll take you over to the club and we'll pile into a couple of fast brews and a steak," Deke said as he drove the pickup towards a cluster of low buildings.

"Thankee kindly, Majuh, Suh. Youse mighty good to us pore ol' field hands."

Deke grinned. "You can leave the joining routine until this afternoon. Hope you're still pretty good at aerobatics. They've got you down for Wild Weasels . . . Buick Flight . . . mine."

At McConnell, Court had flown the modified F105s known as Wild Weasels. With a full bomb load, the F105 Thud was slow to maneuver. Taking evasive action against the surface-to-air SAM missiles which were encountered with increasing frequency on **deep penetration** raids into North Viet-Nam proved difficult. The attrition rate of Thuds had been unacceptably heavy. As a counter to this threat, the Wild Weasel was introduced.

The F105 designated in this category was modified to include sophisticated electronic detecting equipment, and an Electronic Warfare Officer in addition to the pilot. They carried no bomb payload, but Shrike air-to-ground missiles were added to the ordinance.

Tactically, a flight of Wild Weasels, normally four aircraft, preceded the bombers into the target area. When the EWO reported a ground radar-lock, the pilot swung onto the bearing and dived to the attack. With the energy-seeking Shrike released on its downward path to the SAM site, the pilot, unencumbered by bombs, took evasive action.

Taking advantage of the confusion created by these Wild Weasel countermeasures, the following F-105s carried through on the bomb run. The tactics had succeeded in reducing the high rate of bomber losses. With the Wild Weasels, however, it was a different story. In their nose-down attitude of attack, they presented a poor SAM target, but were vulnerable to conventional anti-aircraft fire from the SAM site's outer-ring defenses. The losses were heavy.

Well, baby, Court thought, you wanted action. You're sure as hell going to get some.

* * * *

Deke, Court, and another Buick Flight captain by the name of Jay Grant, became known as the Three Musketeers. Off-duty, they were inseparable. Together, they could be seen in the club, or in one or another of their favorite bars in the town of Takhli. When Buick Flight enjoyed a stand-down of Compensatory Time Off, they could be found as a terrorizing trio in Bangkok in a select number of bars and night clubs, or availing themselves of the services of the same massage parlor. Rumor had it that they even shared the favors of the same Sani Chateau night club hostess. The latter allegation was not based on fact.

It was Court who discovered the hostess. Her name was Dang. She was a well-stacked little nymphet with a sunny disposition, a reasonable command of English, and a healthy sexual appetite. When the three jet jockeys hit town, one of their first ports of call was the Sani Chateau. They would ask for Dang. If she was entertaining another customer, she would excuse herself and join their table. While she enjoyed the banter and company of all three, it was understood that she was Court's exclusive property as bed companion.

It was not that the inclinations of either Deke or Jay were celibate. On the contrary. But their tastes ran to variety — quantity as opposed to quality. They relied on little Dang to produce fresh faces from her wide circle of friends and hostess associates. As a procuress, Dang proved without peer. Harried though she was by changing specifications, she still managed to come to light with something reasonably close to the stated requirements; at least young, willing, and undeniably female.

The exploits and escapades of the unholy trinity became legend on the airbase.

*　　*　　*　　*

On November 28th, Court celebrated his promotion to

captain with a party in the Officer's Club. It was on this happy occasion, when the celebrants had been reduced to a handful, that Deke disclosed his theory. He didn't claim to have originated it, but modestly asserted that over many years of dedicated study he'd added certain refinements. With the owlish pedantry imparted by many bourbons, Deke held the floor.

According to Deke, life was like a giant pool table. The analogy was simple. The game was snooker, but instead of the balls being neatly racked at the beginning of life's game, they were scattered at random over the table. The individual whose life was to be played out was represented by the cue ball, which could be placed anywhere on the table to start.

The celestial pool shark chalked His cue, studied the lay of the balls, and stepped up to the table to execute His shot. As Deke explained, one of the beauties of this theory was that it was all embracing; applying equally well to a good Catholic boy like himself, a Black Protestant bastard like Court, or an undisciplined agnostic such as Jay. The godly pool hustler could be called God, Allah, Tiki, Vishnu, or just plain Fate, take your pick.

A deft stroke of the cue set the cue ball off on its initially appointed course. Of course, in the event of a godly miscue, the individual was the victim of a miscarriage, stillborn, or died in infancy. Presuming, however, an unerring stroke, the game was in progress.

In its path over the table, the cue ball would strike a number of colored balls, and rebound off the various cushions. And that, Deke stated, is life. A carom off a cushion indicated a change of direction over which the individual exercised no control. Impacts with the colored balls were to be considered as decision points in life. A red ball, for example, constituted a minor decision which might well go unnoticed. The six other colored balls were another matter. Striking one of these represented a major decision point, the relative importance of which being directly related to the ascending value of the colors. The yellow ball was thus the least important of the major decisions one would be called upon to make during the course of life; the black ball, the most crucial.

The game was over when the cue ball either came to rest somewhere on the felt, or dropped into one of the pockets. The former case was the general slowing down of old age with eventual death; the later, an unanticipated demise.

Now, Deke stated, if you took colored chalk matching the various balls, and traced out on the table top the courses taken by all the balls set in motion, you had a composite picture of life. The white chalk line represented the course life actually took. The colored tracings, from the points of collision, represented the probable courses life could have taken had other decisions been acted on at these crossroads of life.

Jay and Court seized on Deke's theory gleefully. It was an appealing concept which allowed both predestination, and the option of a personal control at the impact points of decision.

Over the weeks that followed, the trio embellished and enlarged upon Deke's fanciful analogy.

It was Court who hit upon an explanation for precognition.

"The probable courses exist as mathematical options," he argued. "From any given decision, the optional course commences to trace out along with the actual path. Okay, say you strike a red ball. It veers off on a tangential course down the table. The cue ball, however, cuts across the table, bounces off a cushion, hits the green ball, and eventually crosses the red ball's traced path. But the red ball arrived there much sooner in time. At the exact point of intersection, you would experience the fleeting sensation of having been there before and witnessed the scene or action. And in fact in the probable life that's exactly what happened."

"Dunno," Jay said sceptically. "Sounds confusing. Still, it could explain why all these Thai chicks look alike to me. I think I've been the same route before."

Jay's contribution was an application to the concept of reincarnation. "Simple," he opined. "Your diety of misspent youth plucks the cue ball from the pocket, and lines up another shot. Same old balls, but a brand new game."

"Why not?" conceded Deke admiringly.

Embroidering on the theme provided them with amusement. Their daily conversations became studded with cryptic references to the theory. Someone they disliked was referred to as a *miscue*. Their errors and mistakes became *cushion caroms*, beyond their powers of control and therefore attracting no blame. Petty annoyances were *tapping a red*. A difficult position was being *snookered*. The numerals from 2 to 7 were designated by the ball sequence *yellow, green, brown, blue, pink*, and *black*. A difficult decision was labeled *lining up on the black*.

Those of their companions who had not been initiated into the theory found their conversation confusing. The pool-hall jargon was put down to a mild form of mental aberration. Nonetheless, and in most cases unsuspecting of the significance, a good many of the non-coms and officers started to pick up some of the expressions. A CTO pass to Bangkok became known as a *brown alert*, and it was generally accepted that the Base Commander was definitely a *miscue*.

*   *   *   *

At 0800 on the morning of Friday, January 5th, 1968, Court awoke feeling like something that had been dredged up out of a klong.

Warm contact against his thigh alerted him to the fact that he was not alone in the bed. Before opening his eyes to investigate, he tried, without conspicuous success, to reconstruct events.

There had been relatively little activity at Takhli in air strikes over the Christmas, New Year's period of undeclared truce. Then, the previous day, January 4th, Buick Flight was scheduled for three days of CTO standdown from operational duties. Court, Jay and Deke planned a run into Bangkok. At the last minute, Deke begged off, complaining of intestinal cramps and diarrhea which he termed: "A touch of Ping River Polka." If the ailment showed signs of improvement, he said he'd catch the Klong, the C130 shuttle aircraft, and join them the following day. That, Court thought, would be sometime today.

Court and Jay drove down in the Datsun Court had purchased a couple of months earlier. They arrived in the late afternoon, checked into the Siam Intercontinental, took in a movie, dined at the Two Vikings, had a couple of drinks at the Cat's Eye Bar in the President Hotel, and for some reason decided to leave the Sani Chateau until the next evening. They dropped by the Chao Phya's BOOM Club, and stayed until the bar closed, arguing with another couple of jet jocks the relative merits of tactical doctrine. From that point, Court's memory became unreliable. He seemed to recall a bar on Patpong, and had a dim recollection of an after-hours joint somewhere off Sukhumvit.

Cautiously, he opened one eye. Within his immediate range of vision was a bedside table upon which stood a lamp with a singed shade, an empty quart Singha beer bottle, a glass, with about an inch of stale beer, an ashtray containing several crushed butts, and his wrist watch and wallet. Although sunlight slanted through faded cotton curtains drawn across a single window, the bedside lamp was lit. While nothing but his watch and wallet looked even vaguely familiar, he was certain of one thing. He was not in the Siam Intercontinental.

He sat upright in the bed. A sudden sharp throbbing in his head made him wince and wish he'd deliberated before this modest exertion. He subjected the room to a cursory inspection.

His clothes were strewn carelessly on a chair. Trailing across a scrap of bedside rug, were his socks, shoes, and underwear shorts. On a low dresser, primly neat, were placed the girl's cothing, a small red purse, and a brown paper bag. On the floor, near the foot of the bed, was a cheap aluminum tray containing two bowls, a plate, to which adhered some lumps of glutinous rice, and one set of chopsticks. At least, Court thought, she had the good sense to get fed before being bedded.

He looked curiously down at his bed companion. Her back was towards him, the rumpled sheet barely covering her rounded buttocks. By leaning over slightly, he could see the swelling of a ripe young brown-nippled breast and discern enough of her features through the obscuring tangle of jet-black hair to determine that she was young, fairly pretty, and a total stranger.

Court sighed, eased himself out of the bed, paused to snap his watch onto his wrist, noting that it indicated 8:10, and padded into the small bathroom. Two crumpled towels were draped over the end of a rust-stained tub. The flexible shower-head lay inertly hanging into the bath like a dead metallic snake. Court retrieved a cake of pink soap from the edge of the tub, noticing with distaste that several curly black hairs adhered to the soap's surface. He turned to the washbasin.

As he let the water run over the cake of soap to wash away the hairs, he regarded his image in the mottled mirror. He didn't look nearly as bad as he felt. He needed a shave, and his eyes were slightly bloodshot, but otherwise he looked reasonably healthy.

He dressed quickly. Before putting his wallet in his pocket, he extracted three 100 baht notes. He hesitated, and glanced at the girl in the bed. She had moved only slightly from the time he'd left the bed. Either she was still asleep, or was feigning sleep. He couldn't remember how much money he'd started out with, but the billfold seemed much thinner. Very likely, she'd helped herself to some of his money while he slept. What the hell, he thought, sleeping with a drunken GI is a pretty tough way to hack a fast baht. As he slipped the three bills under the beer glass on the bedside table, he wondered idly where he'd picked her up. As he looked once again at the tangled mop of hair on the pillow, he speculated upon where she would spend tonight. Maybe this same sleazy hotel. Probably she got some kind of a cut from the management.

As he opened the door, his mind turned to more immediate problems. He had no idea where he was, or where he'd left Jay, or, for that matter, where in hell he'd left the car. The only thing he knew with any degree of certainty was that he had a monumental hangover.

The door of the room opened onto a small landing with concrete steps leading down to a carport beneath the overhang of the hotel. One mystery was resolved. His Datsun was angled into the carport. And, as he descended the steps, a second question was answered. Jay was curled up asleep in the rear seat.

He shook Jay unceremoniously.

As the recumbent form uncoiled, it emitted a muffled groan.

"Shit, I don't recommend this as a kip," Jay grumbled, massaging the back of his neck and twisting his head gingerly from side to side. As he stretched his legs, Jay shivered. "Damn it, gets cold this time of year."

"Why in hell didn't you sack out in this hot-bed hostelry?"

"I was," Jay said sarcastically, as he got out of the back and moved to the front seat, "being true to my adoring wife and kiddies. Besides, not only did you have a corner on the only available talent, you said you were only going to be about a half hour."

"Did I," Court said mildly, as he inserted the key in the ignition. "Must have overslept."

"You sure as hell did."

They emerged into a side street off Sukhumvit Road. The distance to the Siam Intercontinental was not great, but they were caught up in the morning crush of traffic which served to compound their hangovers.

Court stopped at the hotel desk to collect the key to their double room. The desk clerk handed him a number of telephone message slips.

"Who called?" Jay questioned, as they walked towards their room.

"MACTHAI switchboard. Want either one of us to call back as soon as we come in. Looks like they've been trying to reach us half the night. Probably Deke advising which shuttle flight he's coming in on, and wants us to meet him at Don Muang."

As soon as they were in the room, Court requested the

telephone operator to try and get the call through to the Military Assistance Command operator. When the connection came through, Jay was in the bathroom shaving. Court took the call.

The message was that Takhli Operations had been trying to reach them. Court waited while the operator put the call through to Takhli.

"Major Burns, Operations."

"Captain Palmer here. Someone was trying to get through to me and Captain Grant."

"Palmer. Yes, we tried to reach you at the Siam Intercontinental. Where are you now?"

"Siam Intercontinental. We just got in."

"If we could have contacted either of you last night, we wanted you back on base. You couldn't make it back in time now, so you might as well relax and enjoy yourselves."

"Thanks."

Court replaced the telephone on its cradle.

Jay poked his head around the bathroom doorway. "Deke?" he questioned through shaving soap lather.

"Nope. Ops. They wanted us back on base."

"Now?"

"No. Whatever they have on the burner, we couldn't make it back in time. Suggested we relax and enjoy ourselves."

"Good man. Sound advice. Glad we didn't make it back here last night," Jay replied as he ducked back into the bathroom.

Court sat on the bed, staring moodily at the telephone. He rubbed his face thoughtfully, then picked up the phone and requested MACTHAI for the second time.

It took almost ten minutes to get the connection through to Takhli the second time, and another five minutes before

the operator finally located Deke Maloney at the club.
"Deke, Court here."
"Sound like you had a rough night."
"Yeah. A touch on the excessive side."
"Keep up the good work."
"Sure . . . what's the panic back at the ranch?"
"No problem. They just decided to call on a few experts.
Ross and I are slotted in."
"You feeling Okay?"
Deke laughed. "Shit hot." After a significant pause, he
added, "Might say I'm in the pink."
"Rog . . . Keep the faith."
"What else? See you Sunday."
Jay was standing by the dresser, buttoning his shirt as
he watched Court cradle the phone. "Didn't sound like
much of a conversation from this end. Glean anything from
our peerless leader?"
"Maximum effort raid in Pack 6," Court answered.
Jay's eyebrows shot up. "He told you *that?*"
"Hell no. He worked in the word pink . . . the old six ball
routine. Since Ops wanted us so badly last night, and since
Deke and his new EWO Ross are slotted in, it has to be
a pretty big strike. Ergo — Pack 6 and a max effort."
For administrative purposes, 7th Air Force had divided
North Viet-Nam into target areas known as Route Packages,
familiarly reduced to "Pack" followed by a numerical
designation. Pack 1 was at the Demilitarized Zone; Pack
6 represented the Hanoi-Haiphong area. By coincidence, the
anti-aircraft defenses became increasingly heavy as the
numbers rose from 1 to 6. Deke's casual reference to
"experts" suggested Pack 6; his use of "pink" merely
confirmed it. Of Court's 48 completed missions, 17 had
been in Pack 6. Deke and Jay were even more familiar

with this most hazardous of all the target areas.

They had breakfast delivered to the room. While they ate, Jay planned a busy day. First, he would go to Star of Siam to buy some Thai silk for his wife. Next, he would stop by a jewelers where he'd previously left a star sapphire to be mounted. Concerning a good place to lunch, he was undecided and invited suggestions from Court.

"Jay, don't want to spoil your plans, but I think I'll go on back to the base. If you'll run me out to Don Muang, I'll grab the Klong flight. You can hang on to the car and drive back Sunday."

Jay took a long swallow of coffee before answering. "Figured something like that was going through your little pointed head. Shit, if you want to go back, I might as well tag along. Hate driving in this country anyway. Would we have time to stop by the Star of Siam on the way?"

"Sure," Court answered absently.

* * * *

CHAPTER SIX

Court unlatched the washroom door and eased it open a fraction of an inch. Above the drone of the jet engines, an excited murmur of voices from economy class was clearly audible. Court heard the door to the flight deck close. The broad back of one of the aircraft's officers came into view as he moved through the first class compartment heading aft. The stewardess trailed behind him. One of the passengers, Court thought it was the Indian Ambassador, questioned the officer in a querulous voice. The officer didn't pause in his stride, but the stewardess stopped to offer soothing assurance. All eyes of the first class passengers followed the officer as he moved purposefully into economy class.

This was Court's moment. He swung the door open and stepped forward to the unlocked flight deck door. As he twisted the knob, he pulled the revolver from his pocket. Here goes the old college try, Deke, baby, he thought.

* * * *

The briefing was held at 0930 on the 5th of January, 1968.

The Weatherman, a lieutenant, presented the meteorological picture. There would be a stratus cloud layer of 500 foot thickness at an altitude of 6,000 feet over the target area. Minor turbulence could be anticipated over the Annamite Chain of mountains.

The Wing Intelligence Officer took over the briefing. The situation was that over the past weeks cargo off-loadings from Russian, Polish and Czech freighters at the port of Haiphong had been particularly heavy. The North Vietnamese had taken advantage of the festive season bombing lull to move the bulk of this equipment — mobile guns, rockets, missiles, tanks, and associated military hardware

— to a marshaling area at Hai Duong. Intelligence reports to 7th Air Force Command at Saigon's Tan Son Nhut indicated that it was the intention to start moving the material southwards through Nam-Dinh and Than-Hoa to Vinh and Dong-Hoi. The method employed would be by truck convoys moving only at night. Last minute information indicated the movement was scheduled to commence on the night of January 5th. The decision at Command had been to hit the concentration of material, and hit it hard, before it became strung out along the delta and coastal roads.

The mission would involve bomber squadrons from Udorn, Ubon, and Korat, in addition to the F105s from Takhli. Fighter cover would be provided by Udorn. Rescue and recovery would be by helicopters of the Jolly Green Giants from NKP and 7th Fleet units from Yankee Station in the Gulf of Tonkin. Carrier based aircraft from the fleet would mount co-ordinated diversionary strikes against Hon-Gai and Haiphong.

The routing, turn points and egress from the target were outlined. Refueling tanker call signs were given. Refueling would take place over Laos along the "green anchor" line on the way in. Egress from the target would be to seaward over the Gulf of Tonkin where refueling would take place along the "brown anchor" track. The routing would take them north to a point near Yen-Bai, where they would turn onto a southeasterly course following behind the screening mountain range known as "Thud Ridge", before breaking out over the delta. The attack would be carried out below the stratus cloud cover at an altitude of 4,000 feet. They were to start cranking up the jet engines at 1100. Take-off would be at 1130, Dodge Flight of Wild Weasels leading. TOT — Time on Target — would be 1330, with flights incoming at intervals of one minute.

The Squadron Commander took over for the general briefing. He touched on details of the terrain and approaches to Hai-Duong and the alternate targets. He outlined anticipated enemy fighter activity and anti-aircraft defenses. From blow-ups, he pinpointed the locations of the camouflaged storage dumps at Hai-Duong and such navigational aids as the railway yards and station, the steeple of the Catholic church, and the prominent glass factory. Since strikes from both Udorn and Ubon would be on target before the arrival of the Takhli Thuds, the storage dumps should be marked by fires, but obscured by smoke.

At the conclusion of the general briefing, the pilots broke up into groups for detailed flight briefings by the concerned Flight Leaders.

Deke and his EWO, Lieutenant Jimmy Ross, had been slotted into Dodge Flight for this particular mission.

*   *   *   *

Court and Jay arrived back at the base at 1430. After checking with Squadron, they went over to the club. There was nothing to do but await the return of the mission's flights.

At about 1530, they heard the wailing of the jet engines of the first returning Thuds. It was a further half hour before the pilots started to straggle into the club from their debriefings.

Captain Zabrovski saw Court and Jay sitting at the bar. He hesitated. Zabrovski was joined by Major Swiggham. Bert Swiggham looked at the bar, pursed his lips, glanced meaningfully at Zabrovski, and nodded. Together, they approached the figures seated at the bar.

Jay glanced up and noticed the two flight suit clad pilots.

"Lo, Jake, Swiggy. How'd it go?" Jay questioned.

"Okay," Swiggham answered laconically.

Court swallowed the dregs of his drink and looked up. "Hi Jake. Deke in yet?"

"He . . . they . . ." Zabrovski's voice trailed off. He looked helplessly at Swiggham.

"Didn't make it." Swiggham finished the sentence in a flat voice. "Flak. Heard him report he'd been hit and lost hydraulics. Then we heard him order Ross to punch out. We saw them eject at about 2,000."

Jay's face was a study in shocked disbelief. To Court, the revelation didn't come as such a surprise. Although he'd said nothing to Jay, he'd had a strange feeling of foreboding all afternoon. Even as he'd asked Zabrovski the question, a knot of icy dread had chilled his guts. His voice was steady as he asked, "Good chutes, Swiggy?"

Swiggham hesitated before answering. Then, his eyes swinging from Court's down to the bar top, he said softly, "One was. The other was a streamer."

"Could you tell which?"

There was a momentary flash of annoyance across Swiggham's face. There was an edge to his voice as he answered, "Hell no. We were pretty busy ourselves."

"Yeah. Sure," Court said. "What'll you have?" As he swung in the bucket bar stool to face the bartender, he was conscious of a strung-out tension within himself, and astonished at his outward calm. He ordered a double on the rocks for himself, and noted as he did so that his hand holding the empty glass was white-knuckled from its rigid grip.

*　*　*　*

It was several days before Radio Hanoi announced the

names of some of the American officers killed in the raid
on Hai-Duong. On the list was Lieutenant James R. Ross.
There was no mention of a Major Desmond K. Maloney.

*　　*　　*　　*

There were some changes in Buick Flight. Major Swiggham took over as Flight Leader. Jay Grant went as Nash 3,
of Nash Flight. Court, who as Buick 2, had flown as Deke's
wingman, became Buick 3, taking over as the element leader
with Zabrovski as his wingman. A Lieutenant by the name of
Clifford joined as Swiggham's wingman. To Court, this internal shifting was incidental to the subtle changes of a
personal nature he was experiencing.

Formerly, as they flew the missions deep into North
Viet-Nam, Court thought of the country beneath him in the
simple terms of an assigned target. The turnpoints and the
ragged crests of Thud Ridge were familiar as landmarks. The
roads, rivers, rail lines, and towns and villages were recognized as lead-in indicators to a specific target. He
was alert to such hazards as the Mig base at Phuc Yen,
the heavier concentrations of anti-aircraft defenses, and the
menace of the ever-changing weather. The winking ground
lights of anti-aircraft muzzle flashes and SAM launches,
the yellowish gray puffs of exploding 37-57 mm flak and the
fireballs and black smoke of the larger caliber shells were
linked together in his mind with the blossoming orange of
their own detonating bombs and rockets and the pall of
greasy black smoke over the targets. He supposed he had
been aware of the seasonal changes of the ripening rice in
the Red River Delta paddy fields, and the black dots which
scurried from the roads as the F105s screamed over the
landscape, but they had not formed an integral part of his

mental picture. The one element missing from the scene as he visualized it was people.

In the five and one-half months since Court had joined the squadron, there had been a good number of aircraft lost, along with a corresponding number of throttle jockeys. For his initial ten missions, Court had been slotted into relatively easy flights over the southern portion of North Viet-Nam. On these missions, when an aircraft was hit by ground-fire, the pilot had a good chance of nursing his sick jet at least into Laos where in most cases recovery could be effected. Those not so lucky crash landed or parachuted into enemy country, where, presumably, they became prisoners of war — guests of the Hanoi Hilton — which was the collective term for prisoner of war camps in North Viet-Nam. Following the break-in period, Court's assignment to Buick Flight was on a regular basis and the major missions deep penetrations into Pack 6. Here, the defenses took a murderous toll. Thuds would disintegrate in an explosive flash when they could not evade the heat-seeking or proximity-fused missiles. Even when the damage was not lethal, there was less likelihood of limping back to Laos. Court had seen a good many of his companions eliminated from the combat rosters. These were of course people — and somewhere down there they existed as POWs, probably reflying their missions with appropriate hand gestures as they had at the Takhli club. But up to the point of Deke's joining their ranks, Court had really not given them too much thought. It didn't pay to dwell on absent comrades. And as for their captors and unwilling hosts, Court had scarcely acknowledged their existence.

But Deke's ejection from his crippled Thud put the matter into an entirely different perspective for Court. Deke was much more than just another comrade-in-arms. To

Court, he was friend, companion, confidant, and the brother he'd never had. No longer were those black dots fleeing to the safety of fields and shelters faceless creatures, scampering ants. They were suddenly people, very real people. They were the executioners or captors of Deke Maloney. And even when the months failed to bring confirmation that Deke was in fact an unwilling guest of the Hanoi Hilton, Court totally rejected the thought that Deke could have been killed.

Now, on the missions over the north, Court was acutely aware of the countryside beneath him, and its people. In his off duty hours, he started to read avidly all the available background material on Viet-Nam and the Indo-China conflict. Where before it had been of little interest, he now wished to learn all he could of the conditions, traditions, culture, and political aspirations to which Deke would be exposed.

Court's new preoccupation had little or no affect on his flying. His awareness of the terrain as a living entity did nothing to impair his alertness or automatic responses. He drove his Thud with the same unerring judgement, the same reflexive ability to "jink" — the term applied to the twisting evasive tactics on egress from a target area. It was by no means a purely mechanical process. As before, he maintained rapport with the Flight Leader and responded automatically to commands. He was as alert as ever to the many variables which could affect the strike. That portion of his mind which studied the region seemed divorced from conscious thought — almost a separate entity. It was as though two pilots drove his Thud into combat.

He didn't avoid Jay's company, but he didn't go out of his way to seek it. They were thrust less into each other's pattern of life now that Jay was attached to Nash Flight. They still met and drank together in the club. They played poker together. But neither sought to re-establish the former close association. To Court, Jay was a painful reminder of Deke's absence. He supposed Jay felt somewhat the same. Only once was the subject discussed between them.

Jay completed his 100th mission in February. He was due to rotate Stateside, and, as a reservist, he was also due for separation back to civilian status. The night before his departure there was a farewell party in the club.

Court was sitting by himself. Jay came over and sank into a vacant chair beside him. He sipped his drink, and looked at Court speculatively.

"I've had the impression that you've been blaming yourself for what happened. Do you think that if we'd returned to the hotel, received the message from Ops, and gotten our asses back here in time for the mission, that Deke wouldn't have been slotted in?"

The directness of the qestion disconcerted Court momentarily. He had dwelt on such a possibility. He looked at Jay. "Deke wasn't feeling too well. If I hadn't been carried away with pussy that night, we'd have made it back. Had we been here, Deke probably would not have been included. Yes, I've thought about it."

"Balls. A little case of the galloping shits wouldn't have stopped Deke. He would have gone anyway. Do you think you could have changed his mind?"

"Never could," Court admitted.

"Look at it this way. Deke was lined up on the pink ball and nothing you or I could have done would have changed it."

"Pink . . . Why not the black?"

"Because he chuted out," Jay answered logically. "Jimmy Ross bought it, but for my money Deke's in the Hanoi Hilton this very minute. So forget it. Enjoy the memory of your piece of ass."

Court smiled thinly. "The hell of it is, I can't even remember screwing the chick."

*   *   *   *

There were significant changes in the air war during 1968.

The Tet offensive at the end of January, which continued to drag out over a week, came as a traumatic shock to the American military commands. To 7th Air Force this was manifestly obvious. Morale at the Thailand airbases sank to an unprecedented low. North Viet-Nam had been able to absorb the countless punishing bombing raids and still be in a position to supply and mount a major, country-wide offensive in the south. If the enemy had so managed to relocate its industrial potential, and could still maintain a logistic flow to support such actions in South Viet-Nam, the cost in men and aircraft of the hazardous strikes seemed prohibitive if not senseless. This was an admission that could not be accepted in its harshest implications. When it became apparent that the offensive in the south could not be sustained — had been something in the nature of a go-for-broke one-shot effort — the doctrine of strategic bombing returned to favor. In some minds, however, doubts persisted.

In March, the fragmentary orders reaching the bases daily started to omit missions of deep penetration into the north. On March 31st, President Johnson announced that a policy of restricting the bombing raids to below the 20th parallel was officially in effect until further notice. If only temporarily, Route Package 6 was eliminated from the daily strikes, which were now confined to the less heavily defended supply routes and coastal cities south of Than-Hoa.

On November 1st, the bombing halt for the entire target of North Viet-Nam went into effect.

The latter edict was of only passing interest to Courtney J. Palmer III — civilian.

*   *   *   *

Court was due to rotate for Stateside reassignment in early June. His five year hitch would be served and his active duty completed by mid-June. He had no clear idea what he wanted to do from that point, but was certain he did not wish to make a career of the Air Force. His one regret was that he would not have completed 100 combat missions before his rotation date. He did, in fact, complete 86.

As the date neared for his departure from Takhli, an idea which had been flitting through his mind for several months crystallized into a firm plan. He decided to take his separation from the Air Force in Thailand, and seek employment within the country. He didn't know quite why the idea appealed to him. He had no intention of becoming a permanent expatriate. He would try it out for a year or two. If he could not avoid, he could at least postpone the pressure he knew would be exerted upon him to enter either the banking or brokerage professions. He conceded that he might one day feel differently, but at this stage of his life, with the harrowing yet exhilarating experience of combat duty an accepted way of life, and approaching his 26th birthday, the thought of a bank or a brokerage office as a venue was repugnant. But why was he thinking of staying in Thailand? That he didn't know, and gave up trying to explain even to himself.

Court was not the first serviceman to opt for separation in Thailand, but he was one of a small minority. Both the military commands and the U.S. Embassy frowned on the practice and tended to quietly discourage such an application. It had been their experience that these requests were prompted generally by romantic rather than practical considerations. Almost invariably, complications arose at a later date. Accordingly, while regulations could not prohibit the submission of such a request, they at least included provisions which acted as some measure of deterrent and provided a safeguard against subsequent difficulties. The applicant must obtain written confirmation from an American firm operating in Thailand that the company guaranteed employment at a stated salary plus logistic support; that it would undertake to obtain the necessary visas and ultimate resident status for the employee; and that, in the event of termination of employment, it would guarantee return passage to the United States. This letter of commitment was to be addressed directly to Pacific Air Force Headquarters, Hawaii.

Court submitted his application for in-country separation through his Squadron Commander to the Base Commander. Although they thought he had taken leave of his senses, they advised Court concerning the conditions of guarantee. He was granted leave to proceed to Bangkok in order to pursue his objective.

It was Court's first visit to Bangkok since January. Apart from the fact that it was now the rainy season, he found the city little changed. But since his purpose was far removed from that of previous visits, he became acquainted with an entirely different aspect of the town.

He obtained a list of American firms operating in Thailand from the American Chamber of Commerce. Returning to the Siam Intercontinental, he proceeded directly to his room and set about studying the list for likely prospects of employment. Almost immediately, his confidence started to ebb.

It dawned on Court that a bachelor of arts degree from Princeton in Physics and History, and the skills acquired to drive a jet fighter-bomber through flak-infested skies, hardly constituted qualifications for employment with the companies listed. He took a pencil, and went down the list crossing off the firms requiring specialized skills. Engineering and construction companies were the first to be eliminated. Trading companies dealing chiefly in the Thai economy, and the branch representatives of major American manufacturing firms followed. The list narrowed alarmingly. All he had left were advertising agencies, insurance companies, and firms dealing in sales directed towards the foreign community and the American military. After some deliberation, he drew a line through the advertising concerns.

Court set up a number of appointments by telephone. Hiring a hotel car and driver, he set out on his rounds. He returned to the hotel at the end of the first day, hot, tired and discouraged. It appeared that the services of an F105 throttle jockey were not much in demand in the local business community.

He showered, changed and had a couple of drinks in the Naga Bar. He dined early at the nearby Swiss Inn. After dinner, he considered dropping by the Sani Chateau, or searching out some action on Patpong Road. He abandoned both ideas as having little appeal in his present mood. By 10:00 p.m., he was in bed in his hotel room.

He had been preoccupied with his thoughts throughout the evening. Now, as he lay with his hands locked behind his head and stared into the gloom of the darkened room, he pondered the significance of the day's happenings.

Wealth had never been much of a consideration with Court. It was simply an accepted fact of life. Over the span of his recent years in the Air Force, he had rarely thought on the subject except when he had received advice from the bank concerning dividends, deposits from the family trust, expenditures concerning his property holdings, or notice of shareholders' meetings. Suddenly, however, he was very much alive to his financial position and its implications.

He recognized that had he disclosed his position and offered to invest in any of the firms he had visited during the day, or for that matter many of the concerns he'd crossed from the list, he would have been offered employment even if it meant creating a new position. He could, if he so desired, start some Thailand-based enterprise of his own. But either of those courses would defeat his purpose.

It wasn't that he was imbued with a burning desire to renounce his family background and make a name for himself solely on his own guts and ability. In all honesty, apart from a certain expertise in driving a jet fighter-bomber, he wasn't at all sure what those abilities might be. He realized that he was facing a crucial point in life; one of those big colored-ball decisions.

Wealth carried with it not only privilege and power, but a burden of responsibility. One day, he would employ this wealth to some useful purpose. Before that day came, he was determined to explore his own capabilities. And his studies of Southeast Asian background had whetted his interest in the area and its problems. He strongly felt that some, if not all, of the answers concerning his destiny lay in the region. He wanted to test himself in this arena, and gain first-hand knowledge of its complexities.

As Court slipped into sleep, it was with a confidence

that the morrow would prove more rewarding.

On Court's third appointment the following morning, he met with success. The company which provided the desired offer of employment was Amerthai Investment Associates, Limited.

The managing director received Court affably. His name was John C. (Just call me Jack) West. He was a fleshy, balding man in his early forties. There was a slight trace of an accent which Court couldn't place but led him to suspect that West's name was more than likely a shortened version of something longer and less easily pronouncable.

It seemed that Amerthai were expanding their sales force. Court was just the sort of man West was looking for. The Air Force background would be a definite asset. It didn't matter that Court had little knowledge of mutual funds, investment issues, and real estate developments in Florida and California (and a real sweet proposition in Arizona). Amerthai would not only train him, provide him with qualified leads, but assist him through the provision of a first-rated sales supervisor. With diligence and application, Court could expect to earn two, maybe three thousand a month easily. In addition, there were incentive bonuses in the form of Amerthai stock. Court should have no trouble, no trouble at all, in advancing from trainee to supervisor (with overriding commissions which should bring him to at least $4,000 a month) within a maximum of six months.

It all went a little too fast for Court. Jack West was familiar with the required letter of guarantee. He'd be happy to send it along to PACAF, Hawaii, without delay. Of course, Court understood, West chuckled, the guarantee of salary would just be a formality to satisfy Air Force regulations, since it would be a straight commission deal. Better that way, of course. Court would make more money on commissions then he could hope to make on any salary. And as for logistic support, well West had no doubt that an Air Force captain could find much better accommodation than Amerthai could provide.

Court left the Amerthai offices in the Bangkok Insurance Building in a slightly dazed condition. He had employment which would, at least on paper, satisfy the Air Force conditions. The training program would get underway as soon as Court could come to Bangkok on a permanent basis. Resident status was no problem, but would cost Court US$1,500.00 to look after the formalities (on this piece of information, West had not only chuckled, but winked).

Court had the uncomfortable feeling he'd been conned. He also suspected that West had known exactly who Court Palmer was. He was right on both counts.

*　　*　　*　　*

PACAF Headquarters in Hawaii acceped and approved Court's application with a minimum of delay. It was unusual for an officer to request separation in Thailand and they doubted that Court's stated reasons for wishing to become more familiar with Southeast Asian economy was his motivation, but they considered there was little risk that Courtney J. Palmer III would become a charge on, or an embarrassment to, the U.S. Embassy, Thailand.

*　　*　　*　　*

CHAPTER SEVEN

The transition from military to civilian life was not as difficult as Court had anticipated. Nevertheless, he encountered hurdles he had not expected.

His initial adjustment was one of winding-down. When you're uptight and living constantly on your nerves as were all the fighter-bomber pilots, it becomes an accepted way of life. Separated from that atmosphere, Court now recognized and appreciated the extremes of tension to which he and his comrades had been subjected. While the release from that strain was a welcome change, there is a peculiar fascination in participating in the game where Fate throws the dice each day with life and death as the stakes. Court found the role of spectator rather than player something of an anti-climax.

Any foreign minority community tends to be insular in character. Where the religious, cultural and language barriers are widely disparate, the predisposition towards a ghetto-like foreign community is particularly strong. This was much the case with the Causasian *farangs* resident within the teeming Asian city of Bangkok. And of all the expatriate group, the Americans exhibited this tendency in the most marked degree. There are good reasons why this should be so. In the main, Americans have less experience than Europeans in living abroad. The adjustment seems more painful for the American. Then, the major portion of the American community is composed of families on relatively short contractual engagements attached to the embassy, embassy agencies, or military missions. These people purchase from military commissaries and PXs, utilize the postal facilities of the U.S. Army, coagulate in military clubs, entertain in strictly stratified levels within themselves, resist mixing outside their own groupings, and, in general, without meaning to, they have created an almost hermetically-sealed existence. The behavior pattern of this American community bears a striking resemblance to small-town U.S.A. It is suspicious of newcomers, rife with gossip, and merciless in its censure of real or suspected transgressions. It was into such an expatriate community that Court intruded.

He had hoped that he could embark on his new civilian status as a non-entity; simply an ex-Air Force reservist, Court Palmer. These hopes were dashed within the first week. That he was Courtney J. Palmer III was known to the embassy, which gave Court an automatic if undesired entree into the upper social strata of the American community. He was included on the invitation list for all major embassy functions. Even had this not been the case, his chances of retaining discreet anonymity were nil. Amerthai's Jack West had known Court's family connections. While West didn't claim any direct connection or affiliation, he lost no opportunity to disclose the identity of his newly acquired addition to the sales force, the implication being that Amerthai Investment Associates Ltd., was in some way associated with the renowned Wall Street firm of Crandell, Topeler, Fitzpatrick & Palmer, and the Knickerbocker Trust Bank.

To the vocation of investment salesmanship, Court brought a number of assets, and one distinct liability.

On the credit side, were Court's amiable disposition and his easy assurance. He genuinely liked people and inspired in them both instinctive empathy and confidence. These attributes were of great benefit in any sales presentation.

Then too, although Court had not suspected it, during his boyhood and adolescence he had absorbed a good deal of background in both the financial worlds of banking and brokerage. From Lucinda, he had also acquired a fair grounding in real estate. This knowledge was to stand him in good stead. There was another factor of even greater value. Since he was known as the scion of a prominent financial family, Court went to some pains to assure his clients that the issues being promoted by Amerthai were in no way endorsed by anything even remotely connected with the Palmer interests. He knew of West's hints to the contrary, and was aware that many of his clients did not believe his own disclaimers. Unbeknownst to West, Court wrote to Mr. Cready at the Knickerbocker Trust Bank's Manhattan Branch and had periodic checks run on the issues and real estate developments being presented by Amerthai. Following Cready's recommendations, Court offered his clients sound guidance. If West noticed that Court displayed a marked preference for the less speculative propositions, he said nothing.

Investment selling was by no means the breeze West had pictured. Court's training consisted of familiarizing himself with brochures and prospectuses advertising the projects and issues in glowing terms. This was coupled with instruction presented by West and a sales supervisor named Trasker in the art of the sales introduction, the sales pitch, and the close. Court appreciated that the instruction was sound. He followed the precepts with some success. But the qualified leads and the supervisory assistance so glibly promised by West were inconspicuously short supply. Left to struggle on as best he may, Court quickly learned another cardinal lesson. Sales are in direct proportion to the number of sales presentations.

Far from moving from trainee to sales supervisor within the six month time frame indicated in his initial interview with West, Court found that he barely attained full salesman status within the stipulated period. As for realizing the commission earnings West had so confidently predicted, Court's best month earned him $720; his average running below $500. In the decorating and furnishing of a three bedroom house on Soi Chidlom, trading in his Datsun on an air-conditioned Holden, and entertainment and travel expenses, Court had eaten up his Air Force savings and had been obliged to transfer funds from his New York account to the Chartered Bank in Bangkok.

Court was honest enough not to attribute has lack of earnings to any fault in Amerthai. He knew that he was being overly cautious in his presentations and losing out on the investment plungers who were attracted to the quick-return speculative issues. Had he been hurting for a buck, as were most of the other salesmen, he could and would have changed his tactics. But open, pitch, and close pattern wasn't the real culprit. Had Court devoted more time to daily calls on prospective clients, his personality and assurance would have achieved a higher average. It was his consuming interest in the history and culture of the surrounding region which acted as a brake on his sales performance. During the first six months, Court found every excuse to travel. By car, he drove over most of Thailand — not only to the military bases in search of prospective buyers, but also to the southern isthmus and Malaysia, and to Northwest Thailand, where it was highly unlikely he would locate investment purchasers. He also visited Vientiane and Savannakhet in Laos, and Saigon, Danang, Nhatrang and Vung Tau in South Viet-Nam. In fact, he made it a practice to journey to Vientiane and Saigon once each month. True, these junkets were not devoid of sales results, particularly with Air America pilots in Laos and well-heeled contract employees in Viet-Nam, but they could have been much more productive had Court's interest not been diluted by explorations into the local economic and cultural background.

It was March, 1969, before Court's monthly commissions topped the thousand dollar mark. From that point, his income showed a slow but steady increase.

What had happened was not surprising. Court's clients consisted chiefly of the more conservative investors. He had early established a practice of reviewing their entire investment portfolio and, from time to time, making recommendations based on the private information he received regularly from Cleary in New York. Court's advice concerning Amerthai offerings, and his counsel with respect to general investments and market conditions, were sound. As his clients gained confidence, they recommended Court to their friends and associates. Gradually, Court was building upon a solid base.

*   *   *   *

Amerthai's managing director, Jack West, was by no means averse to his sales force earning big commissions. The more they made, the higher the return to West and his associates. But there are pitfalls inherent in the system. Generally, the temperment which produces a top salesman is that of a gregarious individual with a low tolerance for a confining routine and administrative detail. The salesman earns big money and blows it as fast as it comes in. He may not exhibit much loyalty to the firm which employs him, but while his production is an asset, his departure for more lucrative fields is a disruption which can be readily offset by the introduction of new personnel. From experience, West knew that a sales force was essentially a fluid organization. That is normal and presents only minor problems. Where the danger lies is in the emergence of that rare individual who possesses not only sales ability but also a talent for administration. When these traits are coupled with ambition, as they frequently are, the man becomes a positive threat. The tendency is for such a man to terminate his employment without warning, taking with him the knowledge of the business, his personal clients, and as many of the top salesmen that he can persuade to accompany him. This man has not dissipated his earnings and has accumulated sufficient capital to set up a competing business across the street from his former parent organization. Jack West was alive to this peril. He should have been. It was in just such a manner that West had parted with Investor's Overseas Services three years earlier. With him had gone Burgess, O'Brien, and young Trasker as the nucleus for Amerthai.

West's method of safeguarding himself against such corporate treachery was to follow the time-honored maxim: "When in doubt — promote."

The promotional ladder was simple and relatively standard. A prospective salesman started on the bottom rung as a trainee at a minimum percentage of commission. When the trainee's sales volume reached a prescribed level, he was automatically promoted to salesman at a slightly higher commission. And at this point, the salesman started to accumulate bonus stock in Amerthai as an added incentive. The large bulk of the trainees never reached the second rung, became discouraged, and quit. The secret of such an organization is to have a sufficient influx of new trainees to compensate for the high rate of attrition. But having made salesman, when the total volume reached the next level, he became senior salesman. Again, his commissions increased, and at this stage a new element was introduced. The senior salesman was allocated responsibility for a number of salesmen and trainees on whose earnings he received a small overriding commission to compensate for the fact that his own sales were reduced by the time spent encouraging and assisting his sales force charges. When the aggregate volume of the senior salesman and his sales group reached another prescribed level, the senior salesman was automatically elevated to sales supervisor. Now, the man was weighted with additional responsibilities. His commissions on personal sales remained at a fixed level, but his stock bonuses and overriding commissions increased. The override was now calculated on the earnings of a number of senior salesmen and their sales groups. While the sales supervisor could reach a high earning figure by close supervision and constant encouragement of the sales force under his jurisdiction, his personal client base normally commenced to shrink. It was at this level of sales development that West started to watch closely for the danger signals. Hitherto unsuspected administrative ability showed up under the organizational stress. And if the sales supervisor was imbued with ambition, he became restless, regardless of income.

When the signs pointed to probable defection, West employed a further promotional device. The sales supervisor could be promoted to branch manager with the lure of eventual regional managership leading to corporate positions such as Director of Sales and Executive Vice-Presidency. As a further curb to overweening ambition, in addition to increased stock bonuses, the branch and regional managers were encouraged to exercise stock options. The larger the participation in dividends and corporate profits, the less likelihood there was of the man spinning-off from the parent structure. It was a policy of calculated dependency.

In Jack West's opinion, a man was motivated by one, or a combination of, three incentives. In descending order of importance, these were bread, broads, and status. In June, 1968, when he had confirmed that the applicant seeking employment was Courtney J. Palmer III, West discounted money and social position as Palmer's reasons for wishing to stay and work in Thailand. He put it down to either an infatuation with some Thai chick, or to a possible fourth motivating factor — whim. Who could account for the eccentricities of the very rich? In any case, West was not particularly concerned. He considered that Palmer would stick with the job no more than a couple of months at best, during which time West intended to take full advantage of the situation by inferring that there was a connection between Amerthai and the Palmer interests. He couldn't care less whether Palmer produced a single account.

When Palmer advanced from trainee to salesman, and showed no intention of terminating his position, West became uneasy. He started to watch Palmer's activities closely. The composite picture which West built up over the months was disturbing.

To begin with, Palmer didn't fit any pattern known to West. That Palmer was living on a scale well beyond his commission earnings was obvious and quite understandable. Still, despite a house boasting a cook, servant, and gardner, membership in the Royal Bangkok Sports Club, and a social entree into diplomatic circles, Palmer's scale of living could not be termed lavish. He rejected more invitations than he accepted, entertained modestly at home, and played the night club and bar circuit sparingly. In the area of amatory adventures, Palmer played the field, rarely dating the same girl more than two or three times. While he did have a number of Thai girl friends and regular sleeping companions none of them occupied a position of favorite. As far as West could determine, there had been no romantic interest involved in Palmer's initial desire to remain in Thailand. Reluctantly, West abandoned his original concept that Palmer's seeking Bangkok employment had been pussy-prompted. In sum, it hardly added up to a playboy image. West would have been happier if it had.

There were a number of other factors which contributed to West's growing concern. Not the least of these was the matter of Palmer's travel throughout the area. He had become thoroughly familiar with Thailand. By regular visits to Laos, Palmer knew the market potential as well, if not better, than Trasker, who had been recently made regional manager in Vientiane. Palmer's knowledge of Viet-Nam was very nearly equal to that of O'Brien, the Saigon regional manager. Even more puzzling to West were Palmer's trips to Malaysia and Singapore, where Amerthai had not yet established sales outlets, and at least three visits to Hong Kong. On only one of Palmer's Hong Kong trips had he bothered to contact Burgess, who operated the Hong Kong head office and acted as Director of Sales. What West had no way of knowing, and a fact which could have somewhat allayed his suspicions, was that Palmer had commissioned the Choy Lee boat yard in Hong Kong to commence construction of a 50 foot Sparkman-Steven's design ketch.

From a slow start, Palmer's sales began to show a steady increase from his ninth month with Amerthai. The nature of these transactions was not lost on West. It only served to add to his mounting anxiety. Palmer noticeably avoided speculative issues. He displayed a much broader grasp of the investment field than West would have credited. From some of the advice West learned Palmer had given to clients, West suspected, but could not prove, that

Palmer was in receipt of market information not available to Amerthai. And West fully appreciated that while Palmer's steadily expanding clientele represented the more conservative element, they were also the more affluent and stable investors.

In June, Palmer's volume of sales qualified him for advancement to senior salesman. By this time, West's concern had passed through the stage of dark suspicion to active worry. Palmer was a potential threat. Of that, West was convinced, even though he had not determined what form the threat might take. He could perceive no reason why Palmer should be content to spend a year in investment sales without some dark ulterior motive. And, worst of all, West could see no way to counter this undefined danger. He considered a number of possibilities and courses of action.

Palmer could well be the advance man for the Palmer interests, exploring the Southeast Asian market potential. At any given moment, acting either for a group, or on his own initiative, Palmer could simply walk out of Amerthai and establish his own investment firm. This, to West, was the likely eventuality. The loss of Palmer's clients would be a severe blow to Amerthai. Then, there was the matter of the sales force. While Palmer had not been on familiar terms with many of the salesmen, he had been friendly and was well-liked. West mentally calculated how many of the Thailand staff could be lured away by Palmer. Ruefully, he concluded that with the kind of inducement Palmer could offer the tally stood close to 100%. Palmer's administrative ability hadn't been tested as yet, but he certainly displayed qualities of leadership suggesting organizational talent. But, after all, what did that matter when Palmer was in a position to import the best administrative brains in the business.

West did consider the improbable possibility that Palmer had no designs whatsoever, but simply enjoyed life in Asia. This would fit with the supposition that Palmer could have been motivated by some inexplicable whim. But could such capricious fancy endure for as long as a year? West thought not. Such conduct was so foreign to his own tenets that West discounted the theory. Still, it could not be ruled out entirely since Palmer was an enigma outside any frame of reference West considered reliable. And since this slim chance could not be discarded outrightly, it compounded West's dilemma. While his inclination was to sound out Palmer warily, prudence dictated that he hold off.

With the advent of Palmer's advancement to senior salesman, West felt he could no longer delay some measure of probing.

*　　*　　*　　*

Court would have been amused if he had suspected the turmoil he was generating within West. When he had first learned that West was implying a connection between Amerthai and the Palmer interests, Court was angry. He had done nothing at the time since he was powerless to prevent the innuendoes which would only be denied by West. Later, Court's annoyance was tempered by the admission that the inferences were undoubtedly of some benefit to Amerthai and hence sound business tactics on West's part. And as Court learned more of the sales force structure, he came to appreciate the shrewd employment of 20th century thralldom utilized to advantage by West. Although he developed a grudging admiration for West, he had no liking for the man.

The company practice on sales force advancement was

to advise the salesman by memo of his new position, commission structure, and, where applicable, those trainees
and sales personnel for which he would assume responsibility. Court was surprised when he was called in by West
for personal congratulations on the advancement to senior
salesman.

West started out by expressing the concern he had
felt with Palmer's sales efforts at the outset. Then, he
indicated how delighted he was with the later performance
which had vindicated the confidence he had always had in
Palmer's ability. Yes sir, the present record of achievement was excellent. West could see no reason, no reason
at all, why Palmer shouldn't make sales supervisor by fall,
and branch manager by no later than the following spring.

Bullshit, Court thought, and wondered what West was
leading up to. He was not left long in doubt.

West grew affably confidential. As Palmer was aware,
the corporate earnings over the past year had been substantial. The next two quarters showed every promise of
being even better. Year-end dividends should be most
gratifying for the shareholding participants — which would
include Palmer by virtue of the bonus stock he would acquire
in his newly elevated status.

West paused for effect. Leaning forward, he lowered his
voice and continued in what amounted to a conspiratorial
manner. Palmer was not aware of the planning that was in
progress. West knew that Palmer would respect his confidence. The intention was to expand into Malaysia, Singapore, Indonesia, and the Philippine Islands within the coming
year. There would be considerable room for regional
managerships for those, such as Palmer, who had displayed
proven ability and initiative. But that was not all. No siree,
not by a long shot. As Palmer knew, West had recently re-

turned from a swing through the South Pacific. Had Palmer any idea of the objectives in such a trip?

Court had not. He had every confidence he was about to be let in on the secret. Allowing his face to register interest, he remained silent.

West chuckled. On the trip, he had managed to tie up options on some excellent beach frontage properties in the New Hebrides Trust Territories, and in Fiji. Land booms were coming to those locations on the heels of expanded tourism. Amerthai — or more properly, Amerthai International, S.A. — were going to be in on the ground floor. They would parcel out the land, prepare brochures, plat maps, and title contract agreements. West had already commissioned an Australian firm to prepare 16 mm color movies as sales aids. They would commence to sell estate-sized plots by Christmas, then contract the property development. West was sure that Palmer would be excited as he was when he had a chance to see the properties and study the growth potential.

West became more serious. It was an ambitious program, as he felt Palmer would agree, but practical and with a minimum of risk. West had mentioned Amerthai International S.A. Since Palmer hadn't heard of this corporation, West would enlighten him, but again, in strictest confidence. Burgess was at this very moment in Zurich setting up this holding company in that tax haven. This would be the holding company through which West would operate.

Court had no illusions concerning West's business acumen. There was no doubt in his mind that Amerthai had done well over the past few years; very well indeed. The plan West had unfolded was both feasible and realistic. Expanding the sales force into the areas mentioned by West was a logical extension. Providing there was sufficient capital to exercise the land options, as well as prepare the necessary promotional material, and at the same time bear the expense of setting up a Switzerland-based holding company and the new Southeast Asian sales offices, there was no reason why West would not succeed. As West had implied, he was too smart a businessman to become involved in the property development with his own capital — at least not initially. As far as Court could determine, the program looked sound on the surface. The available capital was the key, and Court suspected therein lay the hook and the reason for this discussion. He was about to be asked to contribute a sizeable chunk of cash.

As if divining Court's thoughts, West sat back in his chair and pursed his lips.

"I'll be frank with you, Palmer," West said. "The expansion program I've just outlined is no pipe dream. It's the product of a lot of thought and expense. The only limiting factor is capital. We can swing it with what we have, and anticipate, without seeking outside support, but it will take time. I would like to move as quickly as possible. Therefore, I am going to make shares in the holding company available to some of our more senior and productive sales personnel. I think you will agree that it presents an excellent opportunity to grow and prosper with the company.

"I consider you a valued member of our sales team. I am also aware that you have at your disposal considerable investment funds. I don't want any off-the-cuff answer, but I would appreciate your studying the proposition. If it appeals to you, and I think it will, I would like to have you as a participant."

West had made his presentation well. Court was interested and if the project checked-out he would consider a substantial investment. In Court's estimation, West had turned in a polished performance with a balanced shading of confidence, enthusiasm, and restraint. It was no ad lib rendition. West had rehearsed and was almost letter-perfect in his delivery of his lines — almost, but not quite. Court was left with the nagging suspicion that there was some other purpose behind West's disclosures.

Court dismissed this impression from his mind. There had been other reasons why he had wanted to talk with West, and this meeting provided an opportune moment.

"I appreciate your confidence," Court said mildly. "I'd welcome an opportunity to study the matter."

"Certainly. I'm having a prospectus prepared as soon as Burgess returns from Zurich. I'll advise you when it's available."

"Thanks." Court let a moment go by before continuing. "I'm happy to have this meeting since I have a couple of other matters to discuss."

"Oh?" There was a wariness in West's tone and expression.

"I meant to inform you that if it isn't inconvenient at this time I intend to take a couple of months off. It's been well over two years since I've been Stateside. Thought it was about time I went back for a visit."

West hesitated. He hadn't expected this. He wasn't at all sure he liked the idea of Palmer returning to the States at this time. On the other hand, he could do little to prevent it. He had no choice but to accept it with good grace.

"Probably an excellent time, before you become too involved with the training and direction of the salesmen and trainees we've allocated. I'd rather hoped you could pump a little fire into them."

"Sorry. And that's the other thing I wanted to discuss. In my absence, I'll turn over my accounts to Tony DeSantis.

He's been working pretty closely with me for the past two months. But on my return, I would prefer not to have any salesmen or trainess under my jurisdiction. I've developed a number of interests which take up most of my spare time. I'd rather not take on the training responsibility at the moment."

West frowned. This was definitely not to his liking. DeSantis was the only salesman in whom Palmer had displayed a personal interest. He could be trusted to hold Palmer's clientele intact. But over and above that, Palmer's indication of lack of interest in a closer involvement within the sales force organization was disturbing.

"It would mean throwing away considerable override commissions," West pointed out.

Court smiled. "Thanks for your concern, but I hardly think that is of paramount importance."

"Ah . . . Yes. Well, no need to make a decision on that until you get back. When do you intend to leave? When do you expect to return?"

"Thought I'd try and get away next week. Should be back by the end of August. If I get hung-up, I'll cable."

*　*　*　*

When Court departed, West sat frowning darkly at the desk blotter. Outside his office window, the gray curtains of afternoon monsoon rains did little to distract him other than add to an already depressed mood. He reached absently for the humidor and took out a cigar. Chewing on the unlit cigar, he reviewed the meeting with Palmer.

What had he accomplished? Nothing. It could even be worse than nothing. In his attempt to draw Palmer out and induce an interest in the corporate affairs, he had outlined his plans for expansion. It had been a calculated risk, but what had it achieved? Zero. He couldn't even be sure that he had sparked an interest. He could certainly use an injection of capital at this point, and Palmer may even provide it, but at what cost? The object had been to lay the groundwork for a deeper involvement on Palmer's side. Somehow Palmer had managed to sidetrack the conversation into another channel, and in the process revealed that he hadn't the slightest intention of taking on training responsibilities. The Stateside trip had come as a surprise. It could be nothing but a long-postponed vacation, as Palmer stated. It would also be a logical time for Palmer to confer with associates and formulate a plan for setting up a competing business. During Palmer's absence, West would have distributed Palmer's more valued clients to branch managers. In that, he had been neatly forestalled by Palmer's assurance of a turnover to DeSantis. On the excuse that DeSantis would have too much to cope with, West might be able to winnow out a few of the fatter accounts, but substantially Palmer's client base would remain intact. And towards the end of the conversation, Palmer had reminded West that there was no dependence on overriding commissions. It was a reminder West had not needed.

"Shit," West said, flinging his mangled cigar into the waste-basket.

He stared gloomily out the window. There were times, increasingly frequent of late, when he wished to hell he'd never heard of Courtney J. Palmer III.

*   *   *   *

The conviction that he needed a change of scene had been growing on Court for some months.

He was still absorbed in the historical and cultural background of the region, but his initial enthusiasm had commenced to wane. He found that his increasing knowledge made him more and more conscious of the gulf between West and East. He had no real desire to bridge this yawning chasm. It was enough that he recognized its existence and accepted it. There was a side effect to his awakened understanding. He began to appreciate how little was understood by most of his fellow Americans and became increasingly critical of American policy and attitudes. Aware that his inverse intolerance was not a desirable acquisition, he felt it was high time he became reacquainted with his own land and its people in their natural environment.

While Court enjoyed investment sales, here again he was dissatisfied. He had learned enough about the business to recognize that, while gratifying, it didn't hold sufficient attraction for him to consider it his avocation. Yet he had encountered nothing which held more appeal.

He was exploring other avenues which looked promising, but at the moment he felt as though he was treading water. A vacation might give him a fresh viewpoint.

On the social scene, there was little to hold him. He had made friends within and outside the *farang* community, but none whom he would consider as a reason for establishing permanent roots. By its very nature, the Bangkok foreign community engendered feelings of impermanence. One felt like a transient among transients.

Romantically, there had been adventures, but none with lasting impact. He was considered an excellent catch. In consequence, he developed a wariness which inhibited many of his associations with the local crop of post-debutante hopefuls. To forestall gossip, he confined himself to no more than two consecutive dates with the same girl. With the Thai and Thai-Chinese girls, he exercised even more caution. Experience had taught him that Oriental women had a tendency to become embarrassingly possessive. To tell the truth, he had encountered no girl who sparked more than a passing interest. He didn't turn down any opportunity to bed a chick, but didn't go out of his way to seek out the situation. In the sexually permissive atmosphere of Bangkok, one hardly had to search for such opportunities. But, for some reason which he couldn't fathom, the old thrill of the chase seemed to have lessened. At times, this worried him.

Other factors contributed to his restiveness, not the least of these being the Bangkok weather. The parade of seasons from wet to dry, the unremitting heat, and the ubiquitous green of the foliage, palled on him. It had been almost three years since he'd experienced the crisp and colorful days of autumn; snow sifting from the dull-pewter colander of a winter sky, or the exuberance of bursting spring. The constant hot damp summer of the tropics was becoming oppressive. Nostalgic memories of Darien and Maryland tugged at him.

During Court's years in the Air Force, Marcie kept up a desultory correspondence. Her letters were light, touching on amusing incidents in her life, but given mainly to news concerning little Jerry. Court answered religiously, trying to keep his responses in the same light vien. This became something of a strain during his fighter-bomber stint at Takhli. Some of the stress under which he was living crept unavoidably into his letters. Abruptly, Marcie stopped writing. He wrote from Bangkok when he separated from the Air Force, advising her of his intentions. It was six months before Marcie answered. In that letter, Marcie's only reference to herself was to tell Court that she had moved to a charming villa in Mijas. The remainder of that January missive had been confined to a description of Jerry's sixth birthday party. Court had replied promptly, but here it was June, and no response from Marcie.

So, along with Court's waxing desire to visit the scenes of his youth, there was a compelling urge to become acquainted with his son. He would return to the States via Spain's Costa del Sol. He had no idea how Marcie would react to his appearance on the domestic scene. But even if she objected to his presence, Court felt that it was high time that he paid a visit. He wanted to get to know little Jerry. At the rate things were progressing, Court thought glumly, Jerome Kirk might well prove to be his only progeny.

*   *   *   *

Court considered just dropping in on Marcie out of the blue. But perhaps that would be unfair. The day before he embarked on his flight, Court cabled Marcie his flight and date of expected arrival in Malaga.

*   *   *   *

CHAPTER EIGHT

Like most Andersons, he was rarely addressed by his Christian name. To his friends and associates, he was "Andy" Anderson.

He waited until the lavatory door was latched and the *"Occupé"* sign lighted up. Satisfied that DeSantis would not be disturbed, Andy strolled up the aisle towards his seat in the forward section of economy class.

Settling his rawboned frame into the seat, Andy glanced at his watch. Less than thirty seconds to go until all hell broke loose. And at that point in time, this desperate adventure would be irretrievably launched. He corrected himself. It was already in progress, and had been from the moment DeSantis had twisted the cap of the smoke cannister.

It was a damn-fool stunt to pull. He wondered idly how Court Palmer had talked him into it. But in all fairness to Court, the scheme had fired Andy's imagination and in all likelihood it was his own enthusiasm which had prodded Court into action. Andy had to admit that Court's organization had been painstakingly thorough. There was a better than even chance they'd pull it off. If they did succeed, it would be a terrific achievement. If they didn't . . . what the hell. He was fifty-six . . . fifty-seven in just a few weeks. He had no responsibilities. It was a worthwhile gamble; perhaps the finest, and certainly the most stupid, he'd ever taken in a long life of taking chances. He shrugged. Succeed or fail, either way he'd end up an unsung hero . . . and a criminal.

His thoughts were rudely interrupted by pandemonium erupting at the rear of the aircraft. He twisted around in his seat and looked aft. "Christ!" he muttered. He had known what to expect, but the volume of smoke pouring out from under seat 30C was astonishing. Coughing passengers were scrambling from their seats and crowding into the aisle. A woman screamed above the incoherent babble of excited voices. As the smoke eddied forward, panic spread to the cabin mid-section, washing in waves of hysteria towards Andy's section. He watched a white-faced stewardess attempting to calm the milling passengers. The purser pushed his way aft to the aircraft intercom. As a diversionary tactic, the smoke generator was proving remarkably effective.

Andy let his eyes swing to search out Gracier in an aisle seat several rows back. The Frenchman was calmly lighting a cigarette. The woman passenger beside him was trying to crowd past Gracier into the aisle. Placing a restraining hand on her arm, Gracier spoke to her quietly. The woman paused in confusion, then subsided back into her seat.

Andy wondered what Gracier had said to the woman. He couldn't help but admire the Frenchman's *sang froid*. In all the time he had known Gracier, he had yet to see him ruffled. He recalled the time that he and Gracier had cleaned out a bar in Saigon. Gracier had handled three wildly-swinging U.S. Marines swiftly, effectively, and with all the detachment of a bored cop. He speculated curiously on just what it would take to blow Gracier's cool — and hoped he wasn't about to find out.

Evidently, the purser had contacted the flight deck. One of the aircraft's officers strode purposefully down the aisle towards the swirling smoke. Andy followed the officer's progress, noting the calming effect his passage had on the still frantic passengers.

At a point several rows behind Gracier's seat, Andy's gaze shifted from the retreating back of the flight engineer and came to rest on John Begg, the fifth member of the group.

The addition of Begg to the team had been Palmer's decision. It might not prove necessary to call upon Begg at all, but should it be necessary, his role was demanding. Andy eyed the middle-aged, non-descript-looking Begg speculatively. The man was sitting rigidly upright, his normally placid features betraying a tension verging on terror. In Andy's estimation, the introduction of Begg to the team at a stage late in the preparations had been a mistake. Without doubt, Begg was the weakest link in an otherwise strong chain. Andy found himself hoping fervently that it would not be necessary to use Begg.

The smoke had ceased pouring from underneath seat 30C. The officer was on his hands and knees in the aisle, groping beneath the seat. A knot of passengers, including the grim-faced purser and two of the economy-class stewardesses, followed his efforts with anxious concentration. So intent were they on the officer's actions, nobody appeared to notice the lavatory door swing open and the looming figure of DeSantis emerge.

Through the thinning smoke, Andy could discern the far rear of the aircraft. The black-garbed DeSantis, his height augmented by the wire framework beneath the hood, presented an awesome spectacle. As many times as they had rehearsed this action, Andy found himself impressed by the chilling apparition. "Jesus," he muttered under his breath, "this'll scare the piss out of 'em."

Andy watched as DeSantis paused a few seconds, then, despite the restricting garments, moved forward smoothly. The figure seemed to glide, rather than walk. Light from the overhead illumination glinted off the barrel of the revolver. DeSantis lightly tapped the aftermost stewardess on the shoulder with the barrel of the gun.

She turned, to be confronted with the towering apparition

in black. The girl emitted a piercing scream. DeSantis placed a bulky flight bag on the galley pantry shelf. With his gloved hand, he slapped the hysterical stewardess sharply across the face. Her hand flew to her cheek, and the quavering scream terminated abruptly in a choking gasp.

Although Andy couldn't hear DeSantis' terse instructions to the stewardess, he knew the lines by heart. DeSantis motioned towards the intercom with the gun. As though in a trance, the girl moved to comply with his orders. The officer had scrambled to his feet, the gas cannister clutched in his hand. He stood uncertainly in the aisle looking at the hooded figure. DeSantis brought the gun to bear steadily on the aircraft officer. The purser, remaining stewardess, and the passengers watched in stunned silence.

Andy watched the dramatic performance with admiration. DeSantis was playing his part to perfection.

* * * *

Despite every outward appearance of detachment, Clement Gracier was as tense as a coiled spring.

From the moment he had watched Andy Anderson unwind his tall frame from his seat forward, and, flight bag in hand, saunter aft, Gracier had been very much conscious of the Luger strapped at his calf beneath his slacks. The gun almost seemed to burn against his flesh. It wasn't that Gracier was afraid. The time for fear would have been many weeks earlier before he agreed to this undertaking. It was because he knew better than anyone of the group the stiff odds against success.

Eight minutes later, minus the flight bag, Andy had returned to his seat. Gracier had not bothered looking at his watch. He had known that it would be only a matter of seconds before smoke would start to pour from the cannister. From years of experience with airline passengers, he had also known exactly the panic which would grip the plane.

His mind dwelt on the phenomenon of aircraft passenger behavior. No matter how much the airlines had publicized the statistics of the safety of air travel, there was something about being encased in a metal tube, suspended high above the clouds, that spooked even the most inveterate of air travelers. It was very likely only the design engineers, technicians, and the aircrews who drove these big kites who actually appreciated the structural strength and built in features of safety of a bird such as this Boeing 707. Let anything happen at all out of the ordinary, anything at all, even the mild discomfort of passing through minor turbulence, and most passengers were on the thin edge of mortal fear. They hid it, of course, from their fellow passengers by a brave show of casual insouciance. But the too-brittle laughter and glib jokes had a hollow ring. Inside, each passenger harbored grave doubts and secretly plumbed the depths of his or her personal cowardice.

In a moment, this load of passengers would face fear. Panic could produce strange and unreasoning actions. Some people simply froze, like a chicken hypnotized by a python. Others felt the need of curses and motion. Still others, gripped by hysteria, wanted to strike out at something — anything. He wondered idly how these passengers were going to react.

The danger lay in the contagious nature of panic. If the passengers were not brought quickly under control, it could be well nigh impossible to exert authority. The plan had been designed by Palmer. The object was to create a diversion to enable Court to have undetected access to the flight deck. In the resulting confusion in the after section, the element of shock would be introduced by DeSantis. This should bring about a blind obedience to command. It was a sound plan. By all the rules of psychology and human behavior, it should work. But Gracier had known the peculiarities of airline passengers. He had never been as sanguine as the rest, but since he couldn't devise a better scheme, he held his counsel.

He heard pandemonium break out before the first pungent whiff of smoke reached his nostrils. He didn't turn around. The woman beside him started to get up. He restrained her. In a quiet voice, he informed her that he was himself an airline pilot and that there was no cause for alarm. He suggested she remain seated while the aircrew investigated. He added that in a few minutes the aircraft captain would advise them concerning the nature of the problem and the remedial measures to be taken. She hesitated, but resumed her seat.

The flight engineer appeared, heading aft for a look at the cause of the smoke. The emergence of this symbol of authority on the scene served to stem some of the mounting panic. Gracier still didn't turn around. He noted with satisfaction that Andy was closely observing the developments. This was a vital few minutes. If DeSantis timed it according to plan, all should go well. If not, he had privately agreed with Andy beforehand that they would step in to assist DeSantis. It would mean that any thought of concealing their identities would have to be abandoned, but that couldn't be helped in an emergency.

Gracier heard the stewardess' trembling scream, which was suddenly cut short. Gracier watched a shadow of a smile flicker across big Andy's rugged countenance. Now, for the first time, Gracier craned his neck around his seat to observe the tall specter of DeSantis with the gun pointing steadily at the flight engineer. The shocked silence of the passengers was eloquent testimony of De-Santis' success.

Gracier took a deep drag on his cigarette. Some, but not all, of the tension eased from him. For no matter how dramatic the scene being enacted back here, the crucial drama was unfolding up in the flight deck.

He felt the aircraft tilt steeply in rapid descent. The high overcast over the South China Sea came up to meet the jetliner. Then, Gracier noted that they were banking in a turn to port. The rays of the early afternoon sun crept slowly aft in the cabin as they came onto a northwesterly heading.

The voice of Captain Christian LePlattre came over the internal broadcast system:

"Ladies and Gentlemen, this is your captain speaking. I have been assured that the smoke in the after compartment is perfectly harmless. There is no cause for alarm. Please remain calm and return to your seats. Please observe the 'Fasten Seat Belts' sign. We are descending to a more comfortable altitude and altering course. I have been instructed to advise you that this aircraft has been taken over by a group of hijackers. You will be issued certain instructions. Please follow these to the letter, and no one will be in any way harmed."

Gracier exhaled a cloud of blue smoke. His face in no way reflected his relief. He knew LePlattre: a good man, and an excellent pilot. He had been positive that LePlattre would in no way endanger his aircraft and the passengers in his charge by some stupid display of heroics. Still, even a veteran captain like LePlattre, trained to avoid panic in any emergency, was capable of unpredictable response under extreme stress. The sudden appearance of a black-garbed, hooded, and armed Palmer in the flight deck should have created quite a bit of stress.

The mental picture amused Gracier. He resisted an impulse to laugh. In any event, it was a little early for jubilation. The first phase may have gone off well, but the tough part was yet to come.

* * * *

Court's cable to Marcie, advising her of his arrival in Malaga at 4:00 p.m. via the domestic Iberia flight from Madrid on July 6th was a matter of courtesy. He didn't expect to be met.

He stood in the Malaga terminal waiting for his suitcase. He absently swept the crowd beyond the barrier with pensive scrutiny. Then, he saw Marcie. She was standing a little back from the group, a little boy, his curly blond hair sun-bleached almost white, clinging to her right hand. Marcie saw Court's smile of recognition. She smiled in answer, and waved with her left hand.

Six years can be a long time. Court didn't know just what he had expected. He'd thought about it, forming a mental picture during the journey, phrasing and rephrasing the words he would use in greeting Marcie and their son. Now, the carefully prepared scenario suddenly evaporated in a swift surge of emotion. He stood there, grinning foolishly.

He marveled at Marcie's appearance. Like the boy, Marcie was tanned a golden bronze. Her loose, shoulder-length auburn hair glinted with a coppery sheen from exposure to the summer sun. She was wearing a gaily colored open-necked shirt tucked into snug beige jeans which rode low on her slim hips. The wide hand-tooled leather belt with its massive gold buckle was more decorative than functional. Around her neck, suspended from a long gold chain, was a jade replica of a Maori tiki Court had sent her from Hong Kong. She wore no other adornment, and no make-up. She looked radiantly lovely. If Court hadn't known she was nearly two years older than himself, he would never have guessed her to be twenty-eight. She didn't look a day older than she had on their last meeting. If anything, she looked even younger. It was difficult to credit that she could be the mother of the boy at her side.

When Court retrieved his bag, he joined them in the waiting area. Marcie kissed him lightly on the lips, then gravely introduced his son. Court was pleased that she said simply: "Jerry, this is your father."

The boy regarded Court warily with wide blue eyes, then extended a small hand. Court shook it solemnly, marveling at the thrill of pride and affection which washed over him at the contact.

As Marcie drove the little Fiat westward along the main coastal highway, she kept up a running monologue. Jerry sat rather stiffly in Court's lap. He regarded the top of his son's blond head, barely listening to Marcie. She was, he appreciated, merely filling what would have been an awkward silence with her chatter, allowing Court to readjust to the moment and the presence of his son. He was grateful for her consideration.

They drove through Torremolinos, Torre Blanca, and Los Boliches, with Marcie slowing to a crawl in the conjested vacation crowds. She waved gaily to various passersby. Court recognized that as a longtime resident, Marcie was very much a part of the scene. He, on the other hand, was painfully aware of being an interloper.

By the time they reached Fuengirola and turned north off the highway in the direction of the afternoon-shadowed sierra, Court had gleaned quite a bit from Marcie's running commentary. She had been busily filling in the blanks and elaborating on the small amount of information contained in her infrequent letters.

She had operated the beach club bar, The Clipper, for two seasons following the one of Court's visit. In October, 1965, she sold her interest and was undecided what to do next. She considered returning to New York, but somehow, with little Jerome as a responsibility, New York had lost its appeal. Then the decision was taken out of her hands by the death of her grandfather, Senator Kirk. She returned to Minneapolis for the funeral. She stayed on several weeks with her father and stepmother, but had felt that her presence as an unwed mother was an embarrassment. That didn't bother her nearly as much as the approaching Minnesota winter. When Senator Kirk's will was probated, Marcie found that she had inherited a sizeable amount in cash and securities.

For the next year, Marcie traveled, first in Mexico, and then in Europe. She returned several times to the house in Fuengirola, which she considered home and used as a base of operations during her European junkets. Then, at Christmas of 1966, she decided that travel was a drag and that the constant changing of hotels and hired nurses was not a good thing for little Jerry. She had found no place which suited her better than the Costa del Sol, so she returned to Fuengirola.

She bought the house at 22 Avenida Nacional from the Spanish owner from whom she had been renting. Then she rented the villa in Mijas, and set about converting the Fuengirola residence into an intimate restaurant and bar. She had hoped to open in time to profit from the summer tourist traffic, but the work of renovation was agonizingly slow. By the time she was ready to launch The Yellow Door, it was late September and the season was drawing to a close.

Despite the exodus of vacationers, Marcie operated the establishment through the lean winter months, depending on the year-round resident community of expatriates from Fuengirola and the neighboring towns. It was a money-losing proposition, but Marcie considered it necessary in order to retain her key staff; her bartender, an Australian named Richard Downing and described by Marcie as a "perfect dear", the young Swiss chef she'd managed to lure away from a Madrid hotel, and Pepe, a Malageno, who acted as maitre d' and general factotum. Marcie herself doubled as cook's assistant, relief bartender, and hostess. Additional staff needed as waitresses and kitchen help was recruited from the ranks of ever-present young drifters of both sexes who gravitated to the sunny coast from harsher climes.

With the 1968 tourist season, The Yellow Door became popular and commenced to show profit. Last winter, an increase in year-rounders had at least made it possible to retain the staff and break even. Now, the summer flood of vacationers was in full swing. The Yellow Door had gained a reputation for charm and good food. The place was packed every night. She and the staff were rushed off their feet, but the cash flow in pesetas was encouraging inducement.

As they drove along the winding road through olive and fig orchards, and started the steep ascent towards the town and crumbling Moorish fortifications perched precipitously on the cliff face, Marcie concluded her running account. Court noted that there had been no mention of Eric, the gigantic Norwegian. He made no comment, concluding that Eric had been dumped somewhere along the way. He was certain there'd been other Erics.

Marcie parked the car in a small plaza. On foot, they continued on through cobbled streets so narrow that they were little more than footpaths, bounded on both sides by the whitewashed facing of unbroken lines of dwellings. Once more back in these familiar surroundings, Jerry scampered gleefully on ahead. Turning a corner around which Jerry had already disappeared, they started a steep descent in a lane into which series of stone steps had been spaced at intervals. Jerry waited impatiently in front of one of the heavy doors midway down the sharp slope.

Marcie dug a large key from a pocket of her jeans, and opened the door. Inside, was a short tiled hallway which opened onto a mezzanine running to the right and left like the top of a "T". A wrought iron railing ran most of the length, broken to the right by a staircase curving downwards. Court glanced over the balustrade down into a sitting room. Doors opened off the mezzanine on both left and right.

Marcie led Court to the left. She explained that this level was devoted to the bedrooms and bathrooms. Jerry's room and hers, with an adjoining bath were to the left. At the other end were a guest room, another bathroom, and a study. On the lower level, were the sitting room he'd seen, a dining room, kitchen, and servants quarters.

She conducted him into her room. Taking his clothing bag from his arm, she indicated where he could drop his suitcase at the foot of a huge four-poster bed, and showed him the entrance to her bathroom.

When he emerged from the bathroom, after washing his face and hands, Marcie was stacking his shirts neatly on a shelf in the closet. His clothing bag hung from a rod alongside her suspended clothing. There didn't seem to be any question of a hotel on this visit.

She straightened from her task, and smiled. Taking Court by the hand, she led him wordlessly to curtained glass doors at the far end of the bedroom. Swinging the doors wide, they stepped out onto a flagged balcony. Skirting a glass-topped table and wrought-iron chairs Marcie drew him to the whitewashed parapet. He was confronted with a breathtaking spectacle.

The balcony seemed to hang suspended in space. Far below, the rolling hills extended from the base of the sheer precipice toward the coast. The shadow of the mountain behind them spread out over the dusty orchards almost to the edge of the pueblo of Fuengirola. The town was bathed in the golden aura of late afternoon sunlight. Slanting rays painted the whitewashed houses a delicate shade of warm amber; the red-tiled rooftops a glowing hue of bronze. From windows of the tall apartment buildings which fringed the curving beach, the sun was reflected in a blaze of gold. To the right of the town, the ruined castle brooded upon its promentory. Offshore, a gleaming white cruise ship bound for Malaga cleaved a furrow through the cerulean Mediterranean.

Court's gaze returned to his more immediate surroundings. To the left and right, above and below them, villas clung like limpets to this slanting line of the cliff face. Like the others, Marcie's villa had been constructed on a narrow ledge by cutting back into the native rock. Directly beneath the balcony, a steep staircase curved downward to emerge into a small garden on the same level as the sitting and dining rooms. Sliding glass doors gave access to the garden which consisted of a stretch of lawn and a miniature pool bordered at the outer rim of the ledge with a flower-bed of pink geraniums, a screening row of slender cypress trees, and a containing stone wall. Where the wall curved in to meet the side of the house, a bougainvillaea splayed a riot of scarlet blossoms.

Court's eyes moved back to the seaward panorama. The shadow now licked at the edge of the distant town. The golden sunlight was becoming tinged with the pink of evening. Trailing a long wake etched on the smooth surface of the sea, the cruise ship was nearing the far headland. The air was still around him, bearing muted sounds from the village, and carrying a hint of the fragrance of jasmine.

A feeling of infinite peace enveloped Court. He felt suspended both in space and time. It was an odd sensation, as though this were a magical and enchanted moment. His hand rested lightly on Marcie's shoulder. He felt her arm move to encircle his waist.

* * * *

They were having breakfast the following morning on the balcony, when Marcie informed him about Geoffrey Braithwaite.

Braithwaite was an Englishman, and a would-be author. Until two days ago, he had resided in the villa's guest room and utilized the study as the scene of his creative endeavors in the world of letters. When she had learned of Court's pending arrival, Marcie had sent Goeff off to Madrid with instructions to remain there until she contacted him.

Court recognized that Marcie's life was her own and that he had no right to criticize her actions, yet he received her casual disclosure with a pang of resentment. The fact that she was the mother of his son gave him no valid claim on her. He was annoyed, and angry with himself for his involuntary reaction.

His efforts to hide his displeasure could not have been too successful, as evidenced by Marcie. "Surely you're not jealous?" she questioned teasingly, her tone betraying suppressed amusement.

The query disconcerted Court. "Hell, no . . . It's just, well . . ."

"Well, what?"

"I was thinking about Jerry. Wondering how he reacts, I guess," Court said lamely.

Her eyes twinkled mischievously as she posed her next question. "Do you consider me an immoral person?"

Now that he thought about it, Court supposed he had always regarded Marcie as having operated within a rather loose moral code. Not immoral, exactly, but certainly well outside what he considered as normal mores. He had accepted this, but never quite understood her. In framing his answer, he hedged. "I'm in no position to judge."

"No," she said drily, "I don't imagine you are. You must have a pretty active stable of slant-eyed lovelies in Bang-kok."

Since this was fairly close to the mark, Court withheld comment.

Marcie sipped the strong black coffee, and eyed Court reflectively over the rim of her cup. Setting the cup back in its saucer, she said seriously, "I wouldn't really blame you for having a low opinion of me, Court. When we met, I was pretty wild. Sort of rebelling against my father and step-mother, stuffy mid-western morality, and the world in general. I was experimenting with life. To you, I must have seemed kinky as hell. I slept around, but not nearly as much as you must have thought. I was, believe it or not, fairly selective. Not too many of that crowd turned me on.

"You probably won't believe this either, but from the moment I decided to have your child, you were the only stud in the paddock. Don't let it go to your head, lover, but no one has ever turned me on quite the way you did — before or since."

His mind skipped back over the years. Sex with Marcie had been hectic, but wonderful. He couldn't recall any later experiences to equal that ecstasy. On the other hand, last night could hardly be termed a world-shaking performance.

"When I came here," Marcie continued, "I found things were not too much different from New York. If anything, these cats are worse. Ibiza is cluttered up with pseudo-intellectuals dreaming of setting the world on fire, with an assist from pot and kief. Torremolinos is like a zoo; a freak show that just won't quit. Marbella is a bit better, but it's the elephants' graveyard of European royalty and a little hard to take for a gal from the mid-west. Fuengirola struck me as the best compromise in sight. It has its fair share of weirdos, but the year-round set seem a bit more stable. You'll meet some of them while you're here, and I think you'll like them.

"The problem is, as I quickly learned, that a girl without a man as a permanent fixture is fair game. Even a real dog will find action. I may not be the greatest looking chick on the Coast, but I'm not exactly repulsive. It's been quite a struggle fending off both the local Don Juans and the transient Romeos. To the Spaniards, I'm a challenge to their vaunted *macho*. The other studs pick up the habit rather quickly. Fortunately, at least during the tourist season, there are enough Scandinavian broads on hand to satisfy the demand."

Marcie paused to shake a cigarette from a package on the

table. Court leaned over and lit it for her. She exhaled a thin cloud of blue smoke and regarded Court contemplatively through the drifting haze.

"Don't get me wrong," she said, "I haven't acquired the habits of a nun."

Court smiled at her unintended pun, and gazed pointedly at her breasts revealed tantalizingly by the housecoat she hadn't bothered to tie. "Obviously," he observed.

Marcie noted the direction of his scrutiny, and caught the implication of her last remark. She laughed. "Not that habit." Then, sobering, she went on with her explanation. "I'm not hung-up on sex, but from time to time I want and need it as much as you do. There are a few men around here who satisfy those requirements. But I have no desire to give Jerry any wrong impression. I've been discreet, both for his sake and to avoid gossip. And that's where Geoff comes into the picture.

"If he knew you were jealous, he'd be highly flattered. He's a fairy. Not a practicing queen, more a latent homosexual. He's also hooked on heroin, a jealous mistress allowing little room for the indulgence of other desires. To Geoff, I'm about as sexually attractive as a jelly-fish."

"Holy Christ," Court exclaimed. "Do you think a fag junkie is a suitable influence for Jerry?"

Marcie bridled. "Yes, he is. He's fond of Jerry, and good to him. Geoff is really quite sweet, and harmless. Jerry likes his Uncle Geoff and minds him, but the attachment isn't very deep and in no way unhealthy. Geoff *is* good for Jerry. And for me. He needs looking after almost as much as Jerry. I must have one helluva maternal instinct. And Geoff's presence keeps the wolves from the door, which is the object of his tenancy. For your information, you're the first person to share that monstrous bed with me."

It made sense in a cockeyed way, Court admitted to himself. It was just that he found the idea of a homosexual as a permanent houseguest repelling. "And where did you find this paragon?" he asked.

"Ibiza . . . almost three years ago. He was eking out a precarious living on a small allowance from England, and what he could make from a few short stories he'd had accepted. It wasn't even enough to feed his habit. He was a pathetic figure . . . guess I just took pity on him."

"Are you supporting him?"

"In a sense, I suppose I am. He pays nothing for his room and board. He's sold several stories and a couple of travel articles, which brings in enough to keep him going. His stuff is pretty far out, but I think he has talent. He's been working on a novel with a setting in Ibiza. I think it's promising. Not great literature, but saleable. But one thing I refuse to do is support his addiction. If he can't hack enough to buy H, he knows he'll just have to cold-turkey — which would probably kill him."

Court suspected that Marcie wasn't telling the whole truth. Heroin addiction is an expensive monkey to feed. He had little doubt that her generosity went beyond just room and board. This trip to Madrid, for example. He surmised she was picking up the tab. He decided there was no point in voicing his suspicions. Instead, he asked, "Why did you tell me about England's answer to Hemingway?"

She took a deep drag on her cigarette before answering. "Jerry was bound to mention Uncle Geoff, or you'd have been poking around the guest room or study and found ample evidence of a male resident. I didn't want you to draw the wrong conclusions."

She butted her cigarette in the ashtray. Court thought she was about to add to her explanation, but at that moment

Jerry's voice came to them from the bedroom.

"Mummy?"

Her face lit up. "Out here on the balcony with Daddy, darling."

Jerry catapulted onto the balcony. Coming to a halt beside his mother, he blurted, "Can I go over to Jaime's?"

Marcie leaned over and kissed the boy. With her fingers, she smoothed his tousled curls. "Jer," she admonished with mock severity, "where are your manners. Say 'Good Morning' to Daddy."

Jerry turned to face Court. For a moment, the boy regarded this tall stranger uncertainly. Then, his face breaking into a broad smile, he said, *"Buenos Dias, Papa."*

Any residual annoyance Court still retained concerning Braithwaite evaporated. He smiled in response, and said, "Good Morning, Jerry."

Glancing up he caught Marcie's eyes. Her face reflected pride, tenderness, and amusement. Court leaned over and brought his hand to rest on hers. She smiled.

*   *   *   *

Court's intention had been to spend no more than a week on the Costa del Sol. He stayed until the first week in August. Even then, he was reluctant to leave, but since he had written his father and sisters that he would visit them he could no longer postpone his departure.

It was a happy month; the most completely satisfying in his recollection.

It took a few days for the initial awkwardness to wear off, but after that their love-making became both spontaneous and mutually satisfying. If it lacked some of the turbulent passion of the days and nights in New York, it more than compensated with hitherto undreamed of heights of sustained ecstacy. If the frenzied character of Marcie's appetites had mellowed, she had lost nothing of her passionate desire. Court discovered that the vague dissatisfaction he had experienced in sexual gratification over the past couple of years now disappeared as though it had never existed. He accepted this phenomenon without question, as a wonderful gift freely bestowed by Marcie.

During the weeks that passed all too quickly, by unspoken agreement they avoided discussing the past, as though fearing that a reawakening of old issues would rob their reunion of its magic. This moratorium could not endure indefinitely, but they managed to maintain it until the week before Court's departure. Even then, they eased gently into discussion of past differences. And then, to their astonishment, they discovered that areas of anticipated dispute had dwindled into insignificance.

Marcie didn't like to be absent from The Yellow Door during the evenings of this rush season. They confined their exploration of the countryside to daytime excursions. The two exceptions were when they took Jerry and stole off for an overnight stay in Ronda, and a two day visit to Granada.

The Yellow Door hours of business were from 11:00 a.m. to 3:00 p.m. for the noontime trade, and from 10:00 p.m. until 1:00 o'clock in the morning to cater to the heavy evening traffic. Court spent most of his evenings at the bar-restaurant. To occupy himself, he started to help out greeting guests, taking orders, and assisting Richard Downing dispensing drinks at the bar. Before the end of his first week. Court had become an accepted member of the staff. To his surprise, he was popular with the patrons and actually enjoyed the work. And he came to appreciate Marcie's reluctance to play hooky of an evening. She was adored by the staff and customers alike. With the staff, she arbitrated minor disputes effortlessly, and with unfailing good humor. With the patrons, she was considerate and solicitous of their wishes without appearing deferential. Court recognized that the obvious success of the business was largely due to Marcie's charm and personal magnetism. He found himself taking vicarious pride in her achievement.

One thing Court noted with amusement was the fact that at no time did either staff or customer make any reference to Braithwaite. He fully appreciated that this was not due to any deference to his own sensibilities, but to avoid any possible embarrassment for Marcie. It was a mark of the esteem in which she was held.

Court devoted a good deal of his daytime activities to becoming acquainted with his son. It was a rewarding experience. A close empathy quickly developed between them. And to add to his enjoyment of the growing attachment was the fact that Marcie was not in the least jealous of sharing Jerry's affection. The only feature which marred the relationship was Court's awareness that the boy's surname was Kirk and not Palmer. But this disturbing element gradually blurred in his mind to a point where it seemed of little consequence.

*   *   *   *

It was during a discussion of Jerry's future that the past first intruded. It was Marcie who broached the suject.

They were lying nude, sunbathing in the small garden. Since nudity offended the sense of decency of the servants, Marcie always positioned a bamboo screen between herself and the glass doors of the sitting and dining rooms. That they were visible from the bedroom balcony, and in all likelihood from the villas on the rising slope, bothered her not at all.

Marcie was explaining that while she was opposed to marriage in principal, there had been another reason why she had decided to have the baby abroad. She had been afraid that Court's family would in some way exert pressure on her to have the baby legitimized. It wasn't that she had any overwhelming desire to create a bastard child, but that she didn't want either the baby or herself to be submerged in a powerful family dynasty such as the Palmers.

Court had been listening to her, and now raised himself on one elbow. "He's still my son and heir. One day a helluva lot of bread is going to shower down on him. When that happens, he'll know he's part of the clan," Court observed drily.

Marcie turned her head toward him and brushed the hair back from her face. "Yes. But by then Jerry will know his father as a person rather than just the last banger in a chain of sausages."

Court grinned, both at her use of the English slang and the image of the Palmer family as so many links of sausage. "Yes," he agreed, "I suppose the Palmers do come on pretty strong as aristocracy in the pelf sense. Jerry becomes a very little sausage hanging at the end of the chain. But since most of the chain didn't know he was hitchhiking at the tail end, you had nothing to fear."

Her eyes opened incredulously. "Do you mean to say you didn't tell your family about the baby? Were you ashamed to father a bastard? Jesus Christ."

Court chuckled. Patiently, he told her of the family superstition that the advent of a child born to the eldest son of the line spelled death for the male grandparent. "It's crap, of course, but I'm sure Dad believes it implicitly. If he'd known of the happy event, he may not have kicked off, but psychosomatically he'd have been one sick kid. So I withheld the joyous news from all but Sharron and Grandmother. Then, I haven't been in very close touch over the past few years. I'll spring it on Dad on this visit. Without a doubt, he'll be so overjoyed to find the superstition is nothing but myth that he'll overlook the paltry matter of legitimacy."

Marcie smiled at the picture presented of the elder Palmer receiving the news that he had a six-year-old grandson. Then another thought struck her. "But didn't they wonder why your grandmother left Jerry an educational trust?"

"Nope. They probably assumed that Jerome Kirk was a distant relative on her side of the family. I was the only one to be surprised. When you trotted off pregnant, I was pretty choked up about the whole scene. Cried on Lucy's shoulder. I don't think she understood what motivated you, but maybe she did. At any rate, she staunchly defended your action. But the strange thing was that I never did tell her your Fuengirola address. She must have had a private eye track you down. So, when the will was read, the trust bit came as a shock to me. It was Lucy's way of letting you know she understood and approved."

Marcie moved close and pushed him onto his back. She slid her body on top of his. With her weight on her elbows, the nipples of her small firm breasts just grazed his chest. Her hair fanned his cheek as she looked down into his eyes. "Lucy must have been quite a gal," she said softly. "I'm sorry I didn't meet her."

"So am I," he said. His hand moved down the warm

flesh of her slim waist to come to rest on the curve of her buttocks. "Apart from a small difference of about seventy years, you're very much like her." He slapped Marcie lightly on the rump, and added, "Except Lucy didn't make me horny."

She moved her thighs seductively, pressing onto his pelvis. "Am I making you horny, lover?" she asked with feigned innocence.

"Either that, or rigor mortis is setting in."

*   *   *   *

It was when they were driving back from Granada, with Jerry sound asleep in the back seat, that Court asked a question which had puzzled him for some time. "Why did you suddenly stop writing me when I was in Takhli?"

She studied his face for a few moments before answering. "Because, Court, I didn't agree with what you were doing. The Viet-Nam war is a bad scene. I was afraid that I couldn't write without my letters reflecting that feeling. Life must have been rough enough for you without aggravation like that . . . so I stopped writing."

He admitted to himself that her answer made sense. Some of his friends had received letters from home scourging them for bombing and strafing the poor defenseless peasants of North Viet-Nam. The fact that these same peasants were engaged in a ruthless war of aggression, and throwing more flak into the air than Berlin had been able to muster during World War II, was incidental. Such letters hadn't done much for the morale of the troops.

He drove for several kilometers in silence. Then he found himself talking. He tried to picture for Marcie what it was like to go out on a bombing mission. He glossed over the hairier details, and realized that in a sense he was justifying his role and that of his fellow bomber pilots. He dwelt more on the exploits of Deke Maloney and Jay Grant rather than his own. Then he described the mission he and Jay had missed, when Deke had been shot down. He explained that this one event had served to bring the war into sharp focus for himself, and how it had led to his interest in the historical and cultural background of the region.

Marcie listened, watching his face intently. She interrupted his monologue with a question. "Court, I have the feeling that you hold yourself responsible for what happened to Deke. Is that so?"

He was surprised. It was almost the same question Jay had posed to him some months after the fateful mission. What had there been in his recounting of the incident to make her draw such a conclusion? He deliberated a minute before framing an answer.

"No, Marcie, I don't. At the time, I'll admit I felt pretty bad and I suppose guilty for not having been on the mission. Later, I realized that even if I had been along it wouldn't have changed anything."

He told her more. As he drove down the winding mountain highway leading towards Malaga, he recounted how his interest in the regional background had led to his decision to spend more time in Southeast Asia. He told her about his present employment in humorous and self-deprecatory terms. And he told her something of his plans for the future.

What he now confided in Marcie, he had disclosed to no one. For some months he had been exploring the feasibility of starting a Hong Kong based film company to engage in documentary travelogues and scripted feature films to be shot throughout Asia and the South Pacific. He had come to the conclusion that there was an almost unlimited market in TV, theatre presentation, and especially in the just-starting field of TV cassettes. It would require a good many months, and a healthy slice of capital to put the project together. He needed to find capable cinephotographers and directors for the field units, suitable administrative personnel, and set up an up-to-date processing lab in Hong Kong. He didn't intend to rush it, but he'd already made a start. The ketch he was having built in Hong Kong was intended for use as a mobile unit base, particularly in the South Pacific. In the meantime, he intended to hang onto his present job which presented him with an opportunity to travel and widen his contacts.

Marcie smiled at his buoyant enthusiasm. She murmured something in Spanish.

"What?" Court queried.

"Nothing. It's a quotation from Cervantes' Don Quixote."

"Meaning you think I'm tilting at windmills?"

"No," she assured him. "It's hard to translate, but it has to do with high ideals. I think the venture sounds exciting. Think you'll do well at it. Also, I'm very happy that you don't intend to return Stateside to take over the helm of the Palmer enterprises. Your ketch sounds like a far better exercise in helmsmanship. I just hope you don't call your company Palmer Films."

Court grinned. "As a matter of fact, my Hong Kong solicitors are incorporating in the name of Pan-Ocean Enterprises, Limited."

"It has an impressive ring," she observed.

*　*　*　*

On the morning of the day of his departure, Marcie

assisted him with his packing.

Court watched her thoughtfully as she folded his underwear and stacked it neatly in the suitcase next to his shirts.

He decided to voice a thought which had been uppermost in his mind for the past week.

"Marcie, the summer rush will be subsiding in another six or seven weeks. Why don't you and Jerry join me in Bangkok?"

Marcie stopped packing, and sat down on the foot of the bed. She looked at Court reflectively. "I wondered when you were going to ask me that," she said.

"Well?"

"I'm sorry, Court, the answer is no. I've thought about it, and maybe I'll change my mind the minute you board the flight for Paris, but even though the idea is appealing I don't think this is the right time for Jerry and me to try and fit into your orbit."

Court had been pretty sure she would refuse, but he was nonetheless hurt by the rejection. His face must have betrayed his emotions.

Marcie's voice softened. "I have no wish to deprive you of Jerry. I think you're good for each other. I was going to suggest that he spend next summer with you. But me, Court, that's a different matter. A woman needs two kinds of security — financial and emotional. The bread department has never been a problem with either of us. That leaves the emotional scene. You're changed, Court, but in spite of the maturity I have the uncomfortable feeling you're still searching for something; still groping for an identity."

He started to protest, but she stopped him with an impatient gesture. "Look, Court, maybe I could help you find what you're looking for; maybe not. But you don't really *need* me. Right now, I don't think you need anybody. Besides, I don't think it would be good for either one of us. I've made a life here which isn't too bad. Not ideal, of course, but I don't want to give it up just yet. When you settle on what you want and get truly established, and if you still want me, we can discuss it again. I just don't think the time is now."

*   *   *   *

They left Jerry in Mijas when she drove Court to the Malaga airport.

They stood outside the International Flight Departure Lounge, oblivious to those around them. It was time Court checked through immigration, but they clung to the final minutes, reluctant to part.

It could be delayed no longer. Court took her in his arms and kissed her hungrily. She clung to him, her head on his chest. Reaching down, he gently tilted her face up. Her eyes were misty; a tremulous smile on his lips.

Pulling his head down, she said in a soft low voice, "I'll tell you a secret, Courtney Palmer. I've finally fallen in love with Jerry's father."

Her lips brushed his lightly, then she twisted free of his grasp and strode quickly towards the glass doors leading to the parking area.

The loudspeaker was announcing the departure of his flight. Court hesitated a moment. Then, snatching up his suitcase and clothing bag, he strode towards the immigration counter. He suddenly felt as if he was already airborne.

*   *   *   *

CHAPTER NINE

The flight deck door clicked shut behind Court.

Expecting to see Maurice Paquet returning to report on the problem in the economy class compartment, the radio operator looked up. Instead of the flight engineer, he beheld a towering hooded apparition. For a moment, his mind rejected the evidence presented by his eyes. He opened his mouth to object angrily at this invasion of the jetliner's sacrosanct nerve-center. At that instant, the fact that he was staring directly into the muzzle of a revolver registered on him. His righteous indignation vanished, submerged by a chilling wave of fear. His mouth hung open. He emitted a gurgling gasp.

From their positions in the forward bucket-seats, both Captain LePlattre and the second officer swung their heads around. A startled, " *Mon dieu* ", escaped the lips of the second officer. LePlattre said nothing as he absorbed the situation. The stiffened set of his shoulders and the corded muscles of his neck attested to contained anger, as he watched Court unwaveringly through narrowed lids.

Court shifted the 38 slightly to bring it to bear on the captain. Mildly surprised at the steadiness of his own cloth-muffled voice, Court said, slowly and distinctly, "Captain, we have just taken over command of your aircraft. In a moment, this will be confirmed through your cabin intercom. Please instruct your entire crew to carry out our orders implicitly, and to do nothing foolish. You will do the following immediately. Shut down on your reporting frequency, and switch off your altitude transponder."

A muscle along LePlattre's jawline tightened, but he curtly nodded assent and growled something in French to the radio officer and second officer copilot. The tight-lipped second officer inclined his head in acknowledgment. His mouth still stupidly agape, the radio operator sat in an attitude of frozen suspension.

Motioning towards the communication equipment with an eloquent gesture of the gun, Court snapped, *"Vite"*. Galvanized from his trance, the radio operator turned hastily and fumbled with the knobs and panel switches.

Satisfied that the transmitter was switched off, Court returned his attention to LePlattre. "Take her below the overcast, Captain," he ordered.

Court watched as LePlattre disengaged the automatic pilot, grasped the yoke, easing it forward, and adjusted the throttle. The jetliner assumed a nose-down attitude. The sweep hands of the altimeter revolved slowly as the aircraft started the descent from its assigned altitude of 37,000 feet. They were not losing altitude rapidly enough to suit Court. "A more rapid rate of descent, Captain," he ordered quietly.

Beneath his close-cropped iron-gray hair, LePlattre's neck reddened, but he complied with more pressure on the yoke and a further throttle adjustment. The gray cloud-line horizon rose in level against the forward view-screen, and the altimeter hands increased their speed of rotation.

Court's attention was fixed on the instrument panel, but his mind was speculating on the events which would be taking place in the after cabin. He had no way of knowing whether things were proceeding according to plan. Having secured the flight deck door behind him on entry, he was virtually cut-off from the rest of the airliner. The confirmation of the hijack he had so confidently predicted seemed agonizingly slow in coming.

A tensing of LePlattre's shoulders alerted Court to the fact that the captain was receiving some report over his intercom headset. The second officer, also receiving the same message, looked questioningly at the captain. LePlattre growled a terse reply into his lip-mike, turned his head slightly, and shot a venomous glance at Court. Beneath the hood, Court essayed a quick smile. His spirits lifted. The reaction of both the captain and second officer, who was now slumped in his bucket-seat staring dejectedly at the instrument panel, was ample proof that the takeover was going smoothly.

Keeping his eye on the altimeter, Court watched the high broken overcast rising relatively to meet the jetliner. He and Gracier had agreed on a flight level of 10,000 feet for this phase. Earlier, following lunch, Court had estimated the cloud cover to be at about 12,000 feet. Taking the air-craft beneath the cover should bring them to about 10,000, and, while they had not considered cloud in their calcula-tions, it would be advantageous.

Court ran rapidly through the initial sequence in his mind. When the flight failed to give a position report at North Reef, Saigon Control's first reaction would be to alert other aircraft along the route to give visual sighting reports. Hong Kong Control would do the same. There could well be a time lag on the part of Saigon Control of several minutes before any alert went out. Then, it would be at least another ten minutes before any search procedures were initiated. By that time, Air France Flight 194 would have completed the next dog-leg alteration of course and be well north over the Gulf of Tonkin. Any chance of interception by either MIG fighters of the Chinese, Hainan-based Air Force, or American interceptors from the Danang airbase, was improbable if not impossible. Within another ten to fif-teen minutes, they should have penetrated the 50 mile Buffer Zone off the North Viet-Nam coast. By then, it would be a matter of purely academic interest since the whole world would be aware of the hijack.

When the altimeter registered 18,000 feet, Court instructed LePlattre to turn to port onto a heading of 290 degrees. The captain scowled, but said nothing as he banked to port.

Court extracted a stiff piece of paper from the pocket of his gown and handed it to the captain. LePlattre unfolded the paper and frowned as he read the two typed paragraphs.

"Read out the first announcement over the internal broadcast as soon as you've completed the course alteration," Court instructed. "I'll tell you when to give the second bulletin," he added.

For the first time, LePlattre broke his silence. To Court's surprise, the question concerned neither the new course nor the two typed announcements. "My engineer?" LePlattre queried brusquely.

"He'll be okay. We'll return him to the flight deck when his presence is required," Court answered. He hoped his statement was accurate and that the flight engineer hadn't done something stupid during his mission of investigation in the after compartment. Court needn't have worried.

*   *   *   *

DeSantis had matters well in hand.

As soon as the aircraft captain's first broadcast announcement was completed, DeSantis had the purser assemble the five stewardesses, together with the flight engineer, in the space at the after galley.

The big jet shuddered and bucked as it entered the cloud cover. DeSantis waited until it emerged from the few hundred-foot layer of minor turbulence, and was trimmed for level flight. Then, from the two flight bags, he took a number of black bag-like objects. Using one of the stewardesses as a model, he explained the purpose of the bag and demonstrated how it was to be utilized. Each bag was fabricated of heavy cotton, with a double-stitched hem at the open end. Through the hem was threaded a light multi-strand wire with a thimbled eye spliced into one end and a number of eyelets inserted at close intervals at the other. Placed over the head in the manner of a hood, it became an effective blindfold. To prevent removal, the wire was drawn tight enough under the chin to secure the device without restricting breathing. A small padlock was then snapped through the thimble and appropriate eyelet.

Before distributing the hoods to the engineer and cabin crew, DeSantis instructed the engineer to advise the flight deck of his intention. There was a lapse of about 30 seconds before the message came over the broadcast system:

"This is your Captain speaking. The cabin crew are going to distribute hoods to the passengers. While these may cause a certain amount of discomfort and inconvenience, you are assured that it is only a temporary measure for your own protection. Please follow instructions, and no-one will be in any way harmed."

DeSantis waited a few moments for the announcement to register, then handing some of the hoods to each of the crew members he started the group moving up the center aisle.

The operation went smoothly. The stewardesses placed a hood over the head of each passenger, the thimble and eyelets to the rear as DeSantis had instructed. Following behind the crew, DeSantis adjusted the wires and locked the hoods in place.

They had moved almost halfway up the economy class compartment before DeSantis encountered anything other than mild protest from the frightened passengers.

In the window seat of 22F, a hood already placed loosely

over her head by a stewardess, a woman sat rigidly tense. As DeSantis reached behind her to adjust the wire, he became aware of a convulsive jerking of her hands in her lap, and her partially-muffled strangled gasps. The possibility of running into claustrophobic passengers had not been neglected in their planning. DeSantis recognized the symptoms. He whipped the hood from her head. While her agitation abated, DeSantis deduced from the pallor of her face and fear-haunted stare that she was in dread of the consequences of non-compliance with the broadcasted instructions. He acted quickly to avert her mounting panic.

"Don't be alarmed, Madame," DeSantis said quietly. "Please join the group in the aisle. I'll seat you in the forward compartment where a hood won't be necessary."

As she scrambled into the aisle with alacrity, her face registered a mixture of fear and relief. She turned toward DeSantis, essaying a smile of gratitude which froze into a grimace.

By the time they reached Anderson, 43 of the 48 economy class passengers had been masked. Although the operation was progressing rapidly, and he was confident that his absence from seat 31C had gone unnoticed, DeSantis was becoming increasingly edgy. The encasing of a passenger's head in the cloth confinement seemed to have a subduing effect, almost a paralysis. But those who had not yet been hooded were beginning to speculate on the alteration of course and the possible intentions of the hijackers. The shock effect was wearing off, to be replaced by restiveness. DeSantis was anxious to complete the task as quickly as possible. He did not appreciate Andy Anderson's unrehearsed contribution.

When the stewardess attempted to place a hood over Anderson's head, he rumbled profane protest. DeSantis stepped forward quickly and rammed the muzzle of his gun into the big man's ribs. Andy grunted in pained surprise, and lapsed into silence. Meekly, he permitted the girl to lower the bag gingerly over his head.

With the task completed in economy class, DeSantis moved the cabin crews, flight engineer, and the claustrophobia victim forward into the first class compartment. He followed, drawing the heavy blue curtains closed behind himself. As he did so, he rapped the barrel of his gun sharply against the dividing bulkhead.

Gracier and Anderson heard the signal. They waited 15 seconds before removing the hoods which DeSantis had only made a show of locking. In Andy's case, DeSantis had been tempted to snap the padlock, but hadn't.

Moving with silent caution, the two men eased into the center aisle. Carefully retrieving his attache case from beneath his seat, Gracier nodded at Anderson. They walked softly down the carpeted aisle towards the rear of the aircraft.

In passing, Anderson paused to let his hand rest lightly on Begg's shoulder. In Begg's case, DeSantis had locked the hood in place. At the contact of Anderson's touch, Begg started, then slowly inclined his head in acknowledgement.

In the after galley, Gracier worked quickly, but without haste. From beneath his pant leg, he unstrapped the Luger and placed it on the galley serving-shelf. From his brief case, he removed the two costumes from the top compartment, and also a belt and sheathed *kukri*, the traditional killing knife of the warlife Gurkha's of Nepal. He placed this weapon beside his Luger on the shelf.

They donned the black garments and affixed their hoods. Anderson buckled the belt around his waist on the outside of his gown. The lethal Gurkha knife was to be his sole weapon. There is something about cold steel which strikes fear in the heart of the beholder. In the case of the *kukri*, there is an added measure of awe for those aware of the Gurkha tradition that once unsheathed it must not be returned to its scabbard unless blood is drawn. This custom would not be lost on the Indian Ambassador and his party. The theatrical aspects of the blade had been a consideration in its selection, but its true function, if required, would be far more dramatic. Andy tugged at the hilt and the blade slid easily from the sheath. He examined the curved flaring 11 inch surface of lightly-greased steel, the cutting edge honed to razor sharpness. Satisfied, he slipped it back in its scabbard.

They went forward; Gracier to join Palmer in the flight deck, and Anderson to assist DeSantis with the relocation of the hooded passengers.

*   *   *   *

Over the weeks of preparation, Court had given the matter of the inspiration for the perilous adventure considerable thought.

Every scheme, great or small, has its particular moment of genesis. Court had no difficulty pinpointing the time and place when the idea suddenly crystallized in his mind. What was by no means as clear was just when the nebulous thought had been conceived and how long it had been in process of gestation. On reflection, he conceded that the seed could well have been planted in some recess of his brain on the fateful day when Deke had been shot down over Hai-Duong. He was not prepared to admit, however, that feelings of guilt had persisted to nurture the seed and bring it finally to germination. That Jay

Grant, Marcie, and, more recently, Andy Anderson, had commented on such a possibility, did not constitute proof to Court's way of thinking. He resented the implication that his decision to remain in Southeast Asia had been prompted by a subconscious compulsion to expiate some fancied sin of omission with respect to Deke. Since his separation from the Air Force, Court didn't think he'd dwelt much on memories of his fighter-bomber experiences. He had been reminded of Takhli days and Deke from time to time, such as when he'd received one of Jay's infrequent letters, or when he had encountered one of his erstwhile companions, but he wasn't aware of having indulged in reflections, morbid or otherwise. He had considered that portion of his life a closed chapter, or almost closed. That the memories were not too deeply buried, had been demonstrated by the vivid recall evoked by Marcie's gentle probing. But with regard to Deke, until fairly recently Court hadn't even known whether his old friend was alive or dead. Officially, Major Desmond K. Maloney was still listed as Missing in Action.

It was in the latter part of September, a couple of weeks after Court's return to Bangkok, that he received a telephone call from Lieutenant Colonel Blair, 7th and 13th Air Force Liaison Officer attached to headquarters of the Military Assistance Command, Thailand. Blair called from his office at JUSMAG/MACTHAI on Sathorn Road.

"Court, Jim Blair."

"Hello, Jim. What can I do for you?"

"Nothing. You remember asking me to let you know if we ever picked up anything about Major Maloney?"

Court experienced a sinking sensation. "Yes."

"It isn't official, but he's been mentioned in a recent intelligence report. Seems he was hospitalized in Haiphong and was transferred from a convalescence camp to a POW camp near Hanoi a few weeks ago."

"Report reliable?"

"Yes. He probably won't appear on any North Vietnamese POW list. Normally, they don't include medical cases. If they botch the patching up job, they don't want any embarrassing questions at some future accounting. But if Maloney's been transferred to a regular camp, he can't be in too bad a shape. Officially, we'll still show him as MIA, but unofficially we're now listing him as a POW. Thought you'd like to know."

"Thanks, Jim."

Court's initial reaction to the news was one of relief. It wasn't until a little later that he started to speculate on the nature of Deke's injuries. After a few days of this fruitless occupation, he gave it up as senseless. If Blair had known, he would have disclosed the information. At any rate, there was nothing Court could do about it anyway. But if thoughts of Deke had been dormant over the past months, they now sprang again to the forefront. At least Deke was alive, which was some consolation.

*   *   *   *

On October 8th, Court received the telegram informing him that Anderson would be arriving the next morning on the Air Vietnam flight from Saigon.

Roy Anderson was a civil engineer employed in Danang by Emerson Engineering on the big navy port development project. Court had met Roy "Andy" Anderson in Danang on one of Court's first exploratory trips to Viet-Nam. Anderson, who had worked on foreign contract assignments almost exclusively since his army discharge at the end of

World War II, had acquired considerable savings over the two and one-half decade period. As Anderson put it, from his first contract with Aramco in Saudi Arabia, back in 1946, he'd been a professional globe-trotter. When you once get that goddamned sand in your shoes, he opined, it's hard to get it out. And there was a certain appeal to high earnings under virtually tax-free conditions. From Aramco, Anderson had worked for practically every major engineering firm and consortium — Morrison-Knudson; Vinell; Bechtel; Johnson, Drake & Piper; Dillingham; RMK; Philco; and now Emerson. Apart from a year Stateside, following his Arabian contract, he had spent most of his adult life in odd corners of the globe. For the past ten years, except for one contract in Cambodia, his activities had been confined to South Viet-Nam.

Anderson had married during his sabbatical sojourn in Oregon in 1948. It hadn't worked out. Andy admitted that this was largely his fault since he couldn't seem to settle down to life in the States, and his young wife had been unwilling to set up housekeeping in any of the isolated project sites abroad. Their union had produced one son. The boy grew to manhood with little or no paternal contact. He was now 21, a veteran of Viet-Nam as a helicopter pilot, married with a son of his own, and completing an engineering degree at UCLA. Even though both father and son had been in Viet-Nam at the same time, Andy had seen little of his son. The grandson, he had never seen — and wasn't even mildly curious concerning him. Andy's marriage hadn't been severed abruptly, but had simply withered slowly due to almost constant geographical separation. Eventually, his wife had obtained a divorce and remarried a druggist in Salem. In Andy's expatriate pattern of life, the legal termination of what constituted a marriage in name only, had little effect.

By all odds, Anderson should have been a wealthy man. He was well-off by any standards, but a penchant for investing in hair-brained schemes had made inroads into his capital. Anderson was 56 when he met Court, and while he had no regrets concerning his unprofitable ventures of the past, he was beginning to think seriously in terms of sound investment for the future. For both Courtney J. Palmer and Roy B. Anderson, it was to prove a decisive encounter.

Court had handled Anderson's investment portfolio for over a year. Anderson, at first cautiously skeptical, had gained confidence to the point where he vested in Court complete discretion. His trust was rewarded. In the 13 month period, Court very nearly doubled Anderson's net worth.

The relationship between the two men became much more than that of client and investment counselor. Despite a disparity of background, and a difference of almost thirty years in their ages, they discovered a mutual empathy which grew into friendship. It was, at least insofar as Court was concerned, nothing like a father-son tie. If Andy found in Court something of the paternal bonds he had missed in kinship, it is doubtful that either one of them recognized the fact.

Roy Anderson was the antithesis of Court's father. Andy was six foot three inches of rock-hard muscle; ebullient, outgoing, and possessed of the slowness to anger common in most big men confident of their prowess. Only once had Court seen big Andy in action. It had been a devastating spectacle. Provoked beyond his limits of tolerance, Andy had proceeded to flatten the offending barroom detractors with the swift efficiency of a sickle cutting a swath through a field of standing grain. In the process, Andy had demolished a good percentage of the bar fixtures. The fight had subsided within minutes, leaving Andy grinning through a swelling lip, nursing bruised knuckles, cheerfully paying for the material damage, and buying drinks for those of his opponents of a moment earlier who were still ambulatory. Court could not picture his father in a similar situation. And there were other points of marked difference. Andy, despite his belated concern for financial security, gave scant heed for the morrow, and dwelt not at all on the mistakes of yesterday. He lived each moment, whether working, drinking, fighting, or making love, to the fullest. It was difficult for Court to conceive of Andy and his father as belonging to the same generation. In some ways, Andy reminded Court of Deke Maloney.

*　　*　　*　　*

Picking up Andy at Don Muang Airport, Court drove directly to the house. It was the cook's day off, but Court had persuaded her to stay and serve lunch.

On the drive in from the airport, Andy disclosed that he'd just felt like getting away from Viet-Nam for a couple of weeks. He intended to spend a few days with Court in Bangkok, then visit Singapore and wind up lolling on the beach at Penang for a week. He had no fixed itinerary, and may even grab a flight to Sydney. It had been an oppressively hot summer in Danang, and the recent spate of Viet Cong rocket attacks on the town hadn't helped matters, Andy explained. A little change of scenery, he felt, was in order.

No stranger to Court's residence, Andy was greeted like a member of the household by the servants and the dog. Disdaining assistance, he lugged his two bags upstairs and deposited them in the guest room.

Following lunch, Court had a number of appointments. He dropped Andy at Patpong, where the big man indicated his intention of stopping by several of his favorite bars before visiting a massage parlor to get, as he put it, "steamed and creamed." Court arranged to rendezvous with Andy at 5:30 in the Derby King.

Court was a quarter of an hour late in meeting Andy at the Derby King. It was shortly after 7:00 p.m. before they left the bar and drove to the officers' club at the Chao Phya Hotel to dine.

While it is interesting to speculate on cause and effect; on the manner and method by which fate conspires to set in motion a chain of events, it is often a profitless exercise. It could be argued that if Anderson had not arrived in Bangkok on the particular day, when Court's cook was off-duty; or if Court had selected another eating place; or if he hadn't been a few minutes late at the rendezvous and he and Andy had arrived at the Chao Phya earlier, or for that matter, later, their lives would have pursued a different course. That is always a possibility. But it is more likely that, in the analogy of life as a billiard table, Court was rolling smoothly down the table towards a point of collision with a major colored ball. If the circumstances hadn't arisen as they did at this particular time and place, destiny would have contrived an equally effective alternative. The fact remains, however, that it was during dinner that an event took place which was to have far reaching consequences. The catalysts were three flyers on R&R from the airbase at Udorn, dining at a table adjoining that of Court and Andy. The occurrence was their chance recounting of an improbable episode.

There was a lull in his conversation with Andy. From the table behind him, Court overheard the conversation.

". . . You gotta be kidding," one of the men said.

"Hell, no," another voice protested. "One day Hank and Gary were bombing the piss out of Hanoi, and they very next day, there they were sitting right in the middle of the Hanoi airport. They came down to Bangkok on R&R on Friday morning, and caught an afternoon commercial flight for Hong Kong."

"So how in hell did they get to Hanoi?"

"Damned if I know. Gary told me the flight was diverted due to some sort of emergency. Suppose Hanoi was the closest strip."

"And they got out without any problem?"

"Yep. They were less than an hour on the ground. Got to Hong Kong that same evening."

"Jesus. Must have been a funny feeling sitting on one of their own targets."

"Yeah. Sure must have been. Gary told me he was scared shitless his own squadron would draw a mission to bomb the strip. Wouldn't that be the shits. On leave, and get knocked off by your own buddies."

Court glanced at Andy, and noted the big man's rapt attention to the same discourse.

He waited until the three men had left before he commented to Andy.

"Bullshit," Court said.

"What?"

"That story about the guys on leave landing in Hanoi."

"Why? Sounded like it could have happened. The kid telling the story sounded pretty convincing."

"Yeah, almost had me convinced. But it's been well over a year since we bombed anything north of the 20th parallel, so he could only have gotten the story second or third hand. And we never did bomb the Hanoi airport anyway."

"Okay, but a commercial flight could have been diverted to Hanoi, couldn't it?

"I'm damned if I can see how. Suppose some emergency developed when they were somewhere over the South China Sea. On the commercial routing, Hanoi would be about the same distance as Hong Kong. If they couldn't make it to Hong Kong or Manila, they'd be diverted back to South Viet-Nam. Danang would be the best bet, but in an emergency they could be cleared for Phu Bai, Chu Lai, Phu Cat, Cam Ranh or Phan Rang. Christ, even Saigon would probably be closer than Hanoi. Can't you just see the North Vietnamese letting a PanAm or TWA flight land in Hanoi? It would have to be one helluva emergency."

"Suppose you're right. But they might let other airlines in . . . Air India, Air France, BOAC, or Cathay Pacific."

"They might. But what airline captain in his right mind would try for Hanoi? Under the worst possible conditions, Danang would be about 200 miles away as opposed to Hanoi at 400. Some emergency."

Andy grinned. "It still makes a good story. I think the kid believed it, bullshit or not."

Court laughed. "Yeah, I think he did. And I think he convinced his pals. But the only way you could get a commercial flight out of Bangkok, bound for Hong Kong, into Hanoi, would be to hijack the mother."

"And who would want to do that?" asked Andy, signaling the waiter for more coffee.

"Oh, some Commie nut, a Vietnamese defector, an American deserter, or . . . " Court paused. His voice lost its bantering tone, as he said almost wonderingly," or someone who wanted to ransom the airliner and its passengers for POWs."

Even as he voiced the thought, his mind leaped ahead to visualize the action. "Godammit," he said softly, "it could be done."

Through the remainder of the evening, back once more at the Derby King, and then at his house, where Court warmed up coffee and served cognac, the conversation between himself and Andy centered around the feasibility of hijacking a jetliner to Hanoi. The more they discussed it, the more plausible it seemed to Court. For every argument Andy advanced against such a suicidal project, Court found some kind of counter-argument. It almost seemed to him that in some secret compartment of his mind the adventure had been planned already in minutest detail.

*　　*　　*　　*

Court was already seated at the breakfast table, nursing a hangover, when Andy clumped down the stairs.

"Good morning," Andy said cheerfully.

"Who the hell asked you for a weather report?"

"That's the trouble with you youngsters — no stamina. Suppose you're hung," Andy replied, as he pulled up a chair and settled himself at the table.

"And I suppose you're not? Slept like a baby? You should have been anaesthetized considering the amount of cognac you gargled."

Andy gulped down a large glass of orange juice, and sat back to let the cook place a plate of bacon and eggs before him. "Now that you mention it, I didn't sleep too well. Got to thinking about that damn fool hijack plan of yours. Couldn't get it out of my mind." Attacking the bacon and eggs with enthusiasm, Andy eyed Court thoughtfully. He chased a mouthful down with a swallow of hot coffee, and added, "You're serious about it, aren't you?"

Court deliberated a moment. While it was true that in the cold light of day he could recognize many pitfalls, he realized that he was not only serious but that he fully intended to translate the plan into action. "Yes," he answered, "I'm serious."

"That's what I thought. Would it do any good to tell you you've got rocks in your head?"

"Not much."

"Thought that too. You realize that it will cost you a bundle to recruit the three idiots you estimate you would need to assist you in pulling it off?"

"Uh huh."

"Okay. I'll go along with you. That's one fool less you have to find."

Court was startled. He looked at Andy in astonishment. "You! You don't think it has a ghost of a chance. What the hell . . . ."

Andy chuckled, and took another swallow of coffee. "I'll team up with you on one condition."

"What's that?" Court asked suspiciously.

"Okay, so I'm as crazy as you are. I thought it over last night. This morning, it looks the same. It could be worked . . . it just could be. But as I see it, there's one major stumbling block, You may have been a pretty hot jet-jock, but you know from nothing about commercial airline procedures. Couple that with the fact that you have only a smattering of French, and no knowledge of North Viet-Nam — except what it looks like from the air, and you have the big drawback. But if you could recruit someone with that specialized knowledge, I think you might swing the caper. And that's my condition. I know a guy who fits the picture,

Clement Gracier. He's a Frenchman who flew the air-drops into Dien Bien Phu, then for almost 11 years piloted a four-engine Stratocruiser for Aigle Azure, running the International Control Commission back and forth between Saigon and Hanoi. If we can con him into the team, you can count me in."

"And just how do I contact this Gracier?"

"You don't. I will. When the International Commission activity slowed down in '65, Clem hung on for about a year, and then quit Aigle Azure in '66. Went back to Air France, but had to do a year getting checked out in jets. Went copilot on the African run for about six months before he figured it out that on the seniority bit he'd never hack captain. He retired last year and started up a flying school in Singapore. That's where he is now. I was going to visit him anyway. Don't know how his business is, but if he's hurting I think he'll put his ass on the auction block."

"What inducement do you think he'd consider?"

"Don't know. He sure as hell isn't motivated by any goddamned guilt complex like you seem to be. He isn't any half-assed idealist, either. You can bet your sweet ass he won't come cheap. Fifteen grand . . . maybe more. Maybe he won't buy it at any price. I'll have to see when I talk to him. Tell you what. If he goes for it, and I can't hold him down to fifteen grand, I'll meet the difference myself."

"Why, Andy? Why in hell do you want to get involved?"

Andy placed his coffee cup on its saucer, wiped his mouth with a napkin, and looked at Court reflectively. "Damned if I know. I'm bored. Fed up with the present contract and most of the assholes I'm working with. What have I got to lose? Like you, I haven't any responsibilities. Bill doesn't need me. Hell, he doesn't even know me. I've got all the bread I need. I must be almost as nutty as you, but the idea sort of grabs me. Anyway, I think you'd go it alone, then *I* might develop a guilt complex. Think you stand a better chance with me and Gracier in your corner. But anybody else, baby, you'll have to dig up by yourself."

* * * *

Tony DeSantis was with Court when the telegram from Andy in Singapore was delivered. It read:

G AGREES TO JOIN FIRM

Court smiled faintly as he read the cable.
"Good news?" questioned Tony.
"Andy talked Gracier into the deal," Court answered, handing the yellow sheet to DeSantis. "We're off 'n running."

* * * *

Court had found the selection of a fourth recruit for the venture more difficult than he'd imagined.

He considered a number of friends and acquaintances. For a variety of reasons, he eliminated them one by one until the choice was narrowed down to only two names — Antonio DeSantis and Jan DeVeers. Initially, he had considered cabling Jay Grant, but on more sober reflection he had abandoned the idea. Jay was not only married with two children, and another on the way, but had recently been promoted to a responsible position with a West coast electronic engineering firm. Jay might accept on Court's persuasion, but it was hardly fair to expect such a sacrifice. Tony and Jan, on the other hand, were both bachelors and Bangkok residents. Court's final selection was Tony DeSantis, on the basis of the more solid trust and friendship.

When approached, DeSantis didn't evince much enthusiasm. His natural reluctance to participate in such a hazardous undertaking was overcome by the offer of twenty thousand dollars to be deposited to his name in a numbered Swiss bank account. Once committed, DeSantis put aside his misgivings and entered co-operatively into the planning and preparation. If he harbored doubts, he kept them to himself.

As for Court, he embarked on the project with a hitherto unsuspected singleness of purpose. He wasn't deluding himself that this was any game. Too much, too many lives, were hinged on the outcome. If they were to succeed, he recognized, every possible contingency must be covered. Methodically, he set about the construction of a detailed operational plan. It was a grave responsibility, not uncomplicated by emotional stress.

When Andy had alluded casually to the fact that Court had no responsibilities, the reference was on the evidence as Andy knew it. What Andy had no way of knowing was Court's relationship with Marcie and his new-found attachment to his son. And, to further complicate matters, there had been a more recent development. Marcie's letters had become much more frequent since Court's visit. The last letter, early in October, had contained a startling revelation as a casually appended postscript. It was seldom far from Court's thoughts as he proceeded with the serious business at hand.

The postscript read, simply:

'PS: You've scored again, lover. The doctor in Malaga advises that Jerry should have a little sister — or brother — as an Easter present.'

* * * *

CHAPTER TEN

Three sharp raps, a pause, and then a fourth knock, sounded on the other side of the flight deck door. Court unlatched the door to admit Gracier.

The conversational exchange was brief.

"Okay?" Court questioned.

A low chuckle came from behind Gracier's hood. "Good, so far," he answered. "I'd say Air France will be faced with a pretty stiff laundry bill. And here?"

"Came onto 290 degrees at 1315. Altitude 9,500 feet. Air speed 500 knots. No coastline indication on radar yet."

Gracier lifted his left arm and checked the time. With a motion of his Luger, he indicated the captain and aircrew. "Them?" he asked.

"No problem."

"Fine. I've got it."

*   *   *   *

The door clicked behind Court as he entered the forward section of the first class compartment. He heard the slight rasping sound as Gracier locked the door.

To Court's right, two uniformed men sat on the jump seats by the forward access door. They were masked with hoods, but would be the purser and flight engineer. In the four seats of the crew lounge opposite the forward galley sat three of the stewardesses and one of the woman passengers. Two more stewardesses were standing just inside the galley space. The stewardesses all wore hoods. The woman passenger did not. Court concluded that she must have been discovered by DeSantis as someone afflicted with claustrophobia. In the aisle, stood a tall figure garbed like himself. From the *kukri* strapped at the waist, Court recognized this to be Anderson. To the rear of Anderson, the heavy curtains were drawn across the aisle, cutting off the view of the first class passenger section.

An eerie silence pervaded the scene. Here, in this relatively confined forward space, there were ten people, including himself and Anderson. The only sound came from the gentle murmur of the external jet engines. Court had known what to expect, yet he found it oddly frightening to see these people, motionless, isolated beneath their confining hoods. The one person not masked, the claustrophobia victim was equally isolated by her non-conformity. She sat in stunned silence staring at the hooded stewardess seated opposite her.

In rehearsing the operation Court had instructed the group to wear their gowns and hoods for extended periods in order to become thoroughly accustomed to the restricting garments. They had all commented on a strange phenomenon. In spite of the fact that the gauze-like cloth in the face of the hoods did little to obstruct their vision, once encased in the garb they had experienced a strange loss of individual identity. As they went about the various tasks they would later perform in the actual hijack, there had been a marked tendency to avoid bodily contact, and to speak in muted tones little more than a whisper. It was, as DeSantis had remarked, not too difficult to imagine themselves as monks bound to an oath of silence.

Then, they had tried out the hoods which would mask the passengers and crew, other than the flight crew. Court had insisted that they wear the hoods for a continuous 12 hour period, and then record their individual reactions. The experiences had been remarkably similar and disconcertingly revealing. Each of them recorded that the initial reaction had been one of total isolation. There had followed a period of depression and extreme lethargy bordering on a catatonic state. All sense of time had been suspended. They had had no way of calculating when the next stage had affected them, but all had reported it in varying degrees of intensity. The inward turning imagination had commenced to play strange tricks inducing confused fancies and nervous agitation.

At the conclusion of the experiment, Court had been forced to alter his original intention, which was to keep the passengers and cabin crew hooded throughout the operation. It would have been excellent if the passengers could have been kept in a state of tractable stupor, but this was obviously an impossibility. And what would their reaction be if compounded by uncertainty and fear? Court had no way of knowing, but had suspected it could be injurious, particularly for anyone who happened to be at all mentally disturbed. At all costs, the passengers must recall their ordeal without rancor, or as little as possible. Court had settled on a compromise whereby the passengers and cabin crew would be masked for as long as it was required to put the first phase in motion, and thereafter only at intervals as and when the necessity arose.

Snapping out of the reverie brought on by the spectacle of the trance-induced crew members, Court walked aft, parted the curtain, and entered the first class passenger compartment. Anderson followed. They were joined by DeSantis, and the three men threaded their way silently aft.

Starting at the rear of economy class, they shifted many of the passengers into other seats. The passengers offered no resistance, allowing themselves to be guided and reseated without protest. Twelve of the passengers, five from seats in close proximity to those which had been occupied by Gracier and Anderson, and seven others selected at random, were shepherded forward to first class. From first class,

Lucille Montgomery, the French businessman, and the Indian Ambassador's male secretary were led aft and reseated in economy class.

DeSantis went forward to conduct the two first class stewardesses back to economy class. While he performed this task, Anderson stationed himself forward and Court retrieved his leather bag from the forward lavatory.

From DeSantis, Court picked up a masking hood and padlock. Removing his hood, wire frame, and outer garments, he stowed them, along with the Seiko watch and 38 in the bottom compartment of his bag. Snapping the Longine on his wrist, Court quietly took a seat directly in front of the one in which he'd situated Lucille Montgomery. He glanced quickly around the cabin. Satisfied, he nodded at DeSantis. While DeSantis was unlocking the hoods from the two stewardesses, Court slipped his hood over his head, adjusted the wire at the rear, and snapped the padlock.

With the stewardesses assisting, DeSantis moved slowly up the compartment unlocking and removing the passenger's hoods. Gradually, the ghostly silence which had prevailed was replaced by a babble of voices.

Lucille leaned forward in her seat. "I thought they'd missed you," she said.

"When I looked out of the washroom and saw what was happening, I ducked back in hoping they'd forget about me. Thought they had until one of those black monsters ordered me to open up. I didn't argue," Court answered.

"Where are they taking us?"

"Damned if I know. China, maybe."

The jetliner started to lose more altitude. Court listened to the changed pitch of the engines, and watched the movement of the wing flaps. The wrinkled surface of the gray sea rose towards them.

* * * *

When Court left the flight deck, Gracier motioned the radio operator to seat himself at the small navigation table. "Tell me when you pick up land on the radar scan," Gracier ordered.

Moving closer behind LePlattre, Gracier let his eyes drift their gaze slowly over the crowded instrument panel.

"North Viet-Nam?" LePlattre queried laconically.

"Hanoi," Gracier replied brusquely.

"Not on this heading."

"Don't worry, *"Mon vieux,* we'll alter course in a few minutes."

The radio operator broke in. "Coastal blip at 250."

"Range?" Gracier snapped.

"Just under 100 miles."

"Anything to starboard?"

"No...yes, somethings showing up now at about the same range, bearing 350."

The port hand radar indication would be either the islands off Danang, or the high headland of Monkey Mountain on the Presque'Isle de Tien Sha. The starboard indication would be the southern tip of Hainan Island. Checking his watch, Gracier computed 12 minutes more on the present course before the alteration to 340 degrees.

To LePlattre, Gracier commanded, "Take her down to 2,000 feet."

"Merde," LePlattre exploded. "We'll burn too much fuel at that altitude."

"Stop worrying. I know your consumption."

"Do you think the North Vietnamese are just going to let us fly into Hanoi? Don't you think they might scramble a reception committee to turn us back? I haven't the fuel reserves to play such games."

It wasn't true. LePlattre had ample reserves in hand. They would require refueling in Hanoi for take-off and the onward journey, but there was no cause for alarm at this point, even with the low altitude flying gulping kerosene at an excessive rate. LePlattre knew it, and by now must suspect that the hijackers were no novices.

"We anticipate fighter interception, Captain," Gracier said mildly.

"You're all mad," LePlattre growled.

Gracier watched as the captain depressed the yoke, throttled back, and ordered the necessary degree of flaps to put the jetliner into a shallow dive. Clem knew Christian LePlattre. He had met the senior Air France pilot on a number of occasions both in Saigon and Paris. He liked LePlattre, and respected his ability. Clem had also encountered the second officer, but couldn't recall his name. Placing himself in their position, Clem could understand and sympathize with their chagrin and frustration.

"Sans doute," Gracier said, in mild agreement with LePlattre's last statement. There was more conviction in Clem's voice than he'd intended.

* * * *

The morning was hot. October sun streamed down on the hangar and through the open front to illuminate almost a third of its interior. The face of the hangar bore the legend: "Lion City Flying Club".

Inside the hangar, just within the shaded area, Clem Gracier was standing on a frame metal ladder, working on the engine of one of the Cessnas. He didn't hear the approaching footsteps on the concrete hangar floor. The first intimation he had of the man's presence was the voiced statement:

"I can lick any French cunt in the house."

It had been almost two years since he'd heard either the voice or the expression, but Clem recognized both immediately. A slow smile lighting his face, Clem straightened from his task and turned. At the foot of the short ladder, Anderson grinned up at him.

Picking up a rag from the engine cowling, Gracier wiped grease from his hands and descended the three steps.

"Morning. Clem," Andy drawled, shaking Gracier's outstretched hand.

"Andy. Good to see you. What brings you to Singapore?"

"Pleasure, and business. Thought I'd pay you a social call, and I have an interesting proposition for you."

"Who do you want killed?"

"No one...I hope. I suggest that you tear yourself away from that engine and come with me to the Goodwood Park where we can discuss the project over a few drinks by the pool."

"Why not tell me here?"

"Because I think you'll need a couple of drinks when I tell you what I have in mind."

"Okay. It's your party." Gracier turned and hollered, "Lee."

A Chinese scrambled out from behind the undercarriage of a Beechcraft Bonanza. "Yes, Mr. Clem."

"Where's Willie?"

"He went out for coffee."

"When he gets back, tell him I'm going into town for a couple of hours. He'll have to take the 10:30 lesson."

"Okay, Mr. Clem."

* * * *

Clem Gracier slouched in the rattan chair, staring moodily at the empty glass in his hand. For several hours now, he'd been mulling over Anderson's offer, and berating himself for accepting it. Andy had offered fifteen thousand, and ultimately gone to twenty-five. Clem suspected he could have held out for an even higher figure. On the other hand, if Andy had known how badly Clem needed money, the big ape could have stuck to the fifteen.

Gracier looked slowly around the living room with an expression of distaste. His eyes dwelt for a moment on the pile of movie and fashion magazines scattered carelessly on the table beside the rattan sofa. His gaze swung to the Japanese doll in its perspex case on the mantelpiece. Momentarily, at the thought that Angelique would be returning from the night club in about an hour, his spirits lifted. Then they plunged back into a mood of black depression. If it hadn't been for Angelique, he'd never have considered Anderson's proposal.

Easing himself out of the chair, Gracier traversed the short distance to the bar in the corner. As he fixed himself another *fine a l'eau,* he glumly regarded his reflection in in the wall mirror.

Staring back at him was a countenance of planes and angles, with deep lines running down from the nose to the jaw line. The close-cropped black hair grew low on the forehead, lending the face a simian aspect. It was a rugged face of indeterminate age. Clem had heard it described as an interesting face, full of character. In his estimation, it was just plain damn ugly. He was proud of his body, though. The strong neck, broad shoulders, swelling biceps, firm pectorals, slim waist, and flat belly, were the physique of a man twenty years younger than his 48 years. But what the hell; he *was* 48, and Angelique, the 20 year-old half-

French, half-Chinese, night club singer who was living with him as his mistress, must look upon him as an old man. To the girl, he represented security and gratification of her expensive tastes. He wasn't kidding himself that it was love that held her.

He thought of her closet in the bedroom, crammed with smart modish dresses and shoes she hadn't even worn, and of the teakwood chest on her dresser filled with expensive jewelry. His mind dwelt on their vacation in Bali two months ago, and the trip to Hong Kong he'd promised her for Christmas. A sigh escaped him.

He knew that one day he'd lose her. She was a ravishingly beautiful little creature who attracted adulation like a magnet. She could not sing worth a damn, but that wasn't why the club continued to employ her. Customers flocked to see, not hear, her. Clem was insanely jealous, which was the reason he stayed away from the club. One evening, some wealthy client would arouse her cupidity, or some young stud attract her. In either case, she'd come back to the apartment just long enough to collect her wardrobe and baubles. Clem knew with sure instinct it would happen that way. He couldn't see how he could prevent it, but was by no means resigned to it. He wanted her desperately, and wasn't going to give her up — not yet. Indulging her whims was the only way he knew to hold her. He kept from her the fact that he was verging on bankruptcy.

He shouldn't be broke. When he'd resigned from Air France, he'd had substantial savings. The pension they paid was no hell, but he hadn't been relying on it anyway. Even though he had to give up his French pilot's license on resignation, he'd kept his British license valid since the days when it had been granted when he'd joined the Free French Air Force in 1940. He'd come to Singapore and had started the flying club. It had taken every franc of his savings and all he could borrow to purchase the two Cessnas, the twin-engine Beechcraft, and the Beechcraft Bonanza, but it had been a sound investment. The business had been slow at first, but after the first six months they had been breaking even. If he'd been content to live within his income, by now he'd be showing a modest profit.

He hadn't considered anything like Angelique in his calculations. He'd met her during his first month in Singapore. The attraction was instant, and fatal. Gracier was no stranger to attractive women. He had witnessed many of his friends make fools of themselves over a pretty face and an appealing body. He'd considered himself immune. He wasn't. He was perfectly aware of the fact that he couldn't afford her, and equally aware that he wanted her badly. Caution flew out the window. He moved from a modest apartment to a larger establishment. Angelique was persuaded to move in.

Now, with the Hongkong and Shanghai Banking Corporation breathing down his neck, a damaged undercarriage of the Bonanza, and the twin-engine Beechcraft in need of a major overhaul, his affairs were more than just tight, they were desperate. Anderson's twenty-five grand had proved a convincing argument.

But it didn't make it any easier to accept. He'd been a flyer all his adult life; 28 years — 29 next month, he'd devoted to flying. It was all he knew. And now, because he was short of money, and unwilling to give up a girl who didn't even love him, he'd committed himself to an action which was contrary to all his principles. It was not only repugnant, it was against his better judgement. He was about to take part in a skyjacking operation. It didn't matter that he considered the objective praiseworthy. What mattered was that to a career flyer the action was anathema.

And he felt passing guilt on another score. He'd stalled with Andy. He'd stated that it would take two weeks to put his affairs in order. Hell, he could turn over the business to Willie Bates in a day. The truth was that he wanted to postpone his leave-taking from Angelique.

* * * *

On October 14th, Court walked into Jack West's office and announced that he was terminating his association with Amerthai Investment Associates.

West's immediate reaction was one of shock. When Palmer had returned from his two month vacation, West had spent several uneasy weeks, fully expecting to be advised that Palmer had conferred with associates in New York and was about to set up a competing investment service. Then, when more than a month had gone by with no indication that Palmer intended anything other than settling back into his established routine, West had breathed easier. Now, his worst fears were being realized, and he was ill-prepared. He felt as though he'd been jabbed in the ass with a red-hot needle. He did his best to conceal his inner turmoil.

Noting the conflicting emotions displayed by West's features, Court hastened to assure him that the reasons for termination had nothing to do with the employment. It was, Court stated, simply that he was planning another venture in a totally unrelated field. That much was certainly the truth. He added, that as soon as he could dispose of his furniture and set his affairs in order, it was his intention to locate in Hong Kong. Before leaving, he said, he proposed to turn his accounts over to DeSantis. He did not add that within two or three weeks DeSantis would be taking an extended vacation.

Almost as an afterthought, Court stated that he had studied the prospectus prepared by West and his associates. It appeared to present a soundly balanced blueprint for corporate expansion. Accordingly, Court had instructed his bankers to invest $50,000.00 in the newly-formed holding company.

When Court left the office, West was positively beaming.

* * * *

Court addressed himself to the planning. To facilitate his task, he broke the problem down to seven broad questions. True, all of the questions were interrelated. Answers to some would provide at least partial answers to others. Some answers would in themselves pose yet other questions. But it was a starting position. His questions were: 'What airline to hijack?' 'How to conceal the identity of the hijackers before, during, and following the operation?' 'When, where, and how to effect the hijacking?' 'How to provide reasonable assurance that the aircraft would be permitted to land in Hanoi?' 'How to persuade the North Vietnamese to part with prisoners of war?' 'How to provide logistic support for the hijacked airliner on the ground and for its onward flight?' 'And what precautions to take to minimize later repercussions?'

The answer to the first question, what airline to hijack, proved to be the simplest. The conditions to be met were that it must be an airline that stopped at Bangkok; that it was a flag line of a country which enjoyed, if not diplomatic, at least friendly relations and possibly commercial interests in common with North Viet-Nam, that its routing took it close to North Viet-Nam, and that it was a flag line of sufficient importance to merit world-wide attention. Air France met those conditions, with the added advantage that Gracier was familiar with Air France procedures. Later, in consideration of other factors, Court would narrow it down to a particular flight, Air France 194, the weekly Saturday flight which stopped at Phnom Penh enroute to Hong Kong.

The question concerning concealment of their identity was more complex. The obvious answer was some form of disguise. He considered a number of possibilities before settling on the pullover section to cover shoes and trousers, the loose surgical gowns, and the hoods. There was a good deal of difference in their individual heights. In order to present uniformity of appearance, they would all have to seem the same. In a sense, it was unfortunate that Andy was so tall. Court hit on the idea of a wire cage-like contraption to fit under the hoods. In some cases, such as De-Santis at five foot ten, the wire framework would also raise the shoulder level. As yet, Court hadn't met Gracier so didn't know whether the same would apply in his case. They would all be of the same height, an awesome six foot four inches. The phsychological impact was a feature which did not escape Court. He decided that the costumes must be a frightening jet-black.

He worked out the manner by which the costumes would be carried on board the aircraft, how and when they would be donned, and their ultimate disposal. This introduced the necessity of blindfolding the cabin crew and passengers. Court designed the masking hoods, and the method by which they would be secured. It wasn't until later, when he ran a test of the hoods, that he had to modify his original concept concerning their usage.

The three-part question of when, where, and how to conduct the hijack was somewhat complicated. The 'when' depended not only upon when all the planning details had been worked out and Court was confident they'd been sufficiently rehearsed to ensure a successful operation, but also upon questions related to the ultimate persuasion of the North Vietnamese concerning the release of the POWs. For this purpose, Court considered he would require a hostage, or hostages, of sufficient importance to heavily weight his demands. Such a person, or persons, would have to be passengers manifested on the flight finally selected. It was one of those imponderables which couldn't be resolved in advance.

'Where' to conduct the hijack was much easier. Court obtained a current IAL Aerad Flight Guide of the appropriate ASI/8 Section from an Air America pilot friend. He used the pretext that he was researching an intended book, and at the same time talked his Air America friend out of a Let-Down Plate for Hanoi's Gia Lam airport. Studying the IAL guide, Court determined that the optimum position for takeover would be immediately after passing the reporting position designated as Papa Echo 8. The details of their flight levels and actions following takeover, he would work out with Gracier. The considerations at this stage would be to avoid, if possible, detection and interception by the Chinese on Hainan Island, the Americans in South Viet-Nam, and the U.S. 7th Fleet in the Gulf of Tonkin.

This brought him to how the hijack was to be effected. He worked it out in rough, and would polish the step-by-step procedures later with Gracier. The first requirement would be to create a diversion which would allow one of their number to don his disguise in the after section, and permit another member of the team to do the same up forward and gain access to the flight deck.

Up to this point in his calculations, the questions were

reasonably amenable to solutions. Now, a good many imponderables entered the picture. Court reasoned that since every known factor and probability would have to be painstakingly examined, the further planning should be, for the most part, open to discussion within the team. He would reserve the right of final judgement, and pray to God that his decisions were correct. In the final analysis, the responsibility for success or failure would be his, and his alone.

* * * *

Court rented a beach house at Bang Saen, where he was joined by Tony DeSantis at the end of October.

On November 3rd, Court met the MSA flight from Singapore. Andy introduced him to Clem Gracier. Court had formed a preconceived image of Gracier. The man didn't fit the picture. From the background Andy had recounted, Gracier had to be somewhere in his late 40's. The craggy face could belong to a man anywhere between 30 and 60, but the black hair was unflecked by gray and the lithe muscular physique was that of a young man. Somehow, Court had expected a taller man and was surprised that Gracier was very little taller than Tony DeSantis.

Stopping in Bangkok only long enough to purchase a supply of groceries and liquor, Court drove directly to Bang Saen. During the 105 kilometer drive, Andy dominated the conversation recounting his amatory adventures in Singapore, where he'd encountered an English girl, conveniently also staying at the Goodwood Park, and fortuitously afflicted with nymphomania. Andy had been happy to sneak up to Penang for a few days of well-deserved rest. On his return to Singapore the previous evening, the eager young lady had nailed him the moment he entered the hotel lobby. He had, he stated, scarcely a moments sleep prior to catching the plane. Court thought the happily-beaming Anderson looked remarkably fit despite the harrowing encounter.

Court found Gracier coolly detached, almost withdrawn. Nevertheless, he was impressed and found himself warming to the Frenchman.

Bang Saen, Court explained, was a beach resort, but not as popular or well frequented as Pattaya. The house he'd rented was large, with extensive grounds, insuring privacy. As a precautionary measure, he'd dismissed the servants. In order not to attract undue attention and the local speculation which might arise from four men staying in a servantless house, Court had arranged for DeSantis and Anderson to stay at the Nipa Lodge in Pattaya. They would commute the 42 kilometers daily, or as necessary, using DeSantis' Toyota. Gracier, since his knowledge was more vital to the detailed planning, would stay at Bang Saen with Court. Court apologized for the inconvenience.

"Good thinking. Very considerate," Andy said, with a chuckle.

"By the way, Andy, won't they be missing you in Danang?" Court questioned.

"Nope. Sent 'em a cable saying I'd decided to extend my vacation to a couple of months. Hell, they've got engineers they haven't even used yet."

* * * *

They were gathered in the sitting room of the beach house.

Court placed his bourbon and water beside a file folder on the coffee table, and leaned slightly forward.

"Before I outline what preparation has been undertaken already, and what lies ahead of us, I want to make one thing abundantly clear. None of us have embarked on this project lightly. But whatever our motives, it is nonetheless a criminal act which we are contemplating. I shall take every possible precaution to protect us, but no plan is perfect. You should all be fully aware of the consequences of our venture. Should we fail in our mission in Hanoi, we can expect at best imprisonment, at worst, execution. Should we succeed, we may be applauded by public sentiment, but still face legal prosecution. It is a perilous adventure, with the odds stacked heavily against us. I want each of you to think carefully and if you have second thoughts about participating, now is the time to withdraw. I would not condemn any of you for exercising that option. But I warn you, the choice must be now. Beyond this point, there is no turning back."

Court eased back in his chair. He gave them a minute to digest his remarks, then addressed each of them in turn.

"Andy?"

"I'm in," Anderson stated flatly.

"Tony?"

DeSantis hesitated a brief moment, then nodded his assent.

Gracier had been watching Court intently. From Anderson's earlier outline, Gracier had formed the impression that he was committing himself to a company of naive idiots. He had almost decided that, tempting though the money was, he would pull out. Palmer, he now concluded, may be young and an idealist, but he was no fool. The issue had been fairly presented. He felt growing respect for this young American. Gracier made his decision.

"Gracier?" Court queried, shifting slightly to face the Frenchman.

Gracier contented himself with an eloquent shrug.

The tension which had been palpable in the room, evaporated.

Court smiled. Leaning forward, he flipped open the file folder.

"Okay," he said. "I have only one more thing to add. As we go along with this, I want each of you to be as critical as you wish. I also want any suggestions which may occur to you. But it must be clearly understood that the final decisions will be mine."

For the first time since he'd embarked on the flight in Singapore, Gracier smiled.

*   *   *   *

CHAPTER ELEVEN

Dan Lyons, staffer for Consolidated International Press, slurped up the watery dregs of his iced tea. He signed his check, and left Mizu's Kitchen to plod across the street to the CIP office. The office was located on the second floor, and as Lyons mounted the poorly-lit stairs he was perspiring freely and puffing from the exertion. As usual, he thought sourly, he'd lunched not wisely, but too well. He vowed to curb his appetite, and give up smoking — maybe tomorrow.

As he entered the dingy outer office, with its bank of three clattering teletype monitors, he noted from the wall clock that the time was 2:10. He'd taken longer over his lunch than he'd intended.

In the equally grubby inner office, Lyons skirted a table piled untidily with papers, passed the teleprinter, and plopped himself into the chair behind his typewriter table. He belched loudly.

His assistant, Samporn, poked his head around the inner office door. "Mr. Lyons, a boy delivered this for you. "It's marked 'Urgent'."

Mildly curious, Dan took the letter — actually two letters taped together. It bore no stamp and was addressed simply to 'Mr. Dan Lyons, CIP Office, Second Floor, 87/3 Patpong Road.' Dan ripped open the envelopes and extracted two sheets of paper. He scanned the typed messages, then his eyes widened and he read them again more carefully.

"Samporn," Dan yelled.

"Sir," answered Samporn, appearing in the doorway.

"What time was this delivered?"

"Just before you came back from lunch. Two o'clock."

"Who delivered it?"

"I don't know. Just a boy."

"Okay, okay." Dan had already turned to his desk and was

flipping through a desk directory of important telephone numbers. Finding the one he wanted, he pulled the phone closer and dailed.

"Air France, *ka,*" came the soft·voice of the operator.

"Mr. Gerard, please," Dan requested.

"Who's calling, please?"

"Lyons. Dan Lyons. CIP."

"Just a moment."

Dan drummed his fingers on the desk impatiently.

"Gerard speaking."

"Jacques, Dan Lyons. Look, I just received notification that your flight to Hong Kong was hijacked at about 1310, Bangkok time, from a position of 16 North, 111 East over the South China Sea. It's supposed to be heading for Hanoi. That true?"

There was a moment of hesitation before Gerard answered. "We don't know the exact time and place of the hijack, but you're substantially correct. The flight failed to report its position over North Reef. Search procedures from Saigon and Hong Kong were initiated shortly after 1330. A few minutes before 1400, the aircraft was reported flying at low altitude on a northwesterly course over the Gulf of Tonkin. Sighting was made by U.S. aircraft carrier, the 'Enterprise' A few minutes ago, I received word that the flight's captain had communicated with North Viet-Nam on international emergency frequency. He stated his aircraft had been taken over by hijackers and requested permission to land in Hanoi."

"Any mention of a medical emergency on board the aircraft?"

Gerard sounded surprised. "Yes. Yes there was. The captain reported a cardiac case and requested that an ambulance and doctor be standing by."

"Have the North Vietnamese granted permission to land?"

"Not to my knowledge."

"That flight stops in Phnom Penh, doesn't it?"

"Yes. It was running about 15 minutes late leaving Bangkok, and was still a few minutes late at Phnom Penh. Otherwise, nothing out of the ordinary."

"The other wire services contact you?"

"Not yet, but I imagine they will."

"Yeah," Dan agreed drily, "imagine they will. Since I'm first in line, can you give me priority on anything new that breaks?"

Gerard gave a short humorless laugh. "All right, Dan, I'll do my best."

"If I send my boy over, can you give him a passenger list?"

"Yes, but I don't think it will be of much help."

"Thanks Jacques. I'll let you know if anything else breaks at my end."

When he hung up, Dan shouted for Samporn to send a boy over to Air France to pick up the passenger list.

Seated before the teleprinter, Dan switched on and started to transmit to New York, London, and the Asian Wire.

101A

HIJACK 12/6 BT

BULLETIN

BANGKOK (CIP) — AIR FRANCE REPORTS ITS BANGKOK TO HONG KONG FLIGHT WAS HIJACKED TODAY FROM A POSITION OVER THE SOUTH CHINA SEA. VISUAL SIGHTING OF AIRLINER AT LOW ALTITUDE ON NORTHERLY COURSE REPORTED BY U.S. 7TH FLEET CARRIER "ENTERPRISE" ON STATION IN GULF OF TONKIN.

(MORE) DL1417ANL

Humming to himself, Dan dialed the Indian Embassy. He was connected with the First Secretary.

"Understand your ambassador was on today's Air France flight to Hong Kong," Dan stated.

"Yes, that is correct."

"His Excellency was accompanied by his wife?"

"Most certainly."

"Can you disclose the nature of His Excellency's mission?"

"Oh no. That is most confidential. Very high level diplomatic discussions. His Excellency will most certainly issue a press release from Hong Kong."

Balls, thought Dan. Probably nothing but a shopping expedition. Into the mouthpiece, he said, "Thanks. Perhaps you haven't heard, but that flight was hijacked over the South China Sea and is heading for Hanoi."

"My God. Goodness gracious."

"Can you add anything concerning His Excellency?"

"Good heavens. No. Oh Dear, this is most distressing . . . most distressing."

"Yes," Dan said, cutting short the conversation.

He had no sooner cradled the telephone, when it rang. "Lyons, CIP."

"Dan, Jacques Gerard. Captain Christian LePlattre of the hijacked flight communicated with Gia Lam on the tower frequency. He was granted authority to land. The plane was escorted over the Red River Delta by MIG fighters and landed at 1416."

"Thanks, Jacques. Anything else?"

"No, that's all we know. I'll try and keep you informed."

"Thanks again."

Dan returned to the teleprinter:

102A
   HIJACK 12/6 BT
URGENT
1ST ADD HIJACK BANGKOK 101A XXX TONKIN.
   CHRISTIAN LEPLATTRE, CAPTAIN OF THE AIR-
LINER, COMMUNICATED WITH HANOI REPORTING
HIJACK AND MEDICAL EMERGENCY. NORTH VIET-
NAMESE GRANTED PERMISSION TO LAND AT HA-
NOI'S GIA LAM AIRPORT. AIR FRANCE CONFIRMS
AIRLINER WAS ESCORTED OVER RED RIVER DELTA
BY MIG INTERCEPTORS AND LANDED SAFELY AT
1416 LOCAL TIME.
   AMONG FLIGHT PASSENGERS IS H.E. KRISHNA
RATHNASWAMI, INDIAN AMBASSADOR TO THAILAND,
WHO WAS ON AN UNDISCLOSED DIPLOMATIC MIS-
SION TO HONG KONG.
   (MORE) DL1424ANL

Dan grinned happily. Bangkok was something of a backwater, newswise. It had been over a year since he'd put out a five-bell bulletin. And, thanks to his unknown benefactor, it looked like he had a CIP beat. On the Asian Wire, it was also copied to New York and London. By now it was on the domestic trunks. Within minutes, the other wire services, AP, AFP, Reuters, and UPI, would be asked to match the CIP story. Any minute now, Dan expected call back from the Asian desk in Hong Kong, and from New York and London. He wished the boy would hurry up with that damned passenger list.

Dan lit a cigarette, and stared at the large area map which covered an entire wall of his office. His eye located the position of 16 North latitude, and 111 East longitude, and traced an imaginary course northwest to Hanoi.

He glanced at his desk, where the typed messages lay.

There was a signature typed beneath each text. It was 'Quixote'. Dan couldn't see any connection between the texts and the whimsical pseudonym. Whoever Quixote might be, it was someone intimately connected with the air piracy; a person who could pinpoint time and place of the hijacking, knew of the presence of at least one important passenger, and was endowed with the miraculous faculty of being able to predict a heart attack in advance.

Dan suspected that the inclusion of the medical emergency information was to establish the credentials of Mr. Quixote beyond question. He had no idea why CIP, and himself, had been singled out to break the news of this event to the world, but he was damned happy to be so honored. He had a strong hunch he would hear more from Mr. Quixote.

Dan kissed the tips of his fingers, and raised them towards the 'ceiling. "Señor Don Quixote," he said feelingly, "whoever you are, and wherever you are, I love you."

*   *   *   *

"Hey," said the passenger in the window seat, "look at that."

Court craned his neck. On the gray sea beneath them, about a mile off to port, was steaming an aircraft carrier flanked by destroyer escorts. It would be the 'Enterprise' on Yankee Station. From this low altitude, the carrier looked mighty big.

"Sleep peacefully tonight, your fleet is guarding the sealanes," Court murmured.

"What?" queried the window seat occupant.

Court grinned. "Nothing. Talking to myself."

They had anticipated encountering units of the 7th Fleet.

It had been one reason for selecting the wave-skimming altitude. The other reason was to avoid coastal radar detection from Danang and Hainan Island. They wouldn't have appeared on the fleet radar scans with sufficient advance warning to fly off interceptors. It wasn't that they feared that interception might deter them, or that absolute secrecy was essential. It was, however, desirable that the North Vietnamese be given as little advance indication as possible in order that when the hijacked airliner reached the 50 mile coastal buffer zone and started inland, the Communist authorities would be forced to make rapid decisions. Court and Gracier had reasoned that the more limited the reaction time, the better the chances that they would be permitted to land in Hanoi. It was this thinking which had determined their low level approach over the Gulf of Tonkin.

The hum of the jet engines took on a deeper note. The seat belt sign flashed on. Court looked at his watch. It read 2:06. They would be starting their climb back up through the overcast to an altitude of 12,000 feet. They were entering the buffer zone. Up forward, Gracier would be instructing the radio operator to announce their presence to the North Vietnamese, and the world, over the emergency frequency.

If they had desired to approach the delta undetected, the reverse was now the case. From this point on, they wanted the entire world to be watching their progress anxiously. The North Vietnamese must be made aware of this fact. They would not long be left in doubt that the attention of the world was focused on the drama being enacted at Gia Lam airport.

By now, back in Bangkok, Dan Lyons would have received the first of the letters. In a few minutes, the story of the hijack should be breaking world-wide.

Court smiled faintly, imagining Lyons' reaction. Andy had wanted all the wire services in Bangkok advised simultaneously. Court had not agreed. His argument had been that most of the Bangkok-based news services operated on a fixed-time radiocast and teletype communications with their Asian desks in Hong Kong, Manila, or Tokyo. CIP had teleprinter facilities which would get the newscast directly on the wire with no loss of time. Then, it would only be a matter of minutes before all the other services were under pressure to get onto, and stay on top of, the CIP story. It was a convincing argument. What Court had not added was that he knew Dan Lyons slightly, considered Lyons a first-rate newsman, and was sympathetic to the fact that CIP was the poor cousin of the wire services. Being Number Five, CIP should try harder. And having a beat on the story wouldn't exactly hurt Lyons.

The method of relaying the messages to CIP was simple. Court had sent the two sealed messages in an outer envelope to a Bangkok Direct Mail Service. By telephone, he had instructed that the envelope marked 'Urgent' was to be delivered first. The enveloped marked 'Confidential' was to be hand-delivered four hours later. The exact times and date for the delivery would be communicated later. If the American manager of the direct mail company had been curious concerning the originator of the messages, 1,000 baht in cash in the outer envelope, and a promise of another 1,000 upon delivery, had been sufficient inducement for him to accept the commitment without inquiry or further credentials. Before the flight's departure, John Begg had telephoned to instruct that the first envelope be delivered at 2:00 p.m. today, and the second at 6:00 p.m.. If, by any chance, the deliverers were detained, the letters could only be back-traced to the direct mail service — and no further.

If they didn't land the hijacked jetliner in Hanoi, the second letter would be meaningless. Lyons would know what they had intended, but it would have little value as news.

Court had debated the inclusion of advice concerning the medical emergency in the message to CIP. Lyons would immediately recognize that such advance knowledge of a heart attack was impossible. But when this was broadcast for the benefit of the unsuspecting Hanoi officials, Lyons couldn't help but grasp the significance. It would authenticate the message as coming from the planners of the hijack. He would be inclined to give credence to the second message from the same source.

The signing of the messages as 'Quixote' had been inspired by Court's conversation with Marcie. The name might mystify Lyons on the first message. It would have a clearer application in the second.

The seat belt sign winked out. They were above the cloud cover and leveled out at 12,000 feet. In a few minutes, Court would know if they'd correctly gauged the North Vietnamese reaction. He watched the clouds beneath the airliner, scanning the billowing blanket anxiously. There they were. Breaking free of the obscuring mists, two jet fighters rose swiftly towards the airliner.

The moment was crucial. The next few seconds would establish whether or not they had a chance of success. Up in the flight deck, Gracier would be the first to know. Court's palms were sweating. With an effort, he controlled his quickened breathing.

* * * *

Gracier watched the aircraft carrier and its screening destroyers emerge through the haze which clung to the surface of the sea. Rapidly, they closed the distance until the fleet units were on the port hand then sliding astern to be once more enveloped in the haze. Gracier checked his watch. One minute to go.

"Alright, Captain. Take her up to 12,000 feet," Gracier ordered quietly.

Turning to the radio operator, Gracier commanded curtly, "Switch on and tune to emergency frequency."

Shifting the Luger to his left hand, Gracier reached into the right hand pocket of his gown. He brought out two folded pieces of paper and a black plastic object slightly larger than a cigarette package. He placed the object on the navigation table and examined the papers. They were marked with numerals. Tapping LePlattre on the shoulder, Gracier handed him the paper marked with the number 1.

"Captain," said Gracier, "you will broadcast this message over the emergency frequency . . . now."

LePlattre turned over control of the climbing aircraft to the second officer, took the paper from Gracier's gloved hand, unfolded the single sheet, and read its typed message. He frowned. Turning his head to look up at the hooded figure, LePlattre questioned, "What heart attack?"

"None," snapped Gracier. "Please broadcast the message exactly as it's written."

LePlattre shrugged.

Listening to the voice procedure as Le Plattre called Hanoi and identified himself, then, Hanoi's acknowledgement and LePlattre's delivery of the message, Gracier's thoughts dwelt on the probable reaction in Hanoi.

If Hanoi was monitoring communications of the 7th

Fleet, which was undoubtedly the case, they would have had by now a few minutes advance warning of the approaching flight. This would cause speculation, and consternation. By now, MIG interceptors should have been alerted. Now, the airport commander was receiving the blunt message advising that Air France Flight 194 had been taken over by hijackers and ordered to proceed to Hanoi. In addition, the message was reporting an emergency cardiac case and requesting that a doctor and ambulance be made available on landing. In effect, LePlattre wasn't *asking* for permission to land at Gia Lam; he was merely stating a series of conditions which gave him no other option.

In a few minutes, the same message would be relayed over the Hanoi airport tower frequency, with one important addition.

"Tune to 118.1," Gracier ordered the radio operator.

He picked up the plastic object and stepped up close behind LePlattre.

"Do you know what this is?" Gracier asked the captain.

LePlattre looked closely at the object in Gracier's hand. "Looks like a transistor radio," he observed.

"It's a transistorized low-frequency transmitter," Gracier said flatly. "Beneath one of the seats in economy class is a brief case containing five kilos of plastic explosive. If I depress this button, a detonating time-mechanism will be activated. It is set for a four minute delay. On the ground, that would allow time to evacuate the aircraft. In the air..." He left the sentence unfinished. Leaving a significant pause, Gracier continued. "In the luggage compartment there is a suitcase loaded with twenty kilos of explosive. The delay mechanism with that is set for sixty seconds. It can be triggered by a similar transmitter in the possession of one of my associates in the after cabin.

I want to impress upon you that we are determined men, Captain. Should we fail in our objective..." Once again, Gracier allowed the sentence to remain open to interpretation.

The effect of this information on LePlattre was evidenced by perspiration beading his forehead.

"Captain," Gracier said evenly, "you will now repeat the message you just sent on the emergency band. This time, you will transmit on the Gia Lam tower frequency. In your own words, you can add the information I've just given you."

As LePlattre complied, his voice betrayed the agitation and anxiety Gracier had intended.

There it was. In this hand of the desperate game, they'd just played their last card. It was now up to their Vietnamese opponent to raise, call, or fold.

In the planning, Gracier had cautioned Court concerning the North Vietnamese. The regime in the Democratic Peoples Republic of Viet-Nam was rigidly totalitarian. There could be little freedom of decision at any level beneath the controlling oligarchy. Decisions, even from the top strata of the ruling clique, were unpredictable since they were often colored by chauvinistic xenophobia rather than cold reason. In his years of experience of flying the International Control Commission aircraft into Hanoi, Gracier had encountered obstacles which appeared to have been dictated by purest malice rather than any practical considerations. It was highly unlikely, except under extreme circumstances, that the airport commander would have the authority to grant the hijacked aircraft permission to land. And, when relaying such a request to higher authority, it did not follow that logic would prevail. What they must do, was create a situation where the airport commander was given as little time and option as possible. Their planning had been to arrive at such a condition.

Mentally, Gracier ticked off the planning sequence. The hijacked jetliner was an Air France plane, representing a flag line owned and controlled by the French government. Under the guise of a 'Cultural Mission', the French government maintained quasi-official diplomatic relations with North Viet-Nam. There existed a reciprocal exchange of news media representatives between the two countries. A limited bilateral trade was still being conducted. And, for a little over a year, peace talks had been in progress in Paris. While the North Vietnamese may not harbor much love for the French, there was every reason for them to treat this hijacked aircraft with consideration.

That the presence of the approaching pirated airliner had been announced first over the international emergency frequency, and had been sighted and reported by the U.S. 7th Fleet, meant that the circumstances were common knowledge. The entire world would be watching developments. While the North Vietnamese might not be swayed particularly by world opinion, they couldn't totally disregard it.

The presence on board the hijacked aircraft of a high-ranking diplomat had also been announced. The fact that it was in this case the Indian Ambassador to Thailand was a matter for added concern for the North Vietnamese, since the Indians were the chairmen of the International Control Commission's observing teams. While the North Vietnamese had done everything to circumvent the provisions of the 1954 Geneva Accord, as a signatory to that agreement they were careful to present a facade of compliance with its terms. Any disaster that befell an Indian diplomat within their domain would be a distinct embarrassment to North Viet-Nam's government.

The medical emergency, and the fact that the aircraft was a flying powder keg, had been introduced to lend urgency. The North Vietnamese were not notably humanitarian, but they couldn't ignore these factors. Without doubt, the airport commander and his superiors might wish fervently that the jetliner would disintegrate in mid-air, but they couldn't afford to be held accountable for such a catastrophe.

Gracier was confident that the approach over the Gulf of Tonkin had given little advance warning. They were presenting the airport commander with a bewildering array of excellent reasons why the aircraft should be permitted to land, and little time for him to confer with higher authority. There was certainly no time for any lengthy debate.

There was one last factor which they had not overlooked. This was of a different character from the other reasons they had considered in the planning, but probably no less compelling. It was the simple human factor of curiosity. To this point, the North Vietnamese would have no idea why a hijacked aircraft was being directed to Hanoi. It had not called at Saigon, which ruled out unwelcome American deserters. The likely probability was a party of defectors. The North Vietnamese didn't normally welcome defectors of any stripe or breed. But this flight *had* stopped in Phnom Penh. And this was an area of considerable North Vietnamese interest.

By all odds, Gracier thought, the deck was stacked in their favor. But was it?

He watched the two MIG fighters approaching, and admitted to himself a decided apprehension.

The loudspeaker crackled with the voice of the Gia Lam tower operator:

"Air France 194, this is Hanoi. Air Force fighters

have been dispatched to escort you over the delta. You have been cleared to land at Gia Lam airport. Please come onto a heading of 342 degrees and commence your descent to 2,500 feet..."

There was more, but Gracier scarcely heard it. Wordlessly, he handed the second piece of paper to LePlattre. It was a photostatic copy of the Gia Lam Let-Down Plate.

For the first time, Gracier realized he was bathed in the dampness of cold sweat.

* * * *

Gracier opened the flight deck door. With a motion of the Luger, he signaled for the flight engineer to approach. Paquet hesitated a moment, then rose to his feet and stepped around the purser.

"We'll be landing in a few minutes," Gracier stated. You'd better take over your duties."

Paquet entered the flight deck. Before following the engineer, Gracier raised his left hand in a mock salute to Andy, who had stationed himself beside the forward galley.

Andy answered the salute, turned, and strode back to the curtains which divided first and economy class. He parted the curtains slightly and slipped through to stand for a moment in economy class. DeSantis, at the rear of the compartment, straightened and acknowledged with a gesture. Satisfied that both Court and John Begg had seen him, as had every other passenger in the section, Andy slipped back to resume his guard position in first class.

Court coughed to mask a profound sigh of relief. Andy's brief appearance indicated that they were being allowed to land at Gia Lam without delay or interference.

Round one goes to the gentleman from La Mancha, thought Court. Now, all we have to worry about is the big one, Phase II of the master plan.

* * * *

CHAPTER TWELVE

Court waited until Tony DeSantis came from the kitchen to complete the group.

"We're as prepared as we'll ever be," Court said seriously. "But let's not kid ourselves. We think we're letter-perfect in our parts and believe we've planned for every possible eventuality, but once we set the actual production in motion, Fate takes over as the director. We could run into some totally unexpected twist in the scenario. If that happens, we'll have to improvise and ad lib, and hope for the best."

"An actor's life is not an easy one," Andy murmured. Begg shifted uneasily in his chair.

Frowning slightly, Court continued. "We've gone over this point many times, but I'd like to stress it once more. At only one period, during the actual takeover, are four of us in costume at the same time. After that, no more than three of us, and generally only two, are involved at any given moment. The rest of us will be masquerading as innocent passengers. If anything comes unglued, that's exactly what we'll be — mystified passengers. Those who happen to be in costume will have to fend for themselves. We all agreed on that, and it's the way it has to be. No matter how strongly any of us might feel, senseless heroics are out."

There was a moment of silence. Each man was absorbed in his own thoughts. Andy stared steadily at Court, opened his mouth to add some comment, then closed it without speaking.

"Right," Court said briskly, "here's the action. Clem, you and Andy return to Bangkok tomorrow morning with Tony. John and I will stay here another couple of days to clean up. Tony, you take the sewing machine with you. Unless you now feel fully qualified as a dressmaker, you can give it to your girl friend for Christmas."

Turning his attention to Gracier, Court said, "Clem, you're booked for Phnom Penh on Air Vietnam the day after tomorrow. If we make it on the 6th, does that give you enough time to fix up the brief case and get props?"

"Yes. More than enough," Gracier answered.

Andy, you're booked Saturday. There isn't much point in your hanging around Phnom Penh unless you want to. You can leave it until Tuesday if you have anything better to do in Bangkok. As soon as you get to Phnom Penh, check with Air France and confirm your booking on 194 to Hong Kong. If you don't get a cable by 9:00 a.m. at the latest on Saturday the 6th, cancel and rebook on the 13th. If there's still no cable by the same time on the 13th, rebook again for the 20th. We have no guarantee we'll luck out with a VIP on any of those flights. That's as long as we can give it. If you don't get a cable by the 20th. we'll be on that flight, hostage notwithstanding. You and Clem can check with each other by phone, but otherwise you don't know each other. Clear?"

"As crystal," Andy replied, with a broad grin.

*　*　*　*

That about winds it up, Court thought as he dropped some scraps of cloth and several sheets of typing paper onto the smoldering fire. With his foot, he scraped more dead leaves onto the smoking ashes, and watched as the tendrils of smoke turned to licking flames. The late afternoon air was still. The smoke rose lazily up through the fronds of a tall palm tree at the foot of the garden.

Court turned and strode back towards the house.

The screen door banged behind him as he entered the sitting room. Begg was on his knees, scrubbing chalk marks from the teakwood floor. He started at the sound of Court's entrance.

"Nervous, John?" Court questioned.

"Uh . . . No," Begg answered, resuming his task.

"Almost finished?"

"Think so. I'll have to let it dry to make sure."

"Take your time. We won't leave for another couple of hours. Want a drink?"

"No thanks."

Court went into the kitchen. There was little evidence of their month of occupancy. The dishes had been washed and put away. There was no food left in the cupboard. They'd cleaned out the refrigerator after lunch. All that remained was an array of almost empty liquor bottles on the sinkboard shelf. Court drained what little that was left in the last bourbon bottle into a glass. He poured the assorted dregs from the other bottles down the sink drain, and stacked the empties underneath the sink. From the refrigerator ice-tray, he pried loose some cubes which he added to the inch of amber liquid in his glass. Leaving the refrigerator door ajar, he unplugged the machine. No one can accuse us of not being neat and thoughtful tenants he thought, as he walked from the room, the ice clinking in his glass.

They had converted the downstairs bedroom into a work-shop. Court examined it carefully. Every shred of evidence had been removed. In an empty beer carton on the table, he'd stored the items to be disposed of on the drive back to Bangkok. In the box were the table vise, pliers, screw-drivers, seaman's dirk, tin shears, electric soldering iron, odds and ends of wire, and the metal thimbles and eyelets they hadn't needed. The last item, which he now added to the box, was the portable typewriter. He had already burned its fabric case in the garden fire.

Court was satisfied that he'd exercised every precaution. If there was any way by which their preparations could be traced back, individually or collectively, he couldn't visualize how.

When he'd decided which airline was to be honored with the venture, Court had made a quick trip to Hong Kong via Air France. As luck would have it, the flight he'd taken had been the Saturday flight by way of Phnom Penh. The purpose of his trip had been to orient himself to the interior layout, determine the passenger capacity, acquaint himself with the number and functions of the aircrew, and to establish the in-flight routine. He had also taken advantage of the trip to make a number of necessary purchases. It had been in Hong Kong that he'd bought a gross of small padlocks, four Seiko watches, the portable typewriter, a stock of typing paper, ten yards of heavy cotton material, and, from a yachting supply store, some light strand wire, a gross of small thimbles, a large quantity of eyelets, and a seaman's dirk.

The remainder of the purchases had been made in Bangkok. DeSantis had bought the Singer sewing machine. The combination lab-coat-surgical gowns had been made up at two different tailoring shops which specialized in hospital garments. The required tools had been obtained from various hardware stores. The small quantity of cotton gauze needed for the face of the hoods had been purchased at a millinery shop.

None of the purchases should have excited any curiosity.

It had been in the matter of weapons that Court had experienced the only real problem. Gracier had brought the Luger with him. It was unregistered. If any super-sleuth could track it backwards in time, Gracier had stated bluntly, he would arrived at a very dead Gestapo major in a Paris suburb, in the year 1945. That left three other weapons to be acquired. Through discreet inquiry, Court had learned of a source in Thon Buri where firearms could be obtained clandestinely. He had paid too much for the old but serviceable revolvers. The Gurkha *kukri* had been acquired later from a dusty little store off New Road.

Court picked up the loaded beer carton, and walked out through the sitting room. As he did so, he noted that Begg had completed his task and was sitting in a chair. Court examined the floor. All trace of the chalk marks had been successfully removed. In rehearsing the movements and timing of the takeover and subsequent action, they'd marked out scaled replicas of the aircraft compartments. There wasn't much likelihood that anyone could interpret the chalk lines correctly, but the landlord would have been annoyed to find his teak floor treated in such a manner.

Court put the box in the back seat of the Holden. As he did so, his thoughts dwelt briefly on John Begg.

The necessity for a fifth member of the team had not arisen until a little over a week ago. One aspect of the planning had troubled Court. It had given rise to considerable discussion. The matter had concerned the methods they would employ to impress upon the North Vietnamese the fact that the hijackers were in deadly earnest. The threat of strategically-placed explosives had already been settled upon, but in Court's estimation this might not prove sufficiently compelling. What was needed, he had argued, was some dramatic act which would convince the Vietnamese beyond any shadow of doubt that the hijackers were desperately intent on achieving their goal. The Vietnamese might not believe that the hijackers were capable of blowing up the aircraft and themselves along with it. To be convinced that such an act was a very real possibility, the Vietnamese would have to be presented with some demonstration of unmistakable impact.

Gracier's chilling suggestion that about the only thing he could think of which would impress the North Vietnamese would be to butcher one of the passengers, every hour on the hour, had not been taken seriously. Finally, Court had hit on a bizarre solution. Even Gracier had grudgingly admitted that, properly staged, it should proved effective. The only trouble with Court's plan was that it introduced a requirement for some props which were not easily obtained — and a fifth member to the group.

Putting Court's suggestion into effect would mean the removal of one of their number as an effective member of the group. They had no idea how long they would be negotiating the release of the POWs. If they succeeded at all, it could take hours, but was more likely to take days. None of them could be expected to stand guard duty over such an extended period without rest. It would be essential that they be able to spell one another on duty. Removing one of their number at any given point, with no guarantee that the negotiations would not still be protracted, was unthinkable. Therefore, Court had no option but to locate an additional man.

It had been no easy task. Court had thought again of Jan DeVeers, but the Dutchman had been in Singapore on business. Then, John Begg had occurred to Court.

Begg was an Australian journalist who had at one time enjoyed an enviable reputation as a newsman. His career in Southeast Asia had gradually gone into eclipse owing to a fondness for liquor, and a steadily increasing inability to fulfill assignments and meet deadlines. Now, at the age of 52, Begg was employed in the editorial department of the Bangkok Times. In his off-duty hours, and when his meager salary permitted, Begg frequented several of the Patpong

Street bars. Begg was tolerated rather than liked. His credit was over-extended. As a consequence, he was afflicted with chronic financial anemia.

Under the circumstances, Court had not found it too difficult to persuade Begg to resign from the newspaper and cast his lot with the hijackers.

Begg hadn't managed to integrate too well with the group. It would have been surprising if he had. In the first place, all of the original foursome were vouched for by an association with at least one other of the group. Over the weeks of planning and rehearsal, they had developed a mutual trust and confidence in each other. Begg was odd man out in this closely-knit organization. And to further complicate his acceptance was the fact that he would not share an equal burden in the enterprise. There was an element of doubt concerning his reliability under stress. Coming late on the scene, as he had, he would take no part in the already established pattern covering Phase I of the operation. As a back-up man, he would only be slotted in on guard duty in an emergency. And the specific task he had been recruited to perform might not prove necessary. He would enjoy a position of relative immunity from the risks inherent in the assigned roles of the others. While Court decried it, he appreciated that a degree of antipathy towards Begg was inevitable. Though the resentment was unspoken, Court was sure that Begg sensed it.

On the positive side, were certain factors in Begg's favor. Fully appreciating that the substantial sum offered by Court represented what could well be his last chance to remove himself from the environment of his humiliation and make a belated start in some other area, Begg was determined to do nothing which could jeopardize this God-given opportunity. He hadn't accepted a single drink during his period of association with the group. He was not unintelligent, and had quickly grasped the essentials of the undertaking. In rehearsal for his particular role, he had displayed a surprising degree of talent. And, in other respects, he was ideally suited. In appearance and manner, he was nondescript and diffident. He would be unlikely to attract attention. Following his performance, it should not be too difficult to reinstate him unnoticed amongst the passengers.

Court closed the car door. He turned to face the house. "John," he called.

"Coming."

"Take a look around and make sure everything's locked and all lights turned off."

"Okay."

Court looked at the front of the house pensively. He would not soon forget it. It had served them well. Upstairs, Tony had mastered the intricacies of the Singer and fabricated the hoods and garments. In the improvised workshop, Gracier had devised and constructed the smoke generating cannister and the explosive timing device. They had all taken a hand at wire splicing, and each had engineered and fitted the false bottoms in their hand-luggage. In the seclusion of the back garden, they had dried the hoods and garments after their immersion in black dye. On the coffee table in the sitting room, he had typed out the various messages and the demands they would present to the authorities in Hanoi. To ensure that his fingerprints weren't in evidence on any sheet, he'd worn cotton gloves. He smiled as he recalled the awkwardness of the chore, and his steady cursing.

Begg came through the front door, closing it behind himself. Court had the key. He stepped forward, locked the door, rattled it to assure himself it was properly secured, then stooped down and slid the key beneath the fiber mat.

"I'll call the landlord in the morning to let him know we've vacated," Court said, as he rose. "He shouldn't have any complaints. Paid him two months in advance."

He turned towards the Holden. "Come on John. We have a couple of stops to make along the way to dump this junk in the irrigation canal. It'll be well past the dinner hour before we hit Bangkok."

*   *   *   *

Gracier closed the attache case, pulled the leather flap across the top, and snapped it shut. He pressed firmly at a point where the flap crossed the top of the case. A muffled ticking issued from the case. Satisfied, Gracier unsnapped the flap and opened the case. He stopped the hands of the cheap alarm clock, and lifted the pressure-activated lever clear of the clock.

Dr. Racine was seated in a nearby lounge chair. He had been watching Gracier with interest. The neatly folded pile of black cloth and the heavily insulated metal box Gracier had removed from the attache case and placed on the table before commencing to tinker with the clock intrigued Racine.

"What's it all for?" he asked Gracier.

"A practical joke. A monstrous practical joke."

"What's in the box?"

"At the moment, nothing. I want you to give me a hand."

"Certainly," said Racine. "Anything I can do to help."

"No, Bernard," Gracier said, smiling at his old friend, "you don't understand. I mean a real hand. A human hand, with about eight centimeters of wrist and forearm attached."

Racine was startled. "But Clem . . . I can't go around mutilating corpses. I can't just . . ."

Gracier cut him short. "For two thousand dollars . . .

in cash," he said softly.

Racine's face froze in astonishment. "You're serious?"

"Dead serious."

Racine thought for a few moments. Gradually, his face brightened. "Clem, for two thousand dollars I can get you a complete cadaver."

"No thanks," Gracier observed drily. "Just the hand. That's what the box is for. I'll also need a couple of pints of blood, and some dry ice."

"When do you need all this?"

"By Saturday morning. Earlier, if we can keep it fresh."

"Oh sure. We can keep it in the freezing compartment of the refrigerator, as long as I instruct the cook not to touch it. It would scare hell out of her — and good cooks are hard to find, even in Cambodge. It shouldn't be too much trouble for me to get the hand and blood from Hopital Preah Ket Mealea . . . for a price."

"No, Bernard. It has to be a Caucasian appendage. I'm afraid a Khmer hand would be a little too dark for my purpose."

Racine frowned. "That makes it a bit more difficult. Have to get it from the Centre Calumette. Still . . . for two thousand dollars . . ." Dr. Racine shrugged expressively. "Don't suppose you'd care to tell me just who is to be the recipient of this joke?"

"No. But I can assure you, they deserve it."

"*Merde alors,* you have a macabre sense of humor."

"Don't I."

As Gracier placed the metal box ,in the bottom of the attache case and started to repack the garments, he thought wryly on the peculiarities of the human animal. It was true that every man had his price. He'd accepted a part in this crazy adventure at a figure he was sure Andy would have bettered. Now Bernard. He had brought enough cash with him to go to more than double the amount Bernard had accepted. He had been fully prepared to bargain. Bernard hadn't put a very high price on his ethical scruples. Well, he thought, Angelique will be the beneficiary. I'll buy her a diamond ring in Hong Kong — if we ever get there.

* * * *

Anderson checked into the Monorom Hotel Tuesday afternoon.

It had been some years since his last visit to Phnom Penh, but he found it little changed.

Wednesday morning, he strolled over to the Air France office and confirmed his booking for Saturday, the 6th of December. Then he walked at a leisurely pace along Vithei Monivong past the Faculty of Medicine and the Catholic cathedral. He turned right at the broad park-divided boulevard of Vithei Daun Penh, and into the driveway before the baroque facade of Le Royal Hotel. At the rear of the hotel, Andy relaxed at a shaded table by the small swimming pool. He ordered a Pernod, and idly watched two young bikini-clad French girls giggling and splashing each other in the shallow end of the pool.

Andy chaffed at inactivity. It occurred to him that if the flight was postponed all the way to the 20th, he'd die of boredom. It was all right for Clem, who at least had a number of close friends in this sleepy community, and was staying with a doctor buddy in a comfortable villa on Vithei Phsar Dek. But Andy couldn't even visit the sonuvabitch.

The selection of Phnom Penh as a transit point had been based on sound considerations. First, Court hadn't wanted them all boarding the flight at Bangkok. Then there was the little matter of an amputated hand. It could have been obtained from one of the hospitals in Bangkok, but Court had considered the risks unacceptable. Gracier had friends in the medical fraternity in both Saigon and Phnom Penh. He had assured them that he could purchase not only the hand, but silence. In Saigon, however, the customs were in the habit of checking outgoing hand luggage thoroughly — in the hopes of surprising illegal currency smuggling. Since Andy was carrying only a load of masking hoods in his flight bag, that shouldn't have aroused anything other than mild curiosity. But Gracier would be another case entirely. In his attache case, Gracier would have the two costumes for himself and Andy, a *kukri,* and the severed hand. Also, at least on his arrival, Gracier would be carrying a substantial amount of U.S. currency. No, Saigon was definitely out. In Phnom Penh, the customs check consisted of a nod and a smile — much better suited to their purpose. And a final consideration had been the fact that Phnom Penh would be the last stop before Hanoi. Court had reasoned, and Gracier had agreed, that the North Vietnamese would initially attribute the hijacking to defection. They should be more favorably disposed to defections from Cambodia than South Viet-Nam.

Andy concurred with the general consensus that Phnom Penh was ideally situated for their purpose. Unfortunately, he had to agree that he was a logical candidate for temporary residence. Court was masterminding the caper from Bangkok. Tony had a finger on the airline manifests and advance bookings. Gracier, with his local connections, would be here anyway. And Begg was at best a cipher. If he'd been sent here, Begg might have succumbed to temptation and be too juiced to make the appointed flight.

Well, Andy thought resignedly, it was a good opportunity for him to get reacquainted with this drowsy little backwater

with its broad uncrowded tree-lined boulevards, its som-
nambulistic pedi-cab drivers, its sidewalk cafes, and its
architecture and atmosphere reminiscent of its late French
colonial status. He could probably talk his way into a
temporary membership in the Cercle Sportif just up the
street, and use its swimming pool and facilities. He could
visit the wat and chedi on Penh's hill — from which the city
derived its name. There would be ample time to wander
through the National Museum near Sihanouk's palace, and
browse through the Street of the Silversmiths close by the
Museum. Lunch, he could partake of at the sidewalk cafe
of La Taverne in the Place de la Poste. Dinners, he could
have here at Cyrene, or any number of equally excellent
restaurants offering French cuisine. And he would definitely
try to locate some of the intimate little bars, with their
soft-eyed accommodating hostesses, he remembered from
his days with Vinell Corporation. Of course, he thought
ruefully, the girls will be about ten years older, but what
the hell, so am I. Then he brightened at the thought that
there must be a brand new crop of young lovelies. No, the
waiting needn't be *too* dull.

* * * *

Apart from a couple of hardly noticeable scratches, it's
as good as brand new, Tony thought, as he placed the sewing
machine in its original packing box. He'd wrap it in Christmas paper. If he returned in time, he'd give it to Sumalee on
Christmas Eve. If not, he'd leave instructions for his servant to deliver the box.

The month of planning and rehearsing the action had gone
quickly. Tony had been caught up in the excitement and
work, and had scarcely noticed the days and weeks slip by.

But now that phase was over. He had time to reflect, and his earlier misgivings crowded in on him.

Court was in the process of turning over his investor accounts to Tony, and they were all gilt-edged clients. And twenty grand was a sizeable chunk of bread. His prospects for the future looked bright. He could marry Sumalee right after Christmas; if he was going to be around for Christmas. And there was the hook, the great big fat hook. What good would twenty grand and excellent business prospects do him if he was rotting in some goddamned North Vietnamese prison?

He thought about the men with whom he'd be associated on the adventure. He couldn't quite understand what made big Andy tick. Tony knew that Andy wasn't in the action for money; had in fact put up some of the expenses out of his own pocket. The big man seemed to be amused by the entire project. Tony couldn't see any humor in the business of risking your life. He hadn't liked it in Viet-Nam, and since he'd come through that episode unscathed, he liked the idea even less now. There was such a thing as crowding your luck. Andy was more than double Tony's age, and maybe that was the answer. Tony, at 25, had a lifetime to look forward to. Andy had used up a fair slice of his allotted span. Maybe he just didn't care as much any more. Gracier, on the other hand, took the project very seriously indeed. Clem was cool, steady, and to Tony, just a little bit frightening. He was glad that Clem was on their side. And Gracier was in it for the money, which made Tony somehow happier. Then there was John Begg. Although it had never been discussed, Tony sensed that they were all uneasy concerning Begg. John was also very much a mercenary in the venture. He probably had a larger stake in its success than some of the others. Yet Tony couldn't bring himself to be sympathetic towards Begg's problems. He couldn't escape the feeling that Begg might prove their undoing.

Had it not been for Court Palmer, Tony would never have accepted any part in the hazardous adventure. To Tony, Court represented an unobtainable ideal. He was envious of Court's education, wealth, social position, and family heritage. It was a jealousy tempered by a healthy respect. These were qualities and attainments which Antonio DeSantis felt had been unjustly denied him, and which he held in deepest reverence. In Tony's preconceived concept of the order of society, Court occupied a special niche. He was the very embodiment of Tony's American dream.

Tony would not have defined his feelings in such terms. He would not have admitted to hero worship, yet essentially it was just that. In Tony's estimation, but two types of men had been placed upon this earth; those born to lead, and those to follow. Into this former aristocratic category, Tony felt Court fitted naturally. In their relationship, there was something of a feudal lord — faithful retainer aspect, although Tony would have denied it hotly had it been pointed out to him. Tony knew, however, that had Court pressed the issue, he, Antonio DeSantis, would have joined the venture, with or without the twenty grand inducement.

Born in Naples on the 18th of August, 1944, Antonio Cesare Mario Borgazzi was a by-product of war. His mother, Carlotta Borgazzi, had been neither prostitute nor street-walker. She had been a simple sales clerk in a millinery shop. A young romantic girl, darkly pretty, and imbued with a zest for life and adventure. Carlotta contended that Antonio's father had been a German soldier named Franz, or Hans, or Helmut. In the recounting of the romantic interlude, Carlotta often became confused. In later years, Antonio examined himself minutely for some trace of Nordic heritage. He concluded that his father must have been a very short slight dark Aryan, or that his mother was mistaken.

Carlotta met Sergeant Vernon DeSantis, U.S. Army, in late 1945. It is a tribute to Carlotta's charms, lack of intolerance, and talent for survival, that despite a policy of non-fraternization she was able to sustain and nurture this romance. They were married in June, 1946. Little Antonio was legally adopted.

The DeSantis family, Vern, Carlotta, Tony, and little Charlotte, arrived at New York's Pier 96 in September, 1947.

They lived first in Brooklyn, for a period of five years. Vern held down a series of low-paid jobs, working on the City payroll. At the outbreak of the Korean War, he re-enlisted in the army. It was the same year that baby Victoria became an addition to the family, and that young Tony started school.

Sergeant Vernon DeSantis sustained a superficial combat wound and rejoined his family early in 1952. He procured a job with the Postal Service. The family moved to Queens.

Tony's formal education came to an abrupt halt in 1961. He was at that time a loyal member of a neighborhood gang who devoted a good deal of enterprise and skill to pilferage from parked cars. They were apprehended one sultry night in July. Tony, as a somewhat inept lookout, and being only 16, was awarded a suspended sentence and placed on probation. He did not return to school that fall.

Tony got a job with the bus company. His function was largely confined to washing the vehicles. In time, he became mechanic's helper, and a pretty fair mechanic in his own right. He aspired to become a driver. A few years later, he was to attain this goal, but with another company and a slightly different vehicle.

In 1965, Tony joined the U.S. Marine Corps in preference

to being drafted into the Army. Surviving a harrowing period of basic training, Tony found himself assigned to a company of the 9th Motor Battalion of the IIIrd Marine Amphibious Force. The location of his company was on a bleak red-scarred hilltop just south of Danang, Viet-Nam.

Driving a groaning six-by through choking dust or seas of mud was not Tony's idea of an enjoyable occupation. He became even more disenchanted when land mines started to take a high toll, and when convoys through to Chu Lai and north to Phu Bai came under increasing ambush and attack. When his year's tour of duty came to an end, he breathed a sigh of relief. He bade a fond farewell to his scarred vehicle and his erstwhile companions-in-arms, and vowed never again to set foot in Southeast Asia.

Tony didn't know quite how it happened. Back in Queens, he found little appeal in returning to the bus company. During his time in the Marine Corps, he had attained High School Graduation certification. He felt life had more to offer than some menial job. He answered an advertisement in the New York Times offering a promising career and travel in auto-motive sales. By February of 1967, he was back in South-east Asia. This time, in Thailand, selling American and foreign make cars at discount prices to the GIs on the military bases.

Tony prospered. The bulk of his sales were on an install-ment basis for Stateside delivery. There were a few exceptions. He sold a Datsun for cash and immediate Thai-land delivery to a Thud pilot at Takhli, Lieutenant Courtney J. Palmer. A little over a year later, Tony was to recall that sale as having been a happy coincidence.

Sumalee came into Tony's life in the spring of 1968. It was a fateful meeting. From that point, Tony's outlook underwent a slow metamorphosis. It started with vague emotional stirrings, and culminated with a firm resolve to formalize the relationship in marriage. Miraculously, to Tony's way of thinking, Sumalee returned his deep affection.

Hand-in-hand with Tony's emotional maturation went an equally disconcerting transformation. For the first time in his life, he started to think in terms of career and future security. True, he was doing reasonably well selling cars to American servicemen, but the market was subject to caprices and could well evaporate overnight. If it was now his intention to settle permanently in Thailand, he must locate a more secure avenue of endeavor. He had little education, no professional, and few technical skills. Salesmanship appeared to be his most promising field. He set about exploring the possibilities.

Mutual funds, securities, and real estate, Tony reasoned were commodities which were likely to endure. It was this thinking which brought him to Amerthai Investment Associates in October, 1968.

Initially, Tony did not do too well in his new milieu. Selling intangible benefits was by no means as easy as promoting the sale of something as tangible and appealing as a new automobile. He didn't do too badly with mutual funds, but his results with real estate and securities were discouraging. It was at this low point, when Tony was beset by grave doubts concerning his abilities, that Fate intervened.

Tony remembered having sold a Datsun to Court Palmer, but didn't know whether or not Court would recall it. Tony was in awe of Palmer, in spite of the fact that Court was very little older, and, like himself, a mere trainee salesman. With the money and background Palmer had, Tony couldn't see why Court was engaged in the business at all. In any event, Tony was not brash enough to inflict himself on Palmer on the basis of a previous brief encounter. Tony was both surprised and flattered by an overture that came from Palmer.

Court remembered Tony well. At the time, he had been impressed with the expeditious way in which DeSantis had handled the customs processing and delivery of the Datsun. When DeSantis joined the Amerthai sales force, Court had been interested enough to keep an eye on Tony's progress. He knew nothing of Tony's background, and was rather surprised that DeSantis' sales were so slow in developing. By February, he came to the conclusion that while DeSantis had grasped the fundamentals of mutual funds, he was out of his depth in the realm of real estate and securities. It was evident that DeSantis was putting forth a good deal of effort, and equally obvious that he was dejected. While Court had made it a rule to remain somewhat aloof from his co-workers, he decided that DeSantis needed assistance.

Slowly, Court initiated DeSantis into the mysteries of such things as puts, calls, warrants, debentures, yields, and the entire range of the stock and bond market. He encouraged DeSantis to study the subject and recommended a number of excellent texts in the field. He was pleased with Tony's response and willingness to learn. And, Court would not have been human had he failed to be flattered by the deference, and thinly-disguised adulation, accorded him by DeSantis.

Under Court's tutelage, Tony made rapid progress. His sales started to embrace a wider range, and his commissions showed a corresponding increase. The entire investment field became a fascinating world for Tony. His depression melted away to be replaced by eager enthusiasm. What was even more to the point was the fact that he could see attainment of his cherished goal in sight.

By May, Court had sufficient confidence in Tony to disclose his Knickerbocker Trust Bank source of confidential market information, and to make this available to DeSantis. Then, when Court decided on a holiday, it was to DeSantis that he turned over his clients.

Mindful of the trust displayed in him, Tony scrupulously serviced Court's accounts through July and August. On his return to Bangkok, Court was pleased. It struck him that with the attention Tony had given the accounts, DeSantis' own clients must have suffered. He did discover that Tony had not added a single new account to his own list of clients during the two month period. Having decided to devote more of his time to Hong Kong and his intended venture into film units, Court commenced to divest himself of his lesser clients. Slowly, he was turning these over to DeSantis.

Then came October, and Court's startling project. It was only natural that he should consider Tony as a prospective and trusted participant. It was equally natural that Tony, against all his instincts, would feel obliged to accept.

* * * *

Thursday afternoon, a messenger hand-delivered an envelope to Tony. It was from Sumalee, and contained a number of airline manifests and advance booking advice slips. Sumalee was employed by an advertising agency. Through her many girl friends, she had been acquiring this information on a daily basis from a number of the major airlines.

Tony's pretext had been that information concerning important arrivals, and the departures of existing and potential local clients would assist him in the investment business. He had hated to abuse Sumalee's confidence in this manner, but there was no way he could disclose his real purpose. The information had been accumulating since early November. Tony's only interest was in the advance booking departures for Air France 194.

Tony discarded the manifests and booking information for JAL, BOAC, PAA, TWA, Thai International, and Air India, retaining only the information pertaining to Air France. Most of this was of no value. The manifests of flights 183 and 186 joined the discarded material. Tony was left with a slip noting advance outbound bookings. A Mr. and Mrs. M. Cosgrove, a Mr. A. Rutengee, and a Mr. and Mrs. K. Rathnaswami were listed for Saturday's flight 194. Penciled opposite these names was the advice that Mr. Cosgrove was a director of Crescent Advertising, Mr. Rutengee was a Secretary at the Indian Embassy, and Mr. K. Rathnaswami was the Indian Ambassador to Thailand. Tony jumped as though he'd been goosed.

He telephoned Court immediately.

"Court, this is Tony."

"Hi. Anything interesting in your daily news bulletins?"

"How does the Indian Ambassador to Thailand grab you?"

There was a moment's silence, then a low whistle. "He's on the December 6th flight?" Court questioned incredulously.

"Sure is, along with his wife and some embassy secretary."

"Jesus, what luck. What incredible luck. I'll get off a cable to Clem and Andy tonight."

"He could cancel," Tony said.

"Yes, he could. We'll have to take the chance he won't. An ambassador doesn't travel without making advance arrangements and setting up a pretty tight schedule at his destination. It isn't that easy to change his plans."

"Yeah. Suppose you're right," Tony agreed reluctantly.

"Tony, you'd better tell Sumalee you won't be requiring any more airline information. I'm sure that will make her happy since her girl friends could get canned for passing out that info. Means they won't admit they've been doing it. Tell Sumalee that you weren't getting the information you'd hoped for and it just isn't worth the risk she and her friends have been taking. I think she'll be glad to get off the hook."

"She sure will be. Didn't go for the idea from the beginning."

"One more thing, Tony. Make sure you destroy all the airline info you now have."

"I sure as hell will."

*   *   *   *

That evening, Court put some typing paper, several plain envelopes, and a pair of gloves in his brief case. He dropped by the home of a friend attached to the Danish Embassy. During the course of the evening, he invented an excuse to use the typewriter in the Dane's study.

Court typed two short notes. The first, signed 'Quixote', advised Lyons that the Indian Ambassador to Thailand would be a passenger on the flight referred to in the attached covering letter. This note he sealed in an envelope which he marked 'Urgent'. The second message was to the manager of the direct mail service instructing him to tape this second letter to the one marked 'Urgent' already in his possession. This message, together with 500 baht and the sealed envelope, Court placed in an outer envelope addressed to the mail service manager.

On his way home by taxi, Court stopped by the direct mail service office and slipped the envelope under the door.

The next morning, Court confirmed by telephone that the

envelope had been received and the instructions understood and complied with in full.

*   *   *   *

CHAPTER THIRTEEN

The cloud layer was more dense over the delta than it had been over the gulf. The jetliner was heading 024 degrees on the final leg of its approach, and below 1,000 feet, before it broke clear of the shrouding blanket. Not that it was clear. A thin rain was falling. Through the misty gray veil, Gracier could make out the southern suburbs of the city and the gaunt black framework of a familiar landmark, the Doumer bridge spanning the Red River. Ahead lay the muddy river, and, on the far side, the concrete runway of Gia Lam.

LePlattre touched down at 1416. He had slowed the aircraft and was heading for the taxi strip as directed by the tower, when Gracier commanded, "Stop her, Captain."

"But we're in the middle of the runway," LePlattre protested.

"I'm aware of that," Gracier said drily. He had taken a folded piece of paper from the left hand pocket of his gown. Handing it to LePlattre, he said curtly, "Read this message to the tower, then shut down on the transmitter."

As the aircraft shuddered to a stop, Gracier eyed the terminal building and rain-slicked parking apron several hundred meters distant. Of the aircraft parked on the apron, Gracier recognized the tail markings of Aeroflot, Czechoslovakian Airways, Chinese and North Vietnamese planes, and a number of military aircraft. There were also some markings he could not recall ever having seen before. Pulled up in front of the building were several vehicles, including an ambulance. On the wide concrete expanse before the building were a number of raincoated figures wearing the faded khaki uniforms and star-insigniaed sun-helmets of the Peoples Army. Their automatic weapons were held at the ready. Other figures in coats and dark suits scurried back and forth between the terminal building and the parked vehicles. Quite a reception committee, thought Gracier.

The tower was calling impatiently directing Air France 194 to proceed to the taxi strip. Gracier listened to LePlattre replying with the carefully-worded message.

They had worked, and reworked the phrasing of this vital message. Gracier listened to LePlattre's delivery intently. Should the captain depart from the prepared script, Gracier would intervene and take over the mike.

It was evident that LePlattre grasped the significance of the typed words. He read slowly, articulating clearly. LePlattre was advising that the cardiac patient had responded favorably to on-board treatment and that the requested medical services were no longer required. Next, he advised that the jetliner would remain parked in its present position on the main runway until the airport officials had complied with certain requests. First, the hijackers would relay their request only to representatives of the International Control Commission, who were to be summoned with as little delay as possible. Second, all passengers and aircrew would remain on board the aircraft awaiting further developments. Third, no one bearing arms was to be permitted to approach the aircraft within a 200 meter radius. Fourth, auxiliary power supply, catering service, and refueling facilities were to be provided immediately. Fifth, essential traffic would be allowed only through the aircraft's forward access door, and a landing ladder was requested. Sixth, the hijackers wish to emphasize that anything construed by them as a hostile act will result in the destruction of the aircraft and the passenger and crew hostages on board.

The message was acknowledged. LePlattre advised that he was closing down transmissions on the tower frequency, but would continue to receive on that frequency. When this was acknowledged, LePlattre nodded to the radio operator. Removing his earphone, LePlattre massaged the back of his cramped neck. With a disgusted sigh, he started to unbuckle his seat belt.

Gracier was satisfied that the message had been relayed exactly as intended. Now, all they could do was wait.

To LePlattre, Gracier said, "Captain, we may have quite a wait before we receive the ICC representatives. I suggest that you and your flight deck personnel would be more comfortable in the crew lounge. Please accompany me. We will leave the flight deck door open in case of important messages."

LePlattre nodded wearily. He stretched, and rose slowly from his bucket seat.

"It is a pity," Gracier remarked mildly, "that for yourself and crew, and those of the passengers who have not visited Hanoi before, that we arrive during this dismal season of the *crachin* rains."

LePlattre made no reply, but shot Gracier a venomous glance.

* * * *

During the next hour, a number of things happened. Auxiliary power was supplied. A landing platform and steps marked "Aeroflot" was wheeled into position at the forward access door. A fuel truck and ground crew appeared on the scene. A catering truck drove up and Vietnamese rushed up and down the boarding ladder delivering prepared food. They were silent, and seemed most anxious to spend as little time as possible on the airliner.

At 3:30, a North Vietnamese Army major, conspicuously devoid of weapons, appeared at the top of the boarding steps.

The NVA officer may have displayed great courage in the face of the enemy, but was visibly shaken when met just inside the entranceway by an awesomely tall hooded figure holding a Luger pointed steadily at the officer's chest. In faltering, but excellent French, the officer reported that the International Commission's team had been dispatched from Hanoi and should arrive at Gia Lam within about 20 minutes.

"Bien," Gracier acknowledged tersely. The officer retreated hastily down the steps towards his waiting vehicle.

The flight engineer conferred briefly with a Vietnamese standing just outside the entrance. Coming into the plane, the engineer was frowning. "He wants to know how much fuel we require," the engineer said to LePlattre.

LePlattre shrugged, turning to Gracier. "Well?" he questioned.

"You may calculate your requirement on the basis of a capacity passenger load . . . and a completely empty baggage compartment."

"He also wants to know how we propose to pay for the fuel," said the engineer.

"Unless you carry petty cash for such emergencies, I would suggest he send the bill to the French mission in Hanoi," Gracier said drily.

LePlattre looked faintly amused. "Tell him to invoice the mission, Paquet."

*   *   *   *

Within the first class compartment, the passengers were becoming restive. They had been on the ground almost an hour and a half. They had noticed supplies being taken aboard at the forward galley, the flight crew seated in the crew lounge, and some comings and goings at the forward access door. They were mystified, and speculated with their neighboring passengers concerning the intentions of the hijackers.

In a penetrating voice, the Indian Ambassador complained volubly to all within his hearing. It was intolerable, he stated, that he, an ambassador, should be subjected to such indignities. He assured his listeners that when the local authorities were apprised of his presence on the aircraft, some action would be forthcoming. His country, he stated smugly, would not stand idly by when one of their diplomatic representatives was being humiliated. These ruffians who had pirated the aircraft, and Air France, would learn to their cost that an ambassador, in the performance of his duties — or otherwise — was not to be trifled with. No indeed. And what was the captain of this aircraft doing about the situation, he wanted to know.

Andy had been standing quietly by the compartment dividing curtains. He was sympathetic with the mood of the passengers. They were understandably edgy. So was he. The Indian's shrill tirade wasn't helping matters. Andy drew the *kukri* from its scabbard and stepped noislessly forward.

The ambassador became aware of the black figure looming above him. He turned his head, and became aware of something even more frightening. The overhead lighting was reflected off the bulbous blade of a Gurkha knife, scant inches from his thoat. The ambassador swallowed convulsively. He paled in mortal fear, his petulant bravado of a moment earlier effectively silenced.

Andy spoke slowly, and loudly enough so that his gauze-baffled voice would carry to all the passengers in the compartment.

"Mr. Ambassador, we regret the delay. We are waiting now to relay our demands to the North Vietnamese authorities, through the good offices of the International Control Comission. We may have quite a wait before our demands are met. I suggest that you and your wife relax and try and make the best of the situation."

The menacing figure above him had spoken politely. Some of the ambassador's irascibility returned. "I demand," he blustered, "that you inform the local authorities of my presence on board this aircraft."

Andy did not alter the civility of his delivery, but the words were all the more chilling by the lack of emotion in his voice. "Mr. Ambassador, I can assure you that the North Vietnamese already know of your presence. They were advised by radio message on our approach from seaward almost two hours ago. At that time, they were also advised that this aircraft is carrying a number of high explosive charges which will be detonated should we encounter hostility, or our conditions are not met."

"What conditions?" questioned the ambassador, in a barely audible voice.

There was no necessity for secrecy. Within an hour or two, not only the North Vietnamese, but the entire world would be aware of the demands.

Andy advanced the blade until the point was just touching the ambassador's neck. The Indian jerked back in terror. "Our conditions, Mr. Ambassador, are that this airliner and its hostages, meaning yourself, all the other passengers, and the aircrew, will be spared upon the unconditional release of sufficient American prisoners of war to fill all the unoccupied seats on this flight. If those conditions are *not* met, Mr. Ambassador . . ." Andy didn't finish the sentence. Instead, he flicked the razor-sharp blade to inflict a slight nick on the diplomat's neck.

Although his vision of the drama had been obscured by

the seat backs, and the partially-drawn screening curtain, Christian LePlattre had followed the entire conversation. Secretly, he was glad that the pompous windbag of an ambassador had been deflated. At the mention of the prisoners of war, LePlattre's eyebrows lifted. This was his first intimation of a motive for the hijacking. It might not make the act of air piracy less reprehensible, but it put things in a somewhat different light. His gaze moved from the black-draped Anderson to the similarly-clad Gracier, standing by the forward lavatory door. LePlattre eyed the Luger-armed hijacker pensively. These men were embarked on a desperate gamble. So far, they had demonstrated a marked degree of competence. If he hadn't been involved personally; if his aircraft, crew, and passengers weren't stakes in this deadly game, LePlattre could have applauded the performance.

*　　*　　*　　*

A convoy, consisting of a gray-green military vehicle and three vintage white-painted sedans sporting fender-mounted identifying flags, rounded the end of the terminal building and approached the jetliner. The line of cars drew up alongside the boarding ladder. A lieutenant colonel and a captain of the Peoples Army, together with a young-looking Vietnamese civilian got out of the military lead vehicle. The sedans disgorged a Sikh colonel, a Canadian major, and a Polish naval commander accompanied by a civilian. The group coalesced at the foot of the steps, held a hasty conference, then mounted the ladder, the Sikh colonel leading.

Gracier had watched the approach of the International Commission team. It was for him a familiar spectacle. Turning to LePlattre, Gracier requested, "Captain, would you and your crew please move into the first class cabin temporarily. We require this area for a brief conference with the ICC representatives."

The three members of the ICC, together with the Polish interpreter and NVA liaison staff, crowded into the crew lounge area. Gracier was joined by Anderson. It was Anderson who did the talking.

From his pocket, Anderson extracted four unsealed envelopes. He handed one to each of the three ICC members, and the fourth to the Vietnamese lieutenant colonel. The NVA officer promptly handed the envelope to the Vietnamese civilian. Similarly, the Polish commander handed his to the Polish interpreter. There followed a few minutes of silence while the contents of the envelopes were read and digested. The Polish member and his interpreter engaged in a rapid low-voiced exchange. The three Vietnamese discussed the letter amongst themselves. Anderson waited patiently, a few paces removed.

The Polish commander was speaking; the interpreter bobbing his head in assent. *"Tak, tak,"* the interpreter agreed. Turning to the Sikh, the interpreter said, "Mr. Chairman, the Commander protests that this is in violation of the procedures established under Article 21 of the Geneva agreement."

The Sikh colonel spoke with a clipped British accent. "I'm perfectly aware of the provisions of the agreement. I fail to see how this attracts any condition specified in Article 21. We will, however, discuss this following control. I take note of the Commander's protest."

Tucking a swagger stick under his right arm, the Indian colonel turned to face the hooded form of Anderson. "What do you expect of us in this matter?" the Sikh questioned.

"Merely that you convey the contents of the letter to

the North Vietnamese authorities as expeditiously as possible, and advise your respective Commissioners of the demands," Anderson replied.

"In other words," interjected the Canadian major, "act as messenger boys."

"Unless you can suggest any other function you could perform," Anderson said evenly.

The Canadian's lips twitched in a faint smile. "Offhand, I can't think of any."

The Sikh colonel frowned disapprovingly. Addressing Anderson, he said, "I understand, Sir, that my Ambassador to Thailand is one of your hostages."

"Yes. Would you like a few words with His Excellency?"

"If you would be so kind," replied the colonel stiffly.

Anderson conducted the colonel into the first class compartment, and pointed out the diplomat. Retreating back to the waiting ICC team, Andy was too far removed to hear other than snatches of the exchange between the ambassador and the Sikh. Although speaking animatedly, the ambassador was employing uncharacteristically subdued tones. Andy made out such words and phrases as: "at all costs", "absolutely essential", and "exert pressure at the highest level." The Sikh, listening intently, wore an expression of distinct discomfort. Beneath his hood, Andy smiled. His object lesson to the ambassador was producing unexpected dividends.

When the colonel rejoined the group, the team prepared to take its departure. At this point, Gracier stepped closer.

"One moment," Anderson said flatly. "I'm afraid we must ask the Polish Commander, and one of you Vietnamese officers, to remain on board as our temporary guests."

Not bothering to refer his remarks to the interpreter, the Pole spoke out angrily. "I strongly protest any such breach of team security. Mr. Chairman, Colonel Tranh, this is unthinkable."

"I'm afraid we must insist," Anderson said. His hand went significantly to the hilt of the *kukri*. Gracier shifted the Luger to bring it to bear unwaveringly on the Vietnamese lieutenant colonel. The Sikh colonel's eyes were fixed on the Gurkha weapon. His eyes, beneath a frown-creased brow, betrayed his anxiety. He did not want to see that blade unsheathed.

"It would appear," the Sikh said in a troubled voice, "that we have little choice, Commander." To the senior NVA liaison officer, he said, "Colonel Tranh, what is your opinion?"

The expression on the Vietnamese's face had not altered perceptibly. He said evenly, "I agree, Colonel. My Captain will remain on board to ensure the security of our Polish colleague."

"And I suppose I'm supposed to guarantee *his* safety," the Pole snapped sarcastically.

"If you like," Colonel Tranh retorted blandly.

*   *   *   *

An afternoon like this makes up for weeks . . . no, months, of piddling news releases, Dan Lyons thought happily as he sipped on a stein of draft beer in the Patpong Cafe.

The minute he'd received the passenger manifest, he'd started checking all along the line. In economy class, F.V. Stolz turned out to be Baron Franz von Stolz, the West German industrialist. R. Blaire, was the noted English playwright, Roger Smythe-Blaire. Mike Cosgrove, local managing director of Crescent Advertising had been important enough to rate a mention; John Begg, on the editorial staff of the Bangkok Times, had not. But if economy class had yielded paydirt, first class was a veritable gold mine. Apart from the Indian Ambassador, already mentioned in his 1st Add, had been M. St-Denis, L. Montgomery, and C.J. Palmer. Marc St-Denis was the Asian Bureau Chief of Agence France-Presse, enroute from Paris to Tokyo. Lucille Montgomery was an English actress who had recently gained some critical acclaim. And C.J. Palmer was none other than Courtney Jerome Palmer III.

Lyons had filed a 2nd Add, and then when he'd definitely confirmed Palmer's identity, he'd given the story a new 'top' with a 1st Lead; AMERICAN MILLIONAIRE, COURTNEY J. PALMER III ON BOARD HIJACKED AIRLINER. It had rated a lead. It was a neat twist, two such prominent examples of capitalist aristocracy, von Stolz and Palmer, on board the same aircraft, and sitting in the middle of a bastion of communism such as Hanoi.

The presence of Marc St-Denis on the airliner meant that AFP would get terrific on-the-ground coverage of the story. Still, Dan doubted that St-Denis would be able to file from Hanoi without some difficulties with censorship and radiocast delays. CIP was still well out in front with the wire service coverage.

Dan was pondering the paradox of von Stolz traveling economy, while St-Denis was riding first class, when Samporn entered the bar. He approached Lyons in a state of obvious excitement.

"Another letter was just delivered," Samporn said breathlessly.

His hunch had been right. Dan checked his watch. It was 6:03 p.m. "Be back," Dan called to the bartender. Leaving his half-finished beer, Dan followed Samporn into the street. The rush hour traffic was still clogging Patpong Road. With Samporn running interference, Dan weaved his way through the jam of cars.

They had reached the upstairs office before Lyons caught up with Samporn.

"Who delivered this one?" Dan questioned.

"The same boy. Found out he works for a direct mail service."

"Did you check?"

"Yes. They don't know anything. They received the envelopes by mail several days ago. Instructions for delivery were by telephone this morning. They don't know who sent them."

"Okay," Dan said. "It figures. I'll check it out later, but it's probably a dead end."

The envelope was marked 'Confidential'. Lyons ripped it open and extracted the several typewritten sheets it contained. There was a short covering letter signed by a typed 'Quixote.' The opening paragraph caused Lyons to smile. It noted that the previously reported cardiac case had responded favorably to on-board treatment obviating the necessity for the medical assistance requested. It was included, Lyons recognized, purely to re-establish 'Quixote's' bona fides. The second paragraph stated simply that the letter attached was an exact copy of a letter transmitted that afternoon through the good offices of the International Control Commission.

Dan turned to the copy letter attached. As he read, his eyes widened. The letter was addressed to 'The President, The Democratic Republic of Viet-Nam, Presidential Palace, Hanoi.' There followed a politely correct salutation. The next paragraph was an apology that circumstances dictated that the aircraft must remain in its location on the runway causing unavoidable disruption of normal airport traffic. Next, it was stated that the passengers and aircrew would be detained on board as hostages, their ultimate safety wholly dependent on the meeting of the request which followed. The next paragraph demanded that 100 American prisoners of war per the attached list, or substitutions to bring the prisoners to the stated number, were to be unconditionally released and transported alongside the aircraft at the earliest convenience of the authorities. The letter closed with a submission that any approach to the aircraft by armed personnel, any interference with the aircraft or the transfer of prisoners, or any action deemed a hostile act, would result in dire consequences for which the originators of the letter would not hold themselves responsible. An acknowledgement was expected within two hours. Any protracted delay in delivery of the prisoners would be interpreted as non-compliance and construed accordingly as a hostile act. The letter was unsigned.

The list of prisoners of war mentioned in the letter was not attached to Lyons' copy. He concluded that this was no oversight. Premature publication of such a list would result in false hopes, agonies of suspense, and possible heartbreak for the families and friends of the prisoners. The stipulated number must be predicated on the load capacity of the aircraft. The numbers of known POWs in North Viet-Nam, to say nothing of those listed as Missing in Action, some of whom must be POWs, was certainly a higher total than the 100 requested. The list, therefore, had to be selective. Publication would bring nothing but despair to the sweethearts and next of kin of the prisoners excluded. It must have been an agonizing choice for the hijackers. Lyons was thankful that he did not have a copy of the list. The decision of whether or not to release it for publication would not rest on his shoulders.

As he dialed the Air France number, Lyons was struck by one ambiguity in the letter. What, he wondered, did the hijackers consider a 'protracted delay'?

Gerard was still in his office. His voice sounded tired. No, he stated, they had no knowledge of the hijackers' demands. The radio communications with the Gia Lam tower had ceased at approximately 1430 and Air France had received no word since that time. Lyons indicated that he was in receipt of what was purported to be the hijackers' demands. Extracting a promise from Gerard that this information would remain strictly confidential until confirmed, Lyons agreed to send a copy.

Placing a long distance call through the Bangkok U.S. Military Assistance Command switchboard, Lyons was connected with the downtown Saigon office of CIP. Luckily, Barton Lynch, the Viet-Nam staffer had not yet left the office.

"Bart, Dan Lyons."

"Hey, baby. Congrats on the hijack bulletin. Great stuff."

"Thanks. How are your connections with the International Control Comission?"

"Pretty good. Have a line to the Canadian Commissioner and his Political Adviser. Couple of reliable sources in the Indian Delegation. Why?"

"The hijackers submitted their demands through the ICC in Hanoi. You'll have to stay on top of your sources until it's confirmed. It will be a new lead with a Saigon dateline. No way I can confirm from here, so over to you."

"Keee-rist. You the only one in on this?"

"Far as I know, so play it cool. I have a copy of the demands. Get a pad and pencil, and I'll lay it on you."

When Lyons completed the dictation and rang off, he sat staring at the telephone. He now appreciated why 'Quixote' wanted the story broken. The free world would be sympathetic to the demanded release of POWs. 'Quixote' needed all the leverage he could get. It was one hell of a news story. TV and radio newscasters would have a field day. By tomorrow morning, banner headlines would be screaming the story all over the world. If it was publicity those crazy bastards wanted, they were sure as hell going to get it. The significance of 'Quixote' as a pseudonym was no longer a mystery. But what still puzzled Lyons was, why CIP?

CHAPTER FOURTEEN

Immediately following the departure of the ICC team, Gracier instructed LePlattre to make a brief announcement for the information of the passengers. Thanks to Anderson's earlier exchange with the choleric Indian ambassador, it was not necessary to impart this information to the first class section, but the economy class had not been a witness to the scene. In the planning, this point had been debated. Was it better to keep the passengers in ignorance, or to advise them concerning the terms and conditions of the demands? The decision had been that wild speculation was likely to give rise to more problems than a disclosure of the actual situation.

The reaction in the first class compartment had been shocked disbelief, then a gradual acceptance of the fact that the passengers were all hostages in a planned extortion of POWs. The fact that the aircraft was a veritable time bomb, loaded with high explosives, was a numbing revelation. At least so far, Gracier had detected nothing that would indicate any passenger was contemplating risking his life in an attempt to escape. The reasoning was likely to be that such an attempt would be courting certain death when dealing with madmen who were prepared to blow themselves to kingdom come along with their hostages. It was better to hope and pray that the hijackers' demands would meet with success. In the planning, this had been the reaction they had hoped for. It seemed to be the case.

Gracier instructed LePlattre to confine his broadcast announcement to the facts that a demand for release of a number of American prisoners of war had been communicated to the North Vietnamese through the International Control Commission; that an acknowledgement was expected shortly; that all passengers and aircrew were to consider themselves hostages to guarantee the demand was met;

that they were all to remain calm; that further announcements would be made as more information became available; and that a meal would be served at 6:00 p.m.

In economy class, the announcement was received in
stunned silence which persisted for several minutes following
the message. This was followed by a general buzz of subdued conversation which gradually died as the passengers
indulged in their individual speculations. An air of shocked
horror pervaded the compartment.

Court was satisfied that the situation was developing
as they'd anticipated. But how long this condition would
prevail was another matter. They had reached no agreement
on that score. How long could the passengers be kept under
almost intolerable pressure without some of them cracking?
At the beach house, they had come up with no satisfactory
answer to that question. The 'protracted delay' on their
demand, which was to puzzle Lyons, was no less worrisome
to Court. How protracted can a delay be before something
has to give?

The detention of the Polish member of the ICC, and one
of the Vietnamese liaison staff, was another calculated
risk which troubled Court. Although they could be considered as additional hostages, that was not the object in their
being forcibly detained. In Court's calculations, only the Vietnamese was required to serve a specific purpose. It had
been decided that only by including an ICC member could
the true intent be masked. The Polish member was an
obvious choice, since as a pro-Communist he would be a logical selection as hostage. Court wished he'd been present
in the forward compartment during the visit of the ICC
team. He imagined that the Pole had been furious, and by
this time was probably a pretty scared Polack.

Leaning back against the headrest, Court closed his eyes.

Might as well get as much rest as he could. They would remask the passengers after the meal had been completed, and reshuffle the seating. Tony, Andy and Clem would rejoin the passengers as innocent indignant hostages. John Begg and Court would take over the vigil. There would not be another shift of passengers until after the morning meal. It promised to be a long night. And in the morning, Court would be faced with a decision concerning Begg's dramatic moment in the limelight.

Court shivered. A chill dampness had crept into the aircraft from the cold drizzle which continued to embrace the delta. Gracier had warned them what to expect of the Hanoi weather at this time of year. Court hoped the captain had enough auxiliary power to permit utilization of the cabin heaters.

*   *   *   *

DeSantis walked up the aisle and parted the curtain. Anderson turned to face him.

"Guy back here says he's a foreign correspondent," Tony said.

"So?"

"Claims he's some high shot with Agence France-Presse. Says they have a stringer here in Hanoi. Gave me this envelope and wants us to try and get it to their man."

Andy took the envelope. "Tell him we can't promise anything, but we'll try."

Andy took several sheets of hand-written copy from the envelope. It was in French. Frowning, Andy walked forward and handed the sheets to Gracier. "Look this over," Andy said.

Gracier stepped into the galley where the light was better.

He scanned the sheets. "Where did this come from?" he asked Anderson.

"Some kook in the rear. Here he sits, worried about getting his ass blown off, and he wants to write a news story. And I thought *we* were nutty. What's it say?"

"It's damn good. Mood piece on how it feels to be on a hijacked aircraft and told you're a hostage. By now, the story's all over the world. This couldn't hurt us. If they send someone to communicate with us, I'll try and get him to deliver it. That's no guarantee it'll get there, or that it will be released if it does, but it's the best we can do."

*　　*　　*　　*

Court woke with a start. He hadn't remembered dozing off, and with the thoughts that had been churning through his mind, he couldn't conceive how it had been possible. What had awakened him, was a grim faced stewardess silently serving dinner. She asked him if he'd like some wine with the meal.

As a test, Court requested a bourbon and water. The stewardess said sourly that she'd been instructed by the hijackers that no alcoholic beverages, other than wine with the meals, were to be served. Court asked for red wine.

There was little point in compounding their problems by allowing any of the passengers to get drunk and revolt against their confinement in a state of alcoholic bravado. They had decided that the liquor supply would be locked up, but that a little wine with the meals might soften the blow. Court hoped there weren't any alcoholics on board.

It was hardly surprising that most of the passengers seemed to have little appetite. Glancing around, Court observed that those within the range of his vision were merely toying with their food. It wasn't a terribly appealing meal: boiled chicken with rice, and a green salad. For desert, there was a slice of papaya. Court hoped it wouldn't attract attention, but he attacked the meal with relish. As he ate, he couldn't help feeling sorry for the three men on guard duty who wouldn't be able to eat unless they could grab a bite during the time when the crew and passengers were hooded for rotation. On the other hand, he and John would be faced with the same problem come morning.

Court was sipping his coffee when the announcement was made.

"Ladies and gentlemen, this is your Captain. I have been instructed to advise you that a North Vietnamese officer has delivered a message to the effect that the demands submitted are under consideration. You will be kept informed of further developments."

As he wiped his mouth on a paper napkin, Court looked at his watch. 6:35 p.m.

*   *   *   *

The Special Political Council had been hastily convened. In the absence of the President due to illness, the Vice-President chaired the meeting. In addition to the Premier and the President of the Committee of Current Affairs of the National Assembly, the ministers of Defense, Foreign Affairs, Interior, Public Safety, Justice, and Communications had been summoned. All but the Minister of the Interior were present.

It was 9:00 p.m., and the meeting had already been in progress for an hour. So far, little had been achieved. Opinions were sharply divided between a faction advocating the destruction of the offending airliner, with or without the evacuation of its crew and passengers, and a more moderate group who counseled acceding to the hijackers' demands, or at least entering into further negotiations. Strangely enough, it was the Minister of Defense who was spokesman for the latter element, while the Minister of Communications was the most vocal proponent of the bellicose solution. Neither the Vice-President, nor the Premier added much to the hot debate.

At 9:03, a messenger delivered a note to the Premier. He read it quickly, jotted a notation in the margin, and passed the sheet to the Vice-President.

The Minister of Public Affairs was speaking. He was suggesting that a build-up of tension within the hijacked airliner was inevitable. If delaying tactics were employed, these tensions should lead the hijackers to modify their demands, or at least consider alternatives. At this point, the Vice-President's grating voice interrupted the Minister's dissertation.

"Gentlemen. We have just been advised that the incident is receiving world-wide news coverage. It is rapidly becoming something of a *cause célèbre,* with, I fear, a good deal of sympathy for the hijackers in their demands. This is an unfortunate aspect which we must consider in our present deliberations."

"The aircraft has been on the ground less than eight hours. The demands have been in our hands less than four hours. How is it possible for this news to be widely disseminated?" the Minister of Foreign Affairs queried testily.

"The marvels of modern communications," the Premier interjected drily. "I imagine that the perpetrators of this crime arranged in advance to publicize their efforts in a vain attempt to place us in an embarrassing position and influence our decision."

"Gentlemen," rasped the Vice-President. "We have not reached accord. The Premier and I shall convey your views to the President. We shall adjourn the meeting until 7:00 tomorrow morning. This will give us all time to reflect on the matter and be prepared to resolve the dilemma with clearer heads."

*   *   *   *

Court was bone weary. It was now 4:00 in the morning, and still more than three hours before he and Begg would be relieved by DeSantis and Anderson. Court was troubled. There were a good many factors contributing to this frame of mind.

Since 6:00 p.m. of the previous evening, when the message that their demands were under consideration had been delivered, there had been no further communication. Court had anticipated that there would be additional word, but by 1:00 a.m. he had accepted the fact that there was little likelihood of anything before morning.

His confining garments only added to his agitation. During the training sessions, he had worn the complete outfit continuously for as much as 18 hours. It had proved irritating, but not intolerable. But that had been under less trying circumstances. Now, he found the peculiar isolation imparted by the hood a source of extreme annoyance.

It didn't help that he was also restricted in his movements. He could not afford to leave the forward access door unguarded. Begg, on the other hand, could move from his position with relative impunity. It had been arranged that Begg was to come forward to check with Court once each hour.

The attitudes of the individual crew members and passengers was causing Court concern. A few were sleeping soundly, but the majority slept fitfully if at all. Court found the silence depressing, and the accusing eyes which followed his every movement increasingly disturbing. The interior of the aircraft, Court thought, was like the inside of a simmering kettle. How long, he wondered, would it be before it came to boiling point?

During the planning, preparation, and rehearsals, Court had been prey to nagging doubts. He had not voiced these, pushing them to the back of his mind. He had not permitted himself to think in negative terms. Now, however, magnified by his tiredness and the prevailing atmosphere, these doubts returned to plague him.

There *had* to be some time limit. It had not been agreed upon. Arbitrarily, Court had established 36 hours as a maximum limit. He wondered now if that had not been overly optimistic. He doubted that the passengers could be kept under control for such an extended period.

And at the expiration of the time limit, what then? He had not been prepared to admit failure as a distinct possibility. But by tacit understanding, all of them had included this eventuality in their thoughts, if not their words. It had been discussed only once, and then not generally. Court had agreed with Anderson that should they fail; should time run out with their demands not met, he and Andy would step off the aircraft and give themselves up to the authorities as the perpetrators of the piracy. Later, Andy had confided this to Gracier. Clem had insisted that he too should accompany Court and Andy under such circumstances. They had not argued with Gracier's logic. Three culprits might be acceptable, where two would not.

The hand they had dealt out in this phase of the operation

was not as neatly stacked as the opening gambit. The cards they had showing on the table looked strong. The hole card was weak. No matter how they looked at it, they were running a colossal bluff. If their bluff was called . . . .?

A doubt which Court had not anticipated was slowly growing on him. As instigator of this mad adventure, the responsibility was entirely his. Had he the right; had he ever had the right, to inflict such hardship on these innocent passengers, or place his colleagues in such a position of mortal danger, no matter how worthy he had considered the cause. Until the hours of this lonely vigil, this consideration had not deterred him. It was a helluva time to be assailed by such misgivings, Court thought glumly.

Dismissing this morbid preoccupation, Court turned to a consideration of Begg. He could no longer avoid the decision concerning Begg's macabre role. The scene must be played, Court decided. It would have to be even sooner than he'd anticipated. The scene would take place during the next rotation of passengers, at about 7:30, directly after breakfast. It should shock the witnessing passengers into a state where they would be less inclined to consider any overt rebellious act. It should serve as a spur to whatever North Vietnamese authorities were considering the demands. When they had last rotated the passengers following dinner, Gracier had removed the ghoulish, plastic-wrapped prop and the containers of blood from the insulated box and stored them at the top of his briefcase in readiness against this necessity. They would now be used. It was the last face-up card they had left to play. It had better be convincing.

The dividing curtains parted, and Begg slipped through.

Court debated telling John that he'd decided on the early morning for the drama. He decided that it was better that

Begg not learn of it until just before curtain time.

"Okay?" asked Court.

"Fine. All quiet," was Begg's low response.

*　*　*　*

CHAPTER FIFTEEN

Eight miles from downtown Washington, Thomas Crone sat in his office gazing out on the bare-limbed trees in the sweeping parkland. It was a gray December day in Langley, Virginia. Crone, as Deputy Director of the Intelligence Division of the Central Intelligence Agency, was in a good mood. The grayness of the day, and the leafless branches of the surrounding forest, did not depress him as they normally did at this time of year.

The door opened, and Gene Faulkner entered, his footsteps silent on the thick-piled rug. Faulkner dropped into the leather chair opposite Crone's desk.

"What do you make of it, Tom?" Faulkner questioned.

"The Hanoi hijack?"

"What else?"

"I'm delighted."

"We're being blamed."

"Certainly. We couldn't expect anything else. We've issued the usual denials; which in this particular case happen to be the truth, the whole truth, and nothing but the truth — so God help us, but no one will seriously believe us. I'm not even sure the Old Man was able to convince the President. But on this one we're 100% clean."

"What difference does it make if nobody believes us?"

"None, Gene. Just a matter of personal satisfaction."

"No possible chance this could be a Plans black operation?"

"No. Cantrell would have had to admit to it the minute the story broke, no matter how secret his plans. We've been all through that supersecrecy bit before, and I don't think he'd have tried to keep it to himself anyway. But in this instance, he's as mystified as the rest of us." Crone tapped the dead dottle from his pipe into an ashtray. As he tamped tobacco into the bole, he chuckled. "And Lew's pretty pissed-off." he added.

"Why?"

"Simply because it *isn't* his show. Guess he didn't even think of such a direct approach. And another thing is that he's got a project on the burner for a commando-type rescue operation on one of the POW camps. This could well louse up his plans."

"You don't think this *could* be a DIA sponsored commando effort?"

"No again. The Old Man would have to know about any such operation. DIA have categorically denied any involvement."

"Do you give it any chance of success?"

"Oddly enough, I do. They've got the North Vietnamese in quite a bind. They were smart enough to hijack an Air France jet. For openers, this is smart. The North Vietnamese don't want to alienate Paris if it can be avoided. Then, they've got the airliner parked spang in the middle of the runway. This must be causing a certain amount of consternation. Can you imagine where we'd be if Dulles was put out of action for a day or two? The presence of the Indian Ambassador to Thailand on board the aircraft couldn't be just a happy coincidence. India has already issued a strong note of protest to Hanoi. Then, they put the snatch on the Polish ICC delegate plus a NVA officer. Warsaw will probably protest, if they haven't done so already. And the speed with which the story hit the CIP wire indicates a deliberate leak by the hijackers. The presence on the aircraft of von Stolz, and young moneybags Palmer gives the story added punch — to say nothing of St-Denis. The AFP release was a great human interest yarn. The presence of St-Denis is probably no accident either. I imagine the hijackers are counting heavily on world opinion as added leverage. All in all, I'd say they've managed to bring a lot of pressure to bear on the Vietnamese."

"Do you think they'd actually blow up the airliner if their demands aren't met?"

"Damned if I know. It must be giving the Viets a headache. Anyone crazy enough to embark on such an adventure is capable of anything. If they fail, they probably consider themselves as dead men anyway. Why shouldn't they take a few more with them?"

"Aren't you forgetting one important point, Tom?"

"What's that?" asked Crone, pausing in the act of lighting his pipe.

"This must be pretty galling for the Vietnamese. One hell of a loss of face. When it comes to a question of face, logic may not prevail in their decision. They could well say to hell with Paris, New Delhi, Warsaw, and world opinion, and blow the damned plane off the runway."

"They could. They could indeed. And that must be the hijackers' big headache. At any rate, we'll know fairly soon which way the old ball bounces. Neither side can afford to let this drag out into a farce. I wouldn't actually bet on it, but I hope the hijackers pull it off. Just for once, it would be nice for us to get credit which we don't deserve."

"How will our position be affected?"

"No appreciable difference. If the hijackers fail, it's a CIA plot that didn't work. If they succeed, the loss of one planeload of POWs doesn't alter the North Vietnamese bargaining position. Who knows, they might even be able to turn the snatch to their advantage. Public opinion is fickle. Today, it may be with the hijackers. Tomorrow, it could well be the reverse."

"You know, Tom, I can't help wondering just what sort of man would undertake the execution of such a crazy scheme.

Have we any idea who the hijackers may be? I assume they're Americans, to be risking their lives for the release of American prisoners. Do you think, for example, that young Palmer could be one of them?"

Crone puffed on his pipe, exhaled a thin blue cloud of smoke, and smiled at Faulkner. "We haven't the faintest idea who they are. I've set the wheels in motion to investigate, but we may never learn who instigated it, or how many are involved. St-Denis is an old-school journalist, a skilled and trained observer, and right there in the plane. He couldn't hazard a guess at identity, and stated in his story that he thought there were two, possibly three hijackers. They were effectively disguised, and have reshuffled the stewardesses as well as the passengers."

Placing his pipe in the ash tray, Crone leaned forward. He rubbed his finger along his nose in a characteristic gesture indicating reflection. "As for Palmer, my immediate reaction would be highly unlikely. There have been a number of wealthy men willing to put their money on the line to ransom the POWs, but I have yet to hear of one who was prepared to stake his life in the transaction. Still, money is no hedge against lunacy, so I can't rule Palmer out completely. On board that aircraft, I would be inclined to eliminate the aircrew, the Indian Ambassador and his wife, the Polish ICC delegate, and the North Vietnamese officer from my list of suspects. But that's about all, and even there I would have to have convincing evidence. You have made a wrong assumption when you confined your thinking to Americans, Gene. It has been my experience that, if the price is right, people can be hired to do almost anything. I can't rule out *anybody* on board that aircraft with the positive assurance that they have not accepted some inducement and are not in some way involved. There is only one positive statement I can make concerning the crazy bastards who planned and executed this mad caper."

"What's that?"

"I wish I had them on my team."

* * * *

News of the hijacking was carried on the noon radio and television newscasts from Madrid. Marcie was lunching at the Marbella Club, and missed both newscasts.

The early evening was one of the most enjoyable times of her day. She could relax over a cocktail or two with friends, and now that Jerry was attending school, these were the hours she could spend with him and listen to his re-counting of the day's adventures. Later, she would change and arrive at the Yellow Door sometime around 9:00 p.m., but these hours between six and eight were hers to enjoy as she wished.

She was curled up on the leather sofa in front of a crackling fire. Nobody had dropped by this evening, and she and Jerry were enjoying each other's company. Jerry sat cross-legged on the goatskin rug before the fireplace, his face furrowed with concentration as he turned the pages of a book. Marcie poured herself another martini from the small shaker.

"Jer," she said, "switch on the TV, and see what's on the seven o'clock news."

"Okay," he said, placing the book face-down on the rug. On all fours, he scrambled across to the TV set to comply with the request.

Marcie sipped her martini and watched an attractive girl extolling the virtues of a new shampoo. Then the news came on. There was a scene of some mountainous snow drifts, while the announcer described the devastating effects of freak snowstorm in the French alps. Marcie was happy that she was sitting comfortably before the fire, and not one of the figures digging at the snowbanks. A shot of an Air France jet taking off filled the screen. The newscaster's voice was mentioning 'hijack', 'Bangkok', and 'Hanoi.' Marcie's full attention was suddenly focused on the TV. She felt a chill of fear. The airliner dissolved to be replaced by the face of the newscaster. Behind his head, was a blown-up map of Viet-Nam. In rapid Spanish, the announcer was recapitulating the account of the hijack and adding that they now had news of the hijacker's demands which were for the release of American prisoners of war in exchange for the safety of the airliner and its crew and passengers. The newscaster continued talking, listing some of the important passengers. As he did so, still photos flashed onto the screen. There was a shot of an Indian diplomat at a reception, a German industrialist seated at a desk, then she heard Court's name, and there he was, clad in a flight suit, standing with another officer beside a jet fighter. It was a slightly younger Court, grinning out at her from the picture tube. Then his image was replaced by that of a lovely young girl who was being identified as an English actress. But Marcie was no longer listening.

"Hey!" Jerry exclaimed, his attention caught by hearing his father's name and seeing the brief image, "that's Daddy."

"Yes dear, it's Daddy."

"Where's Hanoi, Mummy? What's Daddy doing in Hanoi?"

"Nothing, Jer. He's a passenger on an airplane which had to make an emergency landing."

"Oh, is that all." Jerry's attention was now on the next news item concerning a near-fatal goring at a bull fight in

Barcelona.

Marcie wasn't watching the scene of the bullring. Images were flashing in kaleidoscopic fashion across the screen of her mind. Fragments of her conversations with Court accompanied the pictures. She knew with cold and frightening certainty who was responsible for the presence of the jetliner in Hanoi — and why.

*   *   *   *

The passengers in the economy class section had all been hooded. Begg parted the dividing curtains to allow the two stewardesses to move forward into first class where Court awaited them.

"One moment," Court said, loud enough for Begg to hear, "I require assistance up here."

Begg hesitated. He understood. The dividing curtain was drawn closed as Begg retreated back into the economy compartment.

"It is difficult," Court said pleasantly to the puzzled stewardesses, "for me to keep an eye on the forward door and supervise you in distributing those hoods at the same time. We'll just wait for a moment until one of my colleagues can assist."

In economy, Begg moved quickly, the weariness of his long night of duty swept from his mind by the urgency of the moment. From the overhead storage compartment of seat row 18, which had been purposely left free of passengers, Begg took Gracier's brief case, and his own flight bag. Clutching his burden to his chest, he hurried aft, pulling off his hood with his free hand. He joined DeSantis and Anderson in the after galley space.

DeSantis was already fully robed. Andy was zipping up

the back of his gown, and had not yet donned his hood. He looked at the drawn but determined features of Begg, and then at Gracier's brief case. Andy nodded his understanding.

Begg scurried into one of the lavatories. He opened the brief case. From the top, he took the severed hand in its plastic bag, and the container of blood. He placed these objects on the shelf, gingerly, as though contact with them was contaminating. He stripped off the black garments, folded them, and stowed them, along with the wire hood-frame, in Gracier's case. Begg didn't think he'd be needing the disguise again.

The hand was cold to the touch as Begg removed it from the plastic. A shirt cuff, with several inches of material, had been glued to the wrist of the dead hand. Glued to the material was a small plastic envelope filled with human blood. There was an adhesive tab attached to the container of blood. Begg grasped the material and end of the tab firmly between thumb and forefinger. Into the palm of his hand, he fitted a rubber bulb with a short nozzle which protruded between his two middle fingers. Carefully, Begg retracted his arm within the sleeve of his jacket. The amputated hand extended below his cuff. Unless one were to look very closely, the hand looked quite natural.

When Begg emerged from the washroom, Andy scrutinized him carefully. Satisfied, Andy nodded his approval. Taking the arm from which the severed hand hung limply, Andy checked the sleeve to determine the point of termination of the wrist stump. He raised Begg's arm to chest level, and rechecked, making a mental note of the position of the sleeve in relation to the protruding hand.

DeSantis settled a masking hood over Begg's head. He inserted one of the small padlocks, but didn't snap it shut.

With a hand on Begg's shoulder, Andy guided him up the aisle. Just before the pair reached the screening curtain, Anderson selected a second passenger. He instructed the passenger to stand up, and steered him to a position in the aisle alongside Begg. Guiding the hooded men from behind. Andy eased them through the curtain.

Court eyed Begg critically. The left arm seemed stiffly held, and the hand paler than Begg's right hand. Court was satisfied that the difference would go unnoticed in the brief interlude.

Andy seated his second charge. When the man was settled docilely in the seat, Andy moved Begg ahead. At the same time, he gently squeezed John's shoulder. Begg's reaction was immediate, and electric.

Twisting from Anderson's grasp, Begg shouted hoarsely, "No! No more, damn you!" Still shouting incoherently, Begg stumbled against the back of a seat, lifted his left arm slightly, and flailed out with his right.

Anderson growled an oath, and moved with lightning speed. With his left hand, he grasped Begg's left arm, raising it chest high. At the same time, Andy unsheathed the *kukri* with his right hand. He swung the blade up. He held it poised for a second, the light glinting off the steel, then the lethal blade descended in a flashing arc.

Begg felt a stinging pain as the scything blade skinned past his knuckle. He did not release his grip on the tab. The sleeve material was magically whisked from his grasp. He gave a piercing shriek.

Blood splashed over the front of Andy's gown. The bloody severed hand with a sliced off section of shirt-cuff and jacket sleeve landed on the aisle carpeting and slid about a foot, leaving a smear of fresh blood in its wake. Begg's quivering shriek had changed to a howl of agony as he groped with his right hand to grasp the left sleeve. Blood gushed in spurts from the empty sleeve. Begg folded slowly to collapse in the aisle, his howls subsiding to strangled moans. Blood continued to spurt from between the fingers of his right hand where it clutched the left sleeve.

As prepared as he was for the dramatic spectacle, Court could not suppress a shudder. For a fleeting second, he thought that Andy could have made a dreadful mistake and actually lopped off Begg's hand. It wasn't so, of course, but the action was so much more realistic than he had expected; so vastly different from the dress rehearsal where a rolled magazine had served as the hand, and containers of water used to simulate blood, that Court was astounded. And he felt a brief twinge of guilt concerning the doubts he had harbored about Begg. The performance was nothing short of superlative.

The reaction of the spectators was magnified beyond anything that Court had anticipated. Most of them were ashen-faced, frozen in wide-eyed horror. One lady on the aisle was wailing hysterically, her seat neighbor trying ineffectually to calm her. The passenger in the seat closest to the spot where the amputated hand rested had vomited over himself and the floor carpeting. He was still heaving. Two other passengers were retching into air-sickness bags. A grim-faced LePlattre was cursing.

Since the performance had been staged for the benefit of the North Vietnamese authorities, Court checked to see the NVA officer's reaction. There was nothing inscrutable about this particular Oriental. His face was congealed in a grimace of pure terror.

Court stooped down, and picked up the blood-smeared hand. To Andy, he said harshly, "Get the poor bastard out of here. Put a tourniquet on that arm before he bleeds to death."

Andy stooped down and grasped the moaning Begg beneath the arms. As he dragged the feebly-struggling figure toward the curtains, Andy's *kukri* caught on a seat arm. He cursed, dropped his burden, callously wiped the blade clean on Begg's jacket, and sheathed the knife. Begg still clung desperately to his left sleeve. The spurting had subsided, but blood continued to well between the fingers of his right hand.

Court continued to watch critically until the dividing curtains closed behind his two principal actors. He was alone, stage center, and the scene had to be played out.

As though suddenly becoming aware of the grisly object in his grasp, Court turned, strode to the galley, and flung the limp hand on the stainless-steel shelf. It sat there, in a widening pool of blood. The stewardess who had been cleaning up the last of the breakfast trays, was standing just inside the galley. Her eyes followed Court's action, then her eyeballs turned ceilingward. With a faint moan, she sagged and slid to the floor in a dead faint.

Turning to the crew lounge, Court addressed the purser. "Look after her," he said curtly. With a motion of his revolver, he indicated the passenger who had been violently ill. "Then have somebody clean up that mess."

LePlattre had stopped cursing. His face was stony, but his eyes glared venomously at Court.

Court could well appreciate the captain's bitterness. "Captain," he said, "please broadcast an announcement to the effect that owing to the foolish resistance of one passenger there has been an unfortunate incident. To avoid any repetition, we strongly advise compliance with instructions."

"You murderous sons of bitches," LePlattre replied, his voice cold with contained anger.

"Captain," snapped Court, "this is no parlor game. We

don't want trouble of this kind any more than you do. But if it comes, don't expect us to act like boy scouts. One or two lives are of little consequence when we may all be blown to pieces in a matter of hours. Now please comply with my request."

Court's words had a sobering effect on LePlattre. In the graphic display he had just witnessed, he had momentarily lost sight of the larger peril which threatened them all. He rose from his seat resignedly, and walked forward to the flight deck to make the announcement.

*   *   *   *

When Anderson was satisfied that the dividing curtains were fully drawn to cut off the forward compartment, he tapped Begg on the shoulder.

Begg ceased the low moaning. He let go of the sleeve he'd been clutching to prevent any glimpse of his left hand. He eased his cramped arm, and relaxed his grip on the now-exhausted rubber bulb. Fumbling at the back of his neck, he removed the padlock and lifted off his hood.

As he followed Anderson back to the rear lavatory area, he was conscious of the hooded passengers shifting nervously in their seats. Although muffled, the commotion in the first class compartment had been clearly audible back here. Beneath their masking hoods, these passengers muttered in baffled uncertainty. They should not long be left in doubt. As soon as the reseating had taken place, those who had actually witnessed the action would rapidly spread the appalling story.

Andy stopped him before he entered the washroom. With a hand resting lightly on Begg's arm, Andy said in a low voice, "Beautiful, baby. Just beautiful." John smiled wanly in response. You big ham, he thought. Wiping your knife on my coat wasn't in the script. I was scared to death that the bulb would run dry at any second.

Begg surveyed himself in the washroom mirror. He was a mess. The jacket was soaked with blood. His shirt, trousers, and even his shoes were splattered. The black hood was also sticky with blood. Without wasting time, Begg peeled off his garments. Before scrubbing his hands and arms, he cleaned the blood off his shoes and attended to the disposal of the hood, shirt, coat, and slacks. He took a pair of scissors from his flight bag, cut the clothing into strips, and methodically stuffed them down the chemical toilet. This completed, he washed thoroughly. From the flight bag, he took an identical change of clothing and quickly dressed himself.

From Gracier's brief case, Begg removed the insulated box. He rinsed off the bulb, and placed it in the box. Then, sighing heavily with fatigue and letdown, he sank down on the toilet to wait for Court.

*　　*　　*　　*

Awaiting Andy's return, Court located a soiled napkin and wrapped the hand, after wiping the blood from the steel counter. The severed hand had served its purpose well. There was little point in morbidly overplaying the scene.

Having waited a reasonable interlude, Andy pushed through the curtains into the first class compartment. The wrapped hand tucked under his arm, Court stepped into the aisle, taking care to position himself close to the seated Vietnamese officer.

"Well?" Court questioned, as Andy drew close.

"Dead," Andy replied coldly. "Lost too much blood, or

he had a heart attack. The body's in the portside lavatory. Put up a sign saying it's out of order."

"Too bad," Court said flatly. "Better get these passengers hooded. See if you can speed up the crew."

"Okay." Andy turned and walked back to where the stewardesses had resumed the hooding.

Court stood still for a moment, then, pivoting slightly, he loomed over the Vietnamese.

"You," Court said, motioning to the Vietnamese. "Come here."

The officer started, his eyes wide with fright. He scrambled to his feet.

"I gather you speak English?" Court questioned.

The officer seemed incapable of speech, but nodded assent.

"Good," Court said slowly. "I want you to report to your superiors that we are getting impatient. If there is much more delay, we cannot hold ourselves accountable for what happens on this plane. I want you to relay the message that we are now imposing a maximum time limit of 1800 hours for the transfer of the prisoners of war. Do you understand?"

The officer bobbed his head in acknowledgement. Clearing his throat, he managed a faltering. "Yes . . . yes. It is understood."

Removing the blood soaked package from beneath his arm, Court pointed with it towards the access door. "Well," he said, "what are you waiting for?"

The NVA officer suddenly grasped the fact that he was being ordered to leave the dread airliner. He needed no second urging. With alacrity, he moved to the door, swung it open, and half-slipped on the drizzle-slicked metal platform as he started down the boarding steps.

Court watched the unceremonious departure from the

opened door. As he drew it shut, he smiled faintly beneath his hood.

Striding towards the rear of economy class, Court stopped at seat row 18 and retrieved his leather bag from the overhead compartment. As he moved on past the restless passengers, it struck Court that the interior of the aircraft was oppressively stuffy. It stank of stale perspiration and tobacco fumes. The cabin heaters had dispelled the chill damp of the Hanoi weather, but the confined air was now uncomfortably hot.

Before entering the portside washroom, Court spoke quietly to the waiting DeSantis. "Better crack the after access door, and when you go forward, let the forward door stand open for a while. We don't want these poor bastards to suffocate."

In the washroom, Court looked down on Begg where he was dozing, still seated on the toilet. Without disturbing Begg, Court deposited the napkin-wrapped hand alongside the rubber bulb in the insulated box. Removing his hood and wire frame, Court quickly stripped off the outer garments. He folded them and stowed them in his bag. Switching watches, he shoved the revolver and gloves into the bottom of the bag. Then, he gently shook Begg.

Begg awoke with a start.

Court smiled down at him. "Well done, John," he said quietly. "Shall we join the passengers?"

As did Court, Begg took a hood from DeSantis. Moving up the aisle, Begg seated himself in 18C. Carefully placing Gracier's case and his own flight bag beneath the seat in front, Begg placed the hood over his head, snapped the padlock, and sank wearily back in the seat.

Court selected a seat near the rear of the compartment. He adjusted his hood, closed the lock, and with a wave of his hand signaled to Tony DeSantis.

Absorbed in his thoughts, Court scarcely noticed the murmur of voices and rustling as Tony started to shift the passengers.

That foreign correspondent, what was his name, St-Denis, had been one of the spectators of the forward drama. Andy would know better than to assist the journalist in filing any copy on the incident. If the North Vietnamese chose to publicize the brutality of the hijackers, that couldn't be helped. But there was no point in spreading the word if it could be avoided. Such copy wasn't exactly calculated to win public sympathy. Later, when it was disclosed that the macabre scene had been a hoax, St-Denis could make quite a story of the incident.

There was a click as the padlook was unlocked. The stewardess lifted Court's hood from his head. He blinked, and looked about. The passenger in the seat ahead was excitedly recounting the grisly details of the amputation and death of a passenger.

"Who was he?" somebody asked.

"Don't know. He was wearing one of these hoods. About medium height. Could have been anybody. He must have gone off his rocker."

"They killed him?" Court asked.

"Not right out," replied the informed witness. "The one with that crazy knife sliced the guy's arm off. He couldn't have lasted long though. Must have severed an artery. It was ghastly. Blood spraying all over the place."

Court leaned back and closed his eyes. Well, he thought, that's it. We've played our last card. It looked pretty convincing. I just hope it works.

*   *   *   *

CHAPTER SIXTEEN

The 7:00 a.m. meeting of the Special Political Council was postponed one hour, and even then, the Premier was 20 minutes late in appearing. When he arrived, the debate of the previous evening was in full swing. Neither faction seemed to have altered its stand in any appreciable degree during the intervening hours. If anything, the group of which the Minister of Communications was the vocal leader, was more adamant in its demands for immediate direct action.

The Premier slipped quietly into the vacant chair next to the Vice-President. As acting chairman, the Vice-President rapped for silence. It took a few moments before the angry voices were stilled.

"Gentlemen," said the Vice-President. "The Premier has come directly from his conference with the President I propose we yield the floor to the Premier."

The Premier waited patiently until assured of their full attention. They gray light of the rainy morning failed to dispell the gloom of the conference room. Overhead fluorescent lights added a harsh glare. The light was reflected dully from the dark polished table, and from the gold stars gracing the scarlet shoulder boards of the Minister of Defense's uniform tunic. The combination of thin daylight and blue-white fluorescent glare was unflattering. The strain and fatigue on the faces was heightened to a point where most looked haggard. The Premier noted with satisfaction that the Minister of Interior, absent from last night's meeting, was present this morning.

Like the Vice-President, and several of the attending ministers, the Premier was attired in the Mao jacket favored as appropriate revolutionary garb by the President. The Premier's jacket was of a light gray material, and smartly-tailored, but this failed to soften the severity of the garment. The overhead light illuminated his bushy lightly-graying hair, high forehead, prominent cheekbones, and full lips. The light lent an unhealthy pallor to his features, accentuating the shadows of his hollow cheeks and deeply-recessed eyes, and imparting a curious cadaver-like quality to his countenance. While he waited for the voices to subside, his only sign of life was the slow rotation of a pencil grasped lightly between his fingers.

He had complete attention. Placing the pencil in the center of a pad of paper before him, he rested his arms on the table and folded his fingers together.

"Gentlemen," he commenced in conversational tone, "I am happy to report to you that the President's condition is much improved. He sends his apologies that he could not attend this meeting in person."

His voice went a shade deeper. "As you know, I conferred with the President last night and again this morning concerning this matter. The views which I shall now express, and with which I am in complete agreement, are his express wishes."

The Premier turned his head to look directly at the Minister of Communications. "Tich, you have advocated the immediate removal of the airliner by direct action. Your concern is appreciated. You are to be congratulated on the manner by which your organization has diverted normal traffic through the military airbase at Phuc Yen, and Haiphong's Cat Bi. It is certainly inconvenient, and an inconvenience well understood by the President. Nonetheless, he does not agree with your proposed solution."

Disregarding the minister's muttered objection, the Premier turned his attention to the entire assembly. "As you have all observed, our options are limited. One of these, understandably objectionable to our colleague, Tich, was to employ delaying tactics. As I recall the discussion, those who argued in favor of such an approach based their reasoning on the assumption that pressures would build up within the aircraft to a point where the hijackers would be amenable to a compromise of some kind. Just what that compromise was to be, was not suggested. Moreover, the advocates of protracted negotiations were working on the premise that the hijackers would not reach a point of desperation where they would be prepared to blow up the aircraft, killing themselves in the process.

"I am afraid such an assumption is no longer valid. One reason for my tardiness here this morning is that there has been a new development. Word of this was relayed to me at the Presidential Palace directly from Gia Lam. I am assuming that this news has not as yet been communicated to you. Is that correct?"

Blank stares from the assembled ministers answered the Premier's question. He continued, "Shortly before eight o'clock, the officer attached to the Control Commission's liaison staff, the one who was detained on board by the hijackers, was released. He was instructed to advise his superiors that the hijackers had now imposed a time limit of 6:00 p.m. this evening for the fulfilling of their demands. Before his release, this officer, Captain Vinh, was a witness to an event on board the aircraft. Those of you who felt that pressures within the plane would become intolerable are borne out in your judgment. One of the passengers objected to being reseated. For this show of resistance, the hijackers cut off his hand. The passenger died within a very short space of time after the amputation."

The Premier paused to allow the council time to consider the implications of the disclosure.

The Minister of the Interior broke the silence with

a question. "To whom did the captain give this message? Could it have been in any way distorted?"

"To Colonel Ha Van Lo, through the airport commander," answered the Premier, with a trace of annoyance in his voice. "Lo contacted me, and I immediately confirmed the report through Gia Lam. Captain Vinh was still at the airport, and I talked with him myself. It was evident, even over the telephone, that the captain was excited, but he was coherent. He described the amputation scene to me in detail. I must say that witnessing such an action would be a disturbing experience.

"The point is, that we are dealing with fanatics. We are no longer safe in assuming that they are not capable of blowing up the aircraft. Therefore, one of our options has been eliminated.

"This leaves us but two alternatives. Blow up the aircraft ourselves, before the hijackers take that action into their own hands, or submit to their demands. As I have already stated, the President is opposed to the former course."

"What you are saying," said the Minister of Justice, "is that we have *no* option. That we must turn over the prisoners indicated on the list submitted by the hijackers."

"With certain substitutions to the list, that is exactly what the President proposes," replied the Premier.

That the council was being presented with a fait accompli, however unpalatable to some, was fully understood by the Premier. That this would be the case, was known to most, if not all. While, in theory, the Democratic Peoples Republic was governed by the party oligarchy, it was in fact in the final sense an autocracy. Such was the avuncular charisma of the President, that he alone could hold in check the factional rivalries, and he alone make the final decisions. There was no man in this room who cared to dispute this, or the fact that the Premier, as long-time friend, colleague, and confidant, did not speak with the President's voice. That they would accept the fait accompli, the Premier knew. Nonetheless, he would make the acceptance as agreeable as possible.

"We have really had little option in this matter from the moment the airliner entered our airspace, and virtually none from the time that it landed." The Premier picked up the pencil, and tapped it on the pad to illustrate each of his ensuing points.

"We have no desire to alienate the French government, particularly at this time when our delegates, and those of the National Liberation Front, are negotiating in Paris. As long as it was in our power to do so, we had no option but to respect the physical sanctity of the aircraft and its passengers, and equally no option but to supply its logistic requirements.

"The presence of the Indian Ambassador to Thailand, his wife, and one of his embassy staff, have made our position even more difficult. Through their Consul General here in Hanoi, New Delhi has delivered a strong note requesting us to honor any demands made by the hijackers which would ensure the safety of their envoy and his party. I need hardly add that as Chairman of the International Supervisory Commission, established under the Geneva Conference Agreements, to which we were a signatory, India enjoys a rather special position vis-à-vis our government. It is our intention to reply to that note that out of consideration for the safety and well-being of their diplomatic representative we have accepted the outrageous demands.

"The Polish government, through their ambassador, has also handed us a note. It was not couched in such strong terms as that of India, but reminded us that we are responsible for the safety of their ICC delegation while within territory under our jurisdiction. The Foreign Minister has already given the Polish Ambassador verbal assurance that all necessary steps will be taken. We will now give a formal reply in similar vein to that which we are giving India.

"There is also the matter of world-wide public sentiment, which was brought to our attention yesterday. We cannot ignore the fact that, at least at the moment, a sentimental romanticism abroad seems to be obscuring the issue. It has the unfortunate appeal of a David against a Goliath; of Tran Hung Dao pitted against the Mongol hordes of Kublai Khan, or of our own struggle against French colonialism and American imperialism. The fact that this is a criminal act of air piracy is temporarily clouded. It is, therefore, vitally important that we not be cast in the role of the villain of this piece.

"When these facts are added together, it will be seen we have had little choice. The President's decision to accept the hijackers' demands, to submit to this blackmail, I think you must all agree is the only solution."

Although there were a number of scowling faces, there was a murmur of assent.

"We have no choice but to suffer this humiliation," the Minister of the Interior stated resignedly.

"Humiliation, yes," agreed the Premier, "but suffer it in silence, we will not. And it may yet prove less of a humiliation than we think. We have already issued last night's agreed statement decrying this CIA inspired criminal act of piracy, typical of the gangster tactics of the Nixon Administration. We have deplored this callous disregard for the safety of innocent foreign nationals. It is now our intention to issue a further statement. We will publicize to the fullest this infamous CIA act of senseless violence. Robbed of its gloss, the hijacking will appear as nothing but an inexcusable crime. Public sympathy will turn to revulsion."

The Premier's gaunt countenance wore a reflective look; his next words were as thoughts spoken aloud. "I must admit to a grudging admiration for the hijackers. Chance may have been their unwitting ally, but up to now they have managed to place us in an impossible position. This stupid act of violence, however, could well be the one miscalculation which will prove their undoing."

The Premier continued in a firmer voice. "Another statement is being prepared for general release. We will advise the world that we accede to this CIA blackmail for humanitarian reasons; to safeguard the lives of the important personages and other innocent hostages at the mercy of these insane killers, and to demonstrate to the peace-loving American people that while the prisoners of war have committed unforgivable crimes against our innocent people, we nonetheless recognize that they are but dupes of the warmongering Nixon Administration."

Turning to the Minister of Foreign Affairs, the Premier asked, "Were instructions issued to our Paris delegations?"

"Yes. Last night. In protest of this crime, they are boycotting the peace talks until further notice."

"Good. We will have them expand on their protest with this new development in similar terms to the press release."

Nodding in turn to the ministers of Justice, Defense, and the Interior, the Premier stated, "It has not been my intention to usurp your authority, but I deemed time was of the essence. Accordingly, I have issued instructions to the commandants of the prison camps in the immediate vicinity to prepare the prisoners for transfer in accordance with the hijackers' list."

"In accordance with the list?" The Minister of Defense raised his eyebrows.

"Insofar as possible, yes. Since some of the prisoners listed are situated at camps too distant to permit transporting them here in time for delivery, some substitutions will be necessary. Similarly, there will be substitutions for those intransigent prisoners undergoing special treatment. In the substitutions, I have instructed that those prisoners who have responded most favorably to indoctrination be favored. In order to avoid possible delays in acceptance at Gia Lam, I consider it advisable to adhere as closely as possible to the submitted list."

"But," protested the Minister of the Interior, "the list contains names which do not correspond to our official submission in Paris. Surely you don't intend to include any of those men."

The Premier regarded the minister with a steady gaze. "I do," he stated flatly. "The list handed us by the hijackers seems to be a random selection of two or three names from each alphabetical category, with preference given to those longest in captivity. They have also had access to lists of airmen listed as missing in action, and not shown on our official listing. A number of such names have been included, but is a small percentage. Of those, we have records of only a very few. Where possible, I will include them in the delivery. My intention is to demonstrate good faith. In this manner, our 'safe' substitutions will not be questioned.

"I request that those directly concerned with the prisoner question remain behind for a few minutes at the conclusion of this meeting. As I said, I have already issued instructions, but these can and will be amended if any of you comrades have better suggestions. My proposal, with which the President concurs, is to follow the schedule I shall now outline.

"At noon, the hijackers will be advised that we yield to their demands under protest.

"The selected prisoners will be collected from the three major camps by two trucks. These vehicles will be instructed to arrive alongside the aircraft no later than 5:00 p.m. There will be an additional three trucks loaded with prisoners — those not selected, and I trust including those who have been most troublesome. These trucks are to arrive no later than 5:15 p.m. Our stated purpose for this second convoy will be a gesture of good will, in the event that the hijackers can accept more prisoners than initially requested. They may even be able to accept a few. But the real purpose should be obvious to you. Consider the psychological impact of seeing some of your comrades departing to freedom, while you are returned once again to a prison cell. To have hope kindled, and then snatched away, is a refinement which should make these unfortunates bitter, but more tractable.

"The International Commission team will be requested to be present at 5:00 p.m. to observe our compliance with the demands which were transmitted through them. It is also my hope and belief that once the prisoners are delivered, the Polish delegate will be released.

"Two buses will be on hand to transport the disembarking passengers to the Thong Nhat Hotel. Immigration formalities will be dispensed with, but a thorough baggage inspection will be conducted after the departure of the passengers.

"Lastly, as soon as the prisoners are embarked, the airliner will be cleared for take-off." The Premier smiled in the direction of the Minister of Communications. "Then our airport can resume its normal function. You, Comrade, are to ensure that air transport is available Monday morning to fly these disembarked passengers to Canton, from where they can entrain for Hong Kong. This will have to be coordinated with the Chinese through their embassy."

"What leads us to assume that the hijackers will permit any passengers to disembark?" questioned the Minister of Public Affairs.

"A simple matter of space. The passenger capacity of an Air France 707, as we have been advised by Aeroflot, is 124. Captain Vinh was confined throughout his enforced visit to the forward section, where he counted 14 passengers. During his sojourn, however, the passengers were shifted between compartments for reseating. He was not able to·get an accurate count, but estimates that there are close to 60 passengers on board. It is obvious, therefore, from the number of prisoners demanded, that the hijackers intend to disembark some of the less important passengers to make room for prisoners. How many they will retain as hostages, and how many they will release, is of course a matter for speculation."

"Where will we conduct the interrogation of the passengers? At the hotel?" asked the Minister of the Interior.

The Premier looked at the minister coldly. "Unless the baggage inspection reveals something of a positively incriminating nature, there will be no interrogation. The passengers are to be treated with the deference and courtesy accorded a diplomatic mission. They will be dined formally at the Thong Nhat, and are to be our guests at tonight's concert presentation at the Opera House. No restrictions whatsoever are to be placed on their free movement. After their ordeal on board the aircraft, I want them to leave here with the most favorable impression of our hospitality by contrast."

The Minister of Public Affairs nodded his agreement with the logic.

"It occurs to me," the Minister of Justice interjected thoughtfully, "that when a blackmailer meets with success on his initial effort, he is rarely satisfied. What assurance have we that having yielded once to such demands we will not be faced with similar situations in the future?"

"Your point is well taken," replied the Premier. "It was raised this morning by the President. While we agreed that the number of prisoners we now hold is more than adequate for purposes of negotiation, in fact, so large that it is something of an embarrassment, we would not like to see their numbers reduced by continuing enforced attrition. To this end, we are publishing a warning that *any* commercial aircraft entering our airspace without prior authority will be shot down without question or warning. It is hoped that this should deter anyone emboldened by the success of this venture."

"The Gia Lam airport commander?" questioned the Minister of Communications.

"Yes, we discussed this briefly yesterday. Lieutenant Colonel Buu is unquestionably without fault. There was no precedent to guide him. Any one of us here this morning would probably have acted as Buu did." The Premier dwelt a significant pause, before adding, "It is most unfortunate that we require a scapegoat. Buu will be charged with revisionism and a crime against the Fatherland. On these charges, he will appear before a military tribunal. Please see to it that he is relieved of his duties immediately — and that he confesses to these crimes."

*   *   *   *

The Premier's presentation had left little room for argument. The discussion which followed was brief. After a further 10 minutes the meeting was adjourned by the Vice-President.

The ministers of the Interior, Justice, and Defense remained behind to consider the Premier's proposed actions concerning the selection of the prisoners to be released, and their delivery. While this area was properly their divided province, they accepted that the time element had dictated the overriding action. Here too, the discussion was of short duration. They could find little fault with the Premier's instructions. There were minor amendments on only two issues. The times of arrival of the transporting military vehicles were changed to 5:30 and 5:45 respectively to allow the prison commandants as much time as possible to make the necessary substitutions and prepare corresponding lists. And, instead of the trucks pulling up alongside the airliner, where the armed guards could be construed as a hostile act in contravention of the hijackers' terms, the trucks were to remain outside the prescribed 200 meter radius. The prisoners selected would be marched, accompanied by unarmed guards, from the trucks to the aircraft.

All but the Minister of Defense excused themselves.

The general rose to his feet, and methodically stored papers in his briefcase. He glanced across the table, where the Premier still sat deep in thought.

"You do not seem much disturbed by this problem," the general commented softly.

The Premier looked up, and smiled. "Do I not, old friend? Should I be? We cast our lot with the revolution when we were both but youths. Since then, we have traveled a long road marked by many setbacks, disappointments, and triumphs. The road which stretches before us may be considerably smoother than the one we have traversed, but it is hardly likely to be devoid of dismaying obstacles. In my opinion, this incident is, by comparison, only a mild irritant. As a student of the battle plans of Napoleon, would you say, *mon général* that this contretemps exhibits any strategic significance?"

"No," replied the general, his boyish face lit by a smile, "it in no way alters our strategy. You are using it, however, to considerable tactical advantage."

"Perceptive of you. In what way?"

"In your carefully-worded press releases, you have, for the first time, used the term 'prisoner of war'. Does Ho agree with this, or is it on your own initiative?"

"He agreed, most reluctantly. I have convinced him that our contention that these prisoners are criminals, and subject to trial only before our people's courts, must one day be modified. Ultimately, the prisoners of war will become the central issue in peace negotiations with the Americans. They are the key which will eventually unlock the door for us. We are doing everything possible to exploit the growing aversion to this military adventure which stirs now within the United States. In line with our reasoning, you inflict the heaviest possible casualties while we imply that their Administration is leading their essentially peace-loving people down a path of profitless conflict which can only bring shame instead of glory. We cannot be ambivalent with the existing prisoners. They must also be classed as unwitting tools of the Pentagon. Criminals, yes, but we cannot remain adamant. In spite of the fact that this is an undeclared war, we must one day accord them the less demeaning status of 'prisoners of war' in every shade and meaning of the term. To this, Ho has finally agreed. Today will be our first step in that direction."

"Ho, you, and myself, have been dubbed 'the iron triangle'," the general said soberly, "but it has never been suggested that it is an equilateral triangle. Ho, as the man of the people, the visionary architect of our nation, casts the longest shadow. You, as the able negotiator and administrator who has translated the dream into reality, come next. I am but a simple soldier. But, of the three of us, it is you who have been the most recently exposed to western diplomacy and thinking at the Geneva conferences. Accordingly, I respect your interpretations as I would no other's. There are those, however, who do not share my views. It is for this reason that I mention something else which did not escape my attention. I doubt if it was missed by the rest of our colleagues. You went a step beyond the 'prisoner of war' issue, and in this I don't believe you had Ho's concurrence."

The general's reference to himself as a 'simple soldier' had amused the Premier. The general's overweaning ego was a byword. Far from considering himself an unassuming military figure, the general thought of himself as a reincarnation of Bonaparte, or at the very least, a latter day Nguyen Hue. But the amusement was short-lived as the Premier listened intently to the general's words.

"You refer to my inclusion of prisoners we have not officially acknowledged amongst those to be released?"

"I do. It constitutes an admission that we have lied in this matter, or an admission that our controls are so lax that prisoners could exist without the knowledge of our administration. Either, or both, are admissions totally unacceptable to Ho. You could be stepping into grave danger."

"I am aware of that. You are quite correct, in that matter I did not have Ho's blessing. But in this too, he must bend.

It is tied to the whole prisoner question. We do not admit to a lie, merely to facts. There are, of course, a good many of their officers, who they list as missing in action, who are simply corpses. There are others, who for one reason or another we can never disclose. But there are many, notably medical cases who have made satisfactory recoveries, which we should add to our official listing. The CIA is not without intelligence agents within our midst, and a good many of these cases have to be known. If we do not amend our lists, we destroy credibility. And, in the final analysis, it boils down to a simple matter of accounting. How do we propose to dispose of these hidden assets? Ho must see this. At the moment, he does not. The step I have taken is a calculated risk."

"I shall stand with you in this matter," the general stated with simple sincerity. "I am fully in accord with your reasoning. But we may not have an easy time of it."

"We may not, and I thank you for your support."

"Tell me," the general said, frowning, "it struck me that you were not particularly anxious to discover the identity of the hijackers. Surely some of them may be among the disembarking passengers. Yet you do not appear to desire investigation. Why?"

The Premier smiled once again. "I expect some, if not all, of the hijackers to be among the passengers. It is what I would do in their place. It is my hope that they will be clever enough to conceal their identity as they have throughout the hijacking. If that seems strange, let me tell you that I am in no way convinced that this is a CIA operation. To my mind, it doesn't have the stamp of the Intelligence Agency. If I am correct, and it were to be proved that we have been hoodwinked by gifted amateurs, we would look ridiculous. I much prefer that our adversary remain one worthy of our mettle: the CIA."

* * * *

CHAPTER SEVENTEEN

The noon television newscast carried a long shot of the hijacked Air France jetliner sitting on Gia Lam's main runway. In the foreground, Peoples Army soldiers were standing on guard duty in the establishing shot, which then zoomed to the airliner. There were no outward signs of activity, and the aircraft looked dismally forlorn in the thinly falling rain. The picture shifted to the wall map of North Viet-Nam while the newscaster pointed out the alternate airfields which had been pressed into service for commercial traffic. Then the announcer recounted a grim account of an atrocity alleged to have taken place early Sunday morning. The news story was attributed to shocked North Vietnamese officials who gave credit for both the piracy of the aircraft and the incredible act of violence to the CIA. The tone of the story was unmistakably anti-American.

Marcie had been following the newscast with rapt attention. When the picture tube flashed to another news item, Marcie angrily switched off the set. The story concerning the atrocity left her feeling sick.

"Oh, Court, baby, why . . . why?" she murmured, sinking dejectedly into a leather chair.

* * * *

Promptly at noon, a North Vietnamese Army staff car pulled up at the foot of the boarding ladder to disgorge an unarmed major. Anderson met the officer at the opened access door and took from him an unsealed envelope. The major stood waiting on the platform while Andy read the message; a typed statement in English curtly advising that the demands would be met under strong protest and that army trucks would arrive to deliver the prisoners at 1730 hours.

"Thank you," Andy said simply. "Please advise the air-port officials that we will require a second boarding ladder at the after access door no later than 1715. Also, please advise your superiors that we will require an English-speaking liaison officer to stand by from 1715."

"I have been assigned that duty," the major answered with ill-concealed distaste. "I have been instructed to inform you that the International Control Commission will be present to witness the embarkation. In addition, my superiors suggest that there is no longer any necessity for you to detain the Polish Delegation member."

"I'm afraid," Andy stated mildly, "that we must be the judge of that. Assure your superiors that the Polish commander is unharmed."

To Andy's amusement, the major neither acknowledged this statement, nor dignified his abrupt departure with any form of salute.

Sometime during the morning it had stopped raining. Andy stepped out onto the platform. The concrete was drying in patches, although large pools of rainwater still shone dully from the slight depressions on runway and taxi strip. The gods are favoring our enterprise, thought Andy, as he sucked in a lungful of the cool damp air. Exhaling slowly, he thought, by God, we actually pulled it off.

Stepping back into the interior of the plane, Andy walked the few feet to the crew lounge. LePlattre had overheard the conversational exchange in the doorway, and his face registered curiosity, which changed abruptly to a black scowl as his eyes lit on the sheathed *kukri* at Andy's waist. Wordlessly, Andy handed LePlattre the envelope.

As LePlattre scanned the typed message, his features softened into a semblance of a smile. Relief; the release from the terrible pressure was written on his face. He

turned to Anderson. "I may broadcast this news?" he asked.
"Assuredly."

* * * *

Court struggled to wakefulness. He gazed groggily around,
and was dimly conscious of something being broadcast. That
must have been what had awakened him. The words:" . . .
be effected at 5:30 this afternoon." registered. Leaning forward to the passenger in the seat in front, Court queried,
"What did he say?"

"You missed it?" the man asked incredulously.

"Uh huh. Afraid I must have been asleep."

"The Vietnamese have agreed to release the prisoners
of war. The captain said that the transfer'll take place this
afternoon at 5:30."

"Jesus . . . I didn't think they would." And even as he
uttered the words, Court recognized them as the truth.
A vast feeling of profound relief flooded through him. He
grinned foolishly, and realized that he had an overwhelming
urge to urinate.

He moved down the aisle towards the after lavatory.
All around him, the passengers were talking excitedly,
their faces reflecting relief. One of the stewardesses was
passing out luncheon trays. In response to ribald sallies,
she was laughing. The sudden change in atmosphere within
the stuffy cabin was electric.

The seated Gracier favored him with a slight smile as
Court angled past the stewardess.

The hooded figure of DeSantis stood by the after serving galley. Court excused himself, and grinned as DeSantis
stepped politely aside to let him pass. Glancing at the crudely
lettered sign, 'Out of Order', on the port washroom door,

Court's eyes crinkled with increased amusement. An involuntary laugh escaped him.

*   *   *   *

The initial mood of exhilaration wore off quickly. For the passengers, the memory of the morning's ghoulish incident was still fresh enough to exert a decided dampening influence. It had the same sobering effect on the aircrew. For the hijackers, there were different but no less restraining considerations. The Vietnamese may have agreed to comply with the demands, but the prisoners of war were not yet in evidence. Not until the POWs were embarked, the passengers disembarked, and the aircraft not only air-borne, but well clear of the North Viet-Nam coast, could they consider the operation a success. And there was the by no means small matter of a continuing concealment of their individual identities.

As had been agreed upon, duty during the final stages would be confined to Court, Anderson, and Gracier. Gracier, up until the last minute diversion, would keep an eye on the flight deck preparations for take-off. Anderson was to take charge of the passenger disembarkation from the forward door, while Court would supervise the POW embarkation from the after door. DeSantis and Begg would take no part, and from the next, and last, shift of passengers, would be in every respect innocent onlookers. Gracier, during the confusion generated by the curtain-dropping diversionary tactic, would become one of the disembarking passengers. Court and Andy would ride the flight.

They hooded the passengers and crew members following lunch. With DeSantis guarding the forward compartment and access door, Court, Andy, and Gracier held a hurried conference in the flight deck. The purpose of this meeting was to determine the final seating arrangements which would confine the 24 passengers to be retained as hostages to the first class compartment and crew lounge. It was agreed that the Indian Ambassador, his wife, his embassy secretary, Lucille Montgomery, Marc St-Denis, and the unfortunate lady afflicted with claustrophobia would constitute the actual hostages. The remaining 18 would be a random selection. They decided upon a role that the Polish officer would play in the last minute diversion which would neatly dispose of the problem of his release. Then, Court and Andy discussed briefly their own plans for rejoining the body of passengers following take-off. The latter plan, they both recognized, was the weakest part of the entire scheme. That had to be accepted.

Anderson joined DeSantis, and the two men proceeded aft; DeSantis to remove his disguising garments and turn his revolver over to Andy; and Andy to stow the kukri, along with DeSantis' costume, in Gracier's brief case. The latter act, Andy undertook with reluctance. He had grown rather fond of the murderous-looking Gurkha weapon. It had proved to be the most effective and fear-provoking instrument in their arsenal. Still, Andy had to admit, no good purpose could be served in one of them wearing the knife as a constant reminder of this morning's incident.

DeSantis selected a seat, and donned a hood. Andy locked the brief case, stuffed the key into a seat pocket, and carried the case forward to deposit it beneath a pre-selected seat in first class.

The two stewardesses were conducted aft by Court to await the final reseating. This was completed more rapidly than at any previous reshuffling. For one thing, the passengers were by now used to the procedure. For another, the release of the extreme tension under which they had lived for a period in excess of 24 hours contributed to an attitude of cooperation.

Now all the hijackers had to do was wait for the appearance of the POWs. For Court, the hours seemed to drag by with interminable slowness. Gracier, now that he could see the end of the adventure in sight, was thinking of Angelique. Andy, absorbed in a slight change in script he was planning as a finale, was the least troubled of the three.

*   *   *   *

After the sudden release from tension, Christian Le-Plattre had experienced a peculiar lassitude. He felt a curious detachment as he watched the hijackers go about the process of masking the passengers, crew, and himself.

When the hood was removed some minutes later, Le-Plattre's sensation of being purely a spectator persisted. Idly, he wondered what were the hijackers' intentions for handling the embarkation. He knew that his aircraft was intended to take a full passenger load, but since he hadn't seen the list of prisoners requested, he had no idea how many were to be on-loaded. Yesterday, one of the hijackers had stated that the baggage would not be calculated into the take-off-weight. That probably meant that they intended to off-load at least some of the passengers, along with all the luggage. Presumably, they would keep some passengers as hostages — the Indian Ambassador for one.

As it had over the last 26 hours, his mind dwelt once more on the speculation as to the identity of the hijackers. He confessed to himself that he had no more idea now than he had when he'd looked up to see a Luger pointed at his head. He didn't even know how many were involved.

They couldn't have stayed on their feet for this long a period without some rest. LePlattre guessed the number was probably four. He had to admit that they'd organized the operation down to the last detail. They knew the Boeing 707 and its capabilities thoroughly. Quite obviously, they were no strangers to flying and flight conditions. They had correctly assessed the North Vietnamese reaction to their fantastic demands. If it wasn't for the insensate cruelty of the vicious action he'd witnessed this morning, Le-Plattre could admire their achievement.

Of one thing, LePlattre was now convinced. By 1800, or even earlier, his aircraft would be air-borne. His mind turned to the professional aspects. From the Gia Lam Let-Down Plate, he knew the runway to be 6,562 feet. That presented no problem for take-off. The engineer had worked out the fuel with an adequate safety margin. They'd been topped-up yesterday, so that was no problem. The course: he supposed 160 degrees, the reciprocal of yesterday's approach course, would be as good as anything until he could get a position fix. As for altitude; he presumed that the hi-jackers wouldn't be worrying about dodging visual sighting or shore radar now, and he could use a normal rate of climb. As soon as he could establish radio contact with Saigon Control, he'd get an assigned altitude, but assumed that on the easterly heading it wouldn't vary from yester-day's 37,000 feet.

It was at this point that he heard himself addressed by one of the hijackers. It was the one with the Luger, this time.

"Captain," said Gracier, "they're rolling up the after boarding ladder. Our liaison officer has arrived, and we've instructed him to bring carts to handle the baggage. Would you please instruct your engineer to go down and open the luggage and freight bays. I suggest that you and the flight crew can go forward and commence pre-flight checks."

*   *   *   *

At exactly 5:30, a large army truck drew up to a point on the parking apron some 200 meters from the airliner. A minute later, it was joined by a second truck. Watching from the after door, Court observed a number of men clad in pyjama-like garments of loose jackets and trousers descend from the open backs of the trucks. Khaki-clad guards lined the men up in loose formation. Two guards, evidently in charge of the operation, were checking the men against clip-board mounted lists. Faintly, across the intervening distance, Court heard hoarsely-shouted commands. A section in front of the first truck started to move towards the airliner.

During the afternoon, the overcast had thinned and lifted to form scattered clouds which drifted lazily in a southwesterly direction. Late afternoon sunlight bathed the scene in a mellow glow. As the shadow of a cloud advanced down the runway, the ICC convoy of white vehicles rounded the terminal building and paced the shadow as it neared the aircraft. The leading gray-green staff car of the NVA liaison officers came to a halt within a few yards of the after boarding ladder. The white sedans pulled up one after the other and stopped behind the military vehicle. The team emerged from the cars to join the liaison staff. As they watched the approaching prisoners, the cloud shadow slowly engulfed the scene.

The prisoners advanced towards the foot of the boarding ladder in groups of twenty. Each section was escorted by two guards armed with truncheons. The prisoners displayed little semblance of military discipline as they shuffled listlessly towards the plane. Here and there, some of the prisoners hobbled forward on crutches.

The leading group was halted a few meters short of the boarding ladder. A NVA non-commissioned officer strode to the observing ICC team, detached a piece of paper from his clip-board, and handed it to the Vietnamese lieutenant colonel. Saluting, the non-com wheeled from the ICC team and headed in the direction of the boarding ladder. He mounted the ladder, saluted the NVA major standing a few feet from Court, and removed another sheet of paper from the clip-board. After an exchange of a few words, the non-com saluted, turned, and descended the steps. Not once had the non-com as much as cast a curious glance at the hooded figure of Court.

It's all rather unreal and militarily correct, like some kind of parade-ground exercise, Court thought. It's as though we hijackers don't exist. He realized that the bulk of the North Viet-Nam populace would know nothing of the hijacking, and would remain uninformed, but he could scarcely credit that the soldiers on guard duty and those actually taking part in the release of the prisoners could be in ignorance. It was strangely disturbing, but eclipsed by the dismay he was experiencing concerning the prisoners themselves.

The NVA major handed a list of names to Court. With no distinction by rank or number, the names were listed simply in alphabetical order. Court scanned down the list. Under the 'M's, the name he sought leaped out at him: 'Maloney, D.K.'.

"Very well, Major," Court said gruffly, "commence the loading."

The major nodded to the non-commissioned officer at the foot of the ladder. Shrill commands were barked, and the prisoners started to move forward in single file. One by one, they ascended the steps.

What had first struck Court as odd was the almost total silence of the prisoners. Here and there, he heard a muttered word or two, but the general impression was that each man was isolated and remote from his neighbor. If those on crutches stumbled, no hand was raised to assist them. Clad in their loosely fitting jackets and trousers, their bare feet shod only with the so-called Ho Chi Minh sandals cut from discarded rubber tires, the prisoners moved like automatons. They seemed drained of all emotion. Like puppets, they jerkily mounted the steps. For the most part, their eyes remained downcast.

Court scrutinized each face closely. Most of the men looked gaunt and drawn, almost to the point of emaciation, although some looked to be in better shape than the majority of their fellows.

Had Court not been watching attentively, Deke might have passed by unrecognized. He was almost upon Court before something familiar in the features forced Court to take a second look. When he realized it was his old friend, a wave of nausea assailed Court.

Deke's reddish-brown hair was liberally sprinkled with gray. His face was heavily lined, the cheeks shrunken, and the freckles standing out against the pallor of his skin like liver-spots. The sleeve of the right arm of his pyjama-like jacket was pinned up beneath a stump which extended a scant few inches below the shoulder.

Involuntarily, Court stepped forward. Sensing an obstruction in his path, Deke glanced up. The eyes which looked back at Court for a fraction of a second, before they were again cast down, were blank and dead.

Court felt as though he was going to throw up. His hand groped until it found the handrail. With an effort, he steadied himself. Deke moved slowly past to enter the gaping access door.

A movement on the parking apron and taxi strip distracted Court. He shook his head, and forced himself to concentrate. Two buses were drawing up to the forward boarding steps. Further away, on the parking apron, three more army trucks were braking to a stop beside the two which had unloaded the prisoners. It suddenly registered on Court that the three trucks were crammed with prisoners.

What the hell? Court turned to the NVA major. "We didn't request those buses," Court snapped.

"When you unloaded the luggage, we assumed you would require transportation for some of the passengers," the officer said blandly.

"And what the hell are those?" Court pointed toward the trucks.

The major smiled sardonically. "We thought you might be able to accept a few more prisoners."

For a moment, Court's mind refused to function. Christ, there are at least 50 men on each of those trucks, he thought in dismay. The true reason for their presence struck Court like a blow in the stomach. His mind raced. Whirling around, he forced his way through the line of prisoners and up the aisle where the stewardesses were seating the docile POWs.

When he reached the point where the passengers were seated, Court brusquely ordered, "All right. Passengers will disembark from the forward door. Start moving forward, please."

He continued on through to the first class compartment to where Anderson stood. "I've started the disembarkation,"

Court said. "We're going to need more space. Off-load another 14 from this section, and have the purser and two of the stewardesses join them. Got that?"

"Yeah," Andy answered without argument. He too had seen the three additional trucks pulling up on the apron.

Court pushed his way back through the milling passengers and on-coming POWs.

The NVA major stood placidly on the after boarding ladder platform. Court moved up beside the major and pressed the muzzle of his revolver into the officer's side. "All right, you sadistic sonuvabitch," Court snarled, "get 17 prisoners from the closest truck, and if you fuck about with the paperwork, I'll blow your guts out."

The officer didn't flinch. In a calm voice, he gave an order to the non-commissioned officer who still stood at the foot of the ladder. The non-com saluted, and trotted off in the direction of the trucks.

* * * *

Gracier had left the door to the flight deck open. Although he had kept an eye on the pre-flight instrument checks, occasional glances aft kept him advised of the progress. The economy section passengers were crowding up the center aisle. As soon as economy was almost cleared of disembarking passengers, Anderson would draw the dividing curtains partially closed. That would be Gracier's signal, which should come in a very few minutes.

Turning to LePlattre, Gracier asked, "Aren't you going to congratulate us, Captain?"

His communications re-established with the tower, and his instrument checks completed, LePlattre was staring out the window at the straggling prisoners and disembarking passengers. He twisted his head around to stare at Gracier. "I think I could congratulate you if it weren't for your murderous action. How the hell do you think I feel, knowing I have a corpse in the after lavatory?"

Gracier stepped close to LePlattre, and spoke softly. *"Mon vieux,* after take-off, when the purser gives you a head count of the off-loaded passengers, and those remaining on board, you're going to find nobody is missing. There is no dead body in your lavatory."

LePlattre's eyes widened as he understood what he'd been told. He started to say something, then his mouth closed.

Glancing back through the open door, Gracier saw Andy drawing the curtain. Stepping back from behind LePlattre, Gracier's elbow brushed against the navigational table. As it did so, it struck the transistor radio he had placed there. The transistor clattered to the deck. Gracier stooped to retrieve it.

"Merde!" Gracier exclaimed.

"What?" queried LePlattre.

"The detonator. It's activated."

Both LePlattre and the second officer started up from their seats. A white-faced radio operator, his mouth agape, stared up at Gracier. The flight engineer cursed.

"Stay where you are . . . all of you." Gracier snapped, as he stood up, the transistor clutched in his hand. "I'll handle this."

Rushing from the flight deck, Gracier slammed the door closed behind himself.

The brief case was under the second seat on the starboard side. St-Denis was seated in the seat behind. "What in hell's name!" he exclaimed as Gracier's hooded figure reached across him and groped under the seat. As his hand caught the case, Gracier pressed down hard with his thumb on the top of the leather flap. He prayed that with all the shifting about, and opening and closing of the case, that the device would still function. It did. As Gracier pulled the case from under the seat, the ticking of the alarm clock was plainly audible from a few feet away.

"Good Lord," cried the startled St-Denis, "the damn thing's ticking."

Gracier whirled and thrust the brief case into the arms of the Polish naval commander. "Get this off the plane," barked Gracier.

The Pole recoiled. He would have dropped the case if Gracier hadn't been pressing it on him. "It's set to detonate in about three and a half minutes. Move, you dumb Polack, or we'll all be killed. Get it off the plane and out of the airport."

Realizing he had no choice, the commander scrambled to his feet and bolted for the access door. The shocked passengers shrank from him to leave a clear passage.

Andy had moved quietly forward and stood solidly blocking the door to the flight deck. Court, who had come forward on the curtain signal, stood by the lavatory. All eyes were on the Polish commander as he rushed from the plane to push his way down the steps, the ticking brief case held at arm's length.

In the confusion, nobody noticed as Court stepped aside, screening Gracier's quick entrance into the washroom.

It took Gracier only a matter of seconds to pull his flight bag from the used-linen container, strip off his outer garments, and jam them down into the soiled linen. He dropped his Luger into the chemical toilet, followed by his gloves and Seiko watch. The wire hood framework he left sitting on the shelf.

Stuffing the transistor radio into his flight bag, Gracier stepped from the lavatory. The passengers were milling about, craning their necks to follow visually the Pole as he raced for the parked ICC vehicles. Gracier pushed in amongst the excited passengers.

It was at this moment that Court noted something. The purser was standing on the platform of the boarding ladder. He had been engaged in checking the departing passengers against a copy of the manifest. He shouldn't have been there. Court's instructions to Andy had been to include the purser with the disembarking passengers.

Court moved up to Anderson. Before he could speak, Andy brought his hood next to Court's and hissed, "Now you. Into the can. Leave your gun and outfit on the shelf. Fast, and no arguments, or I'll knock you out from under your hood."

There was something in Andy's tone that indicated he meant exactly what he said. Court hesitated only a fraction of a second before slipping into the washroom vacated by Gracier.

As he slipped out of his garments and stacked them on the shelf as Andy had ordered, Court's mind was in a whirl. The purser hadn't been instructed to leave the plane. He, Court, was being substituted. What in hell did the big crazy bastard have in mind?

Dropping the revolver on the pile of black clothes, Court peeled off his gloves and added them to the stack.

When he stepped out of the washroom, the attention of the passengers was still diverted. Court realized he'd taken even less time than Gracier. Through the open access door he caught a glimpse of the Polish commander standing on the concrete. One of the sedans was careening towards the terminal building at high speed. The Pole was no fool, and no hero. Presumably, the vehicle drivers were more expendable than the ICC team members. The Pole was waving his arms and talking excitedly to his interpreter and the Sikh colonel.

Court hesitated. He was a trifle confused concerning his next actions. One thing, he'd have to get his leather bag. Apologizing, he worked his way through the passengers until he reached the first class compartment and the seat row where Lucille Montgomery was sitting next to the port window.

"Pardon me," Court said politely, as he squeezed past the man sitting next to Lucille. At his voice, Lucille tore her attention away from the window to look up at Court.

"Are you one of the departing passengers, or one of our select little group that seem to be continuing on to Hong Kong?" Lucille asked.

Court grinned. "Departing, I'm afraid. Imagine it won't take them too long to find us some sort of transportation out of here though. I hope we can see each other in Hong Kong within a day or two. Will you take a rain check on that dinner?"

"Certainly," Lucille said, smiling. "Considering I didn't think I'd every see Hong Kong, it will be a pleasure."

"Great, I'll look forward to it. But I'm afraid right now I'll have to disturb you. I think my bag is under your seat."

She pulled the bag from beneath the seat, and handed it to Court. Reaching across the aisle-seat passenger, Court thanked Lucille, and took the bag from her.

From behind Court, came Andy's gruff voice. "Snap into it Mac. We haven't got all day."

Glancing to the rear of the first class compartment, Court noted that two stewardesses were already allocating seats in the section to some of the additional 17 prisoners. Up forward, he observed the last few departing passengers moving towards the exit door. Stepping around the black-clad bulk of Anderson, Court started forward.

Lucille watched Court's retreating back, a slight frown on her face. Something was not quite right, but she couldn't think exactly what it was that had given her this impression.

A few feet behind Court, Anderson moved up the aisle. When he came abreast of the front row of seats, Andy paused. He looked down at the Indian ambassador's secretary.

"You," Andy said brusquely.

"Me?" Rutengee queried timorously.

"Yes, you. Come with me."

"Oh . . . Certainly." Rutengee had no intention of questioning this frightening embodiment of authority. Assuming that he was to join the disembarking group, Rutengee retrieved his attache case, stood up awkwardly, and stepped into the aisle. Hesitating long enough to smile apologetically at the ambassador, Rutengee hurried forward in Court's wake.

Andy was close behind Rutengee. Noting with satisfaction that the crew lounge, forward galley, and the area before the access door, were free of crew and passengers, with the exception of Court, Andy drew the curtain which separated this area from the first class section. Catching up with Rutengee, Andy halted the Indian with a restraining hand on the man's shoulder. Rutengee froze in his tracks like a startled rabbit.

Glancing behind himself, Court took in the scene. The frightened Indian secretary, with Anderson at his side, was halted directly in front of the lavatory door. Court immediately recognized Andy's intention. As he stepped through the door onto the platform, Court was hard pressed to suppress a broad grin.

Pausing beside the purser to screen the crew member's

view of the plane's interior, Court said pleasantly, "Thank you for an entertaining flight."

The purser looked up from his copy of the manifest. He smiled. "I wouldn't say it was one of our best, Sir, but I'm glad you enjoyed it."

Taking advantage of Court's small diversionary ploy, Andy opened the washroom door. He propelled the startled Indian into the lavatory, and followed behind him. When the door was closed and secured, the two men had little room in the confined space.

Pointing to the heap of black garments on the washbasin shelf, Andy said briskly, "Get yourself dressed in this outfit."

"But . . . but, how?"

Andy sorted out the clothing, and assisted the trembling Indian in donning the leggings and gown. The Indian was several inches shorter than Court, so Andy selected the wire frame left behind by Gracier. He unfolded the frame and fastened it in place over the Indian's head. Then he slipped the hood over the frame.

"Put on those gloves," Andy commanded.

While Rutengee struggled to get his shaking fingers into the gloves, Andy snapped open Court's 38 and extracted the cartridges from the chamber. "Here," he said, pressing the unloaded gun into the Indian's gloved palm.

"What . . . what?" Rutengee's cloth-muffled voice stuttered.

"Now, listen carefully. Do exactly as I say, and you will come to no harm. You will step out of this door. On your right is the door to the flight deck. Go through it, and close it behind you. Then, all you have to do is stand there and hold your gun pointed at the chief pilot. That's all, nothing more. If anyone speaks to you, don't answer. You just stand there until I come and get you. It will only be a few minutes. You needn't be nervous. Nobody's going to hurt you. Do you understand all that?"

"Yes." came the hesitant response.

"Good," said Andy, then he added grimly, "But bear one thing in mind. That gun you have isn't loaded, but *this* one damn well is."

Andy eased the washroom door open sufficiently for the Indian to squeeze through. When Rutengee was clear, Andy still held the door slightly ajar until he heard the flight deck door open, then close.

Andy crammed his costume on top of Gracier's in the used-towel bin. With his strong hands, he crumpled and twisted the two wire frames, his and Court's, until he could squeeze them into the container. His gun, and the shells he'd removed from Court's 38, he dropped into the toilet. He whistled tunelessly as he stripped off his gloves and pushed them after the gun. He unsnapped the Seiko, and with his handkerchief he wiped it clean before dropping it down the toilet. The chemicals in the toilet were undoubtedly strong enough to remove fingerprints, but there was no point in taking any needless chances.

From his trouser pocket, Andy took his gold Rolex watch, and fastened it on his thick wrist. As he straightened to survey himself in the small mirror, the aircraft commenced to vibrate and the whine of the jet engines drowned his soft whistling.

Well, Andy thought, as he rubbed the course stubble of a day's growth of beard, and grinned at his reflection in the mirror, unless some dumb bastard knocks us out of the sky on the way out, we're home free.

He unzipped his fly part way. As he stepped from the washroom, he was zipping up his trousers. He stopped in feigned confusion and embarrassment. A stewardess was seating the last of the POWs in the crew lounge.

Andy glanced back into the first class section. All the seats appeared to be occupied. He turned to the stewardess. "Hey, he said, "Where am I supposed to sit?"

The stewardess frowned disapprovingly. "There is one unoccupied seat in first class, and one here. I don't suppose it matters which you take."

"Thanks," said Andy apologetically. "Guess I'll sit here."

He settled into the seat, his back to the flight deck. He wondered how his hastily recruited and reluctant surrogate was faring up forward. He smiled happily.

* * * *

LePlattre switched on and one after the other started the jet engines, slowly increasing power until the aircraft trembled like a leashed greyhound. His eyes scanned the instruments. Satisfied he eased off on the throttles. The second officer was busy switching over to generator power. LePlattre looked out of the window. The ground crew was wheeling away the auxiliary generator and booster. He let his eyes swing back to the wing on the port side.

A short distance beyond the wing tip, the passengers were still boarding the buses. A group was standing looking back at the jetliner. LePlattre regarded the group, then suddenly he started. There was a man in dark trousers and a black loosely-knit sports shirt who looked hauntingly familiar. The forward boarding ladder was being pushed away from the aircraft, and momentarily cut across LePlattre's line of vision. Then he could see the man clearly again. The man was looking directly at LePlattre. There was no mistaking those rugged features, that low brow beneath a shock of black hair, and that slow smile.

"*Merde alors!*" exclaimed LePlattre.

"*Comment?*" questioned the second officer.

"Nothing, Paul."

The tower instructed them to proceed to the south end of the runway for take-off. LePlattre acknowledged, eased off on the port brake, and increased power. The engine whine deepened, and the jetliner started to swing slowly to starboard. LePlattre was smiling. Of course, Clement Gracier. Who else knew this airport like the palm of his hand? LePlattre had seen a C. Gracier on the manifest, but hadn't given the name a second thought. Clem Gracier, for Christ's sake, one of the hijackers. If he'd seen Clem amongst the passengers, he'd have known immediately. He must have stayed back in the economy class compartment. LePlattre hadn't caught a glimpse of him. He corrected himself. He'd seen a good deal of Gracier from the wrong side of a very businesslike looking Luger. He wondered if Gracier would have actually pulled the trigger.

Another thought struck LePlattre. He glanced to the rear of the flight deck. A tall black-clad figure stood silently by the door. He wondered who this one was.

* * * *

Court was the last passenger to board the bus. He looked around. There was a vacant seat beside Gracier.

As the bus started to roll towards the terminal building, Court's thoughts were interrupted by Gracier's quiet voice.

"Have you got the time?"

Automatically, Court looked at his watch. His eyes widened in surprise. Sweet Jesus, he was still wearing the Seiko.

"Uh, five minutes to six," Court answered the smiling

Gracier.

Court rummaged in his leather bag. He pulled out a turtle-neck sweater with a muttered comment about it being pretty damn cool in Hanoi. He had used the sweater as a pre-text to cover his locating the Longine and switching watches. He palmed the Seiko, and shoved it into the pocket of his slacks. He'd have to find some way of disposing of it. What a damned stupid mistake, but then Andy hadn't given him much time to think.

*   *   *   *

At almost the same instant that Court made the horri-fied discovery of the wrist watch, Lucille Montgomery, watching the departing buses from the window of the air-liner, recognized what it was that had troubled her. When Court Palmer had reached across to retrieve his bag, he hadn't been wearing the Longine watch. Instead, a stainless steel watch was on his wrist. And it struck Lucille, that she had noticed each of the hijackers wore a similar watch.

*   *   *   *

CHAPTER EIGHTEEN

The white sedan hurtled past a startled sentry at the airport exit guard post. Fifty meters from the exit, the road curved to run beside a broad irrigation canal. The NVA corporal driver pulled the Polish Delegation car to a skidding stop on the loose dirt at the side of the road closest to the canal.

The sweating corporal catapulted from the vehicle, the ticking brief case clutched in his hand. With all his might, he threw it towards the expanse of muddy water. Tumbling end over end, the case described an arc through the air, to land with a splash in the brackish canal. For a few seconds, the case floated half-submerged then it sank slowly to leave a trail of rising bubbles on the surface.

An hour later, when there had been no underwater explosion, it was considered safe to retrieve the brief case.

From a safe distance, an officer directed the operation. The demolition sergeant stood on the bank, while three privates in a sampan probed the mud with bamboo poles. They located an object which proved to be the case. Dripping mud and dirty water, the leather case was deposited on the bank.

Fearing the locked flap could conceal a booby-trap, the demolition sergeant cut through the leather side of the case. Inside the case, they found an alarm clock which had stopped running, two peculiar contraptions of wire, two sets of black cotton garments, a Gurkha knife in a sheath attached to a wide leather belt, and a metal box. In the box, which they opened with caution fearing it could be some kind of bomb, they discovered an empty rubber syringe, and an amputated human hand wrapped in a blood-soaked cloth. The one thing that they were expecting, an explosive charge, was nowhere to be found.

The officer trudged back to the guard post and reported

the findings to his headquarters by telephone.

The information was passed to the authorities concerned, who were already in receipt of the advice that a careful search of the luggage unloaded from the aircraft had revealed no explosives, nor anything which could connect any of the passengers with the air piracy.

The news that there was no evidence that the airliner had been carrying explosives was received with surprise by the majority of the high officials. Neither the Minister of Defense, nor the Premier, evidenced undue concern.

* * * *

Air France Flight 194 received clearance for take-off at 1800.

At the south end of the runway, the aircraft shuddered as the jet engines crescendoed to a throaty roar. Brakes released, the 707 commenced to move down the runway with rapidly increasing speed. It lifted-off, and as it rose steeply and banked to the right, the landing gear homed.

At the best of times, strapped securely in his seat, with no turbulence to mar the flight, Ahmed Rutengee was a poor flyer. It never failed to frighten Rutengee, and he lived in dread from the moment the plane left the ground, until it rolled smoothly to a stop after landing. Under these conditions, encased as he was in confining clothing, his feet on a trembling deck, and his back braced against a vibrating bulkhead, he was in a state of near-panic.

The airliner was several thousand feet up and still climbing steadily, although the angle and rate of climb had been moderated and the roaring pods reduced to a throbbing hum. The nose was swinging onto a southeasterly heading. Through a thin trailing wisp of mist, the airliner rose above the scattered overcast. As it progressed through this layer of slight turbulence, the aircraft trembled with a barely-perceptible bump.

Rutengee lost his balance, and what little was left of his nerve. He flung his left hand out to clutch at an overhead rack. The gun dropped from the nerveless fingers of his right hand. Clattering onto the deck, the gun slid to a stop alongside the left foot of the startled radio operator.

In stupified amazement, the operator looked down at the revolver. He fully expected the hooded figure to swoop down and recover the weapon. Nothing happened. A petrified Rutengee was incapable of any action other than clinging to the overhead rack and pressing against the bulkhead. Inadvertently, he had disobeyed his instructions. He fully expected that at any moment a bullet would come crashing into his back.

The radio operator reached down slowly, and picked up the revolver. "Hey," he yelled, in disbelief, "I've got his gun."

LePlattre pivoted in his seat, and took in the scene. To the copilot, he said, "Take over, Paul."

LePlattre relieved the operator of the revolver. Holding it pointed at the black-garbed figure pressed against the rear bulkead, he said flatly, "We'll find out who at least one of you is. Remove your hood."

"It . . . it isn't loaded," Rutengee's voice came falteringly through the cloth of the hood. "He told me just to stand here and hold it."

"The hood," snapped LePlattre impatiently. The hijacker either wouldn't or couldn't comply with the order. LePlattre stepped forward, grasped the top of the hood, and pulled it off.

A ludicrous spectacle presented itself to LePlattre's

astonished gaze. From behind a wire framework extending a good nine inches above his head, a trembling and white-faced Rutengee stared at the captain with the pleading eyes of a kicked spaniel.

"What do you mean, *he* told you to stand here?" Le-Plattre barked, when he had recovered from his initial surprise.

"The man . . . the man in black. He made me get dressed in this. Took all the bullets out of the weapon. Oh dear . . ." Rutengee's babbling trailed off. He had reached up in an attempt to free himself of the wire frame, and his hand was tangled in the wire.

LePlattre inspected the revolver. True enough, there were no cartridges in the chamber. He believed Rutengee, for the simple reason that he couldn't conceive of such a man as a companion of Gracier's in such a venture. Also, for most of the time LePlattre had been an unwilling guest in the crew lounge, the Indian had been in evidence in the first class section. But not all the time, and stranger things have happened. In spite of the fact that he believed the Indian to be nothing but an innocent dupe, he was at the moment not only the prime, but the only suspect. Turning to the flight engineer, LePlattre said, "For Christ's sake, help him out of that stupid rig." Dropping the empty gun on the navigation table, he added, "And hang onto this, even though the only fingerprints on it are undoubtedly the radio operator's and mine."

As he resumed his bucket seat, the humor of the situation struck LePlattre, His shoulders shook with laughter.

"What's so funny?" the second officer queried.

"Mon dieu," said LePlattre, wiping tears from his eyes, "can you imagine *that* taking over our aircraft. If he really was one of them, maybe we'd better not tell anybody."

LePlattre suddenly remembered Gracier's last remarks, just before the incident of the accidently-armed explosive charge. In the excitement, and the concentration of take-off procedure, it had completely slipped LePlattre's mind. He contacted the after serving galley on the intercom. When the purser came to the intercom, LePlattre instructed him to inspect the after port lavatory and then report forward.

"What did you find?" LePlattre questioned when the purser reported in the flight deck.

"Nothing," replied the bewildered purser. "Absolutely nothing. There's no trace of the body, and no sign of blood. I wonder how they managed to get rid of it?"

"What about the passenger count?"

"Just the one missing."

"Counting him?" LePlattre nodded to the seat in front of the navigation table where Rutengee sat dejectedly.

"Well I'll be damned," said the purser. "With him, that makes a full head count. But who . . . what?"

"What about our newly embarked passengers?" LePlattre said, cutting off the purser's questions.

"Model prisoners. They all look stunned and in pretty sorry shape."

"Do you think they could use a meal. I think we have enough on board for a dinner serving of sorts."

"They certainly look as though they could use a meal. What about liquor? The Hanoi passengers haven't requested anything, but the old bunch that are still on board are howling for booze."

"Serve it to them. I don't suppose one drink would hurt the released prisoners. Give them one on the company. But watch it. It has been a long time since any of them tasted liquor. We don't want a planeload of drunks on our hands.

One drink shouldn't do much harm and may relax them."

As the purser turned to leave, LePlattre stopped him. "When you go aft, have the stewardess make a normal take-off announcement. Welcome our Hanoi joining passengers on board the flight. Advise them that we will be cruising at an altitude of 37,000 feet at a ground speed of 550 miles per hour. Our estimated flying time to Hong Kong is two hours. We anticipate landing at Hong Kong's Kai Tak airport at 9:00 p.m. Hong Kong time. When that announcement is completed, I'll broadcast a message for the benefit of the remaining passengers to the effect that I apologize for the unavoidable delay. I'll add the happy news that we've all been the victims of an elaborate hoax, and that we are not carrying a corpse in the after washroom."

When the purser left to carry out his orders, LePlattre relaxed. He let his eyes rove over the view outside the aircraft. For the first time, he noted that an escorting MIG fighter had joined them and was pacing the flight slightly above and to starboard. Ahead, on the right, he could make out the coastal town of Than Hoa. To port, almost on the beam, lay the city of Haiphong. Between the two, stretched the river-laced Red River delta. Further aft, bathed in the bronze light of approaching evening, LePlattre noted the jagged line of the grotesque limestone formation which marched inland and northward from the Baie d'Along. Inland from those jagged hills, rose the line of mountains which he had heard American pilots refer to as 'Thud Ridge.'

It had been 15 years since LePlattre had last viewed this terrain. And, strangely, there was a marked similarity between that last flight in 1954, and this one. Then, he had picked up a planeload of French prisoners of war released from Viet Minh camps in the northeast. Admittedly, 15 years can cloud the memory, but in retrospect, LePlattre felt that the officers and *poilus,* most of them veterans of the humiliating siege and fall of Dien Bien Phu and the killing 'long march' to the prison camps, had seemed in better shape than the Americans he'd watched filing dejectedly towards the aircraft this afternoon. Perhaps it was because the French were for the most part hardened infantrymen, more accustomed to deprivation and the terrain than these American officers whose first real introduction to North Viet-Nam was the prison camp itself.

They were nearing the coast. LePlattre took a last look to port and the mountain ranges to the north which were falling rapidly astern and fading with the widening distance. From those mountains, from the screening protection of 'Thud Ridge', these American pilots had roared down on the plains like hungry tigers. But these were the ones which had been trapped and caged. Today, they had looked a far cry from the marauding beasts of prey they had once been.

The coastline passed beneath. As LePlattre altered to a more southerly heading, the lone MIG escort banked to starboard and departed inland to return to its base.

About ten minutes later, when the sun was a red ball hanging low in the west, and to the east the purple shadows of evening were deepening, they rose to meet him. Six U.S. Navy Corsairs ranged themselves in tight formation of three on either tip of his wings. Matching the 707's speed, the Corsairs formed close honor-guard for the next ten minutes. Then, they peeled off and fell away astern as they returned towards the carrier. But they had no sooner gone, then they were replaced by nine F4C Phantoms from the Danang airbase. These escorting fighters formed up slightly ahead and above, and again off both wings.

Watching the contrails pluming astern of the fighters' twin tail-mounted jets, LePlattre was suffused with a feeling of warm wellbeing. This tribute by the Navy and Air Force to their returning comrades was an impressive and oddly moving gesture.

After eight minutes, the Phantoms peeled up and outwards to scream homeward into the red-gold glow of sunset.

LePlattre had established voice contact with Saigon Control, and reported his position, course, and speed. He now called to report his estimated time of arrival at the North Reef turn point as 1915. He was a matter of a mere 30 hours behind schedule.

* * * *

On Geoff Braithwaite's return from Madrid, following Court's departure, Marcie had tactfully suggested that Geoff should find more suitable lodgings. She had arranged that Geoff move in with Richard Downing on a temporary basis. She had also continued her subsidy of Geoff by giving him employment at the Yellow Door. It was an arrangement which seemed eminently suitable to all concerned. Yet, while Geoff was no longer a guest, he was a not infrequent caller.

Although Marcie was not in the mood for company, she appreciated that when Geoff dropped by casually at 6:30 p.m. Sunday evening, he was motivated by kindness rather than curiosity. News of the Air France hijacking had gripped world-wide attention. Those of Marcie's immediate coterie, aware of Court's involvement as a passenger on the flight, felt closely related with the unfolding drama. Following the noon television newscast, Geoff undoubtedly felt that Marcie needed a sympathetic companion. She didn't have the heart to tell him otherwise.

Geoff was on the rug, involved in a complicated word game

with Jerry when it came time for the seven o'clock news. Marcie requested their silence as she switched on the set.

The hijacking story was by now the lead item. The station had received both wirephoto stills from Hanoi, and filmed coverage by satellite circuit from Hong Kong. In front of the by now familiar blow-up map of North Viet-Nam, the newscaster was animated and excited. The picture dissolved to a still shot of the POWs boarding the airliner, while the announcer informed the viewing audience that a total of 117 prisoners had been taken on board the jetliner. There was another still of passengers disembarking, but it had been taken at too great a distance for Marcie to distinguish the faces. Then the tube became animated with action as the 707 rolled to a stop on the floodlit parking apron at Hong Kong's Kai Tak airport. Then the passengers and POWs were shown disembarking. Again it was a fairly long shot taken from beyond a cordon of Hong Kong police. There followed three brief interviews conducted somewhere inside the arrival section. The first of these was of a lovely and vivacious Lucille Montgomery. She was delighted to be in Hong Kong after such a harrowing experience. Yes, she had been frightened, especially when she had heard a man had been killed. No, she had not witnessed that terrifying scene since she had been at that time in the economy class section. Yes, she was thrilled to think that the unfortunate prisoners would be at long last reunited with their loved ones.

Marc St-Denis was interviewed next. He required no prompting from the interviewer as he described vividly the mounting tension on board the aircraft, culminating in the shock and horror of the amputation which he had witnessed from a distance of a few feet. He pointed out to the interviewer several splotches of blood which St-Denis claimed proudly had splashed on his lapels during the dramatic episode. St-Denis then went on to describe the profound relief he and the other passengers had experienced when it was learned that the grisly incident had been a fantastic piece of acting and that no one had been even injured, let alone killed.

Captain Christian LePlattre was a more reluctant subject. He confined himself to brusque answers to the interviewer's questions. Yes, it was his first experience of a hijacking — and he sincerely hoped his last. Yes, he had been gravely concerned for the safety of his aircraft and his crew and passengers. Yes, he was damned happy that the ghoulish punitive measure, which he had witnessed, was, as he put it: 'an elaborate hoax'. The prisoners; he understood the U.S. Consulate was looking after those arrangements. The hijackers; no, he could not identify any of them or state with surety their exact number, but he understood that the Hong Kong police were interrogating one suspect. Yes, he knew who the suspect was, but was not at liberty to divulge that information. Yes, he had been advised that the Hong Kong government had received word that the passengers disembarked in Hanoi were to be flown to Canton and would arrive in Hong Kong sometime tomorrow afternoon. Yes, he was very happy to be in Hong Kong.

From the moment when St-Denis had described the incredible act of violence, Marcie had sat tensed on the sofa. When he went on to disclose the event as a fabrication, she was seized with an uncontrollable fit of giggling. It subsided as she listened intently to the interview with Le-Plattre, but she was laughing again as she got up to switch off the set.

"What's funny, Mummy?" asked Jerry.

"Your father," Marcie replied, "is really something

else."

Mystified, Geoff shot an inquiring look at Marcie. She did not elaborate. Jerry digested her cryptic answer and decided it must be an explanation. Grownups often puzzled him.

"Is Daddy coming home soon?"

Marcie sobered, and looked thoughtfully at her son. "I don't know Jer. Your father is a pretty busy man. I just hope he isn't cementing Anglo-American relations with that English bitch. He has an unfortunate weakness for actresses."

*   *   *   *

CHAPTER NINETEEN

Monday, December 8th, 1969

Paris - 9:10 a.m.

At 1, square Max Hymans, 75-Paris 15, the administrative head office of Air France, M. Etienne Fournier, the Directeur-Général, spoke into his desk intercom: "Send him in."

The door opened, and a neat young man carrying a thin black brief case was ushered into the spacious office. He approached Fournier's desk across a wide expanse of carpet.

"Monsieur Binet," Fournier said, rising and extending his hand, "I trust you had a pleasant trip?"

"Excellent, thank you."

"Please be seated, Monsier." When the young man sat down, Fournier resumed his own seat. "I must confess, Monsieur Binet, when I received the call from Lugano at my home Saturday afternoon, I was astonished. Your director, Monsieur Graff, merely indicated that you had been instructed to deliver a rather substantial sum of money to us, and that it would be delivered personally by yourself this morning. I don't suppose you care to add anything to Monsieur Graff's remarks?"

Binet had opened his case, and extracted a slim file. From this, he took a cashier's bank check, and a receipt form. He placed these on Fournier's desk, before answering.

"It is not the policy for us to disclose information concerning our clients, Monsieur," Binet said, with a thin smile, "however, under the circumstances, we can appreciate your curiosity. I am afraid that we could not divulge the information even if we knew, but in this case, Monsieur,

I can assure you that the Overland Credit Bank is as much in the dark as yourself. This sum was transferred to us through another Swiss banking house several weeks ago. We were told to hold the money until we received cabled instructions concerning its disposition. The instructions would bear an identifying code name. That cable was received by us Saturday morning. The cable originated in Bangkok. We know nothing more concerning the sender. As soon as Monsieur Graff verified the code name with the bank of origin, we communicated with you."

"I see. However, Monsieur Graff stated that the cabled instructions advised that this money was to be considered compensation for any inconvenience and expense arising with respect to our flight 194."

"That is correct."

"May I inquire concerning the time the cable was sent?"

"It was sent at 0800 Bangkok time."

"Thank you," Fournier said. He looked thoughtfully at the check in the amount of 600,000 francs, and signed the receipt.

* * * *

Fuengirola - 10:18 a.m.

On her way to the market, Marcie stopped at the Postal Telegraph office. After some deliberation, she sent a cable in care of Air France, Hong Kong.

* * * *

Langley, Virginia - 10:30 a.m.

Thomas Crone stood by the window. Contemplatively, he gazed down on a grove of white oaks at the edge of the woods. A wintry sun had melted the frost which had earlier rimed the bare black limbs, still large patches of hoary white stretched along the brittle grass at the base of the gnarled trunks. From behind him, Faulkner's voice cut into Crone's reverie.

"Well, Tom, your wish has been answered. We get undeserved credit for a highly successful operation."

Crone turned from the window, a faint smile on his lips. "Win, lose, or draw, we couldn't escape authorship. But what pleases me are the unexpected dividends which we could hardly have foreseen. I doubt if they will be noticed or appreciated by the men who actually undertook the mission."

Faulkner chuckled. "No, I suppose you're right. Not being schooled in the intricate steps of the diplomatic minuet, they'll not applaud the North Vietnamese footwork. Using the term 'prisoners of war' in their official releases was revealing, but giving up a few prisoners not on their official listings was something I could scarcely credit. What's your interpretation? How do you think this will affect our position in Paris?"

"Good questions. I don't think we've arrived at any firm position vis-à-vis Paris. My personal thinking is that we've been dropped the hint that one day our negotiations will revolve almost entirely around the prisoner of war issue. When that day comes, we have been led to believe we will encounter a realistic approach from the other side. But that seems to be the extent, unless cautious probing in private sessions reveals otherwise. Again I speak only my own views, but I would caution against undue optimism. The day I mention can be a very long way off. In fact, if events so shape themselves, it may *never* come."

"No one could accuse you of being a Pollyanna, Tom."

Crone walked over to his desk. Still standing, he removed the top of a humidor and commenced to fill the bowl of his pipe. "Bitter experience has taught me skepticism is the safest course. But I will say that, at least on the surface, it looks like there were some in the upper echelon of the Vietnamese hierarchy who welcomed the opportunity presented by the hijacking."

"In spite of the loss of face?"

Crone scratched a match along the side of the large box of kitchen matches sitting next to the humidor. When the pipe was drawing to his satisfaction, he asked, "Coffee, Gene?"

"Thanks."

Pressing down on the intercom, Crone requested two cups of coffee. This amenity attended to, Crone left the desk and dropped into one of the armchairs opposite Faulkner. He puffed on his pipe, and regarded Faulkner across the low glass-topped table.

"Face, the loss or saving thereof, is an intriguing term," he said, returning to Faulkner's earlier question. "I'm as guilty as the next man in making glib reference to the Oriental concept without fully understanding its many nuances. Let's examine its application in this particular instance.

"In the first place, I think you'll agree that while submitting to blackmail may be humiliating, it isn't of necessity demeaning.

"Then we have the status of the prisoners of war. Hell, we haven't been able to justify our presence in Viet-Nam too well to ourselves, let alone abroad. A large chunk of humanity would support the Viet Cong and North Vietnamese thesis that the pilots are guilty of criminal acts and are

therefore criminals; or at best, misguided instruments
of American policy. Taken in that context, releasing the
prisoners by the application of pressure is in effect a sort
of jailbreak.

"And the hijacking itself. Strip it of the glamour of a
noble crusade and it becomes nothing more than a reprehensible criminal act which is becoming increasingly
unpopular as a spectator sport.

"Very well, then we have an act of violence which later
turns out to be nothing but theatrics. It's like rubbing salt
in the raw wound. The world laughs. Those who are friendly
towards North Viet-Nam laugh in embarrassment; those
opposed, with derision, but they all laugh. It is interesting
to note, however, that while we all laugh when we hear
of some outrageous practical joke, our sympathies are
more inclined toward the victim than the prankster.

"The point I'm making, Gene, is just what face is lost —
and whose are we talking about?"

Crone's secretary brought in two steaming cups of
coffee. The men were silent as they sipped the hot liquid.
It was Faulkner who broke the silence. "Tom," he said,
"You're getting to be a pretty cynical sonuvabitch. I haven't
heard you voice one word of sympathy for the prisoners."

"I prefer to think of myself as a pragmatist rather than a
cynic, but perhaps you're right. As for the prisoners, hell,
I have every sympathy for the poor bastards. But I look
at it this way, Gene. Our job in intelligence is to prevent wars. We probe the weaknesses of our would-be opponent, determine his aims and capabilities, and do everything in our power to foster what seems in our best
interests, and alter what isn't. If we succeed, we may not
avert overt conflict, but we may delay it long enough for
reason to prevail. When we fail, the decision to plunge our

country into war is not one of our making. But, in the event that such a decision is taken, our task is to continue to further our cause by every clandestine means at our disposal. We can't prevent the enemy from taking prisoners. All we can do is to bend every effort towards their release. Once released, I feel little further responsibility. I'm happy for the 117 men who soon will be reunited with their families. They will receive the finest medical and psychiatric therapy this country can offer. Yet many of them will remain permanently-scarred casualties. For that unfortunate fact, I cannot and will not hold myself at fault.

"What really bothers me was the St-Denis story of three truckloads of prisoners who witnessed the departure of their comrades. Our high-altitude peeping-Toms confirm his account. The delta was socked-in Saturday and most of Sunday, but cleared enough to allow photo reconnaissance yesterday afternoon. I imagine you've already seen the wirephotos of the SR-71 observation sent over this morning from DIA. It is impossible to determine from the photos the number of prisoners in the trucks, but all five trucks are clearly distinguishable — and they remained there until after the departure of the aircraft. I've thought about that. It is a cruel refinement of torture. I have asked myself if, under reversed circumstances, we would be capable of such sadism. Unfortunately, my answer was that we would. And that, Gene, I will have to admit is cynicism."

Faulkner sipped his coffee without comment. There were times when some of the attitudes of his old friend astonished Faulkner. He did not agree with Crone's detached assessment. It made sense, but Faulkner could not accept it in its entirety. In particular, he was in disagreement with Crone's closing remarks. Old friend Crone may be, but he was still Faulkner's superior officer. Discretion dictated a change of subject.

"At any rate, Tom, you'll have to admit that amputation act was a spectacular ploy."

Crone laughed. "You don't agree with some of my last remarks, Gene. That's your privilege. And now I'm afraid I must take exception to your last statement. Oh, I'll agree it was spectacular, but it was unnecessary.

"That act of violence has puzzled me more than anything else in this whole affair. To me, it represents the one jarring note in an otherwise superbly-polished performance. It's about as subtle as a typhoon."

Crone held up his hand to still Faulkner's protest. "Hear me out, Gene. All the facts aren't in yet, and St-Denis' version is but one point of view, but I think I have enough to formulate an opinion. The scene of violence wasn't anything hastily conceived. For one thing, you just don't find an amputated hand lying about on any street corner. It would be interesting to know where they obtained it, but I somehow doubt we'll ever find out.

"I can assume, therefore, that the scene was carefully planned and rehearsed. The skillful execution of its staging certainly bears that out. But what was its purpose? It could have been a contingency plan devised to shock the passengers into compliant malleability in the event they became unmanageable at some point in the proceedings. When it was used, it certainly achieved that effect. But to my mind, it just doesn't fit with the rest of the scenario. It's too damned heavy-handed. No, to my mind, it was designed to achieve a desired effect on, and reaction from, the North Vietnamese.

"Look at the operation to that point. It was virtually flawless. The takeover was timed to take place between two radio reporting positions which were only ten minutes flying time apart. We have St-Denis to thank for letting us know how this was accomplished. It was done smoothly, with split-second timing. According to St-Denis, about a minute and a half elapsed from the first sign of the smoke diversion until the captain announced the aircraft had been hijacked. In a space of well under five minutes from the initial diversion, the jet was on course for Hanoi.

"The approach was made at low altitude to avoid premature warning of the North Vietnamese. Then, not only was the presence made known by broadcast over international emergency frequency, but a wire-service leak to CIP ensured world attention. The Vietnamese had been presented with limited options, and little time to consider them. It is hardly surprising that they allowed the aircraft to land.

"Then, and only then, did the hijackers disclose their true purpose. And again, by presenting their demands through the International Control Commission, they made sure the world would know of their conditions.

"What they had going for them was impressive. The hostages, in particular the Indian Ambassador, were of sufficient stature to warrant careful consideration. The Air France jet involved almost guaranteed immunity. And, although it wasn't specifically stated in their written demands, the passengers were led to believe the aircraft was loaded with explosives. This must have been communicated to the North Vietnamese authorities. In sum, I would say that the hijackers had presented a convincing argument. The demands would have been met. Then why in hell did they feel they needed a dramatic illustration such as the amputation scene? It was probably a device by which they expected to speed up the process.

"I have tried to place myself in the position of the North Vietnamese. How would I receive news of such an act? My reaction would be to consider the extreme violence as a demonstration of a decidedly unprofessional character. I would be inclined to think that I was dealing with a small group of fanatics as opposed to a sophisticated organization. If a spur to decision was required, I would reason that the CIA would employ a more subtle tactic. This would lead me to the conclusion that I was faced with a desperate bluff; that it was highly unlikely that there was a single ounce of high explosive on board the threatened aircraft. In my estimation, therein lies the inherent weakness in employing such an extreme measure."

Crone laughed softly, before continuing, "But make no mistake, the act would have impact. I may be convinced that I wasn't dealing with professionals; that a reckless gamble was being enacted, and that the airliner was not a ticking time-bomb, but I'd sure as hell hesitate to call the bluff. If molested, men capable of such violence would probably slaughter the key hostages. I would still comply with the demands."

"Then it did accomplish its purpose," said Faulkner.

"In a sense. And it probably had a side-effect never dreamed of by the hijackers. Placing myself again in the shoes of the North Vietnamese, how would I react to the news that I had been the victim of a hoax? I would now have cause to doubt my original conclusions. Could I be dealing with professionals of such skill that an act so out of character with the rest of the operation was a deliberate ploy to confuse the issue? If so, I think I would prefer not to know the answer."

"In essence, then, it was an inspired performance."

"Not so. In balance, I still say it wasn't necessary. I believe it was a miscalculation on the part of the hijackers. It worked, yes, but it could have backfired. However, I'm making rather liberal use of hindsight in arriving at my conclusions. And no matter what astigmatisms may afflict our visual acuity, Gene, hindsight is always 20/20 vision."

*   *   *   *

Hong Kong - 5:20 p.m.

Sibyl Harmon, Production Secretary for Anglo-Continental Films, stirred the pitcher of martinis. Satisfied that the contents were properly chilled, she poured out two glasses, adding a twist of lemon peel to each. She handed one of the glasses to Lucille Montgomery.

Lucille dropped the copy of the script, which she'd been studying, to the floor. Martini in hand, she rose from the chair and walked absently to the windows of her Hilton Hotel suite. She sipped the drink as she gazed down at the view spread before her. To her left, the Bank of China, Hongkong and Shanghai Bank, Chartered Bank, and Mandarin Hotel buildings obscured her view. Before her, the green lawn of the Cricket Club, Statue and Memorial Squares, the baroque Victorian Hong Kong Club, and the ultra-modern City Hall complex were bathed in the golden sunlight of late afternoon. Beyond, between the Star Ferry wharf and the waterfront structures of Kowloon, the harbor was a scene of frenetic activity.

Lucille's mind was not registering the visual presentation. It was, instead, focused inward on the events of the past 24 hours.

At the point of take-off from Hanoi's Gia Lam airport, she had concluded that Court Palmer must be one of the hijackers. The evidence of the wrist watch was not in itself conclusive proof, but she had been intuitively certain he was one of the group. Her initial reaction had been one of hurt bewilderment. She had found Court both attractive and exciting, but the knowledge that he had been party to the dreadful scene of the cutting off of the passenger's hand was a stunning revelation.

Shortly after take-off, the captain had announced that the amputation had been a hoax. As an actress, Lucille had been filled with admiration. True, she had not witnessed the chilling performance, but the graphic descriptions of those who had led her to conclude that it had been worthy of an Academy Award. She had been flooded with relief that Court had not been involved in an act of mutilation and murder. She had wondered what part he had played in the drama. Yet she had still been prey to conflicting emotions.

Should she divulge what she suspected concerning Court to the authorities in Hong Kong? It would be her civic duty to do so. For herself, there would be undeniable publicity value in such a disclosure.

When they had been interrogated by the police at the airport, she had withheld her suspicions. She could not explain why she had done so. Shortly afterwards, she had been glad she had held her tongue.

The name, Court Palmer, had meant nothing to her when he had introduced himself. It hadn't been until Sibyl had given her a file of press clippings that Lucille had realized Court was Courtney J. Palmer III, the American millionaire. She thanked her lucky stars that some heaven-sent impulse had caused her to maintain her silence.

"Sibyl," Lucille said, turning from the widows, "please telephone Air France and find out when they expect the passengers who were left in Hanoi. Find out where I can contact Courtney Palmer."

"Yes, Miss Montgomery."

Sibyl busied herself at the telephone for a few minutes.

Then, cradling the phone, she said, "The passengers should be at the Kowloon railroad station any time now. Mr. Palmer has a suite reserved at the Mandarin Hotel."

"What have I on for tonight?"

Sibyl consulted a notebook. "Dinner party at the Eagle's Nest at 8:30, hosted by Mr. Reichman. Your escort is Rod Reardon. I'll have a list of the local bigwigs for you by 7:30."

"What about tomorrow?"

Flipping over a page in the notebook, Sibyl read out, "Wardrobe fittings all morning, lunch with Reardon and some Shaw Brothers' stars at the Repulse Bay Hotel at 12:30, and a press conference and publicity stills at 3:00. After that, nothing."

Reardon was to be her leading man. The publicity department was fabricating a romance and demanded that Lucille be seen in his company. He was an impressively handsome hunk of Australian virility, but his narcissism left little room for other emotion, and certainly not the homage Lucille felt she deserved. She found him boring.

She finished her martini and held out her glass to Sibyl for a refill. "Call the Mandarin and leave a message for Mr. Palmer to get in touch with me here. Tell the desk that I'm expecting his call and have them relay it to the Eagle's Nest if I'm not in the suite."

Later, sorting through her wardrobe to select something suitable for the dinner party, Lucille was pleased with the plan she had in mind. Anglo-Continental should be delighted to link her name with that of Courtney J. Palmer III, which would relieve her of the odious chore of simpering at Reardon's side. Location shooting didn't start until Friday, and even then, depending on her scheduled scenes, there should be time to devote to Palmer.

She would subtly disclose how she'd kept her suspicion that he was one of the hijackers in confidence. That should be an excellent beginning which could lead to interesting developments.

Hong Kong - 7:40 p.m.

Court was at the desk in the lobby of the Mandarin Hotel, in the act of signing the registration card.

"Hiya, Tiger."

Court grinned in recognition of the voice, and looked up. Andy, in new slacks, shoes, and a Madras cotton sports jacket, stood beaming back at him.

"Andy. Where'd you get the threads? You staying here?"

"Nope. Sacked out at the Hilton. The outfit — American Express card, and instant tailors. Not bad, huh?"

"Great," Court agreed without hesitation. He thought the ensemble looked garish, and like something DeSantis might have whipped together on the Singer, but the big man was obviously pleased with the effect. Come to think of it, this was the first time he'd ever seen Andy in a jacket of any kind. "By the way," he added, "your suitcase was picked up at the Kowloon railroad station by a rep from Air France. Gather it'll be delivered to your hotel."

"No sweat. Let's have a drink."

"Fine. Come on up to the room. You can order from room service while I shower and shave. It's been a pretty rough day."

When the bell captain had escorted them to Court's suite, been adequately tipped, and withdrawn, Court said, "You sonuvabitch."

Andy grinned. "Making you get off. I thought it was a damn good idea. Figured out a little stunt with the Indian, and it was better with just one of us. It worked like a charm."

"I'm happy for you," Court said sarcastically. "You also knew that for those of us off the plane, there was little or no chance of discovery. So you had to play the hero."

"Better one than two. Better me than you. Say, that's not bad poetry."

"You're a regular Ogden Nash. So order a bottle of bourbon and one of scotch, and whatever mixer you want, while I grab a shower."

"Where are the rest of our Merry Band?" asked Andy.

"Kowloon. Tony and John at the President. They're both leaving tomorrow afternoon for Bangkok. Clem's at the Miramar. Plans to spend a few days before returning to Singapore."

While Court showered, Andy recounted how he'd handled the switch with the Indian, and the fact that as unlikely a suspect as he was, the Hong Kong police had detained him overnight before releasing him that morning. Andy described the mood of the passengers once they'd learned that the frightening amputation scene was phony. It seemed that all the passengers, with the exception of the Indian Ambassador, whose pride was hurt, had accepted the situation with good humor. On landing, many of them actually seemed to take pride in the adventure. They had been detained at the airport for an hour, where they were questioned by the Hong Kong police. According to Andy, the questioning had been perfunctory. Air France had had respresentatives on hand who treated the handful of returning passengers like VIPs.

And so they should have, thought Court. He had told none of the others of the arrangements he'd made through his Swiss bank. It had been his hope that if things went wrong in Hanoi, Air France could exert some pressure to assist those apprehended. If things went according to plan, Air

France would not be disposed to press the apprehension of the hijackers. It seemed to be working out that way. He, and the passengers disembarked at Hanoi, had been flown to Canton this morning, and come down to the border crossing into the New Territories by train. Hong Kong police had boarded the train and commenced their interrogation of the returning passengers during the run from Lo Wu station to the Kowloon terminal. The passengers were detained for a further hour and a half at the Kowloon station to complete the questioning. The police had been civil to the point of deference. If Inspector Saunders, who had questioned Court, was any criterion, the attitude of the police seemed to be that the entire episode should be quickly disposed of and forgotten.

The telephone rang. From the shower, Court yelled, "Take it, will you Andy."

When he emerged from the bathroom, a towel tucked around his waist, Court accepted a stiff bourbon and water from Andy. He took a long pull of the amber liquid, then sat on the edge of the bed.

"Who was it, Andy?" Court asked.

"Message desk. Miss Montgomery is staying in 1528 at the Hilton, and would like you to call. C.J. Palmer, Junior has called twice from New York and will call back at 10:00 p.m. local time. Air France have delivered a telegram. Asked them to send it up."

"I'll call Lucille after I blow you to a dinner in the Grill Room. Too pooped to think of meeting her tonight."

Court sipped his drink. "Andy," he said soberly, "night before last on the plane, again last night in Hanoi, and on the way here, I've had plenty of time to think. I've had to accept the fact that I was driven by some sort of obsession, whether I recognized it or not. Came to the conclusion that

I was a damn fool to submit the airline and its passengers to such an ordeal, and an even worse fool for exposing all of you to such peril just because some crazy idea was bugging me. We pulled it off, for which I'll be eternally grateful, but I want you to know that I finally realize what an idealistic idiot I've been."

"Uh huh," Andy agreed noncommittaly.

"When I saw the prisoners, I began to wonder if it was worth it. Jesus, Andy, they were zombies, nothing but walking corpses. I felt sick, and when I recognized Deke, I nearly puked." Court gave a short humorless laugh. "Wouldn't that have been one hell of a mess inside the hood? I damn near did. Then I saw those other trucks pulling up and got so goddamn mad I forgot about it. I nearly blew it, Andy. If that NVA major had given me any argument, or made one false move, I'd have blown his head off. Never felt anything like that before. I *wanted* to kill him. So bad I could taste it."

Andy was smiling. "Kid," he said softly, "you've just pulled off the caper of the century. So now the dry rot's set in. It's only natural, I suppose, but I think I'd better straighten you out on a couple of points.

"I've got to admit the POWs looked pretty bad boarding the aircraft. They didn't look much better getting off in Hong Kong. But what you didn't know was that when they came on board, none of them had any idea they were on their way to freedom. All they'd been told at the camps was that they were being transferred. A good many of them had been transferred several times before — and each time it was to the same thing, or worse. During the flight here, I circulated amongst them. They sure as hell weren't great conversationalists, except for a few fat-cats who wouldn't shut up, but I gleaned a lot.

"You'd think that getting on an Air France jet, complete with round-eyed hostesses, that they couldn't figure they were being sent to another prison camp. But that's just what they did think. They thought they might be on their way to China, or Siberia. They'd been conditioned to the point where they couldn't conceive of freedom. Even when the stewardess made an announcement after take-off, they thought it was some kind of a trick. Some of them started to get the message when a drink and dinner were served. Still, a good many of them didn't really believe it until they stepped off at Kai Tak.

"I wanted to buy them drinks, and got pretty pissed-off when the purser wouldn't let me. He explained that the captain had given strict orders that the prisoners were to have no more than one drink. When I thought it over, decided the captain was smart. A few stiff slugs, and some of those guys would have come unglued pretty quickly.

"Talked with your boy Maloney, or tried to might be a better way of putting it. Best I could get was a couple of nods. He must have had it rough. There were quite a few like him."

Andy watched Court's reaction closely. His drink untouched in his hand, Court listened intently.

"You still feeling guilty about Maloney?" Andy ques-. tioned.

"No," Court answered. "No, I'm not. Thought about that too. What happened to Deke and the rest of them was through no fault of mine. I used to think that I should have been on the mission where Deke bought it. Had some crazy idea I should have been the one to be shot down. But I'll confess something, Andy. I'm ashamed to admit it, but when I saw Deke, sick as it made me, I was suddenly damn glad it wasn't me." Court smiled wryly. "I guess it's safe to say I've finally exorcised the devil that's been driving me."

Andy smiled, but made no comment. He continued discussing the prisoners. "Talked to a couple of consulate and military types at Kai Tak. The prisoners were taken to a hotel in Kowloon. They'll be there for one or two days until they can be fitted out with some clothing. Air Force is standing by to fly them to military hospitals in Guam, Okinawa, Japan, Taiwan, and the Philippines. Maloney is being sent to Clark Field. After the medics get them in a little better shape, they're off home to join their kinfolk and sweethearts.

"So if you're worrying about whether it was worth it, bear in mind that at least 117 of the poor bastards are no longer rotting in North Viet-Nam. As for those still there, it isn't every day that a crazy sonuvabitch like you comes down the pike. They'll have to wait until those who got them into this get them out."

Court sipped his drink thoughtfully.

"Now I'm going to hit you with a few more hard facts," Andy continued with scarcely a pause. "You mentioned dragging us into this. Do you think I didn't know it was a crazy scheme from the start? I sure as hell did, and I didn't give it better than a 50-50 chance. I had nothing to lose. I've enjoyed almost every minute of it, even the times I was scared shitless. Now, I have the satisfaction that I've accomplished something worthwhile.

"As for the rest of them. You laid it on the line in the beginning and they could have backed out then, or at any time during the planning. They didn't.

"Tony thinks of you as some sort of a minor deity. He'd have followed your lead to the gates of Hell - and held the door for you. With him, it wasn't the money, even though I'm sure he can use it. What you did for him was to give him the self-confidence he needs.

"Johnny Begg. What the hell did he have to lose? You gave him a new lease on life. What he does with it is up to him, but I have a hunch this experience has given him a transfusion of guts.

"Clem. He gave this caper even less chance than I did. He went in with his eyes wide open. You pulled his ass out of the fire, but if he doesn't unload that cunt in Singapore, he'll be back in the same spot a year from now. But don't worry about it. He knows it.

"We could have hauled-ass. None of us did. We became a team; a damn good combat team. Your nutty obsession must have been catching. All I hope is that it doesn't become an epidemic."

Court drained his glass. "Okay, Andy, you've made your point. I'll buy it . . . some day I might even believe it."

There was a knock on the door. Court glanced down at the towel draped around his waist. "Get that, will you, Andy. I'd better get dressed."

When Andy returned and dropped a telegram and two message slips on the bed, Court was buttoning his shirt.

"What're you going to do now, Andy?" Court asked, as he glanced at the messages, then started to open the telegram.

"Go back to Danang and finish out the contract. Then, I think I'll go back to Oregon for a spell. It'll more than likely bore the hell out of me, but I think I should see what Stateside living's like. This caper's given me a sudden rush of patriotism. What about you?"

Court was only half listening. A slow smile crept across his face as he read the telegram:

JERRY AND MUMMY REQUEST YOU LOCATE
DON Q   AND TELL HIM TO PLEASE COME
HOME

"What'd you say, Andy?"

"Asked you what you plan on doing?"

"Oh," Court said, "Do a little shopping, then go to Spain for Christmas. I'll stay there at least until after Easter."

Court smiled as he looked at Andy. I guess that Don Quixote bit wasn't too far off the mark, Court thought, but this big ape makes a most unlikely Sancho Panza.

"Come on, Andy, let's eat."

* * * *

This book is dedicated to the many Deke Maloneys who wait impatiently for the moment when their lives can begin again.

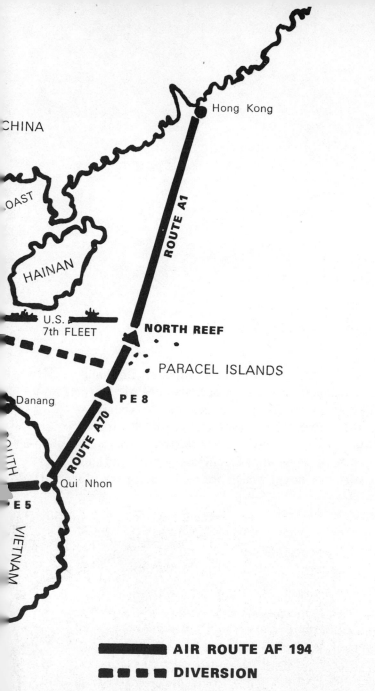

The authors wish to acknowledge with thanks the assistance and cooperation of Air Force and commercial pilots and the local business and diplomatic community. In particular, they express their appreciation to Des Kennedy, without whose continuing faith and support this novel would not have been possible.